# DEVIL'S BLOOD

## SHADE OF DEVIL BOOK 3

## SHAYNE SILVERS

ARGENTO
PUBLISHING

# COPYRIGHT

# DEDICATION

*To that person in front of me at the coffee shop who didn't pay for my drink...
this book is dedicated to someone else.*

*And to anyone who thinks I didn't deserve that drink, I once won a race
against a billion other competitors. It was do or die. If you're reading this, you
probably deserve a coffee, too.*
*And a laugh.*
*Enjoy my words. This book is for you, because you're a winner.*
*I'm not buying you a coffee, though.*

*-Shayne*

# EPIGRAPH

"There is no death. Only a change of worlds."

— CHIEF SEATTLE

# CONTENTS

The Shade of Devil Series—A warning      1

Chapter 1      3

Chapter 2      10

Chapter 3      17

Chapter 4      25

Chapter 5      30

Chapter 6      37

Chapter 7      42

Chapter 8      47

Chapter 9      54

Chapter 10      61

Chapter 11      68

Chapter 12      74

Chapter 13      80

Chapter 14      86

Chapter 15      94

Chapter 16      101

Chapter 17      108

Chapter 18      114

Chapter 19      122

Chapter 20      130

Chapter 21      136

Chapter 22      141

Chapter 23      146

Chapter 24      151

Chapter 25      157

Chapter 26      166

Chapter 27      173

Chapter 28      178

Chapter 29      184

Chapter 30      188

Chapter 31      197

Chapter 32      204

Chapter 33      210

Chapter 34 216

Chapter 35 222

Chapter 36 229

Chapter 37 235

Chapter 38 240

Chapter 39 245

Chapter 40 250

Chapter 41 255

Chapter 42 263

Chapter 43 270

Chapter 44 277

Chapter 45 283

Chapter 46 291

Chapter 47 299

Chapter 48 305

Chapter 49 310

Chapter 50 316

Chapter 51 322

Chapter 52 327

Chapter 53 331

Chapter 54 339

Chapter 55 346

Chapter 56 352

Chapter 57 358

TRY: OBSIDIAN SON (NATE TEMPLE #1) 366

*MAKE A DIFFERENCE* 371

*ACKNOWLEDGMENTS* 373

*ABOUT SHAYNE SILVERS* 375

*BOOKS BY SHAYNE SILVERS* 377

# THE SHADE OF DEVIL SERIES—A WARNING

**M**any vampires were harmed in the making of this story. Like...a lot of them.

If you enjoyed the *Blade* or *Underworld* movies, you will love the *Shade of Devil* series.

**The greatest trick the First Vampire ever pulled was convincing the world that he didn't exist.**

Before the now-infamous Count Dracula ever tasted his first drop of blood, Sorin Ambrogio owned the night. Humanity fearfully called him the Devil.

Cursed by the gods, Sorin spent centuries bathing Europe in oceans of blood with his best friends, Lucian and Nero, the world's first Werewolf and Warlock—an unholy trinity if there ever was one. Until the three monsters grew weary of the carnage, choosing to leave it all behind and visit the brave New World across the ocean. As they befriended a Native American tribe, they quickly forgot that monsters can never escape their past.

But Dracula—Sorin's spawn—was willing to do anything to erase Sorin's name from the pages of history so that he could claim the title of the world's first vampire all for himself. Dracula hunts him down and slaughters the natives, fatally wounding Sorin in the attack. Except a Shaman manages to secretly cast Sorin into a healing slumber.

For five hundred years.

Until Sorin is awoken by a powerful Shaman in present-day New York City. In a world he doesn't understand, Sorin only wants one thing —to kill Dracula and anyone else who stands in his path.

The streets of New York City will flow with rivers of blood, and the fate of the world rests in the hands of the Devil, Sorin Ambrogio.

Because this town isn't big enough for the both of them.

Now, our story begins in a brave New World...

### DON'T FORGET!

*VIP readers get early access to all sorts of goodies, including signed books, private giveaways, and advance notice of future projects. AND A FREE NOVELLA! Click the image or join here: www.shaynesilvers.com/l/219800*

FOLLOW AND LIKE:

### Shayne's FACEBOOK PAGE:

*www.shaynesilvers.com/l/38602*

I try my best to respond to all messages, so don't hesitate to drop me a line. Not interacting with readers is the biggest travesty that most authors can make. Let me fix that.

**W**inner takes all, I had told Natalie a few moments ago, sending her fleeing across the marble floors of the Museum of Natural History in pursuit of our wily prey—Victoria Helsing, the infamous monster hunter.

Except she was not the hunter at the moment. She was the hunted.

In this chase, both predator and prey would fully sate their greedy appetites.

Their laughter echoed in the halls of the museum, carefree and anticipatory. Genuine, heartfelt, blissful sounds. Now that we had a rare moment of privacy and no immediately pressing dangers, it was finally time to celebrate—to enjoy the fruits of our labor. It had barely struck midnight, and Nosh and Isabella had left a few minutes ago, leaving us the rest of the evening to our own devilish desires.

Thoughts of my recent victories—at the Statue of Liberty and in bringing my old castle here to Central Park—encouraged me, only barely drowning out the very real concerns still on my plate. But I squashed down those persistent doubts. None were time-sensitive—at least not for this exact moment. We had earned a night to celebrate.

Castle Ambrogio—now just outside the doors to the museum and surrounded by an impenetrable blanket of fog—jealously reached out to me in a siren song, eager for her own reunion, but I pushed that sensation down as well, muting our bond. I had another bond on my mind at the moment. And it required my full attention. Maybe even through to sunrise.

The world could surely wait that long. It had waited five hundred years, after all.

I took stock of the Greek Exhibit: the various statues, paintings, vases, and suits of armor celebrating the numerous heroes, monsters, and legends from Greek mythology. Several murals and paintings even depicted the famous Greek succession myth—that the parents were ultimately doomed to be overthrown and replaced by their own children.

I let out a breath, shaking my head. They were also a problem for another day. I sprinted from the Greek Exhibit, pushing down thoughts of my newfound family in favor of my current prey. A vampire needed blood.

But a man needed other things.

Flesh. Sweat. Feverish skin. Agony and ecstasy.

Right now, blood was the furthest thing from my mind, although I was certain it would come into play in the coming hours—if for no other reason than to reenergize the three of us for repeated carnal pleasures when we lay exhausted in a sweaty heap of tangled sheets. Because when I drank their blood, it served to reenergize them almost as much as it nourished me.

I rounded the corner, my feet making no sound as they struck the marble floor. The elevators to the catacombs below were at the far end of the museum from my current location, and the devils already had a head-start.

I tapped into my powers to run faster, following a tantalizing, spicy scent in the air.

Dr. Stein had recently educated me about adrenaline—a hormone secreted by the adrenal glands during conditions of elevated stress. Some called its effects the *fight or flight syndrome*—where the person would need the added power in order to escape or battle the sudden danger.

I inhaled the scent of adrenaline-infused blood from my devils.

It was still incredible to learn how far humanity had advanced since my time. I had always sensed a spicy aroma to my prey's blood if they were fleeing from me rather than willingly offering themselves. But I hadn't known the science behind it—adrenaline.

And it tasted fucking *delicious*—a master cook adding the perfect blend of exotic spices to a carefully prepared meal for a holiday feast.

Like the sweetest music, my enhanced senses picked up on the rapidly increasing staccato of two full hearts pumping blood to muscles and tendons, fueled and ignited by the spicy tang of adrenaline. The sounds of Victoria and Natalie giggling and shrieking playfully as they fled the monster of the museum—me—was a perfect accompaniment to the beating of their hearts.

I listened with a hungry grin as their pulses sped faster and faster, deeper and deeper—the potent blood coursing in their veins like fingers of lightning. The heady whiff of their lust and desire was like a trail of fragrant rose petals, letting me know their exact route.

Rather than fight-or-flight, their adrenaline-fueled bodies hummed a different song.

Fuck-or-flight.

But the sexual tension between us was merely a strange byproduct of our *real* bond.

On a purely magical basis, I felt their supernatural powers reaching out to mine, begging to be stroked and tuned, caressed and strained, plucked and played like the strings of a harp. To see what we were capable of accomplishing together. Because we hadn't yet sat down and analyzed our bond. Despite my current hunger for more...primitive experiments, I was confident that our bond really had nothing to do with sex.

There was something...alarmingly powerful between the three of us, even though we had known each other for less than a month. And it was only in the past few days that we had decided to shift our friendship to something deeper—an actual romantic relationship. But the power between us was impossible to ignore, seeming to encourage such an act. Even more now that I had reclaimed Castle Ambrogio. I wasn't sure how or why, but it almost seemed like the three of us had become one—three sides of the same soul.

And reclaiming my castle had vastly increased the cords of power connecting us—especially after I had tapped into my castle to save Victoria's life a few days ago—with a metaphysical blood transfusion. Almost like my castle had become part of our bond in the process.

Victoria and Natalie could even communicate with my castle now —just like me.

And I didn't know what that meant—what consequences it carried or benefits it offered.

Then again...

The prospect of *actual sex* was its own aphrodisiac. It...well, it had been a long time for me. I felt like my very bones ached with maddening lust. And it's hard to get analytical when hormones are contaminating objectivity. It would be better for everyone if we only cleared our heads. Scientifically, it was the wisest course of action. I was certain of it...

I rounded the last corner in time to see the elevator doors closing at the end of the hall. Victoria and Natalie grinned darkly at me from within. Before the doors fully shut, one of my devils flung an article of clothing out of the elevator.

They laughed as the doors closed.

I skidded to a halt outside the metal doors, glaring down at the blouse Victoria had discarded.

I realized I was actually growling, my own heart beating just as anxiously—and nervously—as theirs. None of us knew what the hell we were doing, but we were willing to give it a try.

I stood impatiently, clenching my fists as I waited for the elevator. I contemplated turning to mist in order to descend to my chambers ahead of them, but I chose against it, relishing in the chase. My phone rang in my pocket, threatening to sideline my evening of pleasure. Without shifting my attention from the closed doors, I calmly withdrew the device and crushed it in my fist, dropping the pieces to the marble floor without looking at who had been calling.

I pressed the button to call the elevator, watching my finger tremble in the process. I sensed movement to my right, and I spun to see Nosh and Isabella—Izzy, as he had taken to calling her—jogging towards me. "Sorin!" she shouted urgently, increasing her pace. Her face was pale, making her fiery red hair stand out even more than normal, and she looked out of breath. She wore a long eagle feather in her hair that I hadn't noticed earlier. "You didn't answer your phone!"

I gritted my teeth, seriously considering shifting to mist to escape whatever the hell they needed. "Now is really not the time, Izzy. Whatever it is can wait—"

"The High Priestess of the Sisters of Mercy has come to New York City," she blurted, cutting me off. "She demands an audience with you. She thinks you're allying yourself with Dracula."

I blinked at her, wanting to grab her by the shoulders and shake her. Violently. Nosh glanced at the elevator doors and then the discarded blouse on the ground. He instantly picked up on the source of my irritation. Like a brother on the frontlines of a war, he gave me a grim nod—letting me know that he empathized with our shared plight, but that duty called. He must have had similar romantic aspirations with Izzy before the Sisters of Mercy ruined everything.

"Battle plans never survive first contact with the enemy," he said sadly. I nodded somberly.

Izzy cocked her head, frowning at the pair of us. "This is serious."

I closed my eyes and took a deep breath. The elevator doors opened with a soft chiming sound. I somehow managed to keep my feet firmly planted, refusing to open my eyes until the doors closed. If I had caught even one glimpse of an escape option, I would have taken it. Consequences be damned. The doors whispered shut, and I finally opened my eyes, turning to face her. "Okay. I'm fine," I rasped, breathing very carefully so as not to bite her head off. Her intentions were good.

She nodded uneasily, discreetly gauging the distance between us as if only now realizing how unstable my emotions currently were. "I wouldn't have come back if it wasn't urgent," she said cautiously. "They are outside the museum *right now*."

I stiffened, my eyes flicking over her shoulder even though I couldn't see the front entrance from here. "What?"

Nosh nodded, and I finally picked up on the sea of violence bubbling beneath the surface of his calm façade. "Three dozen of them."

Nosh *never* lost his calm. For him to be so close to violence meant that the situation was extremely dire. "Okay. You've got my attention. This High Priestess asked for me by name?"

Izzy shook her head, wincing. "They demanded to speak with—and I quote—the fool of a vampire who dared to erect a cursed castle in the center of New York City. The fool of a vampire who gave humans proof that the supernatural is real."

I pursed my lips, reminding myself that she was only the messenger. "Why can none of these witches remember a simple goddamned name?"

"Maybe you need a nametag," Nosh suggested dryly. "Like the tombstones all your vampires wear." I grunted. Since so many of the new vampires we had recently brought back to life at that Statue of Liberty had come from different eras, cultures, and countries, Aristos had given them tombstone-shaped lanyards with their pertinent biographical information: their name, when they had been born, when they had died, and where they had lived. The lanyards served as instant conversation starters, helping everyone get to know each other a little better. The homeless vampires had immediately taken to wearing them as well, since most of them had been strangers a month ago. All-in-all, the lanyards seemed to be producing great results.

We had already seen bonds and sub-groups forming, marrying the two groups of vampires together into one cohesive family rather than keeping them segregated and distant.

I fixed my glare on Nosh until his smile withered. Natalie and Victoria were waiting for me, and they would grow very concerned if I didn't appear soon. If they heard that the Sisters of Mercy were waiting for me outside...

My supernatural vampire senses told me there would be a girl fight. A big one.

Because not only were the Sisters interrupting our privacy, but they were also accusing me of allying with Dracula. I feared the instant obliteration of the Sisters of Mercy. Natalie and Victoria were mildly irrational, where I was entirely focused and objective. The Sisters had inadvertently picked a fight that might result in the end of their precious order. Only my calm, rational mind could save the situation.

"Go outside and tell your High Priestess that *Sorin Ambrogio*," I growled, heavily enunciating my name, "does not respond to demands —from anyone. Reassure her that I *trapped* Dracula. I'm not his damned ally. I will execute him after I have a chance to interrogate him. When I am ready, I will *permit* her to sit in the front row. She can be close enough to catch some blood spray if she really wants proof. For now, send them on their way. I've got important work to do." Nosh abruptly fell into a coughing fit, his cheeks flushing bright red as his eyes darted towards the errant blouse on the ground. I pressed on, ignoring him. "Vampire work. It is very dangerous, and it will require my utmost attention—"

Izzy was shaking her head, licking her lips nervously. "They said their arrival was simply a courtesy," she whispered. "A formality. If you do not meet the Sisters of Mercy right *now*, then you have two hours to deliver Dracula into their custody or they will consider your actions a declaration of war."

I stared at her incredulously. "They don't even know my *name*!" I sputtered. "Are they serious?"

Izzy looked up at me, and I realized that her eyes were red-rimmed —that she was doing all she could to hold herself together. "They have already ex-communicated me," she whispered. "Just for *knowing* you." She lowered her eyes and I watched a tear roll down her cheek. "I am no longer a Sister of Mercy." She wiped the tear away, looking back up at me. "I would say they are pretty goddamned serious," she said with an edge of menace.

Well, shit.

## 2

I somehow managed to bite down on my intense desire to go out there and murder them all.

"Why would they ex-communicate you?" I demanded, struggling to gather my thoughts and continue to think rationally rather than emotionally.

"I have been living in the city while you took over, working *with* you, in fact. At best, they think I'm incompetent for not stopping you. They do not trust me any longer." She shrugged. "The Speaker to the High Priestess addressed me as a messenger, not as a fellow Sister. None of them would look me in the eyes when she handed me the letter stripping me of my title."

I ground my teeth, deciding that I didn't like the Sisters of Mercy or their High Priestess very much. I shared a long look with Nosh, who was squeezing Izzy's shoulder comfortingly. She stared down at the ground and I watched another tear fall from her cheek. I felt the flint arrowhead in my pocket, and I smiled faintly. I discreetly tapped my pocket with a finger and Nosh smiled, looking surprised at my indication. He stared at me for a long moment, obviously torn.

Because it was a token of his trust. A gift he had given me. A gift a son had given his father.

If that story was actually true. Nosh had been delirious when he'd let it slip, and he was a skinwalker, so I had no way to verify his claim. It would be better for him if he wasn't related to the Olympians. Safer. Which was why I hadn't told anyone about it.

Even if we weren't related, he had extended me his trust in letting me have one of his arrowheads—the totem for one of his magical tomahawks. They were somehow tied to his skinwalker abilities, but I wasn't quite sure how.

I leaned forward and gripped Izzy's upper arm. I placed the arrowhead in her palm and closed her fingers over it. "I freely pass on my claim to this tomahawk, which Nosh entrusted to me. I'm not sure if there is something he needs to say to make it official, but my gesture has nothing to do with magic." I cupped her cheek, drawing her focus to my face. Her eyes glistened as she stared back at me. "Forget the Sisters of Mercy. Welcome to *my* family," I said kindly. Because I'd decided that love would no longer be a curse for my family. For Nosh, if he really was my son. But my family wasn't restricted to blood. Izzy had been a good friend, going out of her way to help me do the right thing—even when it went against what the Sisters of Mercy had wanted.

Family was loyalty and trust. Not blood. The irony of a vampire not making blood a priority was not lost on me.

Izzy's chin trembled as she nodded, more tears spilling down her cheeks. "I can feel it inside me," she whispered, staring down at it. "Like Nosh is holding my hand."

I wasn't sure if she knew about him being a skinwalker, but she sensed the magic from the tomahawk. That topic was for him to share at his leisure. I had enough secrets on my mind. "You're a saint compared to the rest of us, Izzy," I added with a wry smile. "We need some good to outweigh the bad."

Surprisingly, she lunged forward and wrapped her arms around me, resting her head on my shoulder. I felt the stiff bulge of pistols beneath her jacket, letting me know that she loved me. The smell of strawberries filled my nose as she tried to suffocate me with her thick red hair. "Thank you, Sorin. Thank you," she whispered, squeezing me tightly. "And I'm glad we are no longer pretending your relationship is a secret." I stiffened in surprise and she laughed, squeezing me tighter. "Which you just gave away if I had any doubts."

I grumbled in displeasure, casting a frown at Nosh. He smiled crookedly. "She's devious. Used some magic to get it out of me."

Izzy pulled away, rolling her eyes at Nosh as she pocketed the arrowhead. "I massaged your ridiculously beautiful hair, shaman. It was remarkably easy. No magic needed."

Nosh sighed, dipping his chin at me. "Thank you."

"She's family. Unless you mess it up," I warned him. "Don't mess it up, Nosh."

Izzy nodded matter-of-factly. "I concur. Listen to Papa Ambrogio." I winced at the term, surprised at the sudden terror that flooded through my stomach at the simple four-letter word.

Nosh held up his hands with a laugh. "Deal."

I folded my arms, staring at her thoughtfully. "If I'm allies with Dracula, why is he currently imprisoned in my castle and unable to get out? Shouldn't we be out on the town, drowning the city in blood?" I asked dryly.

She shrugged. "They do not trust you. They fear that you saved Dracula from their clutches and are now protecting him with your mist. If you could move the castle, you must also have the strength to kill him. Therefore, you must be his ally."

I scoffed. "You're kidding me. What does any of this have to do with them anyway?"

She blinked at me, frowning. Then realization seemed to dawn on her. "Of course," she whispered. "I didn't even think about that. The Sisters protected humans from his castle overseas, making sure humans didn't wander too close. They were an extra barrier to make sure humans didn't wander in, and monsters didn't wander out. It was a permanent siege since no one has ever been strong enough to break in or destroy the castle. It is also why Dracula uses others to do his dirty work—he couldn't afford to step out of his castle and get caught. So, when you came in and stole the whole fucking property, you made them look like incompetence reincarnate. It looked like a prison break."

I blinked at her, turning to Nosh. "And no one thought to tell me this when I was formulating my grand plan to move the castle?" I demanded.

Nosh shifted from foot-to-foot. "I was preoccupied with legal battles," he said lamely.

Izzy studiously avoided eye contact.

"You two didn't think I would pull it off, did you?" I whispered, feeling surprisingly wounded by their lack of faith.

They grimaced, tripping over themselves in an attempt to reassure me with hollow platitudes.

"That hurts," I said, cutting them off. "That really hurts." I began to pace, thinking out loud. "Since I made them look bad, the only way for them to weasel out of ridicule is to point the blame at me. It's a political scheme," I said. Then I burst out laughing. "Just when I thought I was out, they pull me back in! I *invented* these games! They're doubling down on a bad bet, letting their emotions get the best of them."

They were staring at me incredulously. "Did you just quote the Godfather?" Nosh asked.

I stared at him for a few quiet seconds. Then I envisioned a world where he hadn't spoken and made it my reality. Izzy glanced at him with a slow shake of her head. "I think that was all Sorin," she mused. I nodded affirmatively. "Wow. Well, you nailed it. Was that your first pop culture reference?"

I closed my eyes, holding my palm to my forehead as I took a deep, calming breath, vividly aware of the fact that I could be tangled up in damp sheets with my devils right now. I could also be fighting witches.

Both would have been better.

I lowered my palm. "Alright, so I made them look bad and now they want to save face. That about right?"

Izzy sensed my obvious frustration and focused back on the matter at hand. "There is also the chance that they actually believe it," she admitted. "I think it's both."

I nodded absently, thinking. "Of course it is both. That's how you play the game. Always have at least two paths to victory," I murmured to myself, thinking out loud. I paused, glancing over at her. "You mentioned a Speaker to the High Priestess."

Izzy nodded. "The High Priestess never, ever, gets directly involved.

She always uses her Speaker—a carefully vetted witch from the Sisters of Mercy. Even we don't see or speak to the High Priestess. That is why I'm so concerned. For her to come to town and instantly demand a meeting with you—a vampire—is alarming."

I scratched my chin, wondering if Izzy knew as much as she thought she did. Royalty had been using 'Speakers' in some form or fashion for hundreds upon hundreds of years—usually to set them up as a scapegoat if and when they made a poor decision. A quick *I never told them to say that!* and their integrity was safe while the poor speaker was slapped in irons and beheaded or strung up in the city square the next morning. Odds were good that the High Priestess was playing the same game. Maintaining distance from your followers often produced a high level of fanaticism and zealotry, binding the ties of loyalty even tighter, and closing off the weak links in the chain with instant alibis. If no one ever heard the ruler speak, all fingers would point to the speaker rather than the ruler.

Power begets power.

"Okay. She threatens war, which is fine. But what does she really want? Specifically?"

"Um. War is not *fine*, Sorin," Nosh said with a concerned look on his face. "We should clarify that up front."

Izzy took a steadying breath, collecting her thoughts and looking as if she was debating her answer. "She wants Dracula in her custody. Period."

I cocked my head. "If she's not angling to take me down as well, she's even worse at this game than I first assumed." I threw my hands into the air, muttering. "Fucking hobbyists all over the place. Does no one know how to properly set up their enemies anymore? It's embarrassing."

The two of them watched me in silence for a few moments, giving me some time to calm down. "I have been exiled, so I only know what I've been told as a messenger," she said. "But I do know how the Sisters from the Castle Guard detail think. Only the most powerful, most obedient, and most fanatical get that job—like their own noble court basking in the radiance of the omnipotent High Priestess." I grunted my agreement. That sounded right.

"Their potions explode more zealously," Nosh said, smiling.

Izzy shot him a stern look, biting back a grin. "The only vampire they ever speak about is Dracula. The rest of you are not worth their attention. Just another body to bury." Her eyes widened and she winced. "Their words. Not mine. The Sisters of Mercy are rather jaded, being stuck outside the castle for decades. They don't involve themselves with the church or the happenings of mankind. They consider themselves an army with one purpose. To stand between the world and Dracula. That is one reason the lower echelons of the Sisters of Mercy work through the churches—so we know where we need to go to fight the other monsters of the world."

I grunted, scratching at my chin as I processed her words and put myself in the position of the High Priestess. How would I maneuver out of such a predicament? After a few moments, I faced Izzy. "Everyone knows that I am not turning over Dracula, even your High Priestess. This is all just a dance." Nosh stared at me so intensely that it looked like he was trying to video record me with his eyeballs. "They want to drag me out of my home tonight as an act of dominance—a power play in front of my army of vampires and werewolves—only so that we can confirm the real meeting with the High Priestess. Two hours from now, you said?" I asked, not waiting for a response. "Let me guess. It's at a church."

She stared at me, her lips moving wordlessly for a few seconds. "Y-yes," she finally whispered. "Trinity Church in the Financial District."

I nodded thoughtfully. "Okay. I assume my army is surrounding them?" Izzy nodded. "Perfect. Tell this Speaker that I will be out in twenty minutes and ask if they need any refreshments while they wait *outside*."

They blinked in unison. "Just like that?" Nosh asked. "You'll go to their meeting."

I shrugged. "Sure. The whole point of these charades is to make the other party second guess themselves. They'll be wondering why I agreed so easily and why I humbly treated them as welcome guests. But they'll also be annoyed that I'm making them wait on my front steps. Which one is my true angle?" I smiled at him. "The devil is in the details." I turned to Izzy. "What can you tell me about this High Priestess?"

She winced. "I've never met her before, but I know she is very powerful. No one else is even close. She wears a veil over her face when she does make one of her rare appearances, and even then, she does not talk. Sisters have died for accidentally seeing her face or hearing her voice. I knew one of them. Her own Speaker had her eyes gouged out so as not to see what should not be seen."

Nosh blinked at her. "That is monumentally ignorant. Who the fuck does she think she is?"

"Are you up for the task?" I asked, sensing her trepidation.

She nodded firmly. "Oh, I'm going to enjoy the hell out of it." She turned to Nosh. "It would be best if I approach them by myself."

He pursed his lips. "They won't do anything stupid, will they?"

She hesitated. "They won't do anything with an army of monsters surrounding them, and I intend to stick close to the museum doors, just in case."

"I'm going to change and let my devils know what's going on. I'll be out in twenty."

Izzy smiled approvingly. "I think it's cute how you call them that." She cast a suggestive look at Nosh before striding away. He gave me a forlorn look and I chuckled.

"Don't ask me, Nosh. I've got two of my own problems to deal with." I pressed the button for the elevator again, surprised that Victoria and Natalie hadn't come looking for me.

## 3

Nosh stepped into the elevator with me. I pressed the button, wondering why he was following me rather than waiting in the lobby where he could keep an eye on Izzy.

"For the record, I do not appreciate being taken away from my work," I said meaningfully. I pointed at two piles of clothes lying on the floor of the elevator as we began to descend. Natalie and Victoria had finished undressing. Right here, reminding me what the High Priestess' distraction had cost me.

"Work," Nosh said, dryly, nudging one of the piles of clothes with the tip of his boot.

They had even left their shoes. I closed my eyes for a two-count, accepting the pain of knowing that today was just not my day. I opened my eyes and turned to look at him. "I never said it was father-son appropriate work," I admitted with a guilty grin.

Nosh flashed me a hollow smile. "Same boat," he said with a frustrated sigh. "Your relationship with them reminds me of the Brides of Dracula."

I frowned at the abrupt shift of topic. "What?"

He gestured at the pile of clothes, sensing my confusion. "There is a story about Dracula having three brides, written after you were put to sleep. They give him power and live with him inside the castle. Details are sketchy, but it reminds me of your devils," he said absently. "Even though it's not your story, it's like you're rewriting it. Maybe it's a vampire thing."

I studied him thoughtfully. Was it? Was that the explanation for my bond with the devils? Something to do with my power? It had never happened in my earlier life. Did that mean Dracula had a similar power source to mine? Was that why the Sisters of Mercy were so concerned?

Sensing I wasn't going to comment, he let out a breath, his face growing somber. "On that note, the Sisters aren't our only problem. Eve was waiting for me outside when we were leaving. Thankfully, she left before the Sisters showed up or things could have really gone south."

I stared at him, frowning anxiously. I hadn't even considered Adam and Eve in this whole mess. They had been allies to the Sisters—at least to Izzy, anyway. In my opinion, they had been more like willing prisoners, stuck in the sewers below Central Park. But that had all changed when I turned them into vampires. They were much happier with their new life, but Nosh had a solid point. Their transformation into Nephilim vampires definitely wouldn't help my relations with the Sisters. Especially not if they attacked the Sisters on the steps of the museum. They were ridiculously protective of me.

"What did Eve want?"

He must have noticed the panic on my face because he held out his hands in a calming gesture. "It's okay. She went back to the castle gates before the Sisters showed up."

"What did she want?" I repeated in a low growl.

"She was concerned about the castle," he said, scratching at his jaw. "She thinks something is wrong with it, and she wanted your reassurance that all was well. I think she was embarrassed that she might be panicking over nothing, but she didn't want to take the risk since she's still trying to accept the fact that she can now talk to your castle." He glanced at me pointedly. "Which is really fucking weird, Sorin. I've never heard of such a thing."

I waved a hand dismissively. "It's not actually alive, Nosh. Don't worry. It's more of an...awareness. Similar to how a home has an aura about it that soothes and calms, makes you feel safe." He nodded, following along. "Well, I lived in the castle a very long time, and magic and blood is ingrained into the very walls. We have a history, and that history has taken on a personality."

Things like that happened when your house held the answers to thousands upon thousands of unsolved murders.

He nodded thoughtfully. "I feel the same about my tomahawks, actually. Like they are alive."

I nodded as I considered the message he'd relayed. Even though Adam and Eve were new to their relationship with the castle, anything that made them feel alarmed was likely justified. Only one way to know for sure, especially after Nosh's mention of the Brides of Dracula—a separate power source.

I reached out to Castle Ambrogio, idly recalling that I had pushed her away earlier when I'd been pursuing Natalie and Victoria. I'd thought she was just longing for her master, but as our bond opened between us now, I felt sweat break out on my forehead. The castle was afraid and very concerned. She felt taxed and strained as if trying to hold up a great burden. My eyes widened.

"What the hell is going on out there? Are the Sisters doing something?" I demanded.

Nosh shook his head, his shoulders tensing at the alarm on my face. "Not that I know of. This was before they even showed up."

"What a coincidence," I snapped sarcastically. I focused on the castle again, trying to pinpoint the problem. The castle was so focused on her own problems that she didn't even acknowledge my presence. With no other options available, I used our bond to get a look inside the castle itself to see what Dracula was up to.

Almost instantly, a growl bubbled up from my chest. Dracula sat on my throne, and he was feasting on one of his vampires. More of his vampires were lined up before the throne, awaiting their turn. A pair of vampires was dragging the bodies away, forming an alarmingly large pile of corpses against the back wall. He was draining his own vampires, and they were letting him.

Three beautiful women wearing rich gowns were kneeling on the ground, using fresh blood to paint dizzying symbols and designs on the floor. The Brides of Dracula. And they were definitely powerful, although nowhere near as strong as Natalie and Victoria. The blackish-red blood was pulsing with power, seeming to glow with violet darkness, exuding a dark, malevolent, anti-light. Even though the particulars were unfamiliar to me, I knew that it was some kind of ritual, and it was battling the castle walls—straining the power that was keeping Dracula and his horde trapped within.

He was trying to summon someone, but who? I could sense that ingesting the blood of his own vampires was making him stronger as well. Castle Ambrogio still held him, but she couldn't deny the obscene amount of fresh blood spilling within her. Like forcing a drug down a resistant victim's throat, the dark blood was weakening her ability to keep him trapped. Her refusal to consent was not enough to prevent the poison he was feeding her.

He was trying to break out. Right when his old jailors knocked on my door, demanding their prisoner back. Was it a setup? Had I underestimated the Sisters of Mercy?

If the castle lost control, only Adam and Eve and a small army of vampires and werewolves stood between him and a city brimming with prey. Would the mist surrounding the castle keep him trapped or would that also fail? And I had to deal with the Sisters of Mercy on top of it all.

A part of me latched onto the suspicion that the Sisters of Mercy weren't as benevolent as I had thought. What if they were actually here to help break him free, concealing their dark motives beneath the guise of trustworthy custodians? All I knew of the Sisters was what Izzy had told me about them, and what I had just seen them do to Izzy—which spoke volumes.

What if their true purpose in Europe had been to protect *Dracula* rather than the humans? That the reason they had so far failed to kill him was because they had never *intended* to kill him? And now they were trying to bully me into giving them custody of the bastard. The fact that they were willing to threaten me with war was an extremely desperate act.

I finally accepted the fact that sex was simply not going to happen tonight.

"The bond is growing weaker," I finally muttered to Nosh. "He's trying to overpower it from within. We cannot let him get out." That was what the castle had been trying to warn me about earlier, but I had dismissed it, more concerned about my love life. Had my devils sensed anything of the sort from the castle, or had their own hormones distracted them as well?

I didn't mention the blood ritual to Nosh because I didn't have any helpful information to add, and nothing Dracula was doing would be in Nosh's field of expertise. Judging by some of the symbols I had seen, it was looking more like my own area of expertise.

Because I had picked out a handful of ancient Greek letters.

Who was Dracula trying to summon? Who could possibly help him escape?

The elevator doors finally opened, and a tide of purple light suddenly bloomed ahead of us, washing over the entire space in the blink of an eye—even through the walls. I gasped in alarm as the hair on the back of my arms instantly stood up on end. The light rolled over us without harm, not actually touching us. Then it was simply gone, as if I had only imagined it.

Nosh stared wild-eyed, clutching one of his tomahawks in his fist. "What the fuck was that?" he whispered. I was simply relieved that it hadn't been a hallucination. He had seen it too.

Aristos and Valentine were ten paces away, holding hands as they stared down a side hall. Except they were motionless—frozen in mid-stride. I'd only seen something like this one other time—when Selene had visited me. Whatever it had done to Aristos and Valentine, it hadn't affected us.

Which was almost worse. My arms tingled with alarm as I looked over at him. "Olympians," I hissed warily, stepping out of the elevator. Had Selene decided to pay me another visit? Or was it someone much, much worse? Dracula's ritual with the Greek letters suddenly seemed much more relevant. Maybe his brides were more powerful than I had assumed.

Nosh slipped out of the elevator beside me, sweeping his gaze across the catacombs and curling his lip in a grim frown. "First, the castle and the Sisters, and now this. Your trouble comes in threes, father."

I tensed at his use of the word father. We hadn't explicitly spoken about it, but we had danced around the topic a few times.

I slowly shook my head, sensing the air as I began to creep towards my chambers. "Keep your head down, Nosh, and be ready to throw your tomahawk." He nodded, following my lead as I crept from book-shelf to bookshelf, peering high enough to look over them but not become an easy target. I could feel the heartbeats of other vampires throughout the vast space, but they all seemed to be emanating from behind the closed doors of the storage rooms we'd converted to dormi-tories for them. Other than Aristos and Valentine, I saw no one in the halls.

Other than my obvious paranoia, I also sensed no immediate danger. I didn't rely on that, deciding that any visiting Olympian was an instant threat—even if they were alleged allies. Selene had been such a great ally that she had sliced and diced Natalie with her silver claws, almost killing her.

"Any enemy in particular? I'd really rather not meet Zeus again," Nosh muttered, looking ashamed of his admission.

I grunted. "Anyone who survives a fight with Zeus has instant credi-bility, Nosh. Don't take that one personally. And that was a misunder-standing. He didn't know you were his grandson. However, I prefer to run on the assumption that every Olympian is a threat. Even Zeus. My wife almost killed Natalie, and she was trying to help. Supposedly. I have enough friends already."

Nosh grimaced, nodding his agreement.

I paused outside the entrance leading to my chambers. Hugo had hired a crew of laborers to come in and replace the massive wooden doors Adam and Eve had destroyed upon Selene's last visit, but they now stood cracked open. The warm glow of my fireplace cast dancing shadows within, and a few dim lamps had been left on near my reading chair by one of the bookshelves. I heard water running and I tasted humidity in the air. A steaming shower was running.

I shared a long look with Nosh before slipping inside, my claws outstretched and ready for a fight. In the event of any sudden projec-tiles, my cloak was only a thought away—because turning into mist would only allow the projectiles to hit Nosh instead.

I swept the room with my gaze in less than a second, noticing only a single anomaly. And it was impossible to miss.

I stared, trying to wrap my mind around the danger, but I was having a very difficult time doing so. The door to the bathroom was open and I saw a naked Natalie stepping deeper into a cloud of steam—obviously in the process of entering the shower when time had been frozen. I peered past her shoulder to see Victoria already in the shower.

I slowly focused back on the room's only uninvited occupant. "This is bullshit," I finally cursed, glaring at the bear-skin rug before the crackling fireplace. A stunningly naked, olive skinned woman lay on her side, propped up on her elbow and supporting her head in her palm. Her long, wavy hair was streaked with both blonde and brown in equal measure, and long enough to drape over her shoulders without concealing her assets. Her perfectly shaped, Olympian breasts belonged on a twenty-year-old virgin who didn't know any better, even though her dark smile openly flaunted that this woman had orchestrated—and participated in—an unfathomable number of coital acts that would make the most seasoned mortal whore look like a virginal babe. She definitely knew better.

I was entirely sure we were staring at Aphrodite, the goddess of love and sex. My half-sister.

Her appetite for desire broke mortal minds, and her victims loved her for it almost as much as she loved leading the poor lambs to the slaughter. Her other hand rested on her inner thigh, concealing—and simultaneously drawing attention to—her lower temptations. "This is bullshit," I repeated, realizing that I was shockingly furious over the fact that my romantic exploits had been shut down by the naked goddess of sex lounging upon my rug. All while a naked Natalie and Victoria were frozen in the act of climbing into the shower together, waiting for me to come tend to their physical desires.

"It's like that Burt Reynolds picture, but without the body hair and mustache," Nosh murmured, practically drooling at the goddess. I had no idea who Burt was, or why any woman would have body hair and a mustache, but I had long ago given up on trying to decipher every pop culture reference I heard thrown into conversation.

The goddess grinned wickedly, her eyes seeming to shine with flecks of pink and purple light. "I don't have a mustache, but I'd gladly accept a *mustache ride*, my sweet, succulent nephew," the Olympian said in probably the most attractive purr I'd ever heard in my life. I felt it internally. Like she had spoken directly to my groin's spirit animal.

Nosh flinched as if slapped, instantly averting his gaze. His cheeks were beet red, and I didn't blame him one bit, despite my anger.

Aphrodite made bear-skin rugs look sexy.

I clenched my teeth, drowning out my instinctive urgings to grab, grope, and grind the goddess into blissful climax. Because I knew they weren't my own thoughts. She was using her magic, knowingly or not, to influence us. "What is the meaning of this, Aphrodite?" I asked, using her name for Nosh's benefit.

She dipped her chin approvingly at my correct guess of her name. "I came for my brother," she said with a suggestive purr, her words heavy on the double meaning. "Hopefully, more than once, judging by the stories I've heard about you and your bite." She licked her lower lip and winked. "Time is no longer a concern. We should indulge in this precious gift."

Right. This was going to be all sorts of fun. I just knew it.

## 4

I narrowed my eyes, shrugging off her innuendo with a sickened frown. We were related by blood, for crying out loud. I knew incestual concerns had never stopped an Olympian before, but it was still shocking to hear it so blatantly stated. In front of my son, no less.

I'd given much thought to how I would react when I met my next Olympian. I knew how dangerous their involvement could be, and that it was only a matter of time before they began pestering me following my encounter with Zeus.

The Olympians, as pretty and elegant as they appeared on the surface, were actually savage, feral, primitive creatures. They functioned on an instinctual mindset, reading body language and working much like wild predators. They just did so in togas with beautiful coats of skin.

Any show of timidity or awe was instantly filed away for them to later use against you. That was my theory anyway.

So, I turned my back on her and calmly walked over to a nearby armoire. I opened it, pulled out a robe, and then I made my way back to the Olympian. I stopped about six inches away, staring down at her with the same look I would have given a particularly uninspiring pebble on a gravel road. She stared up at me, her smile faltering ever so slightly. I dropped the robe on her head before I turned and made my way over to the bathroom, speaking over my shoulder. "Don't eat him, Aphrodite. He's all bone."

"My favorite body part," she laughed in a lilting chime, sloughing off her momentary unease at my blank assessment of her. Once out of sight, I glanced back to make sure she didn't try to kill Nosh. His face was a dark, dark purple as he studied the toes of his boots.

I walked into the dim, candlelit bathroom to survey my naked devils in their natural habitat. Two candles on the counter filled the steamy room with the scent of anise and fennel, thick enough that I could taste it. Before I dared take a look at Natalie and Victoria, I closed my eyes and shuddered so violently that I almost stumbled to my hands and knees. I gripped the marble counter, squeezing it so hard that it crumbled to dust with a sharp *crack*.

My hormones were firing in full force thanks to Aphrodite's magic. I hadn't acknowledged it before, but my heart was racing, and my hands were shaking. I opened my eyes after a few breaths, confident that I was back in control. Somewhat. My groin already ached worse than it ever had before, and all I had done was *look* at the goddess of sex.

I didn't dare try to snap Natalie and Victoria out of their dazes or take my time trying to find a more comfortable position for them. I needed to get Aphrodite out of here as fast as possible. Any dallying on my part would only encourage her. But I didn't want the girls to catch a chill standing around naked—especially since the room was steamy, and flesh cooled much faster than most people realized. The damp air would cling to the skin and grow chill without some source of heat.

The shower itself was an enclosed, eight-by-six, black marble room that had been wired with the most impressive shower system ever designed—according to Nero. He had belabored the fact to me in great detail, still upset that I'd taken the shower from him when I took over the bedchambers for myself.

Rather than a basic showerhead, the ceiling was almost completely covered with several massive grates that could be adjusted to replicate a curtain of heavy rainfall, light rain, thick mist, or even rotating, massaging jets—and all while illuminating the black enclosure in remote-controlled, colored lighting. The glow was currently set on a rotating function, gradually cycling through the colors of the rainbow at such a subtle speed that it was difficult to pinpoint exactly when one color changed to another. Thankfully, Victoria had turned on the heavy rain function so there was enough falling water to keep the both of them warm without me having to get wet and try to remember how to adjust all the dials on the inner wall.

I faced my first task with all the bravery of an innocent, young noble desperately clutching his full sack of gold at the doors of his first seedy whorehouse.

My eyes settled on Natalie's tight round ass, and I was forced to bite my tongue—hard enough to draw blood—in order to remain focused on their immediate needs, not my fantastical dreams. She had managed to set one foot through the large glass door of the steaming shower before Aphrodite had frozen time.

The blanket of thick steam was billowing out from the shower directly over Natalie. Careful to avoid the falling water, I stepped around her and partway into the shower to see that her breasts were pebbled with goosebumps from the cooler air striking her wet flesh. I winced at the razor-thin pale scar looping over one breast and under the other in a horizontal S shape—courtesy of my wife, Selene.

One of the *friendly* Olympians.

I leaned further into the shower and tested the water with my fingers, making sure it was hot but not scalding. The water heater for the catacombs had been upgraded long ago and was large enough to allow the showers to maintain a steady temperature for hours and hours on end, so I had no fear of the water running cold on them. But if I didn't get them both into the full stream of hot water, they could catch a chill from standing in the mist for however long Aphrodite's visit would last.

I finally permitted my gaze to settle on Victoria, trying to keep my priorities straight while facing the tantalizing landscape of gentle rises and dips of smooth flesh. Limned by the cool blue lights above, Victoria was staring deeply into Natalie's fiery green eyes, and her plump lips were parted so as to breathe easier beneath the falling water. She was frozen in the act of beckoning the petite werewolf closer to her with

one curled finger. Her other hand was outstretched in obvious invita-
tion, palm up. In a mirrored motion, Natalie stared back at her, biting
her lips in a tentative, innocently wicked manner as her own hand
extended far enough so that two of her fingers had only just touched
Victoria's palm.

That skin-on-skin contact was the figurative signature on the
unwritten, unspoken contract that the two women had negotiated with
each other while waiting for me—the binding agreement that the two
of them had taken the first steps into a romantic relationship of their
very own.

Until Aphrodite, the goddess of love and romance, had ironically
ruined it.

Despite Natalie coming off as the more vehement participant in our
own physical entanglements, she looked almost timid and shy now that
she was confronted by the infamous vampire hunter, Victoria Helsing.

It was...endearing. And exciting. And infuriatingly cruel to the
poor, blue-balled vampire.

I closed my eyes and took two slow breaths rather than allowing
myself to envision what trouble they would have gotten into
without me.

What fun might have been had between all three of us if the Sisters
of Mercy and Aphrodite hadn't interrupted what could have been a top
contender for the best day of my immortal existence?

I stared into Natalie's sparkling eyes as I trailed the back of a finger
down her cheek, ending on her lower lip. I gently pressed down on her
lower teeth with my finger to open her mouth so that she could breathe
easier in the shower. Surprisingly, she wasn't stiff. On the contrary, I
barely had to try to alter her position. I picked her up by the waist and
set her down beneath the water, not even caring that my sleeves got wet
in the process. I stepped back, watching the two of them for a few
moments, making sure they weren't in danger of choking on water or
anything. The lights shifted through two full cycles over their flushed
flesh before I felt confident they were both warm and safe.

I gently closed the shower door behind me and let out a gentle
breath, thumping the back of my head against the glass door. "I am the
unluckiest, luckiest man in the world," I complained under my breath.

Thinking about Aphrodite in the next room, I mulled over my knowledge of the Greek gods.

Aphrodite had a reason for freezing time to visit me, and I wasn't sure I wanted any part of it. I flicked a switch to turn on the heat lamps as I left the bathroom, closing the door behind me.

Then I prepared myself for a fight with my sibling.

## 5

I looked up to find Nosh seated in the armchair and Aphrodite sitting on his lap, curling his hair around one of her fingers as she smoked a cigarette with her free hand. Nosh looked like a startled deer, fearful to move in any manner whatsoever. Except for his eyes. They latched onto me as I approached, and they were wild and wide as his fingers clenched the armrests like he was holding on for dear life.

Aphrodite playfully wiggled her rear into his lap, exhaling an unnaturally thick cloud of smoke into the air that somehow managed to portray an image of a woman riding a man in...

An armchair. The apparition looked to be having a lot more fun with it than Nosh.

I decided it was good to let him squirm for a few moments longer—as long as it kept her attentions away from me. She hadn't put on the robe, much to Nosh's torture. She also wasn't completely naked—which would have been easier to manage in comparison.

I had studied up on high-class lingerie thanks to Aristos, but we had obviously missed a topic that had been relegated only to the hallowed pantheons of the gods of sex.

Aphrodite wore a pair of silk ribbons—one was a vibrant pink, and the other a royal purple.

That was the only way I could think to describe her outfit.

The two ribbons crisscrossed her body from shoulder to ankle, wrapping around and over her frame in a truly mesmerizing display. The ribbons also didn't bother to cover up any of her important assets, but rather only served to emphasize them. Even as I watched, the ribbons moved, seemingly of their own accord, shifting and snaking across her body like serpents to form exquisite knotted bows and braids in one area before slowly shifting to emphasize another.

I was confident that I could watch the display for hours—and it had nothing to do with her ridiculous beauty. The ribbons were fascinating —like pieces of living art. They reminded me of my cloak and how it also had the ability to move about of its own accord. I was certain that I could watch for hours and never see the same braided designs two times in a row.

Which meant they were weapons intended to distract.

I cleared my throat pointedly. Aphrodite glanced over at me, draping her hand atop Nosh's head so that her thumb caressed his forehead in slow, sensual circles that made him blink lazily, as if entranced. Aphrodite exhaled another impossible puff of smoke, and this time her smoky puppet show portrayed two males working hard to satisfy their female companion in the cloud above their heads. A suggestion for how we might pass the time, perhaps.

"H-hey, Sorin," Nosh said lamely.

Aphrodite laughed, sounding like faint windchimes. "I was just getting to know my newest nephew," she murmured in a voice like warm, dripping honey. She shifted her rear into a better position, and I watched as Nosh swallowed tightly, closing his eyes for a moment. Aphrodite leaned down close to his face. "Where do you stand on keeping things in the family?" She licked her lips. "Ever slept with an older woman before? You can call me auntie. That sounds fun. I have much that I could teach you, little shaman." She poked his nose gently with her finger. "Just think of all the lessons you could later share with your fire-haired witch."

Nosh grimaced upon mention of Izzy, looking further emboldened now that he was no longer alone and concerned about risking her offense while I tended to Natalie and Victoria. "No thanks. I don't even know where to begin on how messed up that is. Auntie," he added dryly. "Unfortunately, we must be going soon."

She pouted. "Let me know when you are more interested in discussing your comings than your goings," she said with a smoldering look. Nosh's eyes widened in disbelief and he struggled to get out from under her.

He didn't have to try very hard because Aphrodite was suddenly standing directly before me, resting her fingers over my heart as she stared deep into my eyes. She flicked her clove cigarette into the fire without looking. The cloud of flavorful smoke reminded me of the candle in the bathroom—an almost identical scent. She began to circle me, trailing her fingers across my shoulder, the back of my neck, and then all the way around to the other side, murmuring to herself in obvious approval. Not that I cared.

"Aphrodite," I warned. "I had hoped our first interaction would be slightly more professional. Instead, you've attempted to seduce your nephew and your brother. And failed, I might add."

"Yeah," Nosh piped up lamely. "Failed horribly." I ignored him, trying not to be embarrassed by my progeny.

She smiled at me in amusement, leaning close enough so that only I could hear her voice. Her breath hit me like melted chocolate and fragrant rose oil. "They're so cute when they're that young. Do you remember what it was like to be so naive?" she asked softly, sounding genuinely curious.

I thought about it and shook my head. "No, actually," I admitted. "But we had to grow up a lot quicker in our days."

She nodded thoughtfully, eyeing me studiously. "And I'm only your half-sister, Sorin. Life is about new experiences. Keeping things in the family wasn't always a crime, if you recall. It's kind of our motto, to be honest."

"And how has that worked for our family? Has it kept us all close and friendly? No one hunting down their other siblings by any chance?" I asked dryly.

She laughed, looming before me so that her breasts pressed against my chest. She hummed as she massaged my shoulders and studied my face with anticipation. The tension in my muscles melted away like hot butter beneath her expert touch, and I had to force myself to bite back a groan. I was close enough to lick her lips, and the steady throb of the vein at her throat was as loud as a drum. She leaned closer, grazing her cheek against mine as softly as an imagined feather. As she moved, she slowly slid her forearms over my shoulders and clasped her hands behind my neck, trapping me with all the physical strength of a butterfly's wings. I knew I could pick her up and snap her in two. And that she would *let* me.

That vulnerable acceptance was part of the fun for her, after all. She was immortal. Any pains I caused could be later shrugged off.

Yet her very presence was the real danger. Her aura was an enticing prison: a barred cell of cool, silk ribbons; towers of melted chocolate fountains; fiery, sweaty flesh; seductive, breathless whimpers; and a never-ending bed of plush pillows. The prison warden of lust whispered directly into my ear. "Some juice is worth the squeeze, Sorin," she breathed, her hair tickling my nose. "*Trust* me." Her voice was a promise I felt deep within my chest, vibrating like a struck chord.

I focused deep on my blood reserves to withstand her charm, ignoring the fact that my cheeks were inflamed where she had caressed them with her skin. "What are you doing here, Aphrodite?" I rasped, stepping back from her clutches. Like I'd thought, she did not attempt to stop me, but she did wear a thoughtful frown. More of a pout, really. Even that looked sexy. "Not that it isn't a pleasure to meet you, but my trust is in short supply these days."

I didn't know Aphrodite, but Selene had warned me against her fellow Olympians. Aphrodite could be a wolf in sheep's...well, lingerie. I glanced back at the door to the bathroom, desperately wanting to wrap up this conversation so I could check on the devils before confronting the Sisters.

Aphrodite followed my wandering attention with eyes like a hawk. She glanced back at me with an approving look. "Your eyes betray you, brother, but I like the way you think. Pleasure before business, as I always say. That being said, your words are correct. This might be the only time I have ever cautioned against lust—at least for a little while longer. And I'm hating every inch of it."

"Minute of it," Nosh corrected, tugging at his collar as if having difficulty breathing.

"Hopefully longer than *that*, shaman," she chuckled suggestively. "In more ways than one. Double connotations heavily emphasized, of course."

I turned my glare on her. "Explain yourself, Aphrodite. If any harm comes to them, I will choke you to death with your own skimpy thong."

"She's not wearing one," Nosh piped in helpfully.

I shot him a dark, withering glare before turning back to my sister and the slithering ribbons, still sliding across the rises and swells of her body. They had moved down to her legs, wrapping around her feet and calves like knee-high sandals. "If any harm comes to them, I will choke you to death with your own skimpy ribbons."

"You know, there's a fetish for that kind of thing…" she said thoughtfully. I just stared at her, folding my arms. She sighed, walking over to one of the other armchairs. She sat down sideways, dangling her legs over the armrest as she crossed her ankles and leaned back, giving us yet another show. To be honest, it was getting rather old by now. Even though it was pleasurable to witness—a woman who fully owned every aspect of her beauty, not even acknowledging the meaning of the word shame. It was…powerful, actually. "You have several problems, and I don't think half of them are your fault," she said, staring into the fire pensively. The firelight struck her eyes, making the flecks of pink and purple glitter like precious gems.

I arched an eyebrow, seating myself across from her. "How so?"

"Dracula, witches, and Olympians," she said, not looking over at me as she ticked up her fingers with each word. I had to force myself to focus on her voice and eyes so as not to get distracted by the ribbons still slithering across her body.

I waited, wondering where she was going with her explanation. "Dracula is my problem, certainly. I inherited the witch problem and inadvertently made it my own—at least regarding the Cauldron. The Sisters of Mercy are a problem related to Dracula, so that's on me as well. The Olympians…I honestly have no idea how to approach that topic. I've only known for a few days. So, two out of three are on me."

She lifted a finger, clucking her tongue. "Ah. But you are presuming much. You do not have the full answer regarding our family. Even I do not have that, but I know more than you." I waited, not liking the direction our conversation was taking, but knowing that it was important—even if she was deceiving me herself. I wouldn't know that until I learned her angle. "Your story started off with the twins—Apollo and Artemis—setting you up. I don't know if Hades was in on it or if that was just a happy coincidence on their part. But..." she trailed off uneasily and I narrowed my eyes. She sighed in resignation. "You're about to make Hades your problem whether you want to or not."

Nosh let out a long whistle. "What makes you think Sorin will do anything you ask?"

"Because his loving, doting sister batted her eyelashes," she said sweetly. Then, case in point, she turned to me, batting her eyelashes as she spoke in a honeyed, simpering tone. "You need to break into the Underworld and get your soul back."

Nosh burst out laughing. "He's sitting right in front of you! What makes you think he doesn't have his soul—"

Aphrodite was suddenly out of the chair and pressed up against him, not seeming to cross the space between. She licked the side of his neck as her hands gripped a handful of his crotch through his pants. "Say *bonds*," she whispered.

Nosh didn't even hesitate, looking panicked. "B-bonds."

The silk ribbons abruptly whipped off Aphrodite's body and wrapped around Nosh's wrists, lifting them high over his head so that he was forced up onto his toes. My eyes widened in disbelief, but she held out her free hand in my direction, commanding me to remain seated.

Without waiting, she pressed her chest against Nosh and cupped his cheek with her unencumbered hand—the other still had a firm grip on his crotch. It was the main reason I hadn't attacked. What if she castrated him the moment I interfered?

She whispered in a tone that was loud enough to be heard from across the room, and she somehow made it into a moaning, sexual sound at the same time. "I can give you such an orgasm that you will literally want to end your life the moment of release. You will taste heaven before being forced to crawl back to a living hell, your desire for my touch so profound that you literally won't be able to string two syllables together. If you interrupt me one more time, I will give you this pleasure and then I will watch you suffer through the loss of your very soul." Her words rang through the room like a bell. She finally pulled away and gripped his chin with her other hand. "And that, my dear nephew, will be the moment I finally allow *myself* to climax."

He shuddered, his face as pale as a sheet. Aphrodite then kissed him on the lips and spun on the balls of her feet, sashaying back to her chair at a semi-natural pace rather than the supernatural, predatory speed she'd just displayed.

She lifted her hand and the ribbons released Nosh, answering the call of their mistress.

## 6

I shared a long, significant look with Nosh, but he was too busy staring at her and her ribbons in disbelief. And…a perverse curiosity—which I knew was part of her allure. To literally sex a man—or woman—to death, using both her body and her victim's mind to torture them with their own desires.

I could tell that he'd tried to use his magic to stop her, but it had obviously been ineffective. I would never look at a ribbon the same way again.

I cleared my throat. "I appreciate your blunt example, but you will never again threaten a member of my family," I said in a calm, soft tone. "I already warned you once. The same goes for any of my loved ones. If you are here on good faith, you will abide by my terms. If you cannot do so, the door is right there."

She studied me from her chair, peering at me with the lazy gaze of a cat—the deceivingly innocent look before they pounced to kill. She nodded slowly, assessing me with a pensive smirk.

I turned to Nosh. "Control yourself. You asked for that. You know who she is, and you should have had some inkling of the weapons she might have at her disposal. Rise to the challenge, understood?"

Aphrodite chuckled at my phrasing, but I ignored her. Nosh gave me a jerking nod. "Y-yes."

I turned back to the Olympian. "Neat trick with the ribbons. But why did you ask Nosh to say...that word?" I asked, carefully reconsidering saying it out loud so I didn't end up like him.

"Consent matters," she said with a wry smile. "And hands can often be busy with other...matters, so Hephaestus made them voice-activated. He is just as talented at making implements of pleasure as tools of pain."

She was grinning at me triumphantly. She may as well have been a cat unsheathing her claws and raking them against the armchair. I studied her up and down, sighing in disappointment to see the playful, carefree gleam still dancing in her eyes. As much as she got off on teasing and drawing out my lust, I could tell she actually wanted to push me over the edge and break me—to satisfy her own curiosity. I sensed that she was often overlooked by her fellow Olympians in the halls of power, and she wanted to dispel that fact. She wanted to see what it was like to fuck the newest godling who had everyone so up in arms, and to have that godling *beg* for the experience. To personally assess my capacity for giving pleasure by seeing how much ecstasy I could give *her* with my bite.

"I'm not convinced you fully understand the depth of my convictions, sister. Let me show you," I told her, gently.

She cocked her head with curious excitement, sensing she had finally won her little game. I saw the telltale flash of a woman daring me to do my worst. It wasn't her fault. She didn't know me. And she had underestimated me.

She didn't know that I preyed on the overconfident. They were my greatest conquests.

And I was feeling more sexually frustrated than I had at any point in my life. The perfect storm. She wanted to see what I could do? How experienced I was in the act of destroying while delivering pleasure?

Okay.

Completely motionless, I focused my powers, sinking to the very depths of my blood reservoir. I scooped up one of the strange blood crystals I had managed to form the last time I had fed upon Natalie. I held that dark ruby of blood, sensing the immense power within. Then I coated the ruby in Victoria's incredibly potent blood, enveloping the crystal in a metallic shell of Olympian-infused power. Oddly enough, I found some of the metaphysical blood Castle Ambrogio had given to Victoria in order to save her life, adding a clear coat to the metallic ruby.

Still motionless, I marveled at my creation, not entirely sure how I had done it. Then I figuratively crushed the precious blood gem into priceless powder and fixed my gaze upon the Olympian goddess of love and sex. A hurricane of power roared through every fiber of my being, almost taking my breath away. I focused my entire self on Aphrodite. The moment my eyes met hers, she visibly flinched, as if I'd struck her cheek with my palm.

I didn't react. Instead, I let unseen ribbons of my own power slither over her body as I swept my gaze over her nudity, starting at her feet and absorbing every single inch of her, permitting myself to openly appreciate every facet of her form. I didn't hold back, and I didn't allow guilt or shame to touch my face or my soul. This wasn't of the heart—that belonged to Victoria and Natalie and...my castle, strangely enough.

This act was of the mind and the body. My weapon was blood—my specialty.

This was an attack, even if Aphrodite didn't quite realize it yet. But she had asked for it. I was about to give her a dose of her own medicine and beat her upside the head with her own hypocrisy.

I saw her body as an exquisite, priceless statue designed by a master sculptor; she was infinitely more than a vessel to be used and then discarded once I achieved the pinnacles of my wildest carnal pleasures.

Aphrodite was genuinely the most beautiful human body I had ever —and would ever—see. I wouldn't be surprised to learn that Nosh saw her in a slightly different way, her form somehow molding to his own interests. Maybe taller or plumper, if that was his thing. If I had the necessary skills to mold the absolute perfect companion that would conform to every inch of my own body, I could not have done a better job than Aphrodite as she appeared to me now. Her every curve screamed to be lightly caressed with a feather and raked with my teeth.

Even her veins were perfectly placed for me to sink my fangs into when I would grow thirsty. Physically, she was everything I ever could have wanted. I could define her in one word, but even that would seem incomplete: perfection.

Everywhere I looked was a perfect handhold of pliant flesh designed to fill my palms like a succulent fruit. Every crevice was perfectly sized to invite my tongue or finger.

Even using only my eyes, I knew other parts of her would fit me just as snugly.

If I was blind, I would have still known every line of her body—down to the individual strands of her golden-brown hair. I would have even known the color of that hair despite not being able to *see*. I would have drowned in delirious happiness at the faintest whiff of her every scent. I could not find one single aspect, curve, contour or measurement that was wrong. Not even that, but I couldn't find a single aspect that I could improve.

But...she was too perfect. Like she should sit on a shelf for fear of breaking her.

She was visibly panting, and her skin was now inflamed, her nipples hard and her lips plump as they became engorged with blood. She trembled beneath my gaze like a glass vase attempting to withstand the dangerous vibrations of that single sound that was enough to shatter it. I'd seen someone do that at a party once, using their voice to shatter a wineglass once they reached a certain pitch.

I watched as Aphrodite's hips began to rock, her shifting ribbons converging between her thighs in a slithering tangle of rapidly quivering silk.

"No," I commanded in a calm, gentle, authoritative tone.

The ribbons dropped to the ground in a pile, utterly motionless.

She gasped at the sudden loss of control and the physical source of her pleasure. Her eyes widened as they flicked towards the lifeless pile of traitorous ribbons—how they had obeyed my single word command rather than her own rampant desire. Her attention latched back onto me as I leaned forward, resting my elbows on my knees. I stared deep into her eyes, using the pulverized blood ruby's power to enthrall her. *Not yet*, I thought to myself, relaying the silent command to the goddess of sex. She had threatened to kill Nosh with sex, and she needed to understand that I didn't tolerate such things.

That it would never happen again.

She nodded—more of a spastic twitch than anything. Her lips parted as she struggled desperately to breathe, unable to even blink without my express permission.

*You will sit on the cusp until I permit otherwise. This ends here, sister. You will never again use your powers against me or those I care about.*

She croaked out a desperate, forlorn whimper, unable to speak through her mad lust, and unable to deny my silent commands. I was preventing her from fully enjoying her own pleasure, and her body was covered in a thin sheen of sweat as a result.

She panted harder, her eyes rolling back into her skull as her body went to war with itself. She whimpered, her hands gripping the armrests of the chair like they were the only thing tethering her soul and body together. The wood groaned as she bit her lower lip, her nostrils flaring.

*Do. You. Understand?*

She nodded frantically, her toes curling loud enough for the bones to pop.

I waited three more seconds before leaning back into my chair to watch the effects of her pent-up lust hitting her all at once. I nodded one time.

She instantly cried out, her thighs clenching tight as she snapped both armrests off the chair and flung her head back. She quivered and rocked the chair back on its rear legs, her toes curling as she gasped and moaned. Moments later, her body slowly melted into the chair as if her bones had liquified.

I turned to Nosh. "Aphrodite wishes to wear one of my robes. She's feeling a chill, the poor dear." Nosh stared from me to Aphrodite with a stunned look on his face. "Now, Nosh. They're just tits. You've seen enough of them."

## 7

He stiffened and then rushed over to scoop up a robe that had been tossed onto a couch—the same robe I'd tried to give her earlier. He approached and politely extended the robe to the still-recovering Aphrodite. She took it and awkwardly covered herself. Then she slowly looked up at me, her mouth opening wordlessly as she tried to regain control of her breathing. She looked... alarmed, yet aroused by that alarm. "How..." she whispered, licking her lips. "What...*was*...that?" she whispered shakily.

"A lesson and a warning. The only one you will receive from me."

She stared at me, still trembling at random intervals as echoes of bliss hit her. "I've never felt anything like it," she breathed. "Perhaps because you were in control. But...*how*? No one should be able to do that to me, of all people."

"It only worked because you actually wanted it," I explained. "I wouldn't have done it otherwise. You said it yourself. Consent matters." She nodded dazedly. "In fact, that is *why* I did it. If I hadn't, you would have done something fatally stupid to press the issue." I studied her face. "Right?"

She nodded. "Y-yes. Even with the likely risks, yes," she admitted in a whisper.

I nodded. "I could sense it on you. I figured it was the best solution to our problem. I flex, and you get enough of a taste to satisfy your desire. No one dies. We get back to what actually matters."

She stared at me with an awed look on her face. "If I had any doubt about you being an Olympian before, you just dispelled it."

"Did you?" I asked softly. "Have any doubts, I mean."

She shook her head. "No. But the question would have always lingered in the back of my mind until I saw proof. Until I saw you in action."

I nodded. "That was another reason I did it. Not for you, but for myself. I am not fully sold on Zeus' claim. I assume that no one but a fellow Olympian could have done such a thing?"

She stared at me in complete silence, the fire crackling between us. "Sorin..." she finally murmured. "*No* Olympian could have done that to me. Not with a look and no physical contact. Sweet fucking gods!" she hissed, raking a hand through her sweaty hair. "No wonder everyone is so terrified of you. I thought they were just being dramatic."

I masked my surprise upon hearing that not even a fellow Olympian could have played her like a fiddle with only a look. I'd been curious about how potent the powers Artemis, Apollo, and Hades had given me were. Their curses, as they had been sold to me. Not only was I a blooded Olympian in my own right, but I now had the added curses of three Olympians. So why were those curses making me more powerful?

Was it their curses or the strange blood crystal I'd formed from my castle, Victoria, and Natalie? Then again, I could only use blood as power thanks to Artemis. I didn't let any of that touch my features because I still had no solid understanding of Aphrodite's true intentions.

"Now that we've gotten that out of the way, you are going to tell me —in no uncertain or ambiguous terms—why you came here tonight. What you meant about Hades and the Underworld. And you will do so quickly," I said, suddenly remembering that Izzy and the Sisters of Mercy were waiting for me up above. "I have people waiting for me upstairs."

Aphrodite nodded patiently. "Why do you think I froze time for you two, brother? To everyone within a mile, only seconds have passed since you entered this floor. Even to those outside."

Inwardly, I let out a breath of relief to hear concrete confirmation about the passing of time being frozen. She'd already said as much, but to hear specifics was greatly reassuring to me.

Nosh cleared his throat. "That...is incredible. How did you manage that?"

Aphrodite studied me, picking up on my thoughts, and gave me a subtle nod. "It is night, and my powers are closely tied to nocturnal pastimes." She glanced over at Nosh who had an aloof look on his face. She sighed. "Sex. We're talking about sex. When a daddy loves a mommy very, very much, a little Noshy is made."

He narrowed his eyes angrily. "Really?" he said in a dry, unimpressed tone. He shot me a frustrated look. I gave him nothing, curious how the two would get along now. I'd already interfered once. He needed to take care of himself from here on out or forever be labeled weak. "I get it, Aunt Ho Dye-tee," he said, making the moniker rhyme with her real name.

I grinned, clapping my hands in approval.

Her eyes widened and she suddenly burst out laughing. "Okay. That was good. I'll give you that. But you are too damned innocent for me to help myself, and my brother doesn't approve of my distractions. The adults are talking now, so you can pretend to be a little human again and go play outside the bedchambers." She stood and tossed him the pile of ribbons that had briefly decorated her naked body—which I hadn't actually seen her grab. "A memento. Twirl them around or something. Whatever little humans do," she said, waving a hand dismissively. "Be careful what you say around them, nephew," she added with a playful wink. "Or don't. Bye."

"Kids," Nosh said slowly, as if wanting to verify he had understood her words correctly because they made no sense to him. "Not little humans." He set the ribbons down on a side table, looking uncomfortable about handling them after the section of Aphrodite's body they'd just been working on. His aunt's undergarments, to be literal. Also, they'd strung him up without effort earlier, so he was obviously embarrassed.

"Yes, those creatures," she snapped impatiently, narrowing her eyes and folding her arms at his act of setting down her insulting gift. "Goodbye."

Nosh shot me an incredulous look. "How can the goddess of sex and love be so ignorant about children?"

I slowly stood, frowning thoughtfully at Aphrodite. She had shifted her attention to stare at me intently, looking on the edge of her patience. Almost as if...she was bullshitting her way into getting Nosh out of the room. I met her stare directly as I slowly answered Nosh. "Maybe she's just not a kid person."

She nodded stiffly, but I could sense a deeper pain on her face at the topic. "That."

"Can you give us some privacy, Nosh? Go check outside and make sure everything is okay. Keep an eye on Izzy and check on the Nephilim."

The room was silent as Aphrodite and I continued to stare at each other. I could almost make out features that reminded me of myself. Almost.

"I am a grown ass man," Nosh argued.

"I took you for a tits man," Aphrodite said absently, not breaking eye contact with me.

"That's not what I meant—" He cut off, letting out a frustrated breath. "You know what? I am going to go outside and make sure everyone is okay. Because I'm an adult." He spun on his heel in my peripheral vision.

"Pick up your toys before you leave, young man," Aphrodite snapped, blindly pointing at the ribbons he had set down on the side table.

I finally broke eye contact to see him turn back to us, staring down at the ribbons before shooting each of us a withering look. "How do I do the serpentine lingerie thing? I'm feeling frisky and I'm being sent to my room. Who knows what I'll get up to," he said dryly.

Aphrodite burst out laughing, finally turning to face him. "No words are necessary if you want it to do something—anything—to your own body. Just think it." She winked darkly. "You're welcome."

He nodded curiously, staring down at the ribbons. They suddenly lashed out, each of them wrapping around a different wrist like bracelets. He grunted in surprise, lifting them for a closer inspection. Thankfully, he left it at that. He shot her a curious look, lowering his arms. "Thank you, Aphrodite. I think."

She nodded with an amused smirk. "You're welcome, sweet boy."

Nosh turned and left the room, closing the door behind him.

"Kids," Aphrodite said, her shoulders relaxing ever so slightly.

I nodded thoughtfully. Because Nosh had brought up an interesting point. Aphrodite had conceived children from quite a few Olympians: Ares, Hermes, Poseidon, and Dionysus. Maybe more. So...why was she acting as if she didn't know a thing about children?

"It is a sore subject, brother. I ask that you leave it alone," she said softly, turning to stare into the fire. "I cannot read your mind, but I can feel your eyes. I just needed him gone."

"Okay," I said neutrally, studying her and wondering what trouble she was about to lay upon my shoulders that she didn't even want Nosh knowing about.

## 8

I waited in silence for about a minute before my curiosity and impatience got the best of me. "What was that really about? Do you not trust him?"

My words snapped her out of her thoughts, and she let out a small sigh. "Why would I not trust him?" she asked, cocking her head curiously.

I shrugged. "He is a skinwalker. Maybe that concerns you."

She stared at me for about three seconds, and then her attention shifted towards the door as if she could still see him. "Is he now?" she asked, rubbing her chin thoughtfully. "Is that a Native American thing?"

I frowned uneasily. "You didn't sense it? You felt that he was a shaman, though."

She nodded thoughtfully, still staring towards the door. "I take it that his mother was a shaman? Or shared that bloodline?"

I nodded. "Second generation shaman, but she didn't have any powers. Trust me on that. Her father was quite frustrated over it," I sighed. "She's long dead anyway. She was mortal."

Aphrodite cast me a sympathetic frown. "I'm sorry. That was your second lost love, yes?"

I nodded, not liking the sudden wave of emotions that welled up within me. "How did you not sense him being a skinwalker?" I repeated.

She glanced back at the door again, pursing her lips uneasily. "Many Olympians can change form, Sorin..." she suggested with extreme caution, as if fearing my reaction.

"Fuck," I cursed under my breath. Did she have a point or was it just a strange coincidence? He had the skinwalker blades—his tomahawks. Was he under the impression that he was a skinwalker simply because he had no other explanation? Like me learning that some of the gifts I'd been given by the Olympians may have simply been birthrights—that I had been played, granting Artemis, Apollo, and Hades more credit than they were actually due. It was a great control tactic to make someone think they owed you everything. I'd used it often in my past life.

Dracula was a prime example of how poorly that could work out, even when the gifts were truly given.

Aphrodite slowly sat down on the bear-skin rug at my feet, not looking at me. She somehow made even that look deliciously seductive. She crossed her legs and carefully adjusted the robe so that it covered her tanned skin. "Sit," she said, gesturing at my chair. Her voice had taken on an undertone of sincerity rather than coy playfulness.

I joined her on the rug instead, mirroring her position so that our knees touched. She smiled warmly, obviously having expected me to take the higher ground and sit in the chair looking down upon her as a power play. Had it been a test? Or was I looking too deeply into it? I was fairly certain that it was impossible to look too deeply into anything related to the Olympians.

"Nosh didn't need to hear your personal matters—and your privacy matters to me," she said, smirking proudly at her dual use for the word. "You don't need an audience when enjoying the company of two beautiful women in your bedchambers."

I listened to her words and I knew that she was not just talking about Natalie and Victoria, or about my bedchambers. "Or when talking to my sister," I said, watching her closely.

She smiled and gave me a slow nod. "One never knows who is listening. I'm sure you've learned that lesson in your years. How even bedrooms are not as private as we hope. The most terrific and terrible things often take place during the night."

My fingers clenched tightly into a fist. Was...she speaking about Selene? How she had feared that our conversation had been watched, forcing her to put on a show and harm Natalie? Was that why she kept referencing my bedroom? I kept my face composed. Were they allies? Was that why she wasn't outright saying it?

"I have learned that. Several times," I said with a hollow smile, hoping that it passed for guilt.

"With recent news, I doubt anyone is watching right now," she said carefully. "It is even likely that they are following other leads that someone may have let slip. But better safe than sorry. Names are not dangerous in and of themselves, but when used in certain contexts, they can be...revealing. Even faint echoes of names can be dangerous."

I nodded, feeling my pulse increase. "Yet some harbor less fear than others and choose to directly involve themselves," I said, gently resting my fingertips on her knees in a reassuring and appreciative gesture.

She nodded. "Perhaps they just harbor less common sense, or no longer care more about their own selfish needs over those of another."

I nodded, waiting for more.

"I am the goddess of sex. I do not like stories without a climax. Fuck and let fuck, as I've often said," she murmured, the sudden shift in topic leaving me reeling. I stared at her, not sure I understood her meaning. "I thought you deserved that much, at least," she said, glancing over her shoulder at the door to the bathroom.

My eyes widened and I blinked. "You stopped time so that I could..." I trailed off, not believing I had heard her properly.

She rolled her eyes, amused. "You can say it, Sorin. Fuck, fuck, fuck. It's what you *mean* by the word that really matters, not the actual word used. Please tell me you aren't that much of a prude. You gave me a demonstration, in case you have forgotten."

I blushed, shaking my head. "I know how to say the word, Aphrodite. I haven't decided on which word to use, or even what I want the chosen word to mean. We haven't crossed that bridge yet."

She nodded, grinning mischievously. "Exactly my point. I froze time so that you could fuck your devils, as I hear you call them. Love that, by the way," she added with a conspiratorial wink. "So they could fuck you. So they could fuck each other. Whatever fuckery you were racing down here to do before the Sisters of Mercy showed up outside." She grinned as I shifted uncomfortably. "It's what a good sister does—helps her brother chase some ass and grasp his dreams by the ponytails."

I blinked at her, deciding that philosophy and morals was not a topic I currently wanted to get into with Aphrodite, let alone grasping my dreams. She was my...*sister*—which still sounded bizarre to say, even though I had tested the word out a few times. "Why would you go out of your way to do that for me? What if I wasn't who you thought? Or what if our interests didn't align? Don't take this personally, but I have a hard time accepting that you did this out of the goodness of your own heart. What is in it for you?"

She frowned sadly, her bubble of joy slowly deflating at my lack of enthusiasm. "To be entirely honest?" I nodded. She stared at me unblinking, and I watched as light tears began to well up in her eyes, even though her face didn't change in the slightest. "What's in it for me is probably an early grave," she whispered.

I stiffened. "What?"

She waved a hand, wiping at her eyes with the sleeves of her robe. "I'll get to that in a moment. Otherwise you won't listen to the rest of what I have to say."

I frowned. "Okay."

"As much as it pains me to admit, freezing time wasn't entirely my idea—even though it should have been, what with me being the goddess of sex. But I was...distracted. It took a rational mind to help me see clearly. It took a heart to open my eyes."

I was surprised to see her open up so completely after her outlandish flirting from earlier. Like I was catching a rare glimpse at the woman beneath the lingerie...which was really a horrible simile, the more I thought about it.

"Upon hearing the recent news about you—that I might have a brother untainted by the scheming of Mount Olympus—I sought out some friends of mine. I only have a few. I soon learned about what was done to you in Delphi so long ago. What was taken from you. That you chose a life of half-love, even though it cost you your soul and two other curses," she said, her voice growing alarmingly angry. "I am the goddess of love and sex, and my own brother was denied the full experience of his heart's desire. Not permitted to even *touch* his lover. Not permitted to behold the radiant glow of the sun's golden light kissing her flesh." She looked up at me, her eyes red-rimmed. "Is it true that you wrote forty-four love poems to her? Using the blood of swans as ink since it was the only thing available to you? The only way you could communicate with her?" she whispered, her voice breaking.

I nodded, surprised that she knew such a specific detail as what type of creature I'd been told to hunt. I cleared my throat at my own swell of grief at the unbidden memory. When trying to steal Artemis' bow in exchange for Hades' assistance, I had indeed used the blood of swans to leave love notes for Selene to find every morning, since I was unable to visit her in person—not after the sun burned my skin, thanks to Apollo's jealousy. "Yes."

Aphrodite's fists clenched, causing her knuckles to crack like gunshots. "Forced to live on blood as a reward for your steadfast devotion in the simple act of pursuing love at any cost. Then to be deceived at the very end, promised a hollow reward if you were willing to kill this woman to prove your love." Tears fell down her cheeks and her shoulders shook. "To learn that two of my siblings had tormented my little brother's very heart and soul almost destroyed me. I wanted to meet such a man," she said, smiling sadly at me. "For that was a man I could proudly call brother."

I lowered my eyes sadly, vividly recalling the events that had birthed the world's first vampire. "Selene was worth it."

She shuddered as if my words tore at her soul. "Upon hearing your story, one of my fellow Olympians felt that you deserved some extra time to enjoy some of those stolen joys. Although not the original aim of your heart, my friend sensed that your heart had somehow opened up again to two others." Her eyes drifted towards the door to the bathroom with a crooked smile. "I wish I could take credit for the idea, but I can't. And I didn't want you thinking I was trying to do so."

I stared at her, my fingers tingling. She really *had* frozen time so that I could climb into bed with Natalie and Victoria. That...was unbelievably considerate. Not just on a physical level, but that she had done it to right a wrong inflicted upon me by our siblings, Apollo and Artemis. It wasn't about the sex; it was about the gift of a peaceful moment of reprieve.

And, if I was reading between the lines correctly, it had been Selene's idea. My wife.

Selene was the fellow Olympian whom Aphrodite was referring to; she had convinced the goddess of sex to grant me the time to enjoy a safe moment of pleasure with Natalie and Victoria. Was that out of guilt for what she had done to Natalie, or was it as genuine as Aphrodite was making it sound?

I stared at Aphrodite, realizing that she was watching me attentively.

"It has nothing to do with any recent injuries your devils may have suffered. Those were necessary for reasons you will soon learn, Sorin," she said reassuringly. Her comment fully confirmed my suspicion about Selene. Then she glanced up at the ceiling. "Sex happens most often at night, so I have close ties to the moon. Next time you're fucking under the moonlight, maybe glance up at the moon and howl. I think it would make her smile."

I blinked, entirely sure that such an act would be beyond cruel and not remotely humorous. "Okay," I lied.

"My gift wouldn't be as strong without the power of night. Just like you, brother."

I suddenly realized why she was being so vague. There were various gods and Titans related to the night. She was obscuring the truth as best she could. But I knew she was talking about Selene. And she obviously didn't want Nosh knowing about her aid. But why be so obscure? She had said that context mattered, but we were talking about Artemis and Apollo without any concern. I remembered when Selene had recently frozen time to pay me a visit with her glass chains made by...

"Hephaestus," I gasped. "The glass chains. Your husband made them!"

"My husband makes many things without my knowledge," she murmured carefully, "and his creations most often cause him more pain than they are worth."

"Zeus forced you to marry Hephaestus. Why would you help Zeus' son?"

She nodded. "He did. But we have all done things we regret, and I have a soft spot for the ugly brute, Hephaestus. It took me a few centuries to find that spot. Or for him to find that spot, technically speaking," she chuckled darkly.

I rolled my eyes. "Less innuendo and more explanation."

"Hephaestus and I have an understanding. You're my brother, and I hate those fucking twins more than almost anyone—except Hera, of course. I hated them long before I heard your story, Sorin. But now?" she asked coldly. "I would open the pits of Tartarus and toss them within, whistling as I worked. Your arrival into the family is like a perfect storm. A storm of retribution. A cleansing purge."

I stared at her, wondering again why she had used their names without concern but hadn't used Selene's name. "You do realize that you just gave me reason to suspect your integrity, right? That you have ulterior motives beyond offering me an evening of pleasure."

She nodded unashamedly. "You had those suspicions the moment you saw me. Which is why I spoke of other things first. Maybe I was hoping to appeal to your emotions in order to manipulate you. But maybe I was speaking the truth. I no longer care which way you take it."

I frowned at her sudden defeated demeanor. "Why do you no longer care?"

"Those chains you mentioned...the twins punished Hephaestus for making them. They thought he made them faulty on purpose—in order to secretly help you. They...severed his thumbs for it."

I gasped, staring at her in horror as I felt bile rise up into the back of my throat.

## 9

She used the sleeve of her robe to wipe at her nose. "I hate them, Sorin. More than I've ever wanted to have sex with anyone. I never truly realized how closely hate and love are intertwined. So, believe me or don't, brother. I am at your mercy. Kill me, imprison me, or believe me. I'd rather die by your hand than let the twins or anyone else in our family do it, for I will surely perish for what I plan to do to them. They know that now. I will be their next target."

"Why?" I rasped, gripping her chin. I now had a pretty good idea why she was mentioning some names over others—she was only mentioning names of the Olympians who were openly standing against me. She didn't want to paint a target on any potential allies. "Hephaestus was not at fault for the chains. I swear it."

She nodded. "I know that. So did they," she said woodenly. "They cut off his thumbs anyway. Simply because they *could*."

"The twins," I growled, gritting my teeth. "Apollo and Artemis. Out of all the Olympians, why are they so obsessed with my downfall?"

She shrugged helplessly. "Hera must be helping them, although I've found no proof. She's the biggest bitch on Mount Olympus, and she hates Zeus' illegitimate children with a passion," she said, pointing a finger at her chest and then mine. She didn't seem to notice that her robe had fallen open, giving me a show. Then again, with her, clothing likely felt chafing and unnatural. "The same one who will hunt you down soon, brother. She won't give you a moment's respite, even if you wanted to live the rest of your life in a cave and never see another human ever again. Your very existence is a slap in her face—direct proof of our father's most recent infidelity. And with a mortal woman, no less. In her eyes, the only way to reclaim her honor is to utterly destroy you. Your only chance to stand against your fucked-up family is to get your soul back from the Underworld. You must take it from Hades."

I stared at her, shaking my head. "If I currently don't have the strength to stand against Hera, how the hell do you expect me to take down Zeus' brother, Hades?" I growled in frustration.

"Perhaps you could steal it," she suggested, not sounding too confident. She noticed my frank look and wilted. "I don't know what to tell you, but it is not a choice any longer."

"What do you mean?" I asked, frowning.

"Who do you think Dracula is trying to summon inside your castle? Dracula knows Hades has your soul, right? I can almost guarantee that Hera knows because Artemis and Apollo would have told her after your little stunt at the Statue of Liberty. Luckily, everyone is too busy picking sides to come at you all at once. And they are too busy maneuvering for their own safety to openly pick a side. You have drawn a line in the sand between two of Olympus's most powerful gods, and everyone is terrified about which side to choose. Welcome to the family, brother. We all hate each other while pretending to love each other unconditionally. We put the fun in dysfunctional."

I ran a hand through my hair, clenching my teeth as I considered and discarded half-a-dozen plans before mentally stepping back to let my thoughts work in the background. "How has no one known about me all this time? I haven't exactly hidden my existence. I always assumed my curses were common knowledge. How did no one know who I really was?"

Aphrodite grunted. "Luck. Sheer fucking luck. The curses helped because it trapped your soul in the Underworld—where no other major Olympians reside. Everyone who might have known kept their lips shut or doubted the truth after Apollo and Artemis so deftly hood-winked you. No one saw you as a threat after that—a powerful human, sure. Then you died and Dracula rose to power. No one even remembered your name, so they dismissed the whispered rumor that you might be Zeus' illegitimate son."

I grimaced. "Then I came back. And *then* I picked a fight in the middle of the sky with Zeus."

She nodded. "Brilliant execution, but a terrible plan, brother."

"I didn't know," I argued angrily. "How the fuck was I supposed to know something like that? Especially after believing that I'd been cursed by Apollo and Artemis."

"Which was probably the point."

I sighed, thinking furiously. "So, Dracula is trying to get his hands on my soul to use as a bargaining chip—which is pretty much his only chance at survival." Aphrodite nodded. "Where does Hades stand on the issue? Couldn't he just crush my soul right now and be done with it?"

She shrugged. "No one knows the mind of Hades. He resents us for banishing him to the Underworld. He's an asshole, but maybe he's a different kind of asshole. I wouldn't bank on him being an ally, though. He took your soul in the first place, after all. I bet he's loving the sudden attention—how his family suddenly remembers how special he is. Until they get what they want, anyway."

I nodded pensively. "Break into the Underworld," I muttered under my breath. "I don't have time to travel to Greece to revisit that cursed cave where I first met Hades. And if I don't hand Dracula over to the Sisters of Mercy, they are going to cause all sorts of problems, spreading my resources thin."

She shot me a frightened look at the mention of handing Dracula over. "I can promise you one thing, Sorin. If Dracula leaves that castle —for any reason—every Olympian on Mount Olympus will come after him. It's simple self-preservation. If they get Dracula, they get priceless answers about your true past. They will have leverage with both Zeus and Hera. Dracula is a shield to keep them out of the war—or to get your soul all to themselves."

I grimaced, deciding not to mention that Nero also knew my past. Luckily, Lucian was already dead—which was a chilling thought to have. It hurt my heart to admit it in such a cold manner, but it was the truth. It meant that he was safe from Olympian politics. But now Nero needed protection. If anyone found out what he knew...he would be just as valuable as Dracula. And if anyone spoke to Dracula, I could guarantee he would tell them about Nero as well. I had to keep both of them safe. From everyone.

Which meant I now had multiple reasons to refuse the Sisters of Mercy.

Which would introduce a whole new layer of drama.

And I had to do all of this before Dracula succeeded in summoning Hades to my very castle to help break him out.

"What are the twins doing right now?" I asked. "What are any of the Olympians doing? Any piece of information might help. If I can turn them on each other, I can cause a distraction that it might buy me enough time to get my soul back without them ever knowing it."

Aphrodite considered my question. "The twins are doing something nefarious, but I have no idea what. It is likely guaranteed to cause you or anyone associated with you immense suffering. When it comes to the other relatives, I have no idea. I've been busy taking care of my husband following the twins' cruelty. I haven't even seen Ares in a while, and we usually Netfuck at least once a month."

I arched an eyebrow, wondering if she understood how inappropriate it was to talk about another man immediately after talking about her doting husband. "Netfuck?" I asked.

She waved a hand. "Our take on *Netflix and chill*. But Ares and I don't even pretend to watch Netflix. Or chill. We just screw each other senseless to release some aggression whenever Hephaestus is busy tinkering in his shop and ignoring me." I watched a tear fall from her cheeks. "Which will no longer be a concern. He can't tinker without thumbs."

"Oh," I said as if her answer made perfect sense. I'd have to find out what Netflix was to get the reference. She obviously saw nothing wrong with her open relationship. I wasn't sure if she was crying about Hephaestus missing thumbs or the fact that she no longer had an excuse to have sex with Ares, the god of war. I didn't see how either answer could help me anyway.

"I used to spend time with Hecate, but she's been quiet for a long time. We usually go our own ways for long stretches since the world doesn't really need our constant attention. Hardly anyone worships us anymore."

I nodded, having a dozen questions on that topic—what did gods do when they were forgotten? I had assumed they died or withered away, but apparently not. "Hecate..." I murmured, scratching at my head. Her name was familiar, but I couldn't place why.

"Witchcraft," she said, watching me thoughtfully. "She's the goddess of witchcraft."

I leaned forward. "What kind of witch?" I asked slowly, fearing the answer. "Dark or white?"

Aphrodite blinked. "Yes. That. Have you not been listening? There aren't really any good Olympians. We have powers and we use those powers however our mood suits us. Otherwise there would be two families—the good one and the bad one. Like the Christians with their angels and demons," she said with a vague grimace of distaste. "We're more like a reality TV show in comparison. We don't pick good or bad. We just do whatever floats our boat."

I shook my head. "How long has it been since Hecate involved herself with humanity? The Sisters of Mercy and the Cauldron are both giving me headaches. Could she be behind either? Both? Neither?"

Aphrodite shrugged. "I haven't heard of her helping any human witches in centuries. Maybe longer. Back when everyone still used swords to make friends. Which was a long fucking time ago, so your current witches are likely being idiots all on their own."

She had a point. If Hecate was involved with either group, I would have already heard about it from Izzy. Hell, the Sisters of Mercy were working for the church—one of the various schools of Christianity, since there were about a hundred different factions these days. I doubted Hecate would be involved with that conflict of interest. The Cauldron hadn't mentioned having a goddess backing them up either, and I was certain they would have mentioned it—or that Izzy would have warned me about it.

"Who else?" I asked, wondering why she hadn't mentioned the obvious name—Selene.

She shrugged. "Any name I give you is going to put a target on their spine, and in case you have forgotten, Artemis is a great fucking shot. The best. Literally."

"My Greek mythology is rusty," I lied. "I'm just asking for a rundown of the players, good and bad. I'm not asking you to give up allies." Hopefully that statement would let her slip in a nugget of truth that I could use. "What is Ares up to? You spend time with him."

She scoffed. "We fuck like wild animals, Sorin. We don't cuddle. We don't chat. We don't braid each other's hair. We share similar interests, in a way," she said with a dark smile. "We both convince one subset of humans to penetrate another subset of humans with a phallic object. He prefers his followers to use a metal sword, I encourage mine to use their flesh sword—"

"I get it!" I snapped, quickly cutting her off before she could go into further detail.

She chuckled at my interruption. "Prude," she teased. "Anyway, when I do see Ares, we don't chat. We take out our frustrations on each other. He's probably overseas, stirring up some human war of one type or another. He cares more about mortal wars than his fellow Olympians. Because we are much too refined to go to war, obviously," she said. "Leaves him little to talk about at the dinner table."

I stared at her intently. "Except now the Olympians *are* going to war..."

Her smile slipped and she blinked. "Oh. Maybe...I should reach out to him," she murmured, sounding embarrassed. This kernel of insight seemed to encourage her. "Okay. Maybe there is a point to this feckless reverie."

I blinked at her, surprised at her specific words. I'd thought that exact phrase just before confronting Zeus a few nights ago atop the Statue of Liberty. Had I said that out loud? Had she been there?

"What about Zeus?" I asked, assuming I already knew the answer. He'd told me he wasn't coming near me until it was safe. What if safe meant dead?

"No one sees Zeus. No one sees Hera either. Unless they are about to die. That applies to both of them, by the way." She wiggled absently, repositioning herself as she began idly combing her fingers through the bear rug's furry head. I hid my smile to find that she was scratching behind the bear's ears, not seeming to realize she was even doing it. Almost like she was petting the dead beast. "Hermes is running messages all over, but he never shares what he knows without payment. This is the busiest he's been in a millennium. I see him all over the place," she mused suspiciously. "Who else do you want to know about?" she asked, her eyes distant as she continued stroking the bear.

"SORIN!" Nosh shouted at the top of his lungs from what had to be the elevator. "Trouble!"

I jumped to my feet, already racing for the door.

## 10

Aphrodite grabbed me with a grip like iron. "No!" she snarled furiously, fighting against my forward advance. "I stopped fucking time for you to have some goddamned sex! Whatever he saw is not an immediate concern!"

I skidded to a halt, frowning back at her. "Truly?"

"Yes!" she snapped, trying to fix the tangled robe back into place since my rush to the door had ripped it wide open. "You moron."

Nosh appeared at the far end of the hall, running as fast as he could. "Sorin!"

"Calm your tits!" Aphrodite snapped at him, obviously annoyed.

He halted before us, bending at the waist to place his hands on his knees and catch his breath. "There's a fight. A big one," he wheezed.

Aphrodite sniffed angrily. "And tell me, shaman, are any of them actually *moving*?"

Nosh straightened, seeming to lose some of the wind in his sails. "Well, no. They're all frozen in place."

"Exactly," Aphrodite snapped. She folded her arms beneath her breasts and began tapping her foot impatiently. She had obviously given up on fixing her robe; I'd torn it too severely to repair. Which meant Nosh was staring—once again—at a very pleasant display of female breasts. Add that to the fact that Aphrodite had sent him away so we could have some privacy, and that she now looked frustrated and annoyed by his interruption, and my situation with Aphrodite took on a whole new meaning. "Now, go back outside and wait until we're finished."

There it was. My saving grace. All wrapped up in cryptic words that alluded to the opposite.

Nosh arched an eyebrow at me, his eyes swiftly taking in the Olympian's state of undress as he processed her last comment. I narrowed my eyes. "We were just *talking*, Nosh. Not the other thing," I growled, scowling at Aphrodite's complete lack of assistance or shame at the suspicion.

Instead, my sweet sister smirked. She fucking *smirked*. "Sorin has other business that he must finish before going outside to see the motionless battle," she said, mocking Nosh's concern.

"Who is fighting the Sisters of Mercy, Nosh?" I asked warily, fearing the answer. "And where is Izzy?"

Nosh clenched his jaw. "The Cauldron showed up—most likely while we were in the elevator before she froze time," he said, pointing at Aphrodite. I felt a cold sweat break out over my shoulders. The Cauldron? Damn it all. "They attacked the Sisters. Thankfully, Izzy was safe from immediate harm. I considered dragging her back inside, but I wasn't sure if that would break Aphrodite's magic and resume the flow of time." Aphrodite sighed wearily, muttering under her breath about incompetence. He pursed his lips, obviously hearing her. "Witches are lobbing magic around like Mardi Gras beads."

I let out a sigh of relief to hear that Izzy was okay and assumed— judging by Aphrodite's grumblings—that dragging her inside would have been perfectly safe. "What do beads have to do with magic?"

Aphrodite chuckled huskily. "Oh, trust me, Sorin. Certain beads can be the back door into a truly magical world."

Nosh's face grew the darkest shade of purple I'd seen on him yet. He even stopped to stare at her, his mouth working wordlessly. She arched an eyebrow at him, flashing her teeth in a malevolent grin.

Finally, he shook his head, turning back to me. "Forget the beads. They are throwing around a lot of deadly potions."

"*About* to throw around," Aphrodite corrected, "because nothing is *moving.*"

He ignored her. "It's like someone paused the last fight in a John Wick film. But there's fire everywhere and I saw a Sister frozen in midair—in two pieces."

Aphrodite didn't even bat an eye at that. "See, Sorin? He's overreacting. The poor lamb doesn't even know she's dead yet."

I blinked at her incredulously. "Who cares if she *knows* she's dead? She's dead."

She shrugged resentfully, conceding my point. "A little, I guess. Tell me about your brilliant plan to save the day. You run out there and, what, get a front row seat to watch her body parts splat to the ground?"

Nosh stared at her, shaking his head in disbelief. "She can't be serious."

I held up a hand, cutting him off as I eyed Aphrodite. "Why don't you want me to go out there?" I asked suspiciously.

She pointed a hand back towards the bedchambers. "Because I stopped fucking time so that you could have some goddamned sex! You could spend the next three hours romping and nothing would have changed by the time you finally decided to go see whatever has the shaman so riled up. There is absolutely *no cost* for you to go do your duty in there—because I paid the price *for* you. Until I snap my fingers, the world does not concern you. At all."

Nosh shook his head in stunned disbelief. "Perhaps I didn't make myself clear. Imagine a war between two pissed off factions of witches. There is fire and blood and death everywhere. As soon as she snaps her fingers, a dozen witches will instantly die. What could possibly be more important than addressing that?"

Aphrodite blinked at him as if he was daft. "Sex. Bumping uglies. Hide the milkman—"

I cleared my throat, cutting her off. I was surprised at how incredibly angry she looked. She really took her job seriously.

She aimed that fury directly at me. "You march into that shower before I make you. I will not be disrespected like this. I'm your big sister and I know what's best for you. Our bastard siblings have given you enough pain already. Go to your women. Now. *She* wanted this for you."

I winced at the connotation for multiple reasons. She was obviously referring to Selene, and I wasn't entirely sure how I felt about it.

"Death. Fire. Dismemberment," Nosh reminded me, pointing up at the ceiling. "People are dying. Right now."

Aphrodite snarled. "We already established this. They are *between* life and death, and they will remain so for a few hours. Or until I snap my fingers."

I stared at her, unable to speak. She wasn't just frustrated. She...was hurt. Offended.

Disappointed.

Part of me was right alongside Nosh, wondering how she could be so callous, but the other part of me knew she was exactly right in her claims. And that I was hurting her feelings by not honoring her gift. She had stopped time for me, truly. The goddess of sex was being dismissed, and it was tearing her up inside.

It was insanely heartwarming and endearing. And psychotic. And sweet.

I wasn't sure that I'd ever seen someone so invested in giving me a gift before. Ever.

She noticed my attention and pointed towards the bathroom again. "Please, Sorin. I worked really hard to do this for you," she said softly. "*We* worked really hard to do this for you," she added in barely a whisper.

I stepped closer to place a hand on her shoulder. "The mood has been destroyed, Aphrodite. It would be impossible for me to focus on pleasure right now, and not even because of the fight outside. All the other things we discussed...I can't just turn off that part of my brain. I wish I could—more than you know. I appreciate your gift and wish I was in the right state of mind to accept it, but I'm not. And if they heard any of what you and I discussed, they would feel the same. It would be a lie to walk in there and not immediately tell them everything. I won't lie to them. They would never forgive me for it."

"My brother is an idiot," she breathed, dejectedly, but I could tell she sympathized with my answer. She definitely wasn't pleased about it. "That's the only explanation."

I smiled tightly, just as frustrated about it as her. "Answer me this," I said tiredly. "Why didn't you wait to warn me about everything? You could have let me walk into that shower and told me about everything else later."

She hung her head grumpily. "I thought about it, Sorin. I really did." I waited, watching her intently. She let her breath out in a huff. "Anyone else and I would have. But it would have been a lie and it would have broken your trust—which I was trying to earn. I want a brother I actually like. One I can trust. You're not tarnished by the games we've played for millennia."

I nodded, lifting my palms. "Exactly."

She sighed dejectedly. "I tried, brother. One day, your balls are going to pack up and leave."

I extended my hand with a warm smile, realizing that I truly enjoyed Aphrodite's company. It would be difficult to convince Adam and Eve not to attack her on sight, though. Perhaps she could give them pointers on their own amorous exploits.

Rather than accepting my offer, Aphrodite wrapped me up in a tight hug. She pulled back and kissed me on the forehead. "Don't do anything stupid out there, Sorin. I only just met you, and you're already my favorite brother. Remember that anything could be a set up. Maybe the twins are out there, hoping to draw you out."

I nodded, having already considered it. "Thank you," I said.

Aphrodite frowned suddenly, her face growing as pale as a sheet. "Something is wrong."

"What?" I demanded.

"Someone is poking at my spell! That's not even possible!" she breathed.

"How long do we have?" I demanded.

She thought about it, the purple and pink flecks in her eyes growing brighter as her gaze grew distant. "They're testing it, looking for a weak point. I can hold them off for maybe ten minutes."

"Wake the devils up!" I snapped, preferring to have them where I could see them—and knowing I could trust them more than anyone who might be outside.

She nodded, rushing into the bathroom. I began pacing back and forth, thinking furiously. Nosh did the same, preferring silence as well. Soon, the girls were rushed out of the bathroom, wild-eyed and hurriedly donning robes as they cast furtive glances at the semi-topless Aphrodite.

"Girls, meet Aphrodite. My sister."

"She's a real sweet-tart," Nosh murmured dryly.

Aphrodite grinned, dipping her chin graciously. The devils stared at me wordlessly, struggling to comprehend the sudden change of events. I cleared my throat. "There's a fight about to erupt upstairs. When you're finished getting dressed, would you do me the honor of accompanying me—"

Victoria was already scooping up her clothes and tugging them on. Natalie tightened the sash on her robe, her face set in a stern frown as she eyed Aphrodite's matching attire with a suspicious scowl.

Aphrodite pointed at me. "Blame him. I tried to buy you time for some fun, but he was adamant."

"Come on!" Nosh urged, motioning for them to hurry.

Natalie stared at Aphrodite for a few more seconds before complying. The two of them ran ahead, not bothering to wait. Victoria tugged on a t-shirt and scooped up a holster with daggers and a pistol attached to it. She didn't even bother with shoes. "What the hell is going on, Sorin?" she demanded, her voice muffled by the shirt she was trying to pull over her head.

"At least fifty witches are trying to kill each other on the steps of the museum," I said, pulling her after me. "Neither seem friendly to us."

"Be careful out there, Sorin," Aphrodite said, her voice sounding strained. "I'm not sure how long I can maintain this, and my face out there might have unintended consequences," she said meaningfully.

I nodded, bolting out the doors. Who was messing with her spell? Artemis and Apollo? Hera? I was doubly glad that I hadn't taken Aphrodite up on her offer to spend time with my devils.

I might have been forced to kill someone if I had been interrupted in the middle of my pleasure. Then again, I was fairly certain that a healthy dose of murder was in my immediate future.

Nosh and Natalie had chosen to take the stairs. "Izzy's out there," I told Victoria, noticing her frustrated frown. "Let's hurry. Witches might be the least of our problems."

"Olympians?" she asked warily.

I nodded grimly. "Welcome to the family."

## 11

The elevator doors opened and we spilled out onto the main level, already running towards the front entrance. We rounded the final corner in time to see Nosh and Natalie slip out the center doors leading outside.

I stared, transfixed by a gaping hole in the massive, grate-covered windows above the entrance doors. A cloud of debris, glass, and a somersaulting werewolf hung suspended just within the newly-formed hole—frozen in time.

It was eerie to behold. Especially when I noticed that the werewolf's side was in the process of catching flame, a perfect circle of unburning fire covering his ribs.

I shared a significant look with Victoria—this was bad. Very bad. A werewolf had already been harmed. It was no longer witch versus witch. And they'd damaged my building—a direct attack. My vampires would not stand for that. Neither would the werewolves.

Once time resumed its normal passing, of course.

We burst through the open door and out onto the steps of the museum. I skidded to a halt, my eyes widening in disbelief and wonder. Blood, bodies, projectiles, and eerily motionless flames portrayed a living exhibit of chaos that any museum would have begged to put on display. Nosh hadn't done it justice. The statue of the museum's founder astride his horse at the base of the steps was awash with frozen flame, and part of the stone foundation had been blown away, threatening the structural integrity of the pedestal. Would it hold or would the statue of Theodore Roosevelt fall?

A double line of motionless women in matching white coats stood in the center of the street, facing the museum like an invading army, and they were all frozen in the act of hurling glass vials, firing pistols, or wielding bared blades. Their faces were locked in grim determination; not a single one of them looked afraid.

On the lower section of the steps leading up to the museum—many hiding behind the statue of Theodore Roosevelt—was a ragtag assortment of women in dark, shabby clothing, looking like an army of homeless beggars. The dark witches of the Cauldron. Somehow, the positions of the two witch factions made it seem like the Cauldron was defending the museum from the invading Sisters of Mercy rather than the other way around. A sinister thought raced down my spine, realizing that the Sisters would see the situation the exact same way.

That the Cauldron was working for me.

"Goddamn it," I growled, pointing at the tableau.

Victoria nodded grimly. "That can't be coincidental."

I noticed a horde of werewolves in the near distance, frozen in the act of racing towards the fight, resembling an approaching tidal wave. Vampires with glowing red eyes hung suspended in mid-air, their bodies almost horizontal with the ground so that they appeared to be flying. I'd never felt like that when tapping into my supernatural speeds, but it made sense. Huh.

I spotted a dozen more of my vampires already on the outskirts of the fight, not daring to come between the two lines of witches, but doing their best to neutralize any stragglers—and they seemed to have no preference between dark or white witches. All were a threat.

Natalie and Nosh were easy to pick out at the base of the steps since they were the only other people moving. I scanned the area ahead of them to see Izzy standing between the two factions of witches, obviously having been trapped there by the Cauldron while passing my message along to the Sisters of Mercy. The now ex-Sister fought all by herself, wielding two oversized pistols aimed at a pair of elderly dark witches. Time had frozen in the act of her squeezing the triggers, making it look like her pistols spit fire rather than bullets. I could even see the bullets hanging suspended in the air between her and her foes.

A lot of bullets.

None of the Sisters behind her seemed even remotely invested in backing her up, focused on their own foes and protecting the other Sisters in white coats. They truly had abandoned Izzy, stripping away her standing in more ways than just on paper. Their very actions spoke louder than any words on a page. Izzy was on her own.

I raced down the steps towards the thick of battle, calling up my cloak of shadows and blood for added protection. Once time resumed, all the projectiles now hovering in the air would instantly spring to life, racing towards their intended victims. Victoria ran behind me as Nosh reached Izzy and began carrying her to relative safety. Natalie was dragging a wounded werewolf away from imminent death. I silently debated how I wanted to impact the fight, my mind racing with political ramifications and maneuvering how best to capitalize on the chaos.

Victoria slipped past me and became a hauntingly beautiful angel of death.

She calmly and swiftly made her way down a line of dark witches, slicing their throats without shame. "This isn't so bad," she said with a macabre smile.

I grunted, leaving the line of easy foes to her tender care as I moved into the kill-zone between the two factions. Each row of witches consisted of about two dozen members, with the remainder battling it out in groups of twos or threes, or all by themselves, in the center area between the two factions. A few vampires and werewolves had unwisely wandered into that kill-zone only to be slaughtered by both sides—some even at the same time.

I cautiously covered my vitals with my cloak since the air in the kill-zone was thick with bullets, knives, wooden stakes, and glass vials—all ready to kill whoever stood in the way the moment that time ticked back to normal.

Rather than dispatching the dark witches like Victoria, I made a calculated, tactical decision and began bodily hurling my vampires, werewolves, and any Sisters of Mercy out of immediate harm's way. I needed the Sisters to work with me on the Dracula situation—at least long enough to get them off my back while I figured out the Hades dilemma.

I was hoping that a life saved was worth more to the Sisters than an enemy slayed.

Numbers would matter when this was all said and done. It wouldn't do me any good to kill all the dark witches only to have the majority of the white witches die from inbound projectiles the moment Aphrodite's spell evaporated.

But I did use my claws to kill or fatally wound any dark witch within easy reach.

I ducked beneath an airborne werewolf and made a quick judgment call to pluck a potion from the hand of a Sister of Mercy who had been intending to throw her poisonous brew at him. Coming upon a dark witch in a similar situation, I chose to sever her hand at the wrist, careful to catch the vial before it fell to the ground.

All in all, it was haunting and eerie to move about the battlefield, choosing who lived and who died without fear of detection or retaliation.

As I saved and slaughtered, I couldn't help but wonder where the Cauldron witches had come from. How had they gotten here so fast? Did it have anything to do with whomever was trying to break Aphrodite's spell? That had to be someone far away—or they were extremely powerful—because anyone within close proximity should have been affected by the altered flow of time, thus unable to interfere.

My bet was one—or both—of the dreaded twins, Artemis and Apollo.

The Cauldron had attacked in the moments right before Nosh and I had seen the purple light in the catacombs. Shortly after I had given Izzy the tomahawk and welcomed her into my family. She must have been speaking to the Sisters when the Cauldron—

I froze, almost fumbling the stolen vials in my hand.

"The tomahawk," I breathed. The number one thing the dark witches had wanted a few days ago was Nosh's skinwalker blades.

I spun, searching for Nosh. I caught him trying to drag Izzy up the stairs towards the door without putting her in the path of a lethal projectile. She was also holding pistols that had just been fired, meaning he had to consider the impending recoil and her line of fire. "The tomahawk!" I shouted at him. "They came for *you*, Nosh!"

Nosh froze for a heartbeat. Then he redoubled his efforts, coming face-to-face with a group of dark witches that Victoria hadn't yet dealt with. He would have to run right through them.

"Don't use your magic or they'll swarm you!" I shouted. "Get inside—"

A sharp snapping sound echoed through the night air, cutting me off.

Then everyone and everything exploded into motion as time suddenly resumed. The sudden storm of gunfire made my ears pop, and the pungent scent of hot blood filled the air, making my mouth instantly salivate. I cursed, ducking beneath a flying witch before she tackled me. Blades and stakes struck my protective cloak from every direction, but thankfully none of them struck my flesh. Simultaneously, potions erupted all around me since I stood in the middle of the fight. Victoria screamed my name, but I was too busy holding my cloak over my head to avoid inhaling any poisonous clouds. I blindly ran, peering through a tiny opening until I was certain I was surrounded by moderately fresh air.

I released my grip on the cloak, letting it fall around my shoulders, and I hurled the vials in my hand at the nearest threat. I winced as a Sister of Mercy backed directly into my line of fire, taking one of the vials in the back of the head. The other sailed true, and both of the witches, one good and one bad, vaporized to ash in a single second, not even having time to scream.

Many of the dark witches simply dropped dead from our earlier ministrations, but the fight was far from over. Nosh and Izzy went down in my peripheral vision and I screamed furiously, clawing my way through a trio of unaware dark witches with their backs to me. "No!" I shouted as a group of wild-eyed dark witches noticed Izzy and Nosh falling at their feet. Their confusion was instantly replaced by wicked grins as they dove for the pair.

A lone werewolf tore into them, eviscerating two of them and knocking the other back. Natalie, in full werewolf form, hunkered over Nosh and Izzy protectively. Her long black fur glistened with the blood of the witches she had just killed, and her lips curled back in a savage snarl.

Victoria used Natalie's back as a stepping stone, launching up into the air with two daggers in hand as she flipped into a somersault to bury one of her blades into the top of a dark witch's skull, driving her down to the ground. She left the dagger behind as she rolled to her feet, still running, not even noticing me. I followed her line of sight to see a Sister of Mercy scowling down at a wounded vampire who was struggling to crawl away, judging by the smear of blood behind him. The Sister lifted her hands with a flash of light, aiming for the wounded vampire.

I snarled instinctively, drawing up a blood dagger to sever her hand before she could execute my vampire.

Victoria was faster.

She punched the Sister in the face with the hilt of her dagger, hitting her so hard that I watched her nose shatter and blood splatter across Victoria's face before the witch crumpled to the ground.

Two other Sisters shrieked at Victoria, raising their arms threateningly, but Victoria was already backpedaling away. Before they could do anything stupid, I dove in front of her, protecting us both with my cloak as I held my arms out to keep Victoria back.

I shouted at the top of my lungs. "It's finished! They're all dead!" The area fell as silent as a tomb. Especially when Victoria rested both of her arms over my shoulders, revealing two gleaming pistols aimed at the witches' faces. She thumbed back the hammers one at a time and the sound seemed to echo off the concrete steps like thunder. I probably looked as startled as the witches...because she would blow out my eardrums if she squeezed her triggers.

## 12

The Sisters wisely backed away. The rest of their faction surveyed the scene, not trusting my claim that the fight was over. I saw a handful of them sneer at a pair of bloodied vampires. Two werewolves abruptly growled a vicious warning from directly behind the Sisters, causing them to jump in surprise as they coincidentally reconsidered their actions. The werewolves forcefully shoved past them, one on either side, knocking the Sisters into each other.

No love lost between the survivors. The Sisters angrily slunk back to their group, glaring daggers at the two offending werewolves.

Victoria calmly lowered her guns and stepped up beside me, giving me enough space to do something violent if I felt so inclined. And she didn't put her guns away either. In short order, the surviving Sisters had regrouped—wounded, singed, and furious. Their white coats were torn and covered in gore, blood, and soot. They congregated in a huddle with three of them facing outwards to keep an eye on us like the whole attack was our fault.

They finally turned to face me, none of them making a sound. One woman stepped forward and I winced to see that she had no eyes, just sunken eye sockets. Despite this, she stared directly at me. The Speaker to the High Priestess. She had long white hair and looked noticeably older than the rest of the witches, who all seemed on the younger side.

"One of your servants told us you would be out in twenty minutes," she said in an officious tone. "Then the Cauldron attacked. Then you arrive to conveniently save us—within one minute of the attack, not twenty."

Not sure how to respond to that without mentioning Aphrodite, and not particularly appreciating her referring to Izzy as my *servant*, I chose humble diplomacy. "I think my favorite part about being a hero is the gratitude," I said, matching the Speaker's pompous tone as I scanned the row of Sisters behind her. "After saving someone, there is something uniquely fulfilling about that special look they get in their eyes—" I cut off, locking onto the Speaker's vacant sockets. "Well, this is awkward," I said, clasping my hands behind my back. "I suddenly feel unfulfilled."

She pursed her lips but managed to maintain her composure. "Did you send your Cauldron witches out in hopes that they would resolve the problem on your front steps?" she asked crisply, ignoring my rudeness.

I stared at her. Then I laughed, turning my back on her as I surveyed the damage to the front of the museum. The steps were soaked with blood, rubble, and sooty smears. I let out a sigh and turned back to the Speaker. "Does it look like my problem was resolved? Go ahead and ask one of your Sisters to take a look for you—one of the Sisters I just *saved*."

Someone laughed behind me, but it was quickly cut off as someone else hit them.

The witches collectively bristled, but the Speaker simply stared back at me without reaction. "Answer my question."

I pointed over her shoulder towards Central Park rather than answering.

Someone laughed from behind me again, but I kept my face composed. Several of the witches turned to study the park behind them. Illuminated by the full moon, my castle loomed above the trees, stabbing at the sky. Living mist surrounded the gates and much of the park in an impenetrable ring. A lone statue stood at the edge of the park, facing away from us. The witches turned back to me with matching frowns.

"My front steps are over *there*," I explained, "not here. In my massive castle. The one you lost track of in Europe." I'd already made my decision about Dracula prior to talking with Aphrodite, but now I had additional reasons to stick to my choice. I couldn't afford Dracula falling into Olympian hands.

The blind woman continued to face me, again pursing her lips. "Why send the Cauldron after us? Why have your army surround us when we came in peace? Why tell us you will meet only to attack us a moment later?"

I blinked at her. Then I snorted and shifted my attention to the rest of the Sisters. "I request a new Speaker. One who has at least a basic grasp on reality rather than a blind obsession with conspiracy. Anyone?" The witches glared back as one. I sighed regretfully, turning back to the eyeless waste of space. Her fists were clenched at her sides. "You stand before my museum with an army, threatening me with war if I don't hand over my prisoner, Dracula. Yet you have no ability or authority to back up your threat. You couldn't even handle a few dozen witches without my help. Is this supposed to impress me? All you've accomplished is to somehow further establish your utter incompetence. And that is saying something, because you are only here in my city after you failed at the *one job* you devoted your life to—watching that castle," I said, pointing over their shoulders again. "And now you wish to point blame at *me*? To insult my intelligence with the fallacy that you truly believe you are the only party qualified to deliver Dracula to the cold blade of justice?" I laughed, a harsh, bitter sound. I held my arms out, indicating the wolves and vampires gathering around us as reinforcements continued to arrive from all over Central Park. "These vampires and werewolves are loyal friends of mine, and they are responding to an attack on my museum—an attack brought upon us by both the Cauldron and your Sisters. The Cauldron is not welcome here, in case you missed the part where we just saved you from slaughter." I let my words sink in for a heartbeat. "In my brief time here, the Cauldron has never attacked the museum. That only happened once *you* graced us with your presence."

Victoria stepped forward. "I killed a dozen of them. How many did you kill, witch?"

The Speaker narrowed her eye sockets at Victoria. "Another lost soul. Victoria Helsing, I presume?"

"You!" one of the Sisters closest to the Speaker snarled, pointing at Victoria.

"If you value that arm, you better lower it," Natalie growled, striding out from a huddle of vampires. She was naked and covered in blood, having shifted back into her human form. Except her claws were still out, her forearms covered in fur like she was wearing gauntlets.

The Sister wilted instinctively, taking a step back from Natalie. She seemed to find some of her courage once she was back within the safety of her group of Sisters.

The Speaker clucked her tongue and the Sister lowered her glare to the ground. The eyeless witch stared at Victoria, not even acknowledging Natalie. "You work with this vampire. You, the notable vampire hunter."

"Perhaps that should tell you something about him," Victoria said, still holding her pistols at her side.

"Or perhaps it tells us something about you, traitor."

I turned to Victoria. "Is this really happening? Are they always this blatantly aloof?"

Victoria shook her head. "Usually they can see common sense. But I'm certain that Sister Hazel was born a zealous twat. Then she became a born-again zealous twat."

"Sister *Hazel*? Like the band?" Natalie blurted incredulously. Then she burst into laughter. "You're kidding me."

Victoria grinned, shaking her head. "Hence the groupies," she said, jerking her chin at the witches behind the Speaker.

The Sisters hissed in unison, but the eyeless Sister Hazel merely thinned her lips with disdain. "You used to be one of our greatest allies hunting for Dracula. Yet here you stand with the enemy. And you've formed a *trinity* with him. Much like Dracula did with his brides—a way for him to gain yet more power to defend himself from us."

I frowned at Hazel. "What do you mean, trinity?" She shifted her attention my way, a suspicious look on her face as if she thought I was being willfully ignorant to further vex her. "I'm genuinely asking. Consider it an olive branch."

She was silent for about ten seconds before answering slowly and carefully. "A trinity is a sharing of power, much like a rope is stronger when braided together." I nodded, having already picked up that obvious aspect. "It varies based on what type of magic you have. Typically, trinities are formed between those of the same supernatural upbringing. Until Dracula, it was considered impossible for vampires to form trinities. Since you three are not remotely the same type of supernatural being, I have no idea what could happen, but I imagine it won't be pleasant. Participants in a trinity share both the pleasures and the pains of their partners, after all," she said with a cruel smirk, eyeing Natalie and Victoria.

Natalie and Victoria continued glaring at the witches as if Hazel hadn't said anything. At least they hadn't shown surprise. Hazel had obviously hoped to sow seeds of discord with the comment.

Hazel sniffed pompously. "It is why Dracula hid his brides from us —he knows that if we harm them, we harm him. And the fact that you have chosen only two brides is direct evidence of your subservience to Dracula—who chose *three* brides. You are not permitted to one-up your boss, it seems. You help him escape us in Europe and bring him to a city where you have a vampire army waiting at the ready. You have deceived werewolves—natural enemies to vampires—to follow you. You surround Dracula's fortress in impenetrable mist, and you take over the heart of New York City. So, yes, we are the only ones qualified to bring him to justice. Because you are working for him—whether you believe it or not. Your every action has served to strengthen his goals."

I narrowed my eyes, debating how much information I wanted to share, but needing to get any answers I could from them. I understood her perspective, but I definitely didn't trust her methods. Or her motives.

And I was more interested in her words about my trinity with Natalie and Victoria—our bond. I sure hadn't intended to do any such thing. I hadn't chosen the two of them. The bond had snapped into place all by itself during a fight with the Cauldron when I had been forced to bite Natalie for the power to save us from certain death. And with us each being different types on the magical spectrum, what kind of dangers did we face?

A rapidly growing commotion behind me snapped me out of my thoughts. I turned to see Nosh running around frantically, lifting dead bodies and shoving people out of his way as he desperately searched for something. He gripped a vampire by the shoulders. "Where is Izzy?" he demanded, jostling him violently. The vampire shook his head, lifting his claws.

My heart dropped into my stomach. No...

"Where is she?" he demanded of another vampire. Then another. All to no avail. I heard a cackling laugh from high overhead and I tensed up, ready to dodge in any direction. Instead, I saw a folded piece of paper fluttering down towards me as a flying silhouette zipped away.

The Sisters of Mercy began talking animatedly, huddling close.

I snatched the heavy paper from the air and unfolded it to find a letter.

*To whom it may concern,*

*Hand over the skinwalker and his tomahawks by sunrise if you want the witch to live.*

*Yours,*

*A witchnapper*

I carefully folded the note and closed my eyes, taking a deep breath. "To whom it may concern," I growled testily. "I have a fucking *name*."

## 13

Victoria tried to snatch the note from my hands but I evaded her, shoving it in my pocket and shooting her a stern look. No one could know about this. Not with the Sisters of Mercy here. If they learned that Nosh was a skinwalker, they might turn him over themselves or find another reason to distrust me. The look on my face must have been convincing because Victoria nodded slowly. I discreetly motioned Nosh to stand down. He gritted his teeth and gave me a stiff nod.

"What did your minion need to tell you?" the Speaker asked, drawing my attention.

"If you can read it yourself, Sister Hazel, I'll let you," I said coldly. "But no cheating," I added, indicating the other Sisters behind her.

She narrowed her eye sockets again, obviously not able to read without eyes. "You seek our trust yet you mock me. Repeatedly."

I scoffed. "Don't play the victim, Sister. Those who spend their life specializing in excuses rarely have time to accomplish anything else. Tearing down someone else's castle does not make your castle any larger, because the loudest indignant shouts from self-proclaimed victims are always muted by the whispers of the quietest victors."

She stiffened, looking startled and embarrassed that I had pointed out her cheap tactic.

I leaned towards her, speaking in a low but clear tone to truly emphasize my previous words. "And I seek *nothing* from victims," I whispered.

Her face darkened. I nodded one time and then turned away from her, finally motioning Nosh closer. He hurried over, flexing his fists in idle frustration over Izzy's disappearance. I handed him the folded paper and leaned close to whisper in his ear before he could read it. "Remain calm and do *not* touch your tomahawk," I urged, gripping his arm tightly. "I need to get rid of the Sisters before we can go after Izzy. We can't afford to give the Sisters any leverage." He nodded stiffly. "We will get her back, and we will destroy everyone involved in her abduction," I promised, squeezing his shoulder hard enough to make his eyes tighten.

He unfolded the letter, walking away with a quiet aura of menace surrounding him like a cloud. He displayed no reaction as he read the short message. Then he calmly tucked the note into his pocket and slowly turned to stare at the Sisters of Mercy with a bored expression. No. He was staring *through* them. And they seemed to sense it, judging by their sudden glares.

My gaze briefly flicked over Sister Hazel's shoulder as I sensed movement in the trees of the park. I kept my face blank even though I wanted to burst out laughing.

Instead, I folded my arms. "Thanks to your incompetence, Isabella has been abducted by the Cauldron. Apparently, some of them escaped before I could kill them for you." Sister Hazel didn't react in the slightest. "She is one of the most honorable women I've met in this city. A few days ago, she suffered the displeasure of the Cauldron, withstanding their torture without giving in an inch. She deserves respect. More than you could ever hope to attain, Sister Hazel."

"We do not grant respect to a monster's *whore*." Her attention shifted to Victoria and then Natalie, but only for a fraction of a second, almost too subtle to notice.

Yeah. Okay.

I waited, willing to let the devils respond in any manner they saw fit

—even overwhelming violence. But they surprised me. Natalie laughed, and Victoria rolled her eyes, turning her back on Hazel. She began walking among my gathered vampires and werewolves, speaking in low tones, apparently finished with the Sisters of Mercy.

"You never had any intention of working with me," I finally said. "You came here to pick a fight. You've made that perfectly clear. But I'm finished dealing with subordinates. Tell your High Priestess that she is welcome to visit me if she wants to discuss anything further." I turned away just in time to hide my manic grin from Sister Hazel.

"How *dare* you turn your back on me?" she sputtered. I grinned, winking at Victoria. She showed no reaction, having already noticed what I had seen lurking behind the witches. It was why she had dismissed Sister Hazel's crude indication that Izzy and the devils were nothing more than my whores. Instead of ripping the elderly Speaker's face off with her bare hands, Victoria had instead chosen to mingle with my warriors—to reassure them about what was coming. Because the Sisters hadn't noticed.

I turned just in time to see a giant living statue land on the ground between me and the Sisters. Adam, one of my two Nephilim vampires, crouched low, twirling a massive ruby scythe that was larger than me in one hand. He was at least fifteen-feet tall and built like a master black-smith, layered with more slabs of muscle than I had ever seen on a man —relative to his size, of course.

His nude body was made of a pale white marble, but a root-like system of ruby striations shifted back and forth across his skin like a slow-motion lightning storm of blood, serving to further emphasize his already impressive musculature.

He slammed the tip of his ruby scythe a foot into the street's pavement with as much resistance as a hot sword through a witch's gullet. The scythe flared with crimson light and the witches collectively tripped and stumbled back, crying out in alarm. Since Adam was a giant, his crouched position facing the Sisters put his giant, crimson-veined ass about a foot away from my face.

I grimaced, stepping to the side as the Nephilim vampire growled at the Sisters of Mercy. "You will show him the proper respect or I will line the castle gates with your pretty little skulls," he said, his voice rolling like distant thunder.

The frightened witches clutched at their chests or grasped spare vials in shaking hands as they faced the colossal marble statue. His glowing, fiery eyes and the shifting, serpentine streaks of living crystal snaking over his body—much like Aphrodite's ribbons, now that I thought about it—captivated their fearful attention.

Hazel looked pale but brave, holding out her arms to calm her fellow Sisters. She took a shaky breath, clearing her throat. "We are not afraid of a fallen Nephilim," she said in a shaken tone. "We are merely saddened that the Devil stole his soul."

"Then you are idiots," I muttered. "Look at those muscles." Adam actually flexed instinctively, threatening to embarrass me. Most of the Sisters were doing their best to ignore his obvious nudity—which was made difficult since it was bigger than their arms—but one Sister was staring hard enough that she could have carved her own replica for later repeated worship.

"One Nephilim is no match for all of us," Hazel said with false confidence. "We are not scared of him."

I smiled. "He isn't the scary one," I said softly.

An impossibly loud scraping sound behind them made them spin around. They froze in silent alarm, both transfixed and petrified to see Eve slowly sauntering towards them from the park, rolling her hips back and forth in a seductive swaying motion. She held a scythe in either hand, dragging their tips across the surface of the street at her sides so that she left twin trenches of destroyed pavement in her wake. She was smiling hungrily, her eyes blazing with ruby fire.

"*She* is the scary one," I said, chuckling.

The Sisters began to twitch and whimper as she neared, torn between turning to face Adam and keeping their eyes on Eve—who was now looming over them with a dark smile. Hazel licked her lips anxiously, struggling to maintain control of her Sisters.

"What about two Nephilim?" I asked her. "Because I can play this game all day. Please call my bluff. I've got a few other surprises that you obviously failed to notice or you would have left ten minutes ago."

Silence answered me, but I let it draw on until many of the Sisters were shifting uneasily, their attention darting left and right as if fearing to see more Nephilim pop up out of the darkness. I was bluffing, but they didn't know that. In their eyes, I'd raised a castle in the middle of Central Park, and turned Nephilim into vampires. What *wasn't* I capable of?

"I thought so," I said dismissively. "Now, Hazel, it is time to atone for your cruelty." She scoffed incredulously, but I had already turned to Adam. "Grab her," I said, pointing at Hazel.

Adam didn't even hesitate, snatching her in one hand around her waist. The Sisters screamed, but Eve drew her blades across each other, showering them with sparks. They quieted almost immediately, their eyes darting about wildly.

Adam brought Hazel over to me. I stepped close, leaning towards her eyeless face as I unsheathed my claws. "You crossed a line when you called Izzy a monster's whore. But you really fucked up when you implied the same about Natalie and Victoria. I want to make sure you and your fellow Sisters remember these three mistakes. Forever."

And I used a claw to slice a line down her right cheek, licking my lips at the sight of her blood. She hissed and squawked in terror, unable to escape Adam's grip. "For Natalie," I whispered once I was finished. Then I did the same to the other cheek, ignoring her struggle and her cries of pain. "For Victoria." I placed the tip of my claw on her forehead and then dragged it down her nose, stopping just below her eye sockets. "For Izzy." She hung limply, shaking with fear and shame. I assessed my work critically, nodding at the three lines. "I have killed for less offense, Sister Hazel. Consider yourself extremely lucky." Then I motioned for Adam to set her back among her Sisters.

Even my own army was eerily silent. I wasn't sure how they felt about my actions, but I'd learned long ago that shocking displays of violence were often the only way to make a point.

And I could not tolerate such blatant disrespect. Rumors about tonight would have spread either way—whether it was how Sister Hazel had openly mocked my allies or how she had suffered for doing so. I preferred the latter. It established a precedent.

Sister Hazel stood before her witches, trembling and sobbing. The Sisters were utterly silent, not daring to risk my anger after what I had just done to their Speaker. She finally turned to face me, her cheeks a curtain of blood and tears.

"The only Sister I'm willing to speak with is your High Priestess."

"No one speaks with our High Priestess, especially not a vampire," Hazel whispered softly, but defiantly. "It is out of my hands."

"Then we are finished here. You are fools if you think I'm willing to hand over Dracula to you after your failures today." I turned my back on her again, making my way over to Nosh. He looked on the verge of doing something reckless.

"You have two hours to deliver Dracula to Trinity Church," Hazel snapped. Before I could turn around, I heard a loud whooshing sound behind me. I spun to see the witches disappearing one-by-one, using magic of some kind to transport their bodies away from my presence. I stared at the spot where they had been standing, grimacing.

I had hoped only Nero knew how to do such a thing. What kind of limitations did they have? Could they appear anywhere they wanted? They would be deadly assassins if they could appear anywhere out of thin air. Nero had needed a totem or a solid awareness of his destination.

The Cauldron witches had also seemed to appear out of thin air, according to the Sisters of Mercy. Was that how they had taken Izzy?

The witch with the note had been flying overhead, so I also had that to consider.

Nero needed to get better at using his magic.

## 14

I surveyed the scene in silence for a few moments, no one daring to approach me.

Eventually, Nosh stepped up beside me, staring at the empty street as well. "You did the right thing, calling them out like that and rubbing their noses in their failures."

I glanced over at him, assuming he was being sarcastic.

He shook his head. "I'm serious. They never intended to work with you, they intended to walk over you. This gave them a reason to reconsider."

"My thoughts as well. Of course, it could always backfire and give them a reason to double down on their efforts to kill me. Appearing weak would have carried the same risks, though, so I chose to make an example out of her."

He nodded absently, focusing on Adam and Eve. It still surprised me that Nosh could be so calm and collected when confronted with stressful situations. Maybe he'd gotten it from me. Or his difficult childhood, growing up as an orphan. That was how I'd learned it.

"Thank you for standing up for Izzy. It would have made her smile."

I chuckled. "We do crazy things for our family, eh?"

A ghost of a smile crossed his face and he reached into his pocket to pull out the letter from the Cauldron. He stared at it for a few moments. I gritted my teeth, ready to argue that there was no way in hell I was handing him over to the Cauldron to save Izzy.

"My aunt once told me how important it was to stay in contact with distant family. How it was food for the soul, no matter how inconvenient it might be at the time," he said carefully.

I grew still, reading between the lines—Aphrodite's warning about how important it was for me to go get my soul back from the Underworld. To visit my distant family member, Hades. And...Nosh was already giving me an out, admitting that the timing was inconvenient but that it was more important than me helping him get Izzy back.

"I'm not trading you, Nosh. Even if I'm busy elsewhere, I will see to it that you can't sacrifice yourself. I swear it."

He smirked. "I wasn't suggesting it. I intend to kill them all."

"Oh." I let out a breath, appraising him thoughtfully. "As much as I hate to admit it, I think you are right about distant family. Things will get much worse if Dracula breaks out and tries to sell his knowledge to the highest bidder. The Sisters will obviously take his freedom as an intentional act on my part, and then we will have them to worry about as well."

Nosh nodded grimly. "I will save Izzy. The werewolves should be able to help me find the Cauldron, if anyone can. Their note just said sunrise, not where to deliver the goods. Fucking idiots," he muttered. "Can't even get a ransom note right."

Despite the seriousness of the situation, I laughed. It was just so goddamned ridiculous. I hadn't even noticed it. "Criminals these days," I agreed, still chuckling.

Renfield walked into view, and his once-white shirt was now liberally splattered with blood, making it look polka-dotted. Except the forearms were solid red. I hadn't seen him in the fight, but there had been a lot going on. He was directing a group of reborn vampires to assist with the clean-up. So far, the reborn vampires had all seemed remarkably unflappable over their second shot at life, and almost fanatical in their worship of me. Like they saw me as a living god.

Dr. Stein and Nero had created dossiers on each of them, interviewing them extensively so as to understand their past allegiances—whether they had been affiliated with Dracula or not.

I hadn't read over the files yet, but all of the vampires had been approved to leave Liberty Island and assimilate with the other members of my Kiss living here in the museum. I was confident that my veteran vampires—Renfield, Hugo, Aristos, and Valentine—had them firmly in hand. They were even hosting a vampire ball tomorrow night —a social mixer, as they'd explained it—to assimilate them into the modern era since many of them came from entirely different cultures and time periods.

The thing that concerned me the most about the reborn vampires was the fact that they had various shades of red irises.

All of them.

And I had no idea what that meant. Yet. I shrugged off the grim thoughts.

They glanced at me with fiercely loyal nods before setting about their work with haunting efficiency and zero empathy. Renfield shot me an equally serious look, but his was empathetic for my plight. His gaze fixated on Nosh and his sorrow only seemed to deepen. Renfield had a deep guilt when it came to Nosh because he had been the one to kidnap him so long ago. In reality, Renfield was the only reason Nosh was still alive and free right now, so I didn't hold it against him. Still, to see Nosh in pain as a result of Izzy's capture brought out the monster in Renfield.

Which was exactly what we needed right now.

My devils walked up to us, snapping me out of my thoughts. Natalie mussed Nosh's head playfully and Victoria smiled at his resulting growl. Natalie had found her robe—surprisingly not shredded and without any bloodstains on it, so she must have taken it off before shifting. She looked wildly out of place amidst the chaos.

"Hey," I said awkwardly, not entirely sure where to begin on how badly our night had turned out. Nosh smirked, watching me flounder as the devils studied me, waiting. "I think it's better for everyone if we don't mention my family where anyone else can overhear," I said, flicking my eyes over the swarm of activity.

"Then we should go for a quick walk in the park," she said, grabbing my hand and tugging me towards the street without waiting for my thoughts on the matter.

Natalie grabbed my other hand, and smacked Adam on the ass as she walked by. "Come on, big guy. We're going for a walk. Heel."

Adam and Eve shared an amused look with each other and then followed us. I shot a helpless look at Nosh behind me, but he just shrugged. "Get me Nero!" I hissed, remembering that the necromancer warlock was just as valuable to the Olympians as Dracula was.

The Shaman nodded and walked away.

"I liked what you said to Hazel," Victoria said with a pleased smile. "Perhaps a little overprotective, but it was cute." She squeezed my hand, so I was fairly certain it wasn't a trap.

Natalie grunted. "Could have gone further. God ruined a perfectly good asshole when he put teeth in Hazel's mouth. You should have knocked them down the back of her throat as your charitable donation to the world."

I chuckled, especially when Victoria shot her a surprised look. Victoria reached into a pocket and pulled out a phone, handing it over to me with an amused smile. "I got you a replacement. One of the vampires found what they think was your old one broken outside the elevator."

I accepted it with a faint smile. "Someone interrupted me with a phone call while I was trying to make it downstairs earlier," I admitted with a frustrated sigh. "So, I destroyed it. Didn't change anything, though," I muttered.

The silence stretched on as we walked, and I felt my shoulders twitching, wondering exactly how much to say to them. I couldn't tell if they were upset with me or just at the situation. Did I mention that Aphrodite had pressed me to enjoy their pleasure? Did I avoid talk of the goddess of sex since the last Olympian had almost killed Natalie? Did I mention my plan about going to the Underworld?

Natalie finally sighed, tugging my hand to stop me short. We were almost at the bank of fog surrounding my castle. "If it was up to me, I would let this drag on just to watch you squirm, but I'm not very rational right now. I'm feeling sexually frustrated, so I'll just cut to the chase. Nosh told us everything."

I froze, schooling my features. Part of me was furious at him for him revealing the details, but part of me understood why he had done so. And if anyone deserved to know the truth, it was my devils. In fact, Nosh had actually done me a favor by volunteering to be the messenger.

"Oh?" I asked very carefully.

"He knew we would raise all sorts of hell until we heard the full story, and he said you wouldn't have the time to properly explain it. Or that you might leave some things out. Then he told us about Izzy to guilt-trip us, the sleazy rat bastard."

Victoria nodded sadly. "We are going to help get her back," she said. "Nosh said that we wouldn't be able to join you even if you wanted us to..." She studied me, obviously not understanding what his comment meant.

But I sure did. I was going to the Underworld. Those with souls could not go there.

"I do want you to join me," I said, picking up on the obvious trap. Victoria grinned approvingly. "But Nosh is right," I admitted. "And before you get all worked up—"

"Worked up?" Natalie asked in a frigid tone. Victoria stared at me, arching an eyebrow.

"Slip of the tongue," I muttered. I had been doing so well, too! "I was going to say that it has nothing to do with how tough you are or how dangerous my destination is. Nosh wouldn't be able to join me either. In fact, I can't think of a single person who could make the trip."

Their confusion only seemed to intensify, but I could think of no other way to phrase it without making it sound worse than it really was.

"And if I don't wrap it up in the next two hours, things are going to get a lot worse in New York City. In a few hours, I can tell you all about it, but I can't talk about it right *now*."

They pursed their lips unhappily, but understood my sense of urgency. Adam and Eve very wisely chose to silently creep past us, giving us some privacy.

Natalie stared at the ground. "Do you promise you will be safe?" she asked, obviously concerned. "That you're not running off to sacrifice yourself or anything? Because. Fuck. That."

I smiled, wrapping her up in a hug. "Our lives will always be dangerous, but I promise to be safe and that this is not a suicide attempt. Although suicide sounds preferable to missing out on our shower," I growled unhappily.

She grinned, looking up at me. "And you promise to tell us everything later? What really happened tonight? I could tell Nosh was leaving some juicy bits out."

I chuckled. "Yes. But I really do need you two to keep any mention of my...distant family to yourselves. My sister seemed very concerned that we might not have as much privacy as we believe. That certain topics and names can be overheard," I said meaningfully.

Natalie nodded, and I let her go.

Then I turned to Victoria. "Keep an eye out on Nosh for me. I should be back in a few hours, but Izzy isn't the only one in danger. They want Nosh and his tomahawks more than anything else. Izzy was just leverage. But that should also be kept a secret—as much as possible anyway." Aphrodite's comment about Nosh not necessarily being a skinwalker came to mind, but I dismissed it. He wasn't carrying around the tomahawks for fun.

She nodded. "Who knows? We might even have all their little pretty heads decorating the gates of the castle when you return."

I smiled, wrapping her up in a hug. Then I let her go and stepped back.

There was a pregnant pause between the three of us, and then they simply left. I watched them walk away, frowning at the situation. I could tell that Hazel had gotten in at least one good blow during our heated exchange.

The topic of our trinity hung before us like a dark cloud, smothering our budding romance with a coating of thick frost. Unfortunately, her warnings may have been entirely truthful. The only person I could ask about that was Dracula.

I turned and stared up at my dark castle, frowning. If Dracula was the biggest threat, and the entire reason that I needed to go to the Underworld to steal my soul from Hades...

Perhaps it would be simpler if I went and killed him right *now*.

Killed him before he had a chance to summon Hades or whatever it was he was trying to do.

Adam and Eve abruptly dropped to their knees with matching groans, snapping me out of my thoughts with a hiss. I ran over to them, terrified that I might already be too late. If they were growing so weak that they couldn't stand, maybe their power was no longer poisoning the walls of Castle Ambrogio.

Dracula would be able to walk right out the front door and into the arms of the most ambitious Olympian—whoever that might be.

"What's wrong?" I demanded, grabbing both of them. Their shoulders straightened somewhat at my touch, the physical contact with their master boosting their strength through our bond.

"It feels like we're holding up a mountain with our fingertips," Adam rasped. "He keeps getting stronger and our grip keeps slipping."

Eve nodded, blinking rapidly and clenching her jaw.

I let out a frustrated breath. "Keep holding on. Please. Do you need to feed?"

Eve looked up at me, the fire in her eyes paler than normal. I hadn't noticed how much of a show they'd been putting on in front of the Sisters. They'd been just as tired then, but they'd muscled through it. "We've been trying to feed, but it only serves to make him stronger," she muttered. "Like he's taking the souls and blood from us—at least a large portion of them."

I grimaced. If true, it meant Dracula really was trying to summon Hades, the master of souls. And that connection was siphoning off my Nephilims' reserves. There was only one way to know for sure. I needed to get another look inside my castle and discover exactly what he was up to. Technically, it had only been twenty minutes or so since I'd last checked on him, thanks to Aphrodite's spell.

But something had caused the Nephilim to drop to their knees. Something had changed.

Recalling how much the Nephilim hated the Olympians, even though I wasn't entirely sure why, I decided to see if a little aggression could liven up their weariness. "The Olympians are involved in this somehow. Are you going to let them beat you?"

Adam stiffened, slowly turning his head to face me. His eyes flared marginally brighter, and I heard Eve growl menacingly. As one, they straightened, and I watched as the crystal veins shifting across their arms condensed into tighter knots.

Their eyes flared brighter at the same time, and I could feel the marginal boost of strength it gave them. I frowned thoughtfully, wondering what to make of it. These were the first two Nephilim vampires in history, so I had nothing to base their abilities on.

They gave me grim nods and then strode into the wall of mist to resume their posts at the gate. I watched them, wondering if they could even manage to hold out for the next two hours.

## 15

I focused on the bond with my castle, closing my eyes. I immediately saw a darkened field of shifting grays and reds—living brambles of mist with thorns that threatened to pierce and ensnare the minds of anyone attempting to look within.

Like I was doing right now.

Except we were bonded, so the defense mechanisms did not apply to me. Although, the fact that I saw them at all was cause for alarm. The castle had her defenses up high.

Slowly, the smoke shifted and coalesced to form a hazy apparition of the throne room. A massive pile of bodies now lay heaped behind my throne, and Dracula stood in the center of an intricate circle of blood painted onto the floor. Ritualistic symbols and designs surrounded the circle, many of them looked Greek in origin. Dracula stood in a bathtub of blood, his eyes closed as he murmured to himself, chanting repeatedly.

What looked like a dome of crimson and green glass rose up around the ritual circle, protecting him with a shield of blood and necromantic power. I gritted my teeth furiously, sensing the immense power radiating from that dome of defensive energy.

It was alarming to see how powerful it was. Powerful enough that I wasn't certain I could break it. Entering the castle right now would be a fatal mistake—like poking a hole in a dam. Because the dome of power had roots reaching down through the stones of the castle, and those roots were the source of my Nephilims' current weakness. Dracula wasn't necessarily trying to break out, but his current ritual was like a persistent vine that would grow strong enough to tear down an ancient stone wall.

How long did I have until that happened? Was he trying to break out or was he trying to destroy the castle? The only heartbeats I sensed inside the castle came from the three young women surrounding the ritual circle at equidistant points, chanting at Dracula with their eyes closed.

The Brides of Dracula. They had to be.

I sensed no other pulses within the castle, which meant he had systematically sacrificed every single one of his followers. No wonder he was so strong. It was a measure of his desperation that he would destroy his only real assets—his army of vampires.

My hopeful plan that I could storm inside and kill Dracula once and for all was suddenly dashed against the rocks like a ship in a storm. Whatever powers his ritual had tapped into, I was not strong enough to face them. Even attempting to do so could be the catalyst that ended in the destruction of the castle itself. It was almost as if he was taunting me to do so.

Dracula had established some sort of conduit—that green necromantic power—with the Underworld. By killing every single one of his followers, he'd earned the attention of Hades. He had bought himself an audience, paying for the opportunity with hundreds of vampire souls. That was the only logical explanation.

Strangely enough, I could sense that he was somehow forcing my castle to help protect him. Even though he was a prisoner, the sheer volume of blood he'd spilled had overwhelmed the castle's loyalties. He'd fed her addiction, harboring no regard for her well-being as he forced the blood down her figurative throat, getting her drunk whether she wanted to or not.

He was truly a desperate man. Nothing was sacred to him any longer. He'd killed all his men to buy a chance at survival. I knew that the most dangerous type of foe was a man backed into a corner with nothing left to lose.

I could feel my castle screaming in a soft, breathless protest that haunted the halls like a malevolent spirit. Until I broke that ritual, no one was safe to enter the castle.

I had hoped that I might make my problems go away by simply killing Dracula and delivering his head to the Sisters of Mercy before they decided to do anything to force my hand. If they wanted to take custody of Dracula, I could deliver him dead.

Because I could no longer afford to let Dracula live. Which meant I had to get my soul back. Now. To distract Hades long enough to break the conduit with Dracula.

I let out a breath and opened my eyes, allowing the vision to dissipate.

I glared up at the castle, empathizing with the old girl. It wasn't her fault. It was the bastard within who would pay the ultimate price. "Soon, old friend, but not soon enough," I snarled.

"What was that?" Nero asked from behind me. I spun with a shout, not having sensed his approach. He froze, lifting up his good hand and his stump in a peaceful gesture. The side of his face was covered in blood and I saw something fleshy stuck in his hair. "Easy, Sorin. I heard you say *old friend*, so I assumed you were talking to me, seeing as how I am your only old friend."

I let out a breath, nodding stiffly. "I need you to take me to the Underworld. Now. I have to steal back my soul before any Olympians can get their hands on it."

He stared at my verbal onslaught. "*What?*"

"Only you and Dracula know the true stories about my past—everyone else is dead. Until I get my soul back, you and Dracula are the most valuable assets in the world. And not in any way you would particularly enjoy." I pointed at the castle behind me. "Dracula is already trying to summon Hades to break him out of my castle in order to save his own life."

"How could you possibly know that?" he whispered.

"I saw it through our bond. Dracula has already killed every single vampire inside. It's just him and his brides, now. And a ridiculously powerful necromantic ritual shielding him."

His eyes widened even further upon hearing Dracula had sacrificed his own army.

"If the Olympians get their hands on my soul, nothing will stop them from destroying this city. From using me to destroy this city. Like a puppet." I wasn't sure if that was entirely accurate, but it didn't sound far off either.

He nodded woodenly. "O-okay—"

"How fast can you get me to that cave in Greece where I first traded away my soul?"

He cocked his head thoughtfully and then froze. A ghost of a smile suddenly split his cheeks and he opened his mouth—

"You ate a witch's *face*," Benjamin whisper-shouted to Stevie. "It was *amazing*."

I'd seen the pair approaching, but I hadn't cared to notify Nero, so he jumped up and spun like a startled cat. The two werewolves chuckled at the necromancer's reaction, having assumed I'd told Nero about their approach.

I arched an eyebrow at Stevie. "A witch's face?" I asked. "Sister or Cauldron?"

The alpha werewolf of New York City was a large, imposing man with a beard that stretched down to his chest. He had found time to change into jeans and a hooded sweatshirt—unless he'd been human when he ate the witch. Gross. He shrugged. "Let's not get bogged down with the details. She was trying to kill one of my wolves. Even after I used non-lethal force to stop her."

I sighed, raking a hand through my hair. "It was a Sister of Mercy, then."

Benjamin turned away, realizing he might have gotten his alpha in hot water. Benjamin was a solidly-built, dark-skinned man with a bigger heart and more inherent mischief than anyone I had ever met. He was also dangerously deceptive in that regard. When push came to shove, he was an absolute terror on the field. A fact which many over-looked after witnessing his playful nature.

"Good riddance," I said with a faint smile. Benjamin let out a sigh of relief, making the sign of the cross over his chest and murmuring a prayer under his breath.

"I heard you needed wolves," Stevie said, changing the topic. "What kind of wolves? Hunters, fighters, trackers?"

Benjamin was grinning at Nero. "You have brains in your hair. Is that a necromancer thing?"

Nero glared, still trying to catch his breath. He fumbled his good hand through his hair until he found the pale glob of flesh, and then he flung it at Benjamin.

It struck the wolf in the forehead with an audible splat and stuck there. Benjamin gagged. "What the hell is wrong with you?" he squealed, frantically wiping at his forehead to dislodge the gore and flicked it far away. He wiped his hands on his pants about a dozen times, panting.

Nero folded his arms with a smug grin. "You're already covered in blood," he said, pointing at Benjamin's hands and neck. "What's a little brain added to the mix?"

"You're sick, Nero. You need help," he shuddered, pursing his lips. "It's different when it's your own kill. Who throws brains at people? Honestly."

Nero pointed a thumb at his chest. "I fucking do. That's who."

I ignored them, turning back to Stevie. "I need your best trackers to help Nosh find the Cauldron. To locate Izzy," I added, not sure if he'd been told about that since I hadn't seen him at the fight. Then again, I couldn't tell most of the wolves apart, so I could have walked right past him a dozen times and not noticed.

Stevie opened his mouth but Nero backhanded him across the shoulder and then leaned in close to whisper in his ear. Stevie stiffened, and then slowly straightened to stare at me. "Benjamin will help," he said numbly, looking as if he had seen a ghost. "Whatever you need."

Benjamin eyed him with a thoughtful frown, but he ultimately shrugged, turning to me. "Of course I'll help." He took a few steps closer, extending his hand and looking me right in the eyes to show his resolve. Benjamin was like that—he could turn from playful to focused the moment danger arose. "I will get my best wolves on it. I know a few of their old spots where we can start our search. We will find her, Sorin, I promise. Don't worry about a thing."

I gripped his forearm and gave him a relieved smile. "Thank you. Victoria and Natalie want to help you."

He grinned excitedly, pumping his fist. "Oh, *hell* yeah! The band is back!"

I smiled at his enthusiasm. He had been very close to Natalie back when she was working with the pack. Having the chance to hunt with her again was like a dream come true. "Adam and Eve are watching the castle, but tell Renfield to get every single vampire he can spare to keep an eye on the exits. Have him include the new vampires, too, and keep nullification cuffs on hand in the event you cross paths with an enemy —any witch, no matter if they are dark or light."

Benjamin nodded soberly, focused on the task ahead.

Stevie was still silent, lost in his own thoughts, so I pressed on. "Same with the wolves. Keep an eye on the perimeter of the park, but I also want everyone watching outwards in case the witches return. Use every wolf you can. I don't want to hear anything about wolves choosing to instead protect their turf back in their own boroughs. If this goes downhill, their only hope at survival will be fleeing the state, so their boroughs don't matter."

Benjamin grimaced, his eyes widening ever so slightly. He gave me a stiff nod, glancing at Stevie warily, wondering why the alpha wasn't jumping in with suggestions.

"What about the social mixer?" Benjamin finally asked, turning back to me. "Want me to tell Renfield to cancel it?"

I shook my head. "No. That goes off as planned. I want our enemies to see us celebrating, even though we're being vigilant. It will give them pause, making them wonder why we would be working so hard yet still celebrating. It will make them think we are sitting on some hidden weapon."

He shared one last look at Stevie, but the alpha werewolf of New York City was now staring up at the castle and didn't appear to notice his attention. Benjamin shrugged. "Okay, Sorin. Victoria gave me your new phone number, so I'll let you know when we find Izzy," he told me.

Then he was jogging back towards the museum, lifting his hand to his mouth and letting out a sharp whistle.

I glanced from Nero to Stevie, frowning. "Is everything alright?" I asked. "Did you need anything else, Stevie?" Rather than answering, he turned to Nero with a hopeful grin.

Nero scratched at his beard, a small smile creeping over his face. "I think Sorin is ready to do your favor, Stevie." The alpha werewolf grinned excitedly.

"That's not what I asked you, Nero," I growled angrily.

Nero smiled excitedly. "You kind of did."

"What does Stevie and his favor have to do with Greece?"

Stevie's grin evaporated. "Wait. What?"

"Do you trust me?" Nero asked me, ignoring Stevie.

I frowned, glancing back and forth at the pair. "Not at all—"

"Cool," he said, interrupting me. He grabbed both of us without warning. Then the world snapped to black and we were no longer in Central Park.

## 16

I coughed, bending at the waist as I grabbed my knees, feeling like I may have left my stomach back in Central Park. "What the *hell*, Nero?" I demanded angrily. "I thought you needed a totem to do that—" I cut off, noticing our surroundings for the first time.

We stood on a grassy plateau about halfway up a massive, forested mountain. It ended in a cliff about thirty yards away. I spun in a slow circle, marveling at the drastic change of scenery. Our little plateau more resembled an unfinished bridge leading to nowhere—the cliff yawning out over a forested valley far, far below us. Our bridge met the mountain a short distance away at the tree-line of a thick, dark forest— which was the only safe way down. Or up, technically.

Luckily, it was level and at least fifty yards wide so I didn't fear it snapping off the mountain to send us tumbling down to our deaths in the valley.

There wasn't a hint of civilization in sight. It was breathtaking.

I stared up at the clear, starlit sky and my mouth opened in awe as a sudden wave of nostalgia rolled over me. The sky was huge and brilliantly lit, much like the nights I had spent in the Americas when I first arrived—and this land was just as empty of human life. The luminous full moon shone down upon the surrounding mountains, bathing everything in a pale glow. It was *nothing* like the night sky back in the city.

Stevie was staring out towards the cliff. A ring of large, mismatched boulders formed a circle like a broken, discarded crown cast down from the mountain above.

"I don't think I've set foot out of a city in a decade," Nero said quietly, staring up at the stars. "I almost forgot how big and beautiful it is." Despite speaking softly, his voice sounded like a shout in the pristine, uninhabited landscape.

"Like the best women," Stevie murmured somberly.

Nero chuckled absently at his words, still staring up at the sky. "The lights in the city make it harder to see the stars. They call it light pollution."

I nodded. "It's just like I remember," I whispered.

I listened to them taking deep breaths of the cool, clean air; I had forgotten what that felt like after growing accustomed to the city air. It was incredible and pure. And...

"This is not Greece," I said, turning to Nero. "Explain yourself."

Stevie wisely took a step back, reading the anger in my tone—because he had good instincts.

"It is better," Nero said absently, his instincts not as sharp as the alpha werewolf.

"Whatever this is, it's not better than Greece and I don't have time for it right now. I'm on a very strict timetable, in case you've forgotten. Don't make me push you off the cliff."

"It's a long walk back," he said dryly. I unsheathed my claws with a warning growl. Nero finally turned to look at me, sighing regretfully. "You're right. This is not Greece. We're in upstate New York, and this spot is more important than you realize. More important than I realized. It might just be the key to your victory. I think they call that serendipity."

Sheathing my claws in hopes that it would calm me down, I shot a curious glance at Stevie. He was also frowning at Nero, looking just as confused but for different reasons. He had wanted me here for his favor, but something about Nero's explanation had been a surprise to him as well.

"I don't think you fully understand my priorities right now, Nero—"

"Perhaps it is you who does not understand your priorities. Maybe you need a reminder. Maybe I do as well," he said in a resigned tone, studying the cliff as he idly caressed his stump for a wrist. That gesture, more than his words, drew me up short. He glanced over at me. "We're not leaving this ledge until you hear me out. You'll thank me later. And before you threaten me, I'm willing to die for it."

Stevie's eyes widened and his hand rose up to grip his beard, giving it a sharp tug—a subconscious gesture on his part. "Um. I'm not willing to die for it. It can definitely wait—"

I held up a hand, cutting him off as I stared at the warlock. "You're holding me hostage?"

He shrugged. "I guess so."

I folded my arms. "I don't understand."

He nodded satisfactorily. "That's a good start. For the record, I don't understand either, but I think our very lives depend on us figuring it out. Now, Stevie told me an interesting story, and I think you need to hear it. But you have to pay for it."

I gritted my teeth, feeling my pulse rapidly increasing as I glared at the warlock.

"He really doesn't," Stevie argued, shaking his head firmly. "I'll tell him—"

"He has to pay for it!" Nero snarled, gritting his teeth.

Stevie shook his head. "I don't know what's going on between you two, but—"

"ENOUGH FUCKING BICKERING!" I shouted at the top of my lungs, unsheathing my claws and panting hoarsely. My voice cracked across the twilight valley like thunder, booming loud enough to make the ground rumble. Nero gasped, staring at me with genuine fear.

Stevie had clapped his hands over his ears with a pained wince and he was standing about five steps back from me. His face was as pale as a sheet as he stared at my claws.

"That's n-new," Nero stammered, pointing at my claws as he also backed away a step.

I glanced down to find golden lightning crackling over the tips of my claws, arcing down over my hand and occasionally stabbing at the ground around me where faint tendrils of smoke rose from the blackened grass. I gasped, just as startled as them, and the electricity winked out.

"I..." My vision wobbled and I almost fell as a severe case of vertigo overtook me. I took a deep breath, holding my arms out to maintain my balance. My throat hurt from my shout, and I felt like I had torn my vocal chords. "I'm...sorry," I whispered, turning away as guilt and shame and embarrassment hammered at me. I couldn't make myself meet their eyes.

My friends were silent for so long that I feared they might have fled.

"It's okay, Sorin. I think," Nero said uncertainly. "Is that the first time it's happened?"

I nodded, still unable to look at them.

"Okay. Well. Did you shit your pants, too, then?" he asked shakily.

I laughed unsteadily, turning to look at him. My shoulders were shaking with concern, but laughter helped. "You didn't really, did you?" I asked, feeling a fit of giggles bubbling up inside my chest.

Nero smiled warmly, shaking his head. "Near miss, though," he admitted. "I just wanted to make sure you could still laugh." He motioned me back over. Stevie nodded, still staring at my hands, but with awe now that the...shock had worn off.

I let out an unsteady breath and made my way back.

Nero cleared his throat. "Can I ask a question?" he asked me.

I nodded. "Sure. But I'm going to sit down for a minute. I feel dizzy." I did so, grounding my hands to support my weight as I leaned back, trying to calm my racing pulse.

They sat down beside me so that we formed a row facing the cliff and valley.

"You're surprised, but I saw recognition in your eyes, too. After they stopped glowing, anyway," he said carefully.

I glanced at him, surprised. "My eyes were glowing?"

He nodded. "Just like your hands."

"Looked like...quivers of lightning bolts," Stevie added.

I shuddered. "Yeah..." And before I knew it, I was giving them a very brief but complete explanation of the Olympians and my recent encounters with my distant family. My father. My son. Dracula. Why I had asked Nero to take me to Greece...

Once finished, I let out a breath and fixed my gaze on my hands, waiting for them to speak. I rotated my wrists, wondering what had caused my outburst of power—of lightning. I'd been angry and frustrated plenty of times. What had been different about tonight?

One thing was for certain. I'd just received proof that Zeus might actually be my father.

"So that was why the lightning was so fucking crazy that night," Stevie murmured, tugging at his beard. I nodded silently.

Nero cleared his throat. "In light of recent events, I believe I can concede the point that Sorin has paid for your story, werewolf," he said haughtily. I snorted at his understatement.

Stevie held his arms out, indicating the cliff. "This is a secret, sacred place that only alphas of the Crescent and their seconds-in-command know about. Natalie and Benjamin both know about it—which was why I was so furious about you taking Natalie from me, and why I needed you to agree to this favor if you wanted me to agree to give her away."

I nodded in confused silence, scanning our surroundings pensively.

"Alphas have always come here to clear their heads before difficult decisions—and to hunt in the surrounding forests. It's a Native American tradition, ironically. To commune with our ancestors and talk to the great wolf spirit. I never understood that. Figured we might have had ties to them at one point long ago. Until tonight, no others were permitted to visit this sacred land. You're welcome."

I swallowed, my throat suddenly tight with emotion to hear that the wolves had ties to the Native Americans.

"I've come here dozens of times and I never saw any wolf spirit," Stevie muttered dismissively. His silence stretched long enough for me to glance over at him. He was studying me curiously. "Until after I met you. After the night you destroyed the blood bank," he said meaningfully. I blinked, not sure what to say. He nodded at the look on my face. "Yeah. I came here to think long and hard about working with you—getting involved in vampire politics. Since werewolves don't work with vampires. Ever." I smiled guiltily. "Anyway, I saw the legendary spirit wolf that night. It was only out of the corner of my eye, but I thought I was going to have a heart attack. I immediately went searching, assuming I'd seen a wild wolf and that my mind had exaggerated it as a result of the sacred legend. But I found—and smelled—nothing. Not a track and not a scent."

"That's the part that caught my attention," Nero said. "I told him we had to get you up here at all costs." He was staring intently at the cliff as if hoping to see this spirit wolf. I followed his gaze, frowning. Then it hit me. Lucian had been the first werewolf. Was this ledge...his *grave*? If the werewolves found this spot sacred and shared stories about a great spirit wolf...

They meant Lucian's spirit! And if Stevie had seen Lucian's spirit here...

Then Nero's reason for taking me here tonight suddenly made sense. The veil between life and death was thin enough for a spirit to cross over.

Which meant it was thin enough for *me* to cross over the *other way*!

"Holy shit," I snapped, jumping to my feet. "You saw Lucian's spirit!" I spun to Nero, tugging him to his feet. "Where is the entrance to the Underworld? Maybe I'll see him when I cross over!" I rambled on excitedly, jostling his arm frantically. "Come on, Nero. Show me!"

Stevie was staring at me with a sad smile. "That's the rumor," he admitted, "and why we don't tell other werewolves about it. Otherwise this place would become a tourist destination."

My joy deflated at the look on his face in addition to Nero's silence. "What's wrong?"

Stevie sighed. "It didn't make me feel better. He was just a wolf out of the corner of my eye. No great epiphany or revelation. No sense of peace or recognition. It was actually worse than not seeing him at all. Like learning that Santa isn't real."

I frowned at him. Nero was nodding empathetically. "Ghosts do not bring peace," he said sadly. "That is a cruel myth. They only bring up old pains. I learned that as a necromancer."

I felt a sharp warning sensation at the base of my neck, and the temperature dropped enough for me to see my breath. I spun with a snarl, focusing on the source of the warning sensation just as Nero and Stevie let out sharp gasps of surprise.

My eyes settled on the cliff and I froze, unable to breathe. My heart skipped a beat, and then suddenly thundered in my chest as if making up for the hiccup. I blinked rapidly, wondering if I was imagining things from Stevie's fanciful story.

Because there, atop the tallest boulder, bathed in a waterfall of moonlight, stood the largest natural wolf I'd ever seen in my life. Except he wasn't natural in any form or fashion, because he was easily as large as a car. The pale moonlight made his fur glow like a ghostly apparition.

He watched us with intelligent suspicion. It wasn't an aggressive look, but it definitely wasn't friendly either. His fur rippled faintly in the breeze, and I saw vapor pulsing from his nostrils.

"Spirits do not breathe," Nero whispered.

I nodded woodenly, my heart thumping hard enough that I thought I might be able to see it beating through my shirt if I looked down.

"Lucian," I breathed, "is not a spirit."

The wolf tensed upon hearing his name, his attention locking onto me like I was a rabbit who had suddenly moved in the underbrush. Compared to his current size, I *was* a startled rabbit.

## 17

I remained motionless so as not to provoke him. Thankfully, so did Nero and Stevie. We stared at the king of all werewolves. My other best friend. It was Lucian.

But...it also wasn't Lucian.

He was impossibly huge. Either that or the moonlight and the elevation was making him seem more monstrous than he really was. Because his back appeared to be even with my shoulders, his head rising above my own. Each paw was the size of three of my boots, and I found myself beginning to doubt our discovery—that maybe this creature wasn't Lucian at all.

Maybe this was just a giant supernatural wolf hiding up in the mountains—much like the Nephilim had hidden in the sewers below Central Park. Because werewolves could shift into four-legged beasts, but they never looked quite like natural wolves. Their structure was just different enough that if they stood side-by-side, you would know one of them wasn't *right*.

And that would be the werewolf.

This creature was not a werewolf. It was a giant fucking wolf. Period.

The most obvious oddity was the crude crown on his head. Where precious gems would have been set on a typical crown, this one was set with authentic wolf skulls. And the crown itself seemed to be made of silver. His fur was burned away beneath its perch, making me frown at the contradiction to my theory. Werewolves were allergic to silver.

But this wasn't a werewolf.

One of his ears had a noticeable gouge out of it, causing it to flop down as opposed to standing straight up like the other. His reddish-brown fur reflected the pale moonlight, making the tips glow like living embers, and his golden eyes were fixated on mine in an unblinking stare.

His muzzle was littered with numerous deep scars, and I noticed other wounds decorating his chest and legs—all of them ancient. Were-wolves had incredible healing abilities—more evidence that this wasn't Lucian.

"Is it really him?" Stevie asked, sounding doubtful. "Or something else?" Even the only werewolf in our party sensed that something was *wrong* about the beast. That this creature wasn't a werewolf. "I've never heard of him just standing around for alphas to gawk at," he added thoughtfully.

I continued to stare at the wild beast, shaking my head in denial. Whoever this was, it wasn't Lucian. It was something much, much worse.

"He's the right color," Nero said hesitantly.

"He's at least ten times bigger than our brother ever was," I argued, glancing at Nero.

He nodded absently, licking his lips. "But look at his *eyes*, Sorin. It's fucking *him*. Tell me you don't see it," he said, sounding desperate for me to validate his hope.

I stared at the wolf's golden eyes, suddenly uneasy. Nero was...right. The longer I looked, the more I began to buy into it. This was Lucian. Or had once been Lucian. Except something terrible had happened to him.

"Death really becomes him. It really brings out that murderous twinkle in his eyes," he said, having to force the words out in an attempt at humor. I could tell by his pulse that he was shaken to the core. "It's really him, Sorin. Our brother. Lucian is not *dead*," he sobbed, falling to his knees. The beast tensed, locking onto Nero and curling his lip in a warning snarl.

And in that moment, I thought I heard a silent, spiritual scream coming from the beast's very soul—as piercing as a hawk's screech.

The hair on my arms stood straight up, and I gasped. The sound cut off abruptly, replaced by an irritated growl from the beast himself—and there was nothing spiritual about it. His head shifted slightly, yet the silver crown did not fall, as if it was fused to his skull.

Which had to be the case. Otherwise it would have fallen off long ago.

Despite his obvious displeasure, he didn't flee and he didn't attack. And with each passing second, I began to sense more of Lucian deep within those golden eyes—a flicker of recognition. Twice. He wasn't crying out for help, but he was there. Deep down. Despite how attentively he watched us, I could see that he was profoundly weary and exhausted. Maybe he feared we were a form of madness. A hallucination. That he was waiting for us to fade away just as desperately as we were waiting for him to irrefutably reveal the truth.

"How does no one know about this?" I demanded, turning to Stevie. "Your king lives!"

Stevie looked troubled. "Whatever he is, he is now a lone wolf. I can sense it. He has no concern for any pack. He smells me, recognizes what I am, and he has already categorized me as lesser—potential prey if I annoy him. He wasn't shy about letting me know it either," he added.

I arched an eyebrow, stunned. "You're kidding. Prey?"

He shook his head. "He is no longer a king, despite that mocking crown. He is a wild beast."

Nero stared up at the wolf with a sad, silent expression. The guilt on his face was impossible to overlook—he felt like he had failed his friend. Even he had thought Lucian was dead.

But...if that was the case, why had he brought me here? What hadn't he told me?

"He's obviously waiting for something," I muttered, turning back to Lucian as I felt my anger rise to the surface—both at Lucian's current situation and Nero's shifty deception.

Lucian continued watching the three of us, blinking with his yellow eyes.

"How do you think we get through to him?" Nero asked.

I was sick and tired of waiting for explanations from people—only getting answers after I managed to ask the right questions. I felt restless and agitated. I wanted to hit something beautiful. I stared at the wolf angrily. He cocked his head, staring at me with renewed interest.

"Yeah. That's what I thought," I muttered, rolling my sleeves up.

Then I began striding towards him with bold, confident steps, swallowing all of my fear.

Nero squawked in horror. "No, Sorin! He is not—"

I didn't slow down as I flung a hand up behind me, silencing him. Lucian watched me approach, his muscles locked rigid. His hackles began to rise and a low, bubbling growl rolled out from his mouth as his lips pulled back to reveal teeth that were long enough to stab entirely through me.

Stevie began murmuring a desperate plea. "Don't, Sorin. That's not the same man you once knew. I don't think he even remembers being a man. His thoughts are all over the place, and they make no sense."

I ignored them, closing the distance between us. Lucian leapt down from his perch with surprising agility and the ground shook at his massive bulk. He began hesitantly loping towards me, keeping his body at an angle and his head low to protect his throat. He was just as large and deadly as he'd looked from afar. His jaws could gobble me down in only a handful of bites.

But he didn't attack.

I halted before him, staring into his golden eyes, ignoring the warning growl still bubbling from his throat. This close, I knew for certain that it was my old friend, despite the obvious differences in his body. In those familiar eyes, I saw a once beautiful castle of reflective glass.

But it had been reduced to a castle of broken mirrors, all pointing at unseen darkness and shifting shadows. I heard echoing laughter and crying in equal measure, balanced by the pregnant silence of the moment before an attack—and these sounds somehow happened simultaneously, like thunder and wind and rain.

A storm of madness, sorrow, and chaos.

My brother was hurting.

I took another step, ignoring the rise in volume of his growl. He shook his head violently, his fetid breath blasting over me hard enough to blow my hair back and sprinkle me with drool.

"Stop!" I snapped.

He did, growing eerily still.

"If I wanted a fight, you'd already be whimpering on the ground—just like the old days."

He coughed, and I caught a brief flicker of dark amusement in those violent, merciless eyes. Perhaps he was just luring me in closer. But there was no way to move forward without trust.

I took another step, slowly lifting my palm before me. He chuffed, sniffing at my hand curiously. His cold nose touched my palm for a heartbeat.

Then he danced back a step, snorting in fear.

"Oh, no you don't," I snarled, lunging past his jaws and grabbing him by the broken ear. I capitalized on his surprise, dragging him down to the ground where he wouldn't be so fucking tall. His snout slammed into the ground and his body whipped over me, slamming into one of the boulders. He yelped loudly and I held on for dear life. "It's time we had a brotherly chat—claws optional—because I'm not abandoning you, Lucian."

In response, he whipped his head, snapping his teeth at me. I shifted to blood mist right as his jaws clamped shut where my head had been. He sneezed in surprise, and I solidified in time to punch him in the snout, sending him skidding away.

"Hot damn!" Nero hooted. "Just like the old days!"

"We're all going to die!" Stevie shouted as Nero cackled with glee.

Lucian regained his footing and bolted after me, his eyes glowing with fury. I called up my cloak of shadow and blood to deflect his force like a brick wall, but he shifted his direction and whipped his head up at the last second, sending me flying instead. I skidded across the grass, using my cloak like clawed anchors to slow my tumble. I jumped to my feet, my cloak cracking and whipping at an unseen wind as I squared off against my brother, grinning maniacally.

"Get him, Lucian!" Nero crowed.

Lucian whipped his head around at the sound and snarled. I cursed as Lucian bolted towards the warlock with anything but playfulness. I zipped between them, making my cloak flare out. Lucian halted in his tracks, glaring at me. Then he hunkered low, his tail wagging ever so slightly. I laughed back at him, feeling my heart grow two sizes larger as flickers of memory struck me—of us wrestling like this back in the old days.

"Here, boy," I taunted, licking my lips.

He exploded towards me with shocking speed. I shifted to mist, coalescing directly behind him to grab him by the tail and stop him in his tracks. I drew deep on my blood reservoir, using my boost in strength to swing him high over my head and then slam him down to the ground with a surprised yelp. He jumped back to his feet, snapping his teeth, but my cloak deflected the blows. I flung it wide and kicked him in the chest, sending him flying back into one of the boulders. It cracked in half and he fell to the ground with a wheeze, shaking his head woozily.

I grabbed him by the scruff of the neck. "Not this time, brother."

There was a brief moment when he fought against me, jerking his head back and forth as he snarled in outrage, and then I was falling face-first into his castle of broken mirrors, the only sound the lamenting howl of a wolf.

## 18

I was no longer on a mountain with Nero and Stevie. I felt myself changing, morphing, disintegrating into nothing but a distant awareness. And then, even that began to fade.

I was no longer Sorin Ambrogio.

The wolf was me. I was the wolf.

And I could do nothing about it. I was stuck in Lucian's mind. Buried in his memories. Drowning in his sorrows.

Swimming happily in an ocean of blood and madness.

Everything shimmered, and a waterfall of broken mirror shards crashed down around me.

I STOOD on the warped deck, my balance already well accustomed to the rises and falls of the large ship's motions. I stared out at the black sky and the stars high overhead, wanting to see anything other than the ocean surrounding us.

The spray of saltwater misted my bearded cheeks. "For the rest of my life, my beard is going to taste like salt," I complained, only marginally jesting.

Nero grunted from beside me. "At least you have a beard." Compared to my bulk, he looked small and lanky enough to be my kid brother.

"You have to grow up before you can have a beard," I said.

He shot me a dark glare. "Without me, you two would die from out-brooding one another."

Sorin laughed, glancing over at us. It was a pleasant sound, hearing him laugh. It had been a long time since he'd done so. He'd been reclusive ever since convincing us to join him on this new adventure. He seemed to notice our attention and his humor faded. I glanced at the warlock, shooting him a helpless look. He shrugged tiredly.

I gazed back up at the stars, searching for anything that might help bolster Sorin's rare good cheer. "Look at the three of us, following the stars. Like the Three Wise Men to the Christians," I murmured.

Sorin chuckled, eyeing me sidelong. "Except we're heading the wrong direction. They travelled east."

"And none of us are particularly wise," Nero murmured. "Well, two of us aren't."

I ignored Nero's cynical remark, eyeing Sorin with distant concern. The breeze made his long hair flare out behind him, but the rare smile on his face was a soothing balm to my heart. Whatever he had seen when he went back to the Oracle of Delphi for a second time had changed him. The first experience had changed him for the worse.

My primary purpose was to make sure that his second talk with the cursed seer didn't make him even more of a danger—to himself and everyone else.

There was no question that it had impacted him severely. He'd promptly abandoned his castle and his vampires, not seeming even remotely concerned for their future even though he was their master. He'd left them to the care of Dracula, his old friend. Our old friend.

Although Dracula had changed in recent decades as well. We all had, to be fair.

The curse of a long life, perhaps. But Sorin was allegedly immortal, so would have it much worse than the rest of us. Since I was the first of my kind, I wasn't entirely sure how long I would live—whether I was also immortal or not.

"How much longer until we finally see this mythical world of yours, Sorin?"

Sorin glanced ahead in the direction of our travel. "We're close. I can feel it."

I nodded my agreement. "I think I saw a bird earlier." Sorin grinned at my news, slapping his palm against the ship's railing. "Are you growing bored of our company, Nero?"

"Neither of you have tits, which makes for poor extended company," he muttered dryly. He glanced over his shoulder with a deeper frown. "And we're running out of crew."

Sorin's good humor evaporated like fog kissed by sunlight. I glared at Nero over Sorin's shoulder, and he winced. But he had a good point. Sorin's appetite had been...impressive. At first, he had been able to keep himself to small sips of blood from the crew, but as the arduous journey stretched on, we had left a fair number of them in the wake of the boat, bloodless bodies strewn behind us like a trail of breadcrumbs.

"They knew what they signed up for," I growled unsympathetically. "Half of them were criminals anyway. It's why we chose this ship."

Nero nodded. "I wasn't judging. You know that, Sorin."

Sorin gave the warlock a stiff nod. "I know, Nero. And *more* than half of them were criminals, Lucian. They *all* were. Even the captain. I made sure of it before we set sail."

I arched an eyebrow at him. I hadn't known that. Such an effort was more considerate than the old Sorin would have bothered to put forth. What in the hell had that cursed Oracle of Delphi said to him?

Whatever it was, it had made Sorin choose to abandon his empire and practically beg us to join him on his adventure to this brave New World that had been on everyone's tongue. A virgin land across the ocean. His request had come at an ideal time for me. I'd grown bored of the political infighting of my own werewolves. The constant challenges over dominance. It seemed like I spent more time mediating their childish tempers than actually hunting anything—man or beast. And hearing about untouched forests full of unknown creatures...

Sorin had barely finished asking me before I'd agreed.

I would have done anything for my brother, Sorin, and I could tell he was hurting. He was either chasing something or running from something, and I desperately needed to make sure it wouldn't get him killed.

Nero had been equally simple for Sorin to convince. Then again, all we had to do was tell Nero that there were new things to learn, new exotic women to behold, and undiscovered magic to master.

We had been Nero's only family—the only people who weren't terrified to spend time around a man who could wield magic as easily as snapping a finger.

But I often found myself wondering about Sorin's true motivations. It was another reason I had agreed to come—to keep an eye on my brother and make sure he was okay.

"Well, brothers," I said, speaking with bold, confident cheer, "we are about to start quite the adventure soon, and I couldn't think of better friends to be with."

"That's because no one else would have you as a friend," Nero teased, chuckling. But I saw the slight shift in his posture—his shoulders straightening with anticipation.

Sorin smirked, studying the stars absently. "It's going to be a grand adventure, brothers. Whatever comes, we will face it together. Surely, it can't be worse than what we left."

Nero and I nodded. "Together."

*Shimmer.*

I LEANED back against the log, crossing my ankles before the campfire, belching into my fist. "That was delicious. You're getting better with your arrows," I said, glancing over at Nero.

He nodded. "It became so much easier when I stopped using the bow and started using my magic to hurl them at my target."

I nodded, suppressing a shudder. It was downright terrifying, as a matter of fact—shooting arrows faster, further, and more accurately than any archer I'd ever met. "Your accuracy is impressive. Don't show any of the hunters your newfound ability or they will stop hunting with you, as well," I muttered.

Nero sighed. "You can't blame them, Lucian. You make them look like children with their first bows and wooden knives."

I waved a hand. "I know. I just never thought I'd miss other werewolves. I want a good fight. Wrestling with Sorin isn't the same as a fight for your life."

"That bear was a fun fight. Well, it sounded like a fun fight. I chose not to get too close." Then he grinned wolfishly. "The look on your face when that thing charged out of the cave! I thought you were going to weep with joy!"

I grinned, patting the black-furred hide bundled up behind me. I had already stretched and dried it during our long hunting trip. "The bear will make a fine cloak."

"Not as fine as Sorin's shadow cloak," Nero teased.

I grunted, rolling my eyes. He was right, of course. The fire crackled between us and I heard an owl hooting in the distance, deeper into the endless forest. I'd run across many new creatures to hunt on these excursions, but I still felt restless more often than not. "What will you do when we get back?" I asked, listening to the calming sounds of nature surrounding us.

He pondered my question for a few moments, scratching at his chin. "Maybe I'll see if Deganawida knows anything that I don't. I'm still trying to wrap my head around the shaman and how his powers work. They are so unlike mine."

"I thought you knew everything," I grinned, arching an eyebrow at him. Nero told us that all the time—how incredibly wise he was compared to us.

He chuckled, hurling a pebble at my leg. "I haven't learned necromancy." I tried to hide my instinctive cringe at thoughts of raising the dead. Nero, on the other hand, was fascinated with the most disturbing studies. Thankfully, he seemed more interested in his own thoughts on the matter rather than having a conversation on necromancy. After a few moments, he looked back up at me excitedly. "Oh! I heard a few snippets of an interesting story about something called a skinwalker."

I frowned uneasily, scratching at my thick beard. "What is that?"

"It's not a *what*, it's a *who*," he said eagerly, leaning closer. "A man who can shift like a werewolf, but he can shift into *anything* or even *anyone*." I turned to him with a dubious and somewhat frightened look, ignoring the prickling sensation at the back of my neck. "But they wouldn't answer my questions when I asked. They seemed afraid to even admit it," he muttered in frustration. Nero often complained about such superstitious stances from the uneducated, arguing that every-thing seemed frightening until someone studied it. "Imagine that. Choosing to be anything you want? Anyone you want!"

I frowned at him uneasily. "Shifting into a wolf is bad enough. It's not just the physical change but the mental one that is dangerous. It's a constant battle for control. A wild beast is always lurking beneath the surface, wanting to break free." Nero nodded with macabre fascination rather than empathy. "A man would die of madness at a young age if he was born with that kind of ability," I pressed. "Handling that many inner beasts would cause insanity."

Nero was already shaking his head. "That's just it. Apparently, skinwalkers are *made*, not born. Something to do with sacred blades..." He flicked a twig into the fire as he continued, thinking out loud. "I'll just have to keep digging. Maybe they don't trust me enough yet."

I let him ramble on as I gnawed on a strip of dried deer meat we'd brought with us on our hunt, pretending to listen to the warlock. I shook all thoughts of skinwalkers from my mind.

"What do you think Sorin is doing back there?" I asked absently after a few minutes.

"Probably something much more enjoyable than sitting next to a stinking wolf," Nero muttered. "I'm sure it involves making Bubbling Brook writhe and moan. Lucky bastard."

I smiled, nodding along. I was happy for him, even though I didn't quite understand it. Sorin had found a measure of peace with the tribe —something that had been denied him his entire life.

A chance at love.

"I do miss that," I mused.

Nero scoffed. "You could have your pick of any woman there. I've seen how they all stare at you. The looks I get are of an entirely different sort. You would think I'm one of these skinwalkers they're all so afraid of."

I grunted, my mood sobering in an instant. Nero's casual comment brought old pains to the surface of my mind. I forced them down stubbornly. Nero and Sorin were my family now. Period. The past didn't matter. "No thanks. I'm going to get some sleep. We'll head back tomorrow to see if Sorin finally taught that stubborn little boy of his to walk."

Nero winced guiltily. "Sorry, Lucian. I didn't mean to bring up—"

"It's fine," I growled, tossing another log on the fire. Sparks flared up, forcing him to quickly lean away and cover his eyes. "It's *fine*," I repeated, taking control of my temper. "It's in the past. Where it will stay."

Nero nodded sympathetically. "Okay."

He began shifting his pack and blanket, leaning back against his own log. I did the same, using the motions to clear my head of my sudden outburst. I leaned back with a sigh, staring up at the canopy of trees as the fire crackled on.

"I bet you a bottle of rum that Sorin hasn't taught the boy how to walk yet," I said after a time.

Nero laughed. "You're on. That boy is growing up entirely too fast. He's probably already running, whatever he is. He's not a vampire, that's for sure."

I nodded absently, thinking about the young boy—the miracle boy. That a vampire had conceived a son was an impossibility.

Until Sorin proved otherwise.

Neither of us said it, but a child from a shaman's daughter and the world's first vampire was a frightening thing to consider. He would be a target. And potentially dangerous in his own right. "He's something," I agreed. "Something dangerous." Nero murmured his agreement. "But not yet. Today, he is only a carefree young boy without a concern in the world. He hasn't seen how cruel the world can be."

Nero chuckled. "That's why he has uncles. To keep him on the straight and narrow. And to annihilate his foes. To teach him how to annihilate his own foes," he added with an almost eager glee in his voice.

I burst out laughing. "Our dear brother chose poorly if he thinks we will keep him on the straight and narrow. Get some sleep, warlock. We leave at first light. I miss Sorin. He's much better company than you."

"Maybe Sorin finally decided on a name," Nero said, yawning tiredly. "Anything is better than *boy*."

I smiled, nodding. "Unless he chooses Nero."

Nero had already dozed off, or he was ignoring me.

Before I fell asleep, I made an oath to keep my brother and his miracle son safe.

By any means necessary. The world would hate him and fear him.

"But they will fear me more," I whispered to myself.

## 19

S *himmer.*

I SNARLED, racing through a scene from a nightmare. My paws were soaked with mud and blood. I followed my nose, panicked, terrified, and furious.

Familiar bodies lay everywhere—many in pieces. The tribe that had taken us in had been slaughtered while Nero and I had been off hunting. Vultures and crows circled above, fearing the werewolf below. I'd already shredded three of them too stuffed with remains to escape my swift slaughter. I had spat them out, unable to even eat them as waves of nausea rolled through me.

That I would indirectly be eating the people who had welcomed us into their homes.

I was mad with blood lust. *Sorin!* I growled furiously. *Where are you?*

What hurt the most was that I didn't even have a name to attach to his son. *Boy* seemed woefully inadequate when trying to save a life.

The smell of old smoke, oil, and charred remains filled my nostrils, masking clear scents from me. Nero strolled through the war-torn camp with a grim frown, his sleeves dripping with blood and filth as he shifted dead bodies, checking every severed limb and head. He'd already vomited three times. I bolted for the trees to clear my nose again. I had to find a scent—something to help us track down the survivors. To track down Sorin or Bubbling Brook or...

*Boy.*

My best friend's son. My brother's son.

*Boy.* The word hit my ears like an echoing crack of thunder, punishing me mercilessly.

I had sworn to protect the boy before falling asleep last night.

If I couldn't find the survivors, I would settle for the scent of the attackers. The things I had already considered doing to them frightened even me. Those thoughts raced through the back of my mind, threatening to take over all else.

But I found nothing. I did pick up occasional scents of stale magic and werewolves in the air, but it was too distant and faint to do me any good. And it only served to ignite my concerns further—to an almost manic degree. Because there were no werewolves here. I was the world's first werewolf, and I hadn't turned anyone since coming here.

I continued to race through the woods around the camp, lost in my own fears as I forced myself to run faster, harder, to ignore the burning ache of my muscles.

Boy was out there somewhere. Nero hadn't found his body. Boy was alive! He had to be!

I whined frantically, feeling tears streaming down my furred cheeks.

I had promised to protect him. *Please, Boy. PLEASE!*

I skidded to an abrupt halt, almost crashing into a log in my haste. I sniffed at the air excitedly, tracking left and right. Then I found a familiar scent.

Deganawida.

He had survived! Along with many others. I hadn't been able to smell them through the death below and smoke of the camp. I spun back to the grim graveyard. Our old home.

Sorin had been down there. Bubbling Brook had been down there.

Boy had been down there.

I held onto my small hope—that I would find them safe and sound with Deganawida.

Even though I hadn't noticed their scent alongside the shaman and his escape party.

I lifted my head and howled, trying to put my every emotion into it, convincing myself that if I could, Boy would hear it. That I could save him for my brother, Sorin.

My howl sent the carrion scattering and flapping with raucous caws.

It was a lullaby of lament.

A wail of war.

Nero looked up sharply, spotting me. He held a severed limb in each hand—both of them belonging to children. I howled again, letting him pick up on my urgency. He dropped the limbs and ran towards me. Black smoke suddenly gathered around him, oozing from his feet so that he looked to be wearing clouds for boots. Magic to help him run as fast as me—some dark magic.

I was pacing back and forth, whining frantically as Nero finally caught up with me.

His cheeks were hollow, and his eyes were sunken. "I didn't find their bodies," he rasped.

I snarled, clamping my jaws down over a dead branch, shattering it in my rage.

And my hope. He hadn't found them.

Then I froze as another scent hit my nose. A faint tickle to the air that I almost missed. My world shook and an agonizing whine was torn out of my throat.

Sorin. My brother.

But something was wrong with the scent. So, so wrong...

I didn't even wait for Nero before bolting after the scent, not even caring as branches whipped into my snout or stones cut into my paws, tearing into my flesh.

*We're coming, Sorin. Your brothers are coming!*

*SHIMMER.*

I STARED DOWN AT DEGANAWIDA. The man was bloodied and beaten, horror dancing in the depths of his eyes. Old horrors, but I was eager to fuel them to greater heights.

Nero stood beside me, his chest heaving as a ball of flame hovered in his palm. "Easy, Lucian," he murmured to me. "Answers before violence."

I nodded jerkily, even though I was seriously considering ripping Deganawida to shreds with my bare hands. The women and children huddling behind a nearby stand of trees and a hastily gathered pile of supplies was the only shield the man had against my fury.

And it was only barely enough to hold me—the world's first were-wolf—back.

Because Boy was not here.

Bubbling Brook was not here.

A film of red fell over my vision, casting everything in a bloody hue as my rage threatened to overtake me. "You will show us my brother's body, shaman, or I will personally finish what Dracula started," I snarled, clenching my fists tight enough for my knuckles to crack.

My inner wolf snarled to break free, only able to focus on the fact that our pack of three was now a pack of two. This shaman stood between me and my fallen brother.

The fang of our trinity. The brains and heart of our brotherhood. The man I would have challenged the world for, even though he had found a new family.

But they had also been slaughtered. Or taken. I wasn't sure which.

All because of this shaman's incompetence. And because I'd taken Nero, my other brother, out on a hunt to get away from the tribe for a time. No matter how hard the members of the tribe had tried to include me in their family, I'd stubbornly refused. I hadn't wanted a new family. I already had one.

And their family had failed to protect Sorin.

I wanted nothing more than to see Sorin's body before I continued my hunt for his wife and son. They needed my protection. Not just from Dracula's army—as the shaman had informed us—but from this shaman as well. Because I didn't trust Deganawida. He smelled... wrong. I wouldn't believe him until I saw the bodies.

"I can take you to Sorin," the man rasped tiredly. "But please don't hurt me. I'm all they have left," he whispered, discreetly indicating the frightened faces peering at us from behind the pile of supplies. "We don't have any fighting men left. I have to get my people to safety."

I could smell the fear and the blood and the tears. He wasn't wrong. And as much as I distrusted him, I knew he was not afraid for his own life. His words rang true. I knew he had nothing to do with Dracula, but he was hiding something from us.

The fact that I hadn't determined if it was the typical secrets a man held close to his heart, or something meaningful to me, was the only reason he still lived.

One of the children cried, staring at me from behind a woodpile. Her eyes brimmed with tears, and she was shaking. I took a step back, realizing that her terror was...caused by me. I took another step back, disgusted with myself. Had I resorted to scaring little girls now? I took a deep, calming breath as Nero resumed the conversation behind me.

Deganawida had already told us about the attack. We were a day's ride from the camp where it had all happened. Tracking the fleeing survivors down hadn't been difficult, which was also suspicious. Why hadn't the attackers finished the job? The only logical answer was that it really had been aimed at Sorin.

If it had also been aimed at Nero and me, they would still be around. But other than the faint scents at the scene of the attack, I'd found nothing sinister following the tribe. The attackers had fled far, far away. Too far away for me to track.

"You will give us his body," Nero demanded in an icy tone.

"No!" Deganawida pleaded desperately. "I cannot. Sorin requested that I take care of his remains. Made me swear on it. He wanted to be buried beside his wife and son," he rasped. "My daughter."

"Then where are *their* bodies?" Nero snapped. "We will take all of them."

Deganawida let out a sob. "I have some of the boys searching, but they haven't found them yet. Or, they haven't been able to confirm whether some of the remains were in fact them."

I grimaced disgustedly. That was a fair point. The old camp had been strewn with so many limbs and carcasses that even I'd had a hard time placing them all—even with the use of my supernatural senses. There had been so much blood, offal, oil, and charred limbs that it was impossible to pick out anything specific.

But Nero and I had tried. Wading through a swamp of hell to find any shred of evidence. And we had found nothing.

"We will find them. They are out there. I know it," Deganawida whispered with false hope.

I had found no trail, so I knew the shaman was wasting his time. He was in denial over his own daughter's death, and he was going to drag his tribe down with him. You couldn't rebuild a home on a broken foundation or heal a broken bone without setting it back into place.

Permitting him to continue indulging his denial would get them all killed.

Death by kindness as they nurtured his madness.

Nurture was for the weak.

Deganawida's weakness at not training enough warriors had taken my best friend from me.

I would never be weak again.

"Then show us Sorin," I said, my back still towards them. "I have a hard time believing he is truly dead. He's tricky like that."

I felt the madness creeping over my mind like tendrils of ivy as I imagined Sorin's son dead. The boy I had sworn to protect.

The boy I had failed to protect.

I would never be weak again.

*Shimmer.*

Blood was all I wanted in life. It was all I was good for. Killing.

Anything to keep the guilt at bay. That sharp bite of hot blood striking my tongue as my fangs shredded my prey was my only link to sanity.

Man. Bear. Wolf.

I didn't care.

"Come on, Lucian. You're not alone," a man's voice begged, snapping me out of my thoughts. "We have to accept the facts. They're dead. They are all dead. If Dracula had taken Bubbling Brook and the boy, we would have found a scent."

I snarled, snapping my teeth at the man with the ball of fire floating in his palms. But something was holding me back. Restraints. Chains.

I bit at them, not caring if I chipped my fangs in the process.

The man stared at me sadly, tears streaming down the dried blood and dirt covering his cheeks. "It's been three months, Lucian. I need you to snap out of it. I can't keep you chained up like this forever. You are a man, not a beast. Please..."

With a sudden start, I realized that I recognized him. Nero. And with that recognition, painful memories slammed into me like a pack of wolves—biting, tearing, howling, snarling, clawing...

"Deganawida is gone," Nero said. "He's hidden Sorin's body..."

I fought back against my pack of inner demons—my pack of memories. Nero's words pulled me back ever so slowly, and I realized that he'd been speaking to me for quite some time.

"You have to find a purpose, brother. I can't do this without you."

Purpose...

I growled. My only purpose was death. Vengeance. Protection. I'd failed at protecting everyone. I'd failed to protect Boy. Sorin was gone. We'd waited beside his body for three days. Waited for him to rise back to life. Nero had tried everything to bring him back, but all to no effect.

He'd failed too.

Nero stared at me.

No. I snarled at Nero, snapping my teeth again. My purpose was blood. That was one thing I never failed at. Spilling oceans of blood.

More time passed in a daze.

I woke to find Nero staring at me with a hopeful look. "Lucian? Are...you back?"

"Y-yes," I croaked. I stared down at my hands, startled to see that I was a man, not a wolf. "I think so," I lied, keeping my inner madness locked down deep. Nero let out a sigh of relief. "You can unchain me, now, brother. I...think I've found a purpose," I whispered, telling the truth this time.

Only one word had stayed with me throughout my madness.

Protection.

If I couldn't protect a person, maybe I could find a way to protect a brave New World. To form an empire of werewolves to watch the shores.

To make sure something like this never happened again.

# 20

S *himmer.*

IT HAD BEEN years since I had last seen Nero. He'd gone back to Europe to hunt down Dracula.

I'd established twelve strong packs of werewolves, stretching all down the coast. More settlers were arriving by the day, all looking for new opportunities and new lives.

I gave them more opportunities than they ever wished for.

To stand guard. To become something greater than a man. To walk the world as a werewolf.

I had never fully banished my inner madness—my guilt. I'd just learned to hide it from Nero long enough for him to release me from the damned chains he'd made for me. I'd managed to keep it under wraps, devoting all my attention to building an empire of werewolves. To never let another vampire set foot on our shores.

But now it was self-sustaining.

My life's work was finished, and I no longer felt the pressing need to keep it up.

I was tired. So damned tired.

I had come up here to the mountains of New York to spend the rest of my days in solitude. I stared out at the valley far below. I'd found this cliff jutting out from the face of a much larger mountain. The best part about it was the solitude. No one in their right mind would come out here. The cliff, reminding me of a broken bridge, offered a great view of the moon and stars as well as miles and miles of forest in every direction. I leaned back against one of the boulders, closing my eyes and letting out a sigh. I had taken off my clothes, ready to shift for the last time.

Because now that my life's work—my purpose—was complete, I didn't quite know what to do with myself. And in that lack of purpose, my madness waited for me like an old friend.

The need to hunt. To abandon the world of man for good.

Anything to escape the damning eyes of a young boy—the son of my dead brother, Sorin. The boy I had failed to save. My thoughts always came back to that moment if I didn't keep myself busy. Like now. I opened my eyes.

And I froze in disbelief as an old woman was suddenly standing a dozen paces away near the edge of the cliff. She was humming to herself, carrying a basket as she bent down to dig at the earth with her hands. I climbed to my feet, suddenly embarrassed of my nudity. What would she think, seeing a man on a cliff, stark-naked and obviously alone? I frowned suspiciously. How had I not sensed her? She must have walked right past me to get to the edge of the cliff. Had I dozed off?

And what was she doing? She looked to be digging for something. I hurriedly tugged on my pants before she noticed that I had woken up from my nap. As I dressed, I watched her reach into her basket and grab something with exceeding caution. She set it down into the hole she had been digging. I frowned. Planting flowers? Here of all places?

I approached, careful not to startle her. "Hello, good mother!" I said from a polite distance. "Do you need help?"

She waved a hand flippantly. "Shove off!" she snapped, not sounding old at all.

I froze in my tracks, my smile faltering. "Oh. I..." I scratched at my head, puzzled. "You—"

"Are you having a vowel movement?" she snapped, shooting a glare over her shoulder.

I stepped back under the intensity of her glare. *Vowel movement?* Had I heard her correctly? I cleared my throat. "If you need any assistance, I'll be over—"

"If I needed assistance, I wouldn't be standing on this godforsaken rock in the middle of nowhere. And I certainly wouldn't approach the naked lunatic sitting on said mountain. You are quite hopeless."

I pursed my lips in chastisement. She wasn't wrong. Her words rankled me for other reasons, though. Hopeless...she was righter than she knew. Crazy old woman.

I tried one last time. "What are you doing, anyway?"

"I'm planting mushrooms, of course."

I frowned. One didn't *plant* mushrooms. I was fairly certain of it. "Why?"

"For my sweet Persephone, of course. It's difficult for me to focus with a dog nipping at my heels. Shove. Off."

I nodded, turning away. I took two steps before I paused, glancing back over my shoulder with a frown. "Dog?"

She stood, brushing her hands together as she turned to face me. She was standing alarmingly close to the edge of the cliff. One slip and she would fall. "Werewolf. Whatever. I do love dogs, but they can be quite the bother at times."

For the first time, I truly assessed the strangely perceptive old woman. She...had power. Nothing alarming, but she was more than the typical human. "What are you?"

She arched a stern eyebrow, making me wilt guiltily, not having thought about how crass my question sounded. "I'm a guide. Natural-ly," she said, holding out her arms to either side to indicate the two mushrooms she had planted on her left and right. My breath caught as I studied the mushrooms at the very edge of the cliff. Even from a dozen feet away, they seemed to be glowing with magical light.

One was red and black, and my scalp suddenly tingled with alarm to see that the cliff no longer ended behind it. Instead, a stone path spiraled down out of sight and into a thick, stygian darkness.

The other mushroom was blue and gold, and a staircase of crude stone and stained-glass spiraled upwards from the edge of the cliff, into a cloud of sparkling mist.

I stared, wild-eyed. "What is this sorcery?" I demanded, no longer caring about my manners. "What are you?"

"I offer gifts to the truly damned: lost souls, ambitious warlocks, broken hearts, hopeless heroes..." she trailed off, waving her hand. "Poor bastards, essentially."

I stared, stunned. "What?"

"Aren't you the nosy one?" then she laughed. "Get it?" I did, and I didn't find it humorous. She sighed. "I originally had three gifts to offer, but now I only have one left before I'm permitted to see her again. Since you look good naked but are obviously depressed, how about you take the last one? Put some magic in that tragic," she chuckled, gesturing at my entirety.

"Three...wishes?" I asked. I didn't comment on the person she wanted to visit. This Persephone. A daughter or grandchild, perhaps.

She nodded. "Three is a magical number, even to the likes of me. And you could call them wishes, but that all depends on what you choose, I guess. Semantics."

She'd made this offer to two others. I was the last wish left. Something she had said tugged at my mind. "You talk like my friend, Nero. Are you a warlock?"

She shot me a very dry look. "No cock, no warlock."

I blushed so hard that my ears threatened to catch flame. "Sorry. I didn't mean—"

"I know what you meant, hopeless hero."

I grew still. Hopeless hero. That had been one of her original comments about who she gave gifts to. She had also mentioned ambitious warlock. I cocked my head, studying her. Coincidence? Right after I talk about Nero, the ambitious warlock, she mentioned hopeless hero.

"Do you know Nero? He's quite ambitious," I said, watching her for a reaction.

The old woman just grinned, obviously unwilling to verbally answer. But that smile...

"What are you offering?" I asked, slowly approaching to get a closer look at the mushrooms.

"A choice. The blue and gold will grant you peace, but it will cost you your memory. The red and black will grant you power, but you will have to master or submit to that power."

"Power?" I asked, scratching at my beard. "Why would I want power? I came to this mountain to forget my past."

She pointed at the blue and gold. "If you are certain, then it sounds like you have made your choice already."

I didn't move, still staring at the mushrooms back and forth. "Power," I repeated. "What kind of power? I'm already a werewolf."

She smirked. "Said the ferocious little puppy that everyone thinks is so cute and cuddly."

I narrowed my eyes, ignoring her husky laughter.

She shrugged. "Power to change what harmed you, if you can control it. Oblivion if you cannot."

I looked up sharply. "Oblivion," I mused. That sounded much better than merely forgetting everything and carrying on with my life as if nothing had ever happened. As much as I wanted to forget my pains, they were also closely tied to the only good moments of my life. I wanted to forget the nightmares, not lose the dreams. But oblivion...

I took a step closer to the black and red mushroom, crouching before it. "Which one did my friend pick?" I asked softly, thinking of Nero.

"I don't know what you're talking about," she said in mock denial. "People usually pick one of them," she said dryly. I muttered under my breath at her evasive answers. She pointed at the black and red mushroom before me. "Hope-full." Then she pointed at the blue and gold mushroom. "Hope-less." She frowned, scratching at her chin. "I think."

I decided to stop asking her questions. I calmly plucked up one of the mushrooms and stood, staring at the older woman. I ignored the throbbing pulse of the mushroom in my fingers. It felt like I was holding a beating heart, and it was even oozing a sap-like substance over my knuckles. The woman watched my choice with a curious smile. Her smile began to fade after about ten seconds. "Well, eat it and walk, you idiot," she snapped impatiently, pointing out over the cliff at my chosen path. "Magic still requires a modicum of effort, you lazy sack of bones. Standing around like a moron holding a magic mushroom," she muttered, her voice growing fainter by the moment.

Then she was simply gone. There was no sound or visual puff of smoke. She simply wasn't there anymore, and I couldn't even recall what she smelled like.

I spun in a slow circle, sniffing at the air. I could sense nothing. I shivered involuntarily, staring back at the boulders where my shirt was neatly folded—where I had intended to turn into a wolf for the last time.

There was no harm in a little adventure. I could always come back here later.

I moved towards the appropriate path and tossed the mushroom into my mouth. It tasted like pure sugar, melting onto my tongue within an instant, startling me.

Between one step and the next, I found myself standing in a darkened cavern, the sound of dripping water echoing in the distance. A waterfall of lava suddenly spilled from the rock wall ahead, illuminating a colossal beast with three snarling heads. It was easily as tall as a building.

I glared at the beast, fully expecting to die. Massive gates rose behind the three-headed dog, tarnished and stained. What had I done? And was Nero here?

Or had he made a better choice?

The dog barked—each head hitting a different octave, and my soul was ripped from my body as I exploded into a wolf form unlike anything I'd ever seen.

Still only a pup in comparison to the beast before me.

Cerberus. The guardian of the Underworld.

## 21

I found myself back in my own body.

I stumbled back from the giant wolf, staring at him wild-eyed and gasping for air. The wolf stared back, looking equally stunned. No. Lucian looked back.

Because it was definitely him. No one else would have had those memories.

But...how had I seen his memories? Had I forced the experience upon him, or had he shown them to me? Was he trying to communicate? With each following breath, the full magnitude of his memories pounded into me, seeming to batter me into the ground without mercy. I stared, unable to blink or move. When I'd looked into his eyes, I'd seen a castle full of broken mirrors. Had those memories been the broken pieces of Lucian left on the floor of his once great castle?

Was Lucian calling out for help? Trying to tell us that he was still inside and didn't know how to get out? In a brief moment of clarity, Lucian stared back at me through those massive wolf's eyes. And he was begging my forgiveness with a single word.

*Boy.*

My eyes suddenly misted over, but I was unable to make myself speak.

He wanted forgiveness for failing me. For failing my wife. For failing my son.

Then, ultimately, for failing himself and taking the coward's way out—running from his problems. The wolf narrowed his eyes, suddenly furious at something. I cocked my head with a pensive frown. Had...he read my mind, too? I couldn't read his now, so that seemed unlikely.

Unless...Lucian *hadn't* taken the coward's way out. I hadn't been able to see which color mushroom he'd chosen—that specific memory being blocked off from me—but I'd seen where it had taken him. To be honest, I wasn't entirely sure I understood what each mushroom had signified. The old woman had been slightly insane.

But I had seen Cerberus. I had seen the guardian of the Underworld. Which meant this bridge really was another entrance to the realm of Hades.

I studied Lucian, wondering how he was still alive after so many years. Same with Nero. I'd given up my soul to become immortal—or so I had been led to believe. Unless Hades and the twins had been lying about that—which seemed more realistic. A way to hide the fact that I was a demigod, complete with electric claws, now.

I glanced over my shoulder at Stevie. "How long do werewolves typically live? On average."

He stroked his beard in thought, looking caught off guard by my random question. "I've heard as many as three hundred years, but I'd say two hundred is a fair average."

I nodded, turning to Nero. "What about warlocks? I bet it's less than five hundred years."

He narrowed his eyes. "I already explained that, Sorin. I'm still alive because of dark magic and a light diet."

I didn't comment on his snarky answer. I just stared back at him, my face utterly blank as I watched his eyes, wondering why he wasn't mentioning the mushrooms.

He opened his mouth to speak.

"Nah," I interrupted him. "You sold your souls." His face grew instantly stony, shutting down as he clamped his mouth shut. "Yeah.

Thought so." I turned to Stevie. "If you could make one wish, what would it be?"

"A rich woman. A twofer," Stevie said without a moment's hesitation, but it sounded mechanical, because he was staring at Nero with a wary look, obviously picking up on the tension.

I chuckled. "A clever man knows what he wants—and how to trick the system," I said, nodding. I turned to Nero, scratching my chin thoughtfully. He stood entirely motionless, his eyes darting about as if searching for an exit. "I bet you would pick immortality. Or necromancy."

Nero didn't even move.

I glanced back at Lucian to see that he had his ears tucked back, averting his gaze. I grunted, having no way for him to confirm or deny since he couldn't talk. I turned back to Nero.

"They never tell you about the price, though, do they?" I said, folding my arms.

He licked his lips. "I would imagine that in such a hypothetical scenario, they would not discuss the price. And they would likely forbid any discussion of the topic with others."

Oh, he was being very careful.

I nodded. "That is fair."

Lucian let out a huff and I watched Nero visibly relax.

Stevie stared at the three of us with a bewildered expression. "Is anyone going to explain what just happened?" he demanded.

Nero nodded curiously, studying me. "One minute you were wrestling like the old days, and the next you were both frozen still. Then you suddenly step back, panting as if you'd just finished running a five-mile race. Did you accidentally Taser each other with your magic hands?"

"What do you mean? How long was I out?" I asked, suddenly recalling my timetable.

Stevie and Nero shared significant looks with each other. Nero's calculating gaze briefly flicked past my shoulders at Lucian before settling back on me.

Stevie answered. "You only just touched him when you both froze as if you had been turned to stone. Then you jumped back a few seconds later." He cocked his head curiously, looking at the grass rather than at me. "Did you touch that crown?" he asked.

I glanced back at Lucian, shaking my head. I froze, momentarily startled to find that it was no longer on his head. "I don't think so." I licked my lips anxiously.

Lucian's silver crown now lay in the grass near my feet. I hadn't noticed it falling. From Lucian's sudden whine, he hadn't felt it either. It hadn't looked like it *could* fall off—more like it had been attached to his flesh. And it was now cracked in half, the two pieces lying side-by-side. I crouched down and hesitantly extended my hand towards one of the pieces.

My every muscle was ready to recoil at the anticipated pain as my finger touched the silver.

Except...

All I felt was cold metal. It rapidly grew warmer with each passing second, and I knew it would quickly begin to burn me if I maintained contact for too long, so I jerked my hand back. It should have burned me instantly. Or at least faster.

I'd recently been able to touch silver for longer periods, but nothing like this.

Artemis had initially cursed me for stealing her silver bow, preventing me from touching silver without suffering significant burns. But...not anymore. Did it have something to do with the lightning around my claws earlier?

I looked up to find Nero and Stevie staring at me, their mouths hanging open.

Lucian had promptly sat down, staring at us and making a faint whining sound. He looked troubled by the fact that the crown hadn't instantly made my flesh sizzle, but he also had a dazed look in his eyes, likely wondering how it had fallen off after so long. Had it been his gift from the old woman?

Or had it been the source of him losing himself?

But he was still a giant wolf, even though the crown had broken. What did it mean?

Nero arched an eyebrow, glancing at Stevie. The werewolf folded his arms, studying Lucian thoughtfully. Reverently, now that his legendary king wasn't actively wanting to kill him.

I thought about my purpose for coming here—visiting the Underworld to rob Hades so I could get my soul back. How much time had passed us by? Not much, since my contact with Lucian had only lasted seconds, but we had spent time talking before that. I was on limited time to return to the witches. Limited time to stop Dracula from forming some kind of bond with Hades and breaking free of my castle.

Except now I had new information. Time had frozen upon touching Lucian—and Lucian had spent at least some time in the Underworld after eating his mushroom.

That's when it hit me. Time. The old stories.

The passing of time was *different* in the Underworld—almost non-existent. Did that mean we were already in the Underworld? Was time frozen right now—like how Aphrodite had frozen it for Nosh and me? She'd been the one to encourage me to go after Hades. I suppressed a shudder, shaking off the bizarre hope. And Selene had frozen time to speak with me as well. Did that mean...

The two women were working with Hades? If so, was that a good thing or a bad thing?

Maybe it was a setup. A trap.

## 22

I realized I was glaring at Nero, frowning thoughtfully. He slowly circled around me, making his way towards Lucian with a fascinated look on his face. A sad, heartfelt look of relief.

Nero had thought of this forgotten bridge the moment I mentioned needing to go see Hades. He obviously hadn't known the truth about Lucian, but he had sure known about the bridge's connection to the Underworld or he never would have brought me here. He'd even admitted to not understanding how it was possible that Stevie's favor had coincided with my need. He'd called it serendipitous. He'd originally intended to take me out here with Stevie at a later date to witness the spirit wolf as a favor to Stevie.

But when I'd mentioned needing to go to the Underworld, Nero must have seen the opportunity to kill two birds with one stone. To investigate Stevie's rumored legend—since it happened to be on the same mountain where Nero had once sold his soul—and to help me find a way back into the Underworld.

The only way any of this was possible was if Nero really had eaten one of the mushrooms.

And he was apparently not allowed to talk about that with outsiders. I smiled at a sudden idea.

I turned around and walked past Lucian towards the edge of the cliff, scanning the ground. Nero watched me, suddenly tense and surprised. Because he didn't know what had transpired between me and Lucian—that I had seen everything.

Lucian trotted after me on silent paws, even though his head hung higher than mine. Even if there was no old woman, I was hoping her mushrooms might still be here. I knew Nero had been discreetly searching the ground for them, pretending to be checking on his friend Lucian.

"Hey, Sorin. What are you doing?" Nero asked, sounding anxious.

"Probably not a great idea for you all to be standing on the edge of a cliff!" Stevie said from a safe distance away.

I glanced at Nero. "I'm hungry. Know where I can find any mushrooms?"

He stiffened, and his mouth fell open. "How..." he trailed off, not knowing what he could safely say without breaking his promise to the old woman.

I pointed at Lucian. "He met her as well. Who was she?"

His eyes flicked towards Lucian in stark surprise. "Oh, god. Is that why he's like this? He met the creepy old lady, too?" he squealed. Then he groaned, realizing he'd given himself away.

"Was she a witch?" I asked, not bothering to gloat at his slip-up.

He shrugged defeatedly. "She had power, so she was something. But nothing more than other wizards or warlocks or vampires I've met. Less powerful than you."

I grunted. "Given recent news about my father, that isn't saying much."

He nodded soberly. "Yeah. Good point."

There was nowhere to hide any mushrooms on the edge of the cliff, but there was a long, flat stone, surrounded by fist sized rocks. My only hope was that the mushrooms would be growing beneath. I crouched down, placing my palm on the flat stone as I reached for one of the rocks.

Nero hissed and I leaned back. Because a single glowing mushroom had suddenly appeared out of nowhere, growing right out of the long flat rock. It had a midnight black stem and the deep purple crown had a single golden circle on the peak, reminding me of a halo. The under-side was a shade of crimson that looked like illuminated blood, and the entire mushroom glowed with dark, infernal magic.

It was nothing like the mushroom from Lucian's memory. Either of them.

Still, I let out a triumphant hoot. "I don't see the creepy old broad, but maybe this mushroom still works!"

Stevie coughed from over our shoulders, looking as if he was trying to put as much distance as possible between himself and the edge of the cliff. "I've always heard mushrooms are dangerous. Especially the glowing hellish ones."

Would this different mushroom work? Would it take me to the Underworld like that cave in Greece where I had first traded away my soul to Hades? As if in response, I felt a faint tugging sensation deep within my chest. It thumped out of sync with my own heartbeat, almost like an echo.

Nero bent down, getting a closer look at the mushroom. He let out an uneasy breath. "Very different than the two I had to pick from."

I glanced up and almost let out a shout to suddenly see the two familiar paths before us, exactly like Lucian's memory. One leading up a spiraling staircase of stone and colored glass, and another leading down into darkness. Nero grimaced.

Stevie swore wildly, dancing back a couple steps. "What the fuck is going on here? Will one of you assholes fucking explain something out loud for once?" he demanded, almost hyperventilating. "I didn't even touch the mushroom and I'm seeing shit!"

We ignored him.

Nero cast me a thoughtful look, shifting it to Lucian after a few moments, the question obvious. I kept my face blank, waiting. "Which path did Lucian pick? Hey—"

I plucked up the mushroom, following my instincts.

"Wait! Just hold on a damned minute, would you? There's no creepy old lady to explain the rules! What if the paths mean something else than they did five hundred years ago?"

I glanced back at him, lifting the mushroom to my mouth to antago-nize him. "The gods plan and the devil laughs."

"That's not how the saying goes!" he argued angrily, swiping at my hand. Lucian leaned close, snapping his jaws at Nero's face—close enough to sever a few strands of his long hair. He backed off, letting out a shuddering breath. "Man plans and the gods laugh. That's how it goes."

I climbed to my feet. "Not anymore." I broke the mushroom into thirds and held out my hand to Nero and Lucian.

Nero picked up one of the pieces and met my eyes. I nodded. He turned to point his stub at Stevie. "You still have a soul, you lucky bastard. We don't. So, you're stuck here on guard duty. Make sure you don't listen to any creepy old ladies peddling 'shrooms. They're bad for the soul."

Stevie nodded nervously. "Right. Drugs are bad."

Nero waved his stump angrily. "No. Drugs are great. It's flirting with mouthy old women that will kill you."

Stevie smirked faintly. "Amen."

I tossed him my phone. "In case they call while we're gone."

"I don't have a car, so I would really appreciate it if at least Nero makes it back."

I grinned, and Nero let out a slightly panicked laugh. He glanced up at Lucian, a genuine smile washing away his fears. "Just like old times, eh?"

Lucian growled unhappily.

"Yeah. Fuck you, too," Nero grumbled. But I caught the hopeful smile that almost crossed his cheeks. When Lucian emitted a strange coughing noise that sounded like a laugh, Nero's face brightened into a wide grin.

I was smiling, too.

I popped the mushroom into my mouth and bit down. It dissolved onto my tongue like powdered sugar, instantly making me salivate. Lucian snatched up the mushroom in my palm with his long tongue, and Nero threw his up into the air, catching it in his mouth.

I strode ahead down the dark path. Lucian and Nero followed in silence, all of us anxious for what would come next. Soon, the darkness was all-encompassing, and I could no longer see the cliff behind us.

Nothing happened.

Lucian grumbled a warning, obviously troubled by this fact. In Lucian's memory, it had taken him to the Underworld after only a few steps. In Lucian's memory, there had been two mushrooms—a choice.

But we weren't looking for a choice this time. We were here to reclaim our property.

We kept walking, and my shoulders began to hitch up at every gust of wind. I heard what sounded like the rattle of bones and hisses of steam from the darkness surrounding us.

"You guys feel anything yet?" Nero asked. "Because I didn't walk this far last time."

I shrugged. "No."

Nero frowned. "The first time I ate the mushroom, I was willingly trading my soul to gain entrance and claim my wish."

I nodded. "I know."

He slowly turned to look at me and his face was pale and gaunt. "We don't *have* souls this time, Sorin. What are we going to pay with—"

The ground dropped out below us and we were suddenly falling.

Lucian let out a howl.

Nero let out an imaginative string of curses.

I was laughing.

"I missed my brothers!" I shouted between laughs, my voice echoing up through darkness to a tiny prick of light. Then that disappeared and we continued to fall.

And laugh. And curse. And howl.

## 23

We landed in a pile atop Lucian—thankfully, or he might have crushed us. He wasn't a pleasant pillow, because he bucked us off with a pissed-off snarl and snapping teeth.

Nero and I managed to back away a safe distance, holding up our arms. Lucian shook his head, snapping out of his instinctive reactions—fighting back his inner monster.

Rather than standing before Cerberus, we were in a long, winding tunnel of damp, black rock.

"Is that...elevator music?" Nero demanded incredulously.

Indeed, a simple, annoyingly upbeat tune seemed to be playing from hidden speakers somewhere in the ceiling. I glanced behind and then ahead of us, wary of an attack.

But the only other sign of existence was that damning jingle. It was already grating on me.

I pulled Nero aside. "Are you now free to talk since we all ate the mushroom?" I asked, scanning our dark surroundings, "and since we obviously arrived in the Underworld?"

Nero nodded distractedly, glaring up at the ceiling as if intending to blow out the unseen speakers with magic. "Yes. I don't feel any pressure on my heart anymore. It was hurting like hell when you kept pestering me with your questions, by the way. Asshole."

I winced. "Sorry." I pointed at Lucian. "Other than giving up your soul for immortality, what else happened? If his gift was to become a powerful beast but to wear a crown that locked away his humanity," I breathed, "what happened to you? What did you ask for?"

Nero swallowed audibly. "I learned the art of necromancy," he said. "In hopes that I could use it to bring you back to life." His words struck me in the heart, and I lost my breath. He averted his gaze, looking embarrassed. "Except Dracula found me the moment I returned from the Underworld," he whispered. "I woke up in Greece to the sound of a collar closing around my neck." He glanced at Lucian with a wince. "Not unlike his crown, now that I think of it."

I stared at him incredulously. "Greece? But you entered here in New York." He shrugged. "And how did Dracula know where you were?"

"Great questions, Sorin. No answers." He scratched at his neck as if he could still feel the collar. "Dracula was already aware of my newfound knowledge of necromancy. He wanted me to use it to bring Lucian back to life, since everyone—including me—thought he was dead." He saw the baffled look on my face. "If he could control Lucian, he could control every werewolf in the world."

I gasped, backing up a step. "No...is that true?"

He nodded solemnly, glancing at Lucian—who was bobbing his head slightly to the sound of the beat, not seeming aware he was doing so. "An instant army that would have opened the gates to the Americas for him. Someone told Dracula what I'd learned, and the list of snitches is small. The mysterious old bitch and Hades."

Lucian seemed to understand our conversation, glancing back at us from over his shoulder with a meaningful look. Almost as if...corroborating Nero's words. The equivalent of a nod that Nero's story was right, and that it was why he'd chosen to make the deal. Why he'd chosen to become a beast—to stop Dracula.

I gritted my teeth, staring out at the gloomy cavern.

"You really didn't know about Lucian when you took me to the mountain?" I whispered.

Nero shook his head. "When Stevie told me the legend, I'd hoped to see his ghost, or maybe find his tomb. When he told me where this sacred spot was—that it was the same place I'd sold my soul and couldn't tell anyone about—I almost had a heart attack. Then you come asking for a way to the Underworld." He met my eyes. "Serendipity."

I nodded uneasily. "Or the perfect trap."

Nero sighed. "I considered that as well."

"Why didn't you ever go to the mountain by yourself? To verify Stevie's legend?"

Nero shot me a horrified look. "You think I would have dared go there without you? We are brothers, Sorin. If Stevie's story had any truth to it, I had to have you there at my side," he growled. "I'll admit that the temptation was high. Especially when I didn't dare say anything to get your hopes up. Just waiting for you to finally come help with Stevie's pesky little favor." He was smiling crookedly.

I smiled back, squeezing his arm. "Thank you."

Lucian watched us, wagging his tail happily. I smiled sadly, wondering if the man would ever come back or if this was as good as we were going to get.

"Come on," I said, motioning for them to follow me. I walked down the large stone tunnel, spotting a bend up ahead. The ambient sound—not the maddening music—of the Underworld seemed louder there.

I reached the corner and peered out. I froze, pulling back just as silently. I took a calming breath, not acknowledging the inquisitive look on Nero's face.

Rather than waiting for me to speak, Nero walked out into the open and froze. I walked up beside him and faced the exit of our tunnel, unsheathing my claws. Lucian loped beside me, lifting his hackles as he snarled at our first obstacle in the vast cavern before us. The area beyond was so immense that it reminded me of walking out of a cave under a night sky.

Except the ceiling thousands of feet above us was made of rock, with huge, building sized, spiky pillars pointing down at the ground, ready to fall at a moment's notice.

I glared at the colossal three-headed dog guarding the familiar gates to the entrance of the Underworld. His fur was sleek and black, and even though he was sitting down on his haunches, he was easily three-stories tall. Cerberus. The eyes all glowed with bright fire, and each head was locked onto us—the only living people in the Underworld. Trespassers.

"He...well, he looks a lot bigger than I remember," Nero admitted, licking his lips. "What's the game plan?"

I narrowed my eyes at the guardian. "We're going to tickle his tummy, punch an old woman in the mouth, and then get our souls back," I muttered. Lucian growled his approval.

"Oh. Is that all?" Nero asked grimly, but I could tell he was ready to cut loose.

I thought about it. "I'm probably going to punch my uncle in the mouth, too."

I approached Cerberus, brandishing my claws. Lucian drifted ahead and to the left, growling audibly. I angled my path to the right.

I glanced back to see Nero walking directly towards Cerberus, and his body was bathed in black and purple flames. "Stand there and look imposing."

He shook his head with a malevolent smile. "Nah. I think I'll swing first this time. I've heard that's the smartest thing to do on your first day in the prison yard." He lifted one arm over and behind his head, murmuring a spell under his breath. Unseen wind abruptly screamed through the cavern and slammed into his wrist, forming a black ball of flame around his hand. I stared, transfixed. It was as if he was summoning all the malcontent souls of the Underworld to do his bidding. "They really fucked up when they let a necromancer sneak back into the Underworld," Nero said, cackling over the sounds of screaming souls. "It's like a buffet table of power," he shouted, his voice growing deeper and more powerful. His eyes dimmed to black fire, and the black flames moved from his arm to surround his body and then suddenly wreathed around his head like a crown.

He flung his hand towards Cerberus, and the cavern screamed and blazed with necromantic flame.

The fire roared, hot enough to vaporize the guardian to the Underworld. Halfway there, it struck an unseen, transparent wall, splashing across its surface like paint. The massive dog panted happily, staring at us through the smear of obsidian flame as it flickered and ultimately burned itself out. It looked like nothing separated us from the dog. A hellish, glass barrier of some kind? I shifted my attention back and forth, ready for an ambush. "What the hell—"

The cavern abruptly darkened and all sound ceased. Even with my night vision, I could see absolutely nothing—not even my own hands. Lucian growled threateningly, but the sound instantly cut off with a yelp. Nero hissed from behind me. "What is this, Sorin? I can't see a goddamned thing! It's blacker than Hades' asshole in here!"

"My *what*?" a cold, booming voice demanded, coming from everywhere—and nowhere.

## 24

Nero grunted from somewhere behind me. "Thank *god*. That infernal jingle was driving me crazy," he said, sounding relieved. He didn't even try to address the disembodied voice —Hades.

"That is kind of the point down here," Hades said dryly. "This isn't a five-star kind of resort."

Nero burst out laughing. "Yeah. I guess it's not."

Lucian growled, sniffing at the air in an attempt to locate us.

Hades sighed. "Let me just turn on the lights, then. You already ruined my introduction."

A large brazier flared to life with purple flame directly ahead of us, casting a violet glow on the polished marble floor beneath our feet—definitely not the rough cavern we'd just been standing in. Two more braziers crackled to life on opposite sides of me, equidistant from each other, to form a perfect triangle.

With us in the middle.

Twelve obsidian columns supported exquisitely decorated, connecting lintels twenty feet overhead, forming a perfect circle around us. I gaped at the fine craftsmanship of the murals on the lintels; even though they were too high up to make out specifics, I could tell they were astonishingly detailed. My heart warmed to see familiar Greek architecture after so many years. Granted, this architecture was of an exceptionally better quality than I had ever seen, even in palaces. I finally lowered my eyes, taking in our ground-level surroundings.

The polished black floor was flecked with glittering gems where it wasn't covered by numerous fur skins. The purple-flamed braziers consisted of wide, shallow, silver bowls perched atop waist-high, white marble pedestals. The bowls were each full of burning bones rather than wood—human bones—and cast a warm, comforting glow over the pavilion. The entire space was rather large, maybe forty feet in diameter, and it was surrounded by a sea of purple mist. An endless cloud that stretched as far as the eye could see.

A long, L-shaped, black leather couch was tucked up against one of the columns close to a brazier, and the floor in front of it was liberally strewn with blankets, furs, and pillows to create a lounging space to sprawl out.

Two beautiful young women reclined on those pillows, watching us with amused smiles as they sipped wine from golden chalices. One woman was tall and thin with a long, graceful neck and sharp, prominent cheekbones. She had long, straight hair as black as night, almond-shaped brown eyes, and milk-white skin. She wore a black toga with a golden chain for a belt, and she seemed to embody the definition of feminine. She was idly nibbling a pomegranate seed from a platter of fresh fruit that sat between her and her friend.

The other woman was only slightly older with rich, olive-colored skin, and a thick head of frizzy, auburn hair framing her plump cheeks. Her eyes were a deep, dark purple, and she wore a dark gray toga with no belt. Light, haunting violin music was playing from somewhere nearby, and the women were not the only occupants.

A man in a crisp black dress suit stood before us, his hands clasped behind his back. His collar was undone at the neck, making his suit appear more casual than formal. He was tall and thin, but he had broad shoulders that signified a deceptive strength, and his skin was tanned and unblemished—the kind of tanned from work outdoors rather than any natural skin tone. I wasn't sure where Hades found sunlight in the Underworld, and I didn't really care one way or another.

His hair was jet black and wavy, almost reaching his broad shoulders, and his eyes shone like sparkling sapphires—bright enough to both draw me in and simultaneously trigger my sense of danger. Because an almost physical power radiated from those cool irises.

He smiled pleasantly, revealing a row of dazzling white teeth. "Welcome. We have all the time in the world to get to know one another. Not a single second shall pass during your stay, since I know you have many questions, and I don't want you to feel rushed."

He held a tiny puppy in the crook of his arm, and the puppy had three heads. Two of them were napping, one on top of the other, but the third was gnawing on the god's finger. One of the heads whimpered in its sleep, and I saw one of the rear legs kicking fitfully as it dreamed.

Dreamed of devouring three recent invaders, perhaps.

"Give us back our souls," I demanded in a low, commanding tone, extending my claws in warning as I stared down the God of the Underworld.

He smiled with infinite patience, looking like a kindly old grandfather entertaining a child's temper tantrum. It wasn't that he was condescending, but more that he seemed truly unflappable.

"Is that any way to greet your uncle?"

I narrowed my eyes suspiciously, glancing at the Cerberus puppy. Was it the same one we'd just tried to fight, or were there more of the mongrels running around? "Hello, uncle. Give us back our souls. Please."

He gently patted the non-sleeping pup's head with an easy smile. "Okay." Then he turned his back on us and walked over to the two women, handing the Cerberus puppy to the younger, black-haired woman. "Thank you, Persephone." I had a suspicion of who the second woman was. A very good suspicion.

The two women fawned over the sleeping puppy with cooing, adoring sounds, taking turns to kiss the two sleeping foreheads of the puppy—and avoiding the playful bites from the third with lively giggles. The pup's tail began to wag and the other heads blinked lazily before letting out big yawns, causing the women to emit more affectionate sounds. "Naughty, Cerby," Persephone laughed in a joyful, carefree chime.

I turned to Nero with a look of concern. Was this a different Cerberus? And why were they being so kind to us? From my knowledge of mythology, visitors to Hades' realm usually suffered less than courteous welcomes.

Noticing my attention, but not wanting to shift his wary glare from the puppy, Nero gave a small shake of his head. I turned to Lucian and I barely managed to slap a hand over my mouth as I jumped back a step.

Lucian was also locked onto the puppy, and he looked a lot warier than even Nero. But that wasn't what had startled me.

Lucian was no longer a wolf. He was a man.

A very large, naked man with long, wavy golden hair. He seemed entirely unaware of his current form as Hades approached, offering him a dark silk robe. "I do not permit large dogs in my private chambers. Thank you for your understanding," he said jovially, dipping his chin.

Instead of accepting it, Lucian curled his lips in disdain at the robe, much like a dog might do to show displeasure. His gaze noticed his human feet in his peripheral vision. And then his body. His eyes widened and he gasped, immediately slapping his hands against his skin. He began caressing and squeezing his chest and arms with strong, groping gestures as if to verify that it wasn't some form of illusion.

Nero suddenly seemed to catch on and glanced over. He stumbled back a step, gasping and reflexively slapping his chest with his stump. "The *fuck*?" he sputtered.

Persephone was no longer playing with Cerberus. She had shifted upright, openly appraising Lucian from head-to-toe with a hungry, smoky gaze. She held a ruby-red pomegranate seed to her parted lips as if she'd forgotten it. If she had been a cat, she would have been purring.

Hades noticed my attention and glanced back. He sighed tiredly. "Wife. You're leering."

She spent about ten more seconds to fully complete her threat assessment of the naked Lucian. Finally, she gave him a slow, single nod, sliding the seed—and her finger—into her mouth. "Mmm." She withdrew her finger with a wet popping sound. Only then did she shift her attention to her husband, casting him a sultry smile. "Just because I've ordered dinner doesn't mean I can't look at dessert."

Lucian's face purpled and he hurriedly slipped into his robe, still patting himself as if not quite believing it. I was too stunned by my brother's transformation to overly care about Persephone's wandering eyes. Lucian was a human again. For the first time in hundreds of years. Although, he didn't seem able to make himself talk, and I knew he still had a long recovery.

If this was even permanent. It had sounded more like a courtesy forced upon him for Hades' peace of mind.

Hades sighed in resignation as Persephone resumed her leisurely pose, leaning back down onto the pillows, as she continued eating the pomegranate seeds more rapidly. He shot me a frustrated look and I smiled in spite of my own frustrations.

He shrugged. "You are quite the specimen," he said, smiling at Lucian. "And she would eat you alive."

Lucian's eyes widened and he hastily tightened the sash on his robe swiftly enough that he almost tore the fabric as he lowered his gaze.

"Allow me to formally introduce my wife, Persephone."

"Charmed," she said, staring only at Lucian as she brushed a seed back and forth across her lips in a sensual manner despite her husband standing right in front of us.

I turned to the other woman, who had been entirely silent so far. Although time was no longer a concern, I was impatient to get some damned answers. I took a gamble, confident of my theory.

"You are Hecate," I said, squaring my shoulders. "The mushroom lady."

She stared back at me, her gaze intense but not confirming my claim. "It is considered impolite to not let the host finish introducing his residents," she said gently.

I flashed my teeth at her. "Fuck being polite. I came here to punch you in the mouth for stealing their souls," I said, pointing at Nero and Lucian. Then I formed a fist, lifted it to my mouth, and kissed my knuckles, staring at her the entire while.

Persephone's eyes widened with sudden excitement, shifting her assessing gaze my way. "Hmmm."

I turned to her and eyed her up and down with a faint sneer. "If those eyes wander any further, you might lose them, auntie," I said coolly, remembering how Aphrodite had teased Nosh. It was important for me to firmly establish the fact that I was not their subordinate. Immediately. Or they would attempt to walk all over me. The Olympians had already taken advantage of my past naivety. That trend ended now.

Persephone's smile changed altogether, seeming even *more* intrigued. "I will take that under advisement, dear nephew," she said, popping another seed into her mouth.

Hades sighed unhappily. "It's like back-biting is bred into our very blood."

I had already shifted my attention back to Hecate, waiting, so I didn't respond to Hades.

She gave me an approving nod. "How did you know?"

"I heard that the Goddess of Witchcraft has been gone for a while. Then I learned that a mysterious old woman gave my friends a choice at a crossroads, using magic—or witchcraft, to be more accurate." Her eyes gave away nothing. "Yet you are not an old woman. Thinking back on my mythology, the only other thing I recalled reading about you was that you were known as the three-faced goddess." I pointed at Lucian. "When I saw his memories, you mentioned wanting to visit Persephone."

She reacted to that. "*Saw* his memories?" she blurted.

I nodded. "I broke his crown."

She let out a relieved sigh. "That is glorious news. And impressive."

I didn't acknowledge her praise. "The only other person I knew with a close association to Persephone was her mother, Demeter." I glanced at Cerberus and then Hades. "And I doubted Hades was close enough with his mother-in-law that he'd let her play with his dog. A man only lets those he trusts play with his dog."

Nero and Lucian were both staring at me with stunned looks on their faces.

## 25

She finally nodded. "I am Hecate," she whispered. "Or, I once was."

I cocked my head quizzically, but Nero interjected. "Hecate..." he mused, scratching his chin. "You have three faces—old, mature, and young, right?" She nodded in response. "Yet you used only one disguise with us," he said, pointing at Lucian and himself. "Why?"

"Because everyone seems to know that pesky fact about me. I tried not to make it so obvious, but it seems we have a mythology buff in our midst," she said, smirking at me. "Disguises are so incredibly effective when used as weapons. We do it all the time. Almost like we are skin-walkers," she said with a dry smile aimed in my direction. "Without any of that primitive blade nonsense, anyway."

I narrowed my eyes. "Right." Nosh. She was referring to Nosh. Aphrodite had also hinted on the topic. "So, we're already playing games. I know a game where my fist touches your teeth. The rules are simple—you just stand there and think happy thoughts until the moment of impact. That's the end of the game."

Hades watched with great interest. So did Persephone. Cerberus had grabbed hold of her toga and was tugging on it back and forth, whipping his three heads like it was a game, but she didn't seem to notice.

"Life is a game," Hecate said with zero fear, rising to her feet as if to call my bluff.

"As is death," Hades added with an amused grin.

"I'll let you pick which fist I use," I said. "Or maybe we can do both —one for each of my friends that you lured into your trap."

She shrugged. "I no longer have my powers, so I imagine it will be rather painful."

I smiled. "Good. Don't clench. I heard it helps, but you'll have to tell me if that's true."

"This will not help you make friends," she added, striding closer to me.

"When she's right, she's right," Hades said with a disappointed sigh.

"I've already got enough friends."

"Let's hold off for a few moments," Hades said. "If you feel the same way after we talk, that is between you two. But Cerberus goes absolutely *wild* at the scent of fresh blood."

I gritted my teeth, staring down Hecate. "Fine. Cherish these precious moments thinking about what awaits."

She dipped her chin politely, not reacting to my aggression. "Thank you."

I studied her for a few moments longer, suspicious of her meek obeisance. From what I had seen so far, the Olympians were not calm and collected, and they did not tolerate challenges or threats. Which was one reason I had chosen to be so aggressive right from the onset. To get their emotions high, because emotional people made mistakes. So far, it was not working. It was both reassuring and concerning. Why was she acting so calm? Did she have a trick up her sleeve? Hades watched the two of us pensively but offered no further comment. I noticed that Nero was studying Hecate thoughtfully as well, a nervous frown growing on his face.

I turned back to her, wondering what he'd seen. Then I thought about what she had last said. "Where are your powers—" I cut off abruptly, slowly turning to Nero again. I noticed Lucian was also studying her thoughtfully. Neither of them looked angry—they looked suddenly alarmed. "*That's* what this is all about! You gave them *your own* powers, didn't you? Without letting them know what they were doing."

She nodded tiredly. "I gave them a choice—a facet of me that you missed in your analysis. I am all about choice."

"But...*why?*"

She hung her head, considering her answer. "To hide them." She slowly lifted her head. "To right a wrong. To help them." She finally shrugged. "Why does one like the color blue? Expound." She folded her hands before her, one atop the other, and waited.

I narrowed my eyes. "I did not come here for riddles. You say you wanted to help them yet you harmed both of them."

"There is always a cost to power," she admitted sadly. "Sometimes it is born by the receiver, sometimes the giver. In this case, it was both. I sacrificed *my own powers* to reduce the price they might have to pay. But the alternative was worse if I didn't act. Your nemesis, Dracula, wanted to raise you and Lucian from the dead. I gave him a necromancer to accomplish that goal." She smiled sadly at Nero. She shifted her sad smile to Lucian. "Yet I took the werewolf's soul, refusing to let him die, ultimately stealing Dracula's prize without him ever knowing." Finally, she turned back to me. "And I knew you were not dead, because Hades had already taken measures to protect your soul—a gift that you paid dearly for."

I stared at her, panting heavily as her words struck me like clubs to the gut.

She...was right. Yet wrong.

Nero had told me how raising Lucian would have given Dracula direct control over every werewolf in the world.

"And what about Nero? You sold him out to the very man who concerns you. I don't see how that was necessary."

She slowly turned to look at Nero, and then me. "Did I?" She walked up to Nero, sizing him up and down as she began to circle him. As she passed out of view, she changed, because once she was behind Nero again she was an old woman, shuffling painfully. "Or did his new gift of necromancy shield the mysterious little box of your coffin dirt that he had obtained? A box that Dracula was already on the verge of discovering when it suddenly disappeared from his awareness," she croaked in a rasping tone. Lucian blocked my view for a moment as she continued walking, and then she was suddenly a young maiden barely over eighteen, moving with a slight skip to her step as she danced back before Nero, smiling brightly. "Did Nero know where the world's first vampire's body was entombed, or was he still alive, safe from this nefarious necromancy? Did the new necromancer know where Lucian's body was, or was Lucian actually safe from necromancy because he was still alive?"

I stared at her, dumbfounded. She...was the reason I'd been able to take back my castle?

Persephone clapped delightedly, causing Cerberus to yip and yap as he leapt onto her lap, trying to nip at her fingers, his tail wagging hard enough to throw his balance off kilter.

I settled a stubborn glare on her. "You harmed them without telling them your schemes. Did Lucian know he would be trapped within a beast for five hundred years? Did Nero know that he would be forced to live with his most hated enemy, wearing a collar?"

That young, innocent face cocked her head, studying me. But her eyes were depthless pools of ancient wisdom and pain. "To be crass, do I care?"

I snapped. I lunged forward, grabbing her by the throat and hoisting her up in the air. Her shins kicked violently as she stared down at me, her eyes bulging. "I already told you that I have enough friends." I pointed at Lucian and Nero with my free hand. "And you're looking at them. You harmed them. So, let me ask you again, little girl. Did. They. Know?"

"She is no longer an Olympian," Hades murmured directly into my ear, his hands still clasped behind his back. I slowly turned to glance at him, surprised to see how calm he looked. "She cannot take a beating of the likes you wish to deliver. She is currently choking to death and cannot answer you." Then he stepped back.

I gritted my teeth, lowering her to the ground. I released her, turning my back to her as I took a calming breath. Lucian stepped up to me, gripping my shoulder with one massive hand. His eyes were red-rimmed, and so full of compassionate concern that it made my heart flutter. Seeing that brotherly love when I thought he had been dead...

It threatened to break me.

He opened his mouth, attempting to talk, but he was still unable to do so. He nodded slowly instead.

My eyes widened. "You knew?" I whispered.

He hesitated and finally shook his head. Then he squeezed tightly with his hand, hard enough to bruise. Then he lifted his palms and shrugged in a familiar gesture. As if to say, *who cares?*

"*I* care, Lucian. I fucking care," I snarled. "You didn't consent to selling your soul for centuries of torment."

Hades cleared his throat. I shifted my glare at him, expecting punishment for my actions. He held up his hands. "If you three would sit down and each pet Cerberus at the same time, you will be able to communicate more clearly."

I stared back incredulously. "You're kidding."

Persephone was already walking over to us, nodding eagerly. "He speaks the truth." She held the puppy out in her hands, and the puppy was staring back at us with an awareness so deep that it made me instinctively step back. That was not the same carefree puppy from a moment ago. "Your consciousness passes via contact into Cerberus, and since he is one creature with three minds, he can...translate, relaying your thoughts to each other."

"He is more than he seems," Hades confirmed. "This is one aspect of his being that serves me quite well in the Underworld. This is the land of the dead. Communication is...good for morale," he said dryly. "And I care deeply about morale."

I stared at him. "No. I really doubt that you do."

He smiled darkly. "It helps me refine my punishments so as to extract the best screams."

I shuddered and Nero took a step back from the seemingly gentle god. Lucian nodded his agreement. It would have been less subtle if he'd given the god a pat on the back.

"Join us on the blankets," Persephone said, shoving the puppy into Lucian's arms. The werewolf took it with a panicked look on his face.

Then his features abruptly slackened and he stared down at the three-headed dog in surprise.

Persephone grabbed his arm by the bicep—somehow seeming to latch onto his entire torso with eight non-existent limbs—and guided him over to the blankets and furs where they had been lounging. I saw her shudder as her palm unnecessarily cupped his ass, saving his life from an unseen fall before guiding him down to the pillows. Hades rolled his eyes. "She doesn't forget anything," he muttered.

I arched an eyebrow and he grimaced, not realizing he'd spoken out loud. "Oh?"

He grunted. "It was just a woodland nymph. And nothing even happened."

Nero walked after Lucian, speaking to Hecate in low tones. I sighed joining them. We sat down in a circle, feeling decidedly awkward with three gods standing over us as we...cuddled with a deadly puppy.

With a resigned sigh, I set my hand on the last available head. The puppy grew unnaturally still, nuzzling into Lucian's lap and closing all six eyes as he seemingly went to sleep.

I gasped as I suddenly felt the consciousness of my two brothers.

We spent about five seconds mentally shouting over one another, verifying that we could all hear the other and vice versa.

Lucian stared at me, a single tear spilling down his cheek. *Sorin.*

I smiled, wiping at my own immediate tears with my sleeve. Then I wrapped him up in a tight, one-armed hug.

Lucian withdrew and turned to Nero. He gripped him by the back of the neck and pulled his head forward, pressing his forehead against the warlock's. *I've missed you, brother.*

Nero gasped, closing his eyes for a three-count. His jaw was trembling as he stared at his best friend. *Why can't you talk?*

Lucian shrugged. *I can't seem to make my mouth speak words.* He turned to me. *Did you really see my memories?*

I nodded, my throat feeling raw. *Oh, Lucian. You poor fool.* He lowered his eyes, nodding. *You didn't need to make those promises about Bubbling Brook and my son. You couldn't have known so you can't hold yourself responsible or carry any burden of guilt for it.*

He hung his head, panting hoarsely. *It is what brothers do, Sorin. He looked up at me. How are you alive?*

I sighed, shaking my head. *It's a long story, and I'd rather not sit around, sobbing like idiots while three gods stand over us...*

Nero rolled his eyes. *Ever the bleeding heart, our Sorin.*

Lucian nodded, wiping his face with his sleeve. *He is right. This speech issue is not permanent. Something changed on that mountain when you broke the crown,* he said. *I don't remember much other than hunting, but the moment I saw you two, I felt violently ill.*

Nero grunted. *Wow. Thank you. Nausea and tears.*

Lucian winced guiltily. *Your arrival changed things. Memories suddenly hit me, but all at once. I still felt wild and angry, but I also felt confused.* Nero and I studied him thoughtfully. *But then you touched me and it felt like I saw a lighthouse through an ocean of fog.* He stared at me, smiling happily. Proudly.

I shifted uneasily. *I didn't do anything other than kick your ass.*

Lucian grinned. *Letting you think you won also helped center me. Reminded me that violence without fatality used to be fun.*

Nero arched a dubious eye at Lucian's bold lie about letting me win. *You two are just as insane as always.* But he had a faint smile on his face. He turned to me. *Regarding Hecate, you need to know that I trust her. And not because the ultimate outcome was to get you two back. The choice she offered me that night...I needed it. I knew there would be serious pain and a heavy cost—she told me that much—but the reward was worth it.*

Lucian nodded eagerly. *I just wanted to die, Sorin. She literally saved my life that night. Saved all our lives by neutering Dracula's plan to take me. Locking my mind in that crown prevented him from ever using me even if he had found me.*

I blinked in disbelief. I hadn't even considered that. *You knew she would turn you into a wild beast when she gave you the crown?*

He nodded. *She said that I would have to fight my inner demons to claim the ultimate prize, and then she gave me the crown. I had the chance to decline, even then. I chose not to. I didn't want Dracula using me to control the werewolf empire I had so carefully built in your honor.*

I pursed my lips and closed my eyes at the swift stab of emotion from his words. I finally opened them and turned to Nero to ask a similar question.

But he was already nodding. *She told me that to master the ultimate power, I would need to learn to serve, and that it would be humiliating and painful. She also warned that inner demons would try to stop me.*

I sighed, shaking my head. *What inner demons did she mean? Was she being literal?*

They stared at me, not understanding the question. Lucian frowned pensively. *I have lived with my inner wolf for a long time, Sorin. I knew how to control him. This...was different. I think that I was the inner demon. My own mind.*

Nero snapped his fingers, nodding eagerly. *Yes. That is precisely it. She said that I was my own worst enemy.*

I nodded wearily. *And her gift granted you immortality?*

Lucian nodded. *In exchange for our souls, which she promised to keep safe.*

Nero grunted. *So long as we never mentioned it to those who hadn't eaten the mushroom.*

I nodded. *Does she have any control over you? Can either of you sense some magical way that she might be using you or even controlling you?* Because it all seemed too altruistic to me.

*No*, they both said in unison, shaking their heads adamantly.

Nero gripped my knee tightly. *She is not human, but she is definitely not godly like Hades and Persephone either. She is just a witch.*

*What is your assessment of Hades and his wife?* I asked him.

Nero shrugged. *Nothing to be concerned about, but they are powerful as hell.*

Lucian rolled his eyes at Nero's phrasing, but he did nod. *I think they want to help, but they are being exceedingly careful about it. They smell nervous.*

I narrowed my eyes suspiciously. *Stay sharp. We are not in the clear yet.*

Nero squeezed my knee again. *Don't hurt her, Sorin. Please. I'm asking as your brother.*

I frowned, studying him. He looked...almost defensive. *Why not? Don't tell me you have feelings for her. You only just met her.*

He sighed, shrugging. *I don't know what it is, Sorin, but my gut is screaming at me. I think she's going to be very important to me. Maybe even to us.*

I considered his request for a few long seconds. Finally, I let out a sigh. *Okay, Nero. Unless she does something to change the situation, I'll bury my hatchet.* He nodded, looking relieved.

Lucian was grinning at Nero, making the necromancer blush. I waited a few moments, gathering my thoughts. Then I removed my hand from Cerberus. The pup instantly woke—at least the head I had been touching. It stared at me very intently for a few moments, making me want to jump back a few dozen steps. Instead, I calmly rose to my feet.

And then I turned back to the Olympians, considering what else I needed to know before going back to New York City.

## 26

The gods waited patiently, and I was surprised to see that they had granted us a measure of privacy, retreating to the couch.

I faced them squarely, planting my feet. They turned to look up at me, waiting silently. "Why would you care about our problems? The Olympians do not seem to like me very much—and I was out of the picture, anyway. You went out of your way to help all three of us more than anyone ever has. And that is very tough for me to admit out loud," I conceded.

Nero cleared his throat. "That was an apology. He's doing his best."

I sighed, nodding. "I'm sorry."

The three of them smiled appreciatively. Persephone was grinning. "That is already showing more humility than any other Olympian I've met." She glanced at her husband with a warm smile. "Well, almost."

Hades returned her smile, and I could tell they truly loved each other, despite their banter. Well, Persephone's banter.

Hades turned to me, holding up a finger. "Some of us knew that you were not out of the picture, but the only safe place to discuss such things was in my realm—the Underworld—where our family members could not hear us."

Persephone nodded. "I spend my Spring and Summer above and

hear a great many things. Everyone fights to share the gossip with me. I'm just so gods-damned cute."

"So, I'm supposed to just take you at your word?" I said, raking a hand through my hair. "That although everyone else seems to want me dead, you three care deeply for me?"

"Selene said you had trust issues, but I had no idea they were this severe," Persephone murmured. I looked over at her sharply, and whatever she saw made her lean back.

"You are friends with Selene?" I whispered.

Persephone nodded. "I have tea with her and Aphrodite on Fridays to catch up and complain about men, annoying husbands, abducted husbands, and various other cruelties suffered at the hands of our family members."

I glanced at Hades to find him scowling at her. "I apparently give her ample conversation material."

"You work with Aphrodite as well?"

Persephone nodded with a bright smile. "She mentioned visiting you soon. Something about an important gift she and Selene came up with."

I kept my face composed. "Oh?" I croaked, hoping my face wasn't as flushed as it felt.

She nodded. "She was very excited about it, but they didn't tell me what it was. Aphrodite gives the best gifts, so you'd have to be a fool not to accept it," she said with a suggestive wink. Hades cleared his throat powerfully, coughing into his fist and avoiding eye contact with anyone. Persephone smirked at him before turning back to me. "She is very close with Selene. Especially after recent events," she said, her smile fading. "She was onboard before the twins tortured Hephaestus, but now...she truly desires to bring her passion to the upcoming party." She smiled wickedly. "I've never seen her this excited. You're all she ever talks about lately. I can't wait for you to finally meet her. She'll be walking on clouds for days."

I nodded stiffly. "I look forward to it," I lied, not wanting to admit the truth and discuss the situation from earlier tonight. Persephone would immediately pounce, asking the kinds of questions that I didn't want to answer in front of a crowd of strangers. In front of family.

It was also unnerving to hear that they didn't already know. That the Olympians were not omnipotent. Reassuring, but also concerning.

I turned to Hecate, wanting to change the subject. "Who was the third recipient of your gift?"

She pursed her lips, shaking her head. "I am unable to disclose the information—for their protection, my protection, and your protection." I opened my mouth to argue but she held up a finger. "Also, I cannot. Literally. It was part of the deal. Magic is very particular. If I divulge, all three will drop dead on the spot. Loose lips lose gifts."

Nero and Lucian gasped. I frowned curiously. "But we're talking about it right now."

"You each ate the mushrooms, and you bypassed the rules by reading his mind," she added with a thoughtful frown towards Lucian.

"Earlier, you made it sound like you were no longer a goddess. That you gave away your power in thirds."

She nodded. "Yes. But I still have my magic, and can still use my three forms. Much like Nero before I gave him my gift." She eyed the necromancer with a sincere smile. "We are very similar. It is one reason I chose him. But I am just an immortal witch, now."

He returned her smile, and I sensed an entirely human response between the two. The response of possibility between two consenting adults. I wondered if it had anything to do with Nero's earlier request.

But this wasn't a love story. "I'm currently dealing with a witch infestation. Know anything about that, or how to resolve it? It would be great if you commanded them all to stand down."

She thought about it for a few moments, and I began to get my hopes up. Until I noticed the pain in her eyes. "It has been a very long time since anyone worshipped me, Sorin. It is another reason I chose to give up my gift. My...specialty is more of a hobby than my fellows. Death, war, love, sex, seasons, sun..." she trailed off sadly, and I suddenly felt like a major asshole. "I decided to pass it down to the next generation and enjoy my life on my own terms instead. I haven't felt worship for centuries," she admitted. "I'm sorry."

Nero cast me a grim look as if to say, *happy now? Punching her would have been kinder.*

I winced guiltily. "I'm sorry, Hecate. I didn't think about that."

She shrugged. "It's okay. No one has asked me about witchcraft in a long time. I didn't think it would still hurt. I shouldn't have dumped that guilt on you."

"Of course you should have, sister," Persephone argued. "It's the only way to keep the menfolk in line. Guilt, liquor, and lingerie." I looked over to find her grinning empathetically at Hecate, trying to make her smile. Hecate giggled, sniffling.

I let her regain her composure for a few moments. I still had questions that were pertinent. "What can you tell me about the gifts you gave them? Without killing them, of course."

Hecate considered my question. "That I gave them each an aspect of myself in order to bolster their inner powers."

I nodded, having assumed as much. "You were a werewolf?" I asked, indicating Lucian.

She scoffed. "No. But I do love dogs." Lucian frowned angrily. "No offense."

I realized she hadn't actually answered me, but I could tell it was by intent. It was an answer in and of itself. I studied Nero thoughtfully. "And you gave him magic because you were the goddess of witchcraft."

She sighed, looking frustrated. "I gave them each an aspect of myself in order to bolster their own inner powers," she repeated carefully. "I cannot make something from nothing."

I nodded in understanding, waving off her discomfort. I wasn't trying to trick her, but I was trying to see if I could figure out on my own who the third person was—which was why she wasn't actually answering me. Twice. She didn't dare indirectly lead me to the identity of the third recipient for fear of putting them all at risk.

"You can try to guess, if you wish. I will answer honestly, but you only get one chance—otherwise you would just recite the world's population until you got the right one."

I folded my arms, thinking of anyone and everyone. What other aspects of Hecate were there to consider? Magic had gone to Nero. Dogs had gone to Lucian.

What other new immortals did I know? The answers were obvious. Nosh and Deganawida. They both had explanations for their immortality, but so had Nero and Lucian. I knew both men had secrets and were both tied to events of that fateful night.

It seemed obvious that it couldn't be Deganawida because I had watched him die and then spoken to his spirit. But...coming back from death seemed to be a common reoccurrence these days. And Nosh was a lot more than he claimed to be. More than he had gotten from my bloodline.

"Nosh."

She shook her head with a sad frown. "No."

I punched my hand into my fist. I really didn't need to know the answer anyway. I had plenty of other things to deal with at the moment, and the fact that I'd managed to save Lucian and find a few potential allies for Olympians was better than I had expected when setting out for the Underworld. But I still had a few things to do down here.

Hecate was studying Nero. "You misplaced your hand since I last saw you."

He grunted, pointing his stub at me. "Brotherly squabble. He feels terrible."

I stared at her blankly. "So terrible that I almost can't even tell I feel it," I said, deadpan.

Lucian stared at me, arching an eyebrow. Persephone burst out laughing. "I want a Sorin, Hades. Please?" she asked, clapping her hands together as if begging.

He rolled his eyes. "No. I hear they're almost impossible to raise," he said, shooting me a meaningful look. It sobered me right up. He was absolutely right. Because I'd almost been killed many times growing up, even if I hadn't known it.

Persephone harrumphed, pouting theatrically.

Hecate and Nero had eyes only for each other. "Grow a new hand," she told him. "I recommend a skeletal one. Real conversation starter."

He stared at her for about five long seconds, and I could tell that he wasn't thinking about magic or necromancy. Well, not only those things. "Perhaps you could show me how."

She smiled shyly. "I can no longer do it myself, but I could definitely teach you."

Nero smiled, looking as giddy as a warlock at his first demon summoning. "Please."

"Gladly," Hecate said, climbing to her feet and holding out her hand to Nero.

They left and Nero grinned at me from over his shoulder before following her between two columns and disappearing into the mist beyond the pavilion.

Lucian began to slow clap, grinning at their departure. I laughed, shaking my head.

"They are most likely the only two who can truly understand each other due to their powers," Hades said from directly beside me, making me jump. I hadn't noticed him getting up from the couch. "Well, the powers she gave him. They share a magical bond. Oftentimes, a magical bond can turn into feelings of personal attraction—whether otherwise warranted or not."

I stiffened instinctively, flicking my gaze towards him. He was staring after Hecate and Nero so he hadn't noticed my reaction. Had he been referring to my bond with Natalie and Victoria? The strange trinity we had formed? Was there something to be said about our physical attraction to each other being a result of our magic rather than our hearts?

Persephone approached Lucian, wrapping her fingers through his with an empathetic smile. "I may be able to help speed up your speech problem. Cerberus seems to like you," she said. Despite how she had been looking at him earlier, she sounded as if she genuinely wanted to help him rather than openly flirting with him. As if it had all been a game to get Hades riled up. Lucian nodded and she led him over to the couch, setting Cerberus in his lap and sitting down beside him with an encouraging smile.

Hades pulled me aside. "Walk with me. The women will keep your friends busy."

I eyed Persephone and Lucian with concern. "You sure about that?"

Persephone latched her dark eyes onto mine. "I'm the queen of fertility, not fidelity. Do not meddle, Sorin."

I shot Hades an incredulous glance. He shrugged. "She's all bark and no bite. Trust me. It's strange, but I'm coming to believe that the

Queen of the Underworld delights in tormenting me for some strange reason. I'm not sure where she gets it."

Persephone laughed, grinning at Hades, but he was already walking away, forcing me to follow or remain behind.

Not feeling particularly romantic—in fact, hating all aspects of romance due to my current shortfall in the area—I followed the Lord of the Underworld.

We left the pavilion and walked into the purple mist. Despite the circumstances, the purple mist reminded me of Aphrodite and the gift she had so vehemently tried to give me. One that had been so important to her that she'd even bragged about it to Persephone.

Why had it been so important to her? She hadn't even met me yet.

And why in the world had Selene agreed to such a gift?

The purple mist eddied and whorled around me, taunting me, as I pressed on after the Master of Souls.

## 27

Almost immediately, we had stepped out of the confines of the purple mist. In a way, it reminded me of the mist around my own castle. A protective barrier walling in my most sacred place—my home.

We had walked for ten minutes without speaking a word. Hades seemed to be moving with a purpose, leading me somewhere rather than just trying to get some privacy from those at the pavilion. So, I followed in silence. Whatever he wanted to tell or show me, he didn't want the others knowing about.

Since I still hadn't gotten anything immediately useful for my problems in New York, I was feeling hopeful about Hades private conversation. Although what I had learned about my past filled in more blanks than I'd ever thought I would learn.

And I'd saved Lucian. And Nero.

I had my brothers back. Together, we could do anything.

As we walked, I found myself focusing on the wondrously terrifying landscapes of the Underworld. It was full of countless crystalline formations of every color imaginable. I had witnessed hundreds of skeletons and people—looking nothing like wandering spirits, but rather living, breathing labor workers—hammering away at walls of gemstones, and shoveling piles of emeralds, diamonds, rubies, sapphires, and amethysts into carts that were then carried away by yet more workers.

No one had been whipping or beating them. Some had even waved at Hades, giving him a weary smile before resuming their work—with renewed vigor. I pondered that, frowning. He sure didn't seem like a feared ruler.

He seemed to be loved.

I caught up with him, stepping into his peripheral vision as he continued his swift stride. "If Lucian and Nero and this unknown third person sold their souls for power as a result of accepting Hecate's offer, where do I stand?"

He glanced over at me. "You did not deal with Hecate when you bargained your soul. You bargained with Hades."

I nodded. "Yes." I waited another minute, but he remained silent. "Well? Where is my soul and how much will it cost me to buy it back? I have it on good authority that people are considering stealing it to try and control me."

He glanced over at me, arching an eyebrow. "That's ridiculous. I already told you that you can have it. I was merely holding onto it for you."

"Oh." I frowned, waiting for the catch, but he kept on walking. "What happens if I take my friends' souls back? Do they lose their immortality?"

He skidded to a halt, frowning at me. "Who *hurt* you?" he asked.

I narrowed my eyes. "A lot of people, actually. You were one of them."

He sighed, nodding. "That's fair." He continued walking, gathering his thoughts. "Your friends will not lose their immortality when you take their souls back. They loaned Hecate their souls, earning interest over a long period of time. That interest is theirs to keep even after the loan is paid back to them. Like a bank."

I stared at him, dumbfounded. This was all working out entirely too easily for my comfort. There had to be a catch somewhere.

He continued walking. I hurried after him, cresting a small rise in our surroundings.

"Ah, here we are," Hades said, pointing. "Look at that dumb fucker."

I gasped to see a wide river stretching out before us. The water was mostly black, but there was a perfect circle of bright red water near the shore, and it was diluting downstream, merging with the darker, brackish water. A man stood in the center of it. A familiar man. "Dracula," I hissed, extending my claws.

"The poor bastard looks frightened," Hades commented, sounding amused. "Let's go throw precious sapphires at him," he said, pointing at two lawn chairs on the bank of the river that I hadn't noticed. I gaped to find two waist-high piles of sapphires beside each chair. Hades was already hustling over to them, not bothering to wait for my reply.

I laughed in disbelief, sitting down in the chair with a contented sigh. Dracula stood up to his knees in the circle of frothing red water, and his face was frozen in a mask of horror. Because time was different here. He was stuck. I noticed skeletal hands reaching out from beneath the water to grip his legs, holding him in place—at least a dozen of them. He stood in the exact same posture as the vision I'd seen within my castle, except he was now in a river as opposed to a bathtub.

"He slaughtered every single man and woman who trusted him. And he did it for power," Hades intoned in a cold voice. He reached out to grab a sapphire as big as a grape and then hurled it at Dracula hard enough to break bone. It struck him in the ear and I cringed. But... Dracula didn't even flinch. "Ha!" Hades crowed.

I shook my head, smirking at the childish, cruel, petty—

I grabbed my own sapphire and hurled it at my nemesis, striking him in the nose with a sharp thwack. My chest loosened and I let out a shudder of pleasure, turning to look at Hades. He nodded slowly. "I know. Feels good to take down an evil tyrant, doesn't it?"

I nodded slowly. "Yes. It really does."

He hurled another sapphire at Dracula, missing him this time. "The Underworld isn't about unnecessary cruelty, no matter what everyone seems to think," he said, studying the man in the river. "It's about accepting your dues. Whatever you do up there comes back to haunt you down here. Both good and bad. A man must pay for his crimes, no matter who he is."

I nodded, trying not to think of what was facing me some day.

"Men like Dracula...they relish in their cruelty. They truly enjoy it. I look forward to meeting them more than anyone else."

He hurled another sapphire, cracking Dracula in the forehead this time.

"But this man in particular," Hades growled with an animalistic hunger, "has done worse than most. I cannot wait to meet him."

I chuckled, somewhat uneasy about my participation. Dracula deserved much worse, no question. It was the fact that he couldn't fight back that bothered me. "Can he feel any of this?"

Hades shook his head. "Not until he goes back home. Then he will feel the pain all at once, but he won't experience any lasting physical effects. Just a major headache. We can't really hurt him. Yet."

Feeling better, I chucked a sapphire at him, hitting him in the nuts. "Damn. That's unfortunate."

Hades grinned. "Tell me about it."

I studied Dracula, hefting a large sapphire in my palm. "So, he's not really here?" I asked.

"No. Just an apparition. But he's trapped here just as surely as he's trapped in your castle. In this exact pose." I arched an eyebrow at Hades. He shrugged. "You opened up a connection between me and your castle when you summoned the Eternal Blood to save Victoria's life at the Statue of Liberty."

I stiffened in surprise, not having known there was a name for what I had used to save her, and I definitely hadn't known it was tied to Hades—although it made perfect sense. And...Hades was remarkably well-informed.

"See?" he asked, noticing my reaction. "I'm helping you even when you don't know it. I needed to talk to you away from prying eyes, and I needed to make it look like it was the last thing you wanted—in case any of our relatives heard about it. So, I reached out to Dracula in his dreams."

I realized my mouth was hanging open. "You...tricked Dracula into summoning you?"

"Dreams can be dangerous," he said with a dark chuckle. "Time is fluid in dreams, making them seem to last forever, no matter how much you cry or how much blood is spilled in your torment, the pesky things just never seem to end."

I nodded stiffly, not entirely sure I liked being this man's friend. But it was better than being his enemy. "Time. Again," I murmured.

He pitched another sapphire, striking Dracula in the jaw with a sharp crack. Hades beamed. "Enough about Dracula. He will be waiting for you when you return, remarkably weakened since I am draining all the blood he stole from his followers. Your soul is safe from harm."

I slowly turned to look at him. "You're telling me that...all of this nonsense with Dracula and the witches doesn't *matter*?" I whispered, feeling as if the ground had just opened up beneath me.

## 28

He thought about it, looking torn. "Not in the way you initially thought, no. But it is still a great danger. It is much worse than you initially thought."

"The twins," I breathed.

"They are out there, planning something that even I can't see. And that troubles me." He glanced at me sidelong. "It should definitely concern you."

"Why am I so hated? Not that I care about their opinions, but on a practical level. What is so threatening about me? Is this all a result of Hera's animosity over her husband's well-established infidelity?"

Hades hesitated. "It may have started with Hera's hatred, but it took on a new life with Artemis and Apollo. You are their brother, and a direct threat to their standing on Olympus."

"Why? Other children of Zeus have thrived and joined the ranks of Olympians. Heracles, Theseus, and others."

"Children always complicate things. But you are a wild card. Your older siblings took part in the war with the Titans, so they were tied to Zeus and Hera whether they wanted to be or not. Piss either of them off and maybe you get sent down to Tartarus to silence you." He shrugged. "And our bloodline tends to murder their parents at any opportunity. Parents do not like that. Although, it is often necessary."

I shuddered at his last comment and the distant look in his eyes when he'd said it. "You're dodging the question. Why am I any different from other demigods?" I narrowed my eyes at the obvious answer. "It has to do with my mother, doesn't it?"

He nodded ever so slightly.

I felt my heart flutter at the thought of my mother. "Who was she?" I asked softly.

Hades glanced over at me sympathetically. "I cannot say. I know you do not like hearing that answer, and I do not like giving it, but you need to remove her from your mind. At least for the time being."

I gritted my teeth. "We are safe down here, so why can I not hear the answer?"

"Because you do not intend to *stay* here. You will return to the world above, and certain knowledge stains the mind. That knowledge can then be taken and used against you." He stopped, turning to face me. He gripped my shoulders. "I swear on my power that it is in your best interest—not mine or anyone else's—for your mother to remain a secret for the time being."

I felt a thrum of power between us as his oath seemed to magically bond with his power. The haunted look in his eyes told me he was not stringing me along for any other reason than what he had said. He truly believed it. Maybe knew it for a fact.

I nodded minutely. "For now."

He smiled sadly and released me. He lobbed another sapphire at Dracula and missed. Then he paused, staring out over the river with a resigned sigh. "Did you know that Apollo threatened to kill the Oracle's sister, Selene, if she did not lie to you about your fate?" I froze, feeling a sudden bloom of rage deep within my chest. Hades nodded grimly. "Well, to phrase your fate in such a way that it led to murkier conclusions, at least. Then you fell in love with Selene, tightening the noose around your neck even better than he had originally intended."

It took every fiber of my being to remain seated.

"The twins knew that your Olympian gifts were on the cusp of awakening, so they pretended to gift you your abilities by 'cursing' you, making you think you were tied to them. So that you never learned about your true bloodline. They attached guilt and pain to your blossoming powers, making sure that you always saw them as curses. They created a self-fulfilling prophecy."

I frowned, trying to bottle my rage before I exploded. "But they did curse me. Apollo made the sun burn me, and Artemis made it so that silver burns me and that I must feed on blood."

He nodded. "That is true. Olympians can harm and curse each other. But have you noticed that you are no longer as incapacitated by these curses? That your newfound awareness of your birthright is finally beginning to counteract these curses?" I nodded very slowly. "That is why you are a threat. You...are much stronger than them. Guilt and self-doubt were the real curses."

I nodded, considering his story and trying to find holes. "But you helped them."

"I saw what they were doing, so I tried to help you as subtly as possible. You were much too desperate back then for me to tell you the truth. And your powers hadn't even begun to bloom. You were an easy target." I opened my mouth to argue and he shot me a warning glare. "Just like you pleaded for Artemis to help you when you failed to steal her bow. You gave me up." I sighed, nodding regretfully. "Putting you right into the palm of her hand. Selene's ultimate demise was just sheer cruelty. You could have touched her. It would have infuriated Apollo, but you could have. If only you had known how powerful you truly were. They gaslighted you."

I stared at him, stunned. I...could have touched Selene? That simple act would have changed my entire life, had I known. I took a calming breath, closing my eyes for a few moments.

I hadn't heard the term gaslight before, but I understood what Hades meant.

"I'm a stronger man, now, Hades," I said, opening my eyes. "And I'm not referring to my bloodline."

He nodded. "I know," he smiled. "That's why we are finally talking. Artemis and Apollo never expected any of this to happen. Despite their almost perfect scheme, you somehow managed to flourish. You started taking over the world in your own right, all broody and guilty and hungry. They let it slide but kept a close eye on you in case you ever grew wise to your true bloodline. They didn't tell Hera that you'd actually survived that fire as a babe due to fear of inciting her wrath. As long as you didn't know your bloodline, you were no longer a real threat. Pleading ignorance was a safer bet for them. Because they are devious, cowardly, self-serving twats."

I nodded with a faint smile at his unconditional love for his niece and nephew. Their admission would have started a war, forcing everyone to pick a side between Zeus and Hera. I studied Hades. "Why did you take my soul, though? And why keep it?"

"I already explained that. To keep it safe. And we made a deal— Artemis' silver bow for your soul. That weapon is fatally dangerous to you. It always will be. Heed my words."

I nodded at the stern look he gave me. "Okay. Don't get shot. Got it."

He studied me for a few more moments before relaxing. "I took your soul because you needed time to mature. Time to learn the truth for yourself. Time to grow into your powers. And I wanted to take Artemis' bow so that she couldn't hunt you down with it. It also gave me plausible deniability—or at least sheltered my true machinations. I couldn't risk anyone learning that I was trying to help my brother, Zeus. I couldn't even risk him learning the truth since he thought you were long dead. Any direct act to help you would have drawn attention to you and started the very war we were trying to avoid. A war that would have been your downfall because you were not strong enough to survive a battle with gods."

I frowned, shaking my head. "Then what has changed? I started growing stronger after learning about Zeus—"

"No. Everything changed when you formed your trinity with your devils and your castle. *That* was the catalyst that let me know we finally had a chance to win."

I stared at him, not sure what to say. But I didn't like the direction it seemed to be taking.

"That is why everything has suddenly kicked off at full speed. It is why Zeus got involved. He didn't know exactly what was happening, but he sensed the sudden change in the air and tried to destroy the threat at the Statue of Liberty." He smiled smugly. "Surprised the fuck out of him to find his own son was at the eye of the storm, so to speak. Surprised him in a good way," he reassured me. "Zeus wants this just as much as me. He knows how corrupt Olympus has become. The Olympians are a plague of tyrants who must be eradicated. Just like your Dracula, but far, far worse. New blood is needed." His eyes twinkled as he stared at me. "Hello, vampire."

My heart was racing wildly. "You...want me to overthrow all of Olympus?" I breathed.

"Damned right I do. And Zeus agrees."

I stared at him, licking my lips. "That is insane. Why would you want me to destroy...you?"

"Because I am the old generation, Sorin," he said tiredly. "I might not be like them, but I let it all happen. Guilt by association," he said, hurling another sapphire at Dracula.

I suddenly felt very, very small.

"Now that Lucian and Nero carry the gifts of the Titaness Hecate, the world the Olympians used to rule with an iron fist is beginning to tumble. They just don't know it yet. Why do you think Hecate gave up her gifts in the first place?" I stared at him, feeling numb. "You, Nero, and Lucian are the new breed. The proof is that you bonded Natalie, Victoria, and your castle. Three entirely different sources of power. You represent change. A melding of magic that hasn't been seen since the first creation."

I frowned uneasily. He was talking about the same trinity Hazel had mentioned. Had I really done that? Without even knowing? And was it truly as powerful as he claimed?

I couldn't even make my romantic relationships work, and he wanted me to topple the Olympians? "I don't know, Hades."

"Why do you think Zeus slept around so much?" he demanded. "He was trying to make a child with the correct qualities to birth a trinity— a real one that could span other supernatural classes. Ironically, the right son was hidden from him and labeled a monster."

I'd found the catch I'd been looking for. And it was a big one.

Destroy the world. For your family.

"Shall we?" he asked, rising to his feet and holding out his arm to indicate what looked like a wide cobbled road leading to a massive wooden door set into a marble wall. "Just because the table is set does not mean dinner is ready."

I nodded, eyeing Dracula's predicament one last time before following Hades.

My family was even more fucked up than I'd ever thought. Many of them wanted to kill me.

And the others wanted me to murder them.

## 29

We finally came to a stop beside the massive door. I turned to Hades with a questioning look. He stared at the door, looking as if he was gathering his courage. Bellowing roars could be heard from the other side, and I felt a shudder of instinctive fear. Whoever was making those noises was loud. And very large.

He didn't look eager to talk about it even though he had obviously wanted to bring me here. And after the secrets he had already told me, I was absolutely certain I didn't want to see the skeletons in his closet.

I glanced back at Dracula, deciding to shift the topic from the door until he was ready. "Your scheme with Dracula weakened my Nephilim vampires," I said carefully. "Will they be okay?"

He glanced over at me, as if I had caught him dozing. He blinked a few times, replaying my words in his mind. Then he waved a hand dismissively. "They're just hungry."

I frowned. "They tried feeding but it only seemed to siphon off into Dracula's spell."

He nodded. "Diet makes the man."

I studied him for a moment, thinking. They had consumed souls and blood from their victims, but Dracula's blood connection with the Underworld must have tainted the flow of souls. "Them trying to feed only served to make his spell stronger because the castle feeds off blood."

Hades nodded with an approving smile. "Exactly."

"I need clean souls." I glanced out at the Underworld thoughtfully. "Is there a bulk discount option? I've given you quite a few bodies over the years, and plenty of blood and souls."

"Yes, thank you for being responsible with your waste management," he said dryly. "You can have all the souls you want."

I waited for the catch, but he had returned his attention to the door. "Don't you need them? I don't want to tell you how to do your job or anything, but aren't you supposed to protect them? It would be hell on earth to mess with the natural order like that."

He shot me a frank look. "Imagine that."

Right. I had momentarily forgotten about his insane plan.

He sighed patiently, sensing my obvious reluctance. "I believe in restoring the world. Even if it means destroying all the gods. We've had our turn, and we've done a lousy job. It's time for the next generation to have a go." He was still staring at the door before us.

"Me," I said, not feeling very confident in my role—or even his plan. "Lucian and Nero. Three brothers, just like you, Zeus, and Poseidon so long ago." He shrugged. "Why do the Nephilim hate the Olympians so much?" I asked curiously.

Rather than answering me, he was entirely still for a few moments. "The Alpha and the Omega," he finally murmured, setting his palm on the door. I heard a resounding click from deep within the blackened wood, followed by a series of deep groans from some internal locking mechanism. "Perhaps Zeus isn't just Zeus. Perhaps Hades isn't just Hades. Perhaps the Titans aren't just Titans."

I stared at him. "Wait. What are you doing right now?" I demanded, glancing at the massive door warily.

"We both know you came down here with much grander plans than reacquiring three souls."

I maintained my composure, wondering if he was just fishing or if he had truly seen through me. "Oh? And what else would I want from you or the Underworld?" I asked.

Because it had only been a vague, absently-considered idea.

"Walk through the door, Sorin. It's unlocked."

I licked my lips. "You're serious."

"As serious as a coffin nail," he smiled sadly. He lit up a clove cigarette—just like Aphrodite had been smoking—and began walking away. "Take your time. I'll be waiting back at the pavilion. I'll send Dracula back to your castle after I finish draining him of his stolen power."

I blinked at him. "The river of blood...you really were draining it from him?"

"Can never have enough blood," he muttered dryly. Then he chuckled darkly. "Remember your dreaded prophecy—the first one, anyway," he said with a knowing wink. "*The blood will run,*" he quoted, holding out a hand toward Dracula in the near distance. At the river of blood mixing into the black waters.

"What about the second message the Oracle gave me? When I went back to her?"

Hades glanced back again, and his face was a mask of secrets. "Perhaps that one was authentic. Perhaps it was another lie. But you've had enough truths for one night."

"What do I do on the other side?" I asked, glancing at the door nervously.

He paused, glancing back at me. "Use this," he said, tossing me an inky black ring. I caught it, inspecting it in the ambient light. It was large enough for my thumb and made of a black, heavy stone, as smooth as polished glass. "It's a soulcatcher. Use your imagination."

"Soulcatcher," I repeated thoughtfully. "How many can it hold?"

He smirked, lifting his hand to reveal his own matching ring. "Enough. Why do you think it's so quiet down here? There should be billions upon billions of wandering souls. You've seen maybe fifty, right?" He kissed his ring and flashed me a smile.

"Is there a cost?" I asked, considering my plan in a new light. I could use the soulcatcher to feed my Nephilim.

He stared at me in utter silence, looking as if he was in great pain. "There is always a cost. And the price is always unknown when making epic decisions," he whispered, sounding as if he spoke from a place of personal experience. "It cost me something to help you in that cave.

And perhaps it's costing me something even now. Sometimes it is the one giving the gift who pays the price, not the one receiving it. Like Hecate said about your friends." Then he continued walking away, his shoulders slumped tiredly.

I let out a shaky breath. How had he known my plan? I hadn't told anyone. I hadn't even made a solid decision yet. It had just been a thought after Aphrodite's comment about our family putting the *fun* in dysfunctional.

Talk about understatements. Aphrodite was the sanest one in the bunch.

I turned towards the door, taking a deep breath even though I didn't need to actually breathe.

"Here goes nothing," I said, pushing the door open. Wind that was simultaneously fiery and icy blew at me, forcing me to call up my cloak of blood and shadows. Frosted embers and frozen flames whipped through the screaming wind, and through it all I heard the agonized cries of the damned.

## 30

I took my time walking back, mildly surprised to find Dracula no longer trapped in the river. Had Hades sent him back to the castle already?

The souls working here and there gave me a wide berth, all of them staring at my new soulcatcher ring with nervous frowns. They bowed and scraped as I passed them by, redoubling their work efforts in my wake. Their fears gave me pause, wondering exactly what kind of deadly artifact I had accepted from him. But I didn't dare take it off either.

Not anymore.

It was a perfect fit for my thumb, feeling like it was made of ice.

I'd considered my conversation with Hades in great detail as I walked. It was unbelievably troubling, but...I was in complete agreement. Especially the part about me having other, more pressing, matters to deal with before I needed to address his grand plan.

The table was set, but dinner was not yet ready.

Truer words.

So, I shoved it all to the back of my mind and focused on the tasks at hand.

I returned to the pavilion to find Hades staring into one of the braziers, lost in his own thoughts as he caressed the soulcatcher on his thumb in an absent, familiar gesture. He looked up at my arrival, his eyes latching onto my ring as his breath caught.

He watched me, his silent question obvious.

I nodded discreetly. He closed his eyes and let out a slow breath. Then he opened them and returned my nod.

Nero was leaning over a black marble fountain of purple liquid that hadn't been there earlier; a vaporous mist shifted lazily near the lip of the bowl, but none of it overflowed.

Hecate was speaking to him in low tones, directing him from over his shoulder. He reached out with a skeleton hand—which made me jump in surprise—holding a chalice and scooped up a cupful of the liquid. "Drink," Hecate urged him.

He lifted the chalice to his lips, and I marveled as it appeared to function the same as any other hand of flesh and blood. The joints between the knuckles consisted of a deep violet crystal that seemed to shine with dull inner light. As he sipped the purple liquid from the fountain, he let out a sharp gasp, almost dropping the chalice. He shook as if laughing, and then flung his head back, taking a deep breath. "My soul is back," he breathed, and then he began laughing.

Hecate smiled, gripping his arm warmly. Then she released him, motioning Lucian over.

Persephone tugged Lucian to his feet with an encouraging smile. "Think of loping through empty fields of wheat, the sun at your back," she murmured softly.

He nodded, taking a deep breath and closing his eyes. "O-okay, Persephone," he rasped. I sucked in a breath, relieved to see that she really had begun to help him get his speech back.

Persephone beamed. "Just like that, Lucian! It will get easier with time," she reassured him, shooting a triumphant look at her husband. Hades nodded with a polite smile.

I grunted, shooting Nero an incredulous look. He nodded back at me, lifting his new skeleton hand. "He's working at it, but he's already said a few words. And I have my soul back!"

I stepped up beside Hades while Lucian went to drink his soul back with Hecate.

Hades didn't look over at me, staring down into the brazier again instead. "I'll move the Soul Spring to your castle for you," Hades said, gesturing vaguely. "I'm sure you have an empty corner that could use a decorative fountain."

I nodded. "Thank you. How does this...Soul Spring work?"

Hades was silent for a few moments. "It is well connected to the rivers here. It will offer consistent nourishment to your Nephilim." His eyes flicked to my soulcatcher ring. "Their appetite could increase dramatically soon."

"Am I on any kind of time-limit?" I asked, studying my ring warily.

He shook his head. "No. Time is meaningless when you start dealing in souls. You can even change your mind, if you wish. Just dip the ring into the Soul Spring and say my name. On that note, if *anything* with a soul touches that liquid and you say my name, it is considered an offering to me. A very painful offering," he added, smiling up at me faintly.

I grimaced. "I could use it as a weapon, is what you mean."

"Everything can be a weapon, Sorin." He shifted his attention over my shoulder and cleared his throat. "Your friends are no longer soulless bastards."

"We are now heartless but *soulful* bastards," Nero crowed, "because we can all hear you."

Lucian was smiling gratefully at Hecate. She nodded. "This will make your transition back easier, Lucian, but do not expect a full recovery anytime soon." He nodded in mild disappointment. "Do not cut off that darker, wilder side of you. Embrace it and understand it. Much like cutting off one ear will not make you hear any better, even if you really do not like the way it looks in the mirror. It is a part of you."

He nodded solemnly. "Better," he whispered hoarsely.

"Is my soul in there as well?" I asked, eyeing the fountain nervously, wondering what it would feel like. Hades nodded, gesturing me towards Hecate, who was holding out the golden chalice with an expectant smile on her young face. I took a step in that direction and the fountain abruptly disappeared. Hecate gasped, jumping back. The chalice was no longer in her hand. I stared at the empty space for about two seconds before slowly rounding on Hades. "What is the meaning of this?"

Hades was frowning at the empty space as well. "I...am not sure. Perhaps you must wait until you get back up top." He looked deeply troubled, scratching his chin as he shot a pensive look at Persephone.

She flung up her hands. "Oh, no you don't. I didn't do anything."

Hecate looked startled as well. She shook her head, realizing that Hades had shifted his attention to her. "I couldn't have made it move even if I had tried."

I studied the three gods suspiciously. "I do not appreciate games," I warned them.

They each turned to me with similar looks of concern.

"I set it up to return to your castle," Hades finally said, as if thinking out loud. "Maybe it left early, thinking it was already finished after giving Nero and Lucian their souls back."

He was absently toying with his ring, staring at the empty spot and licking his lips nervously.

"You better hope so, Hades."

He looked up at me, and then down at my ring. Finally, he nodded. And the tension in the pavilion lessened dramatically.

"So, nothing has changed for me—other than the fact that Dracula is no longer on the verge of breaking out. My enemies still wait."

Hades nodded. "Technically, Dracula won't realize the connection has been cut off between him and the Underworld until you return. It will be a very...painful lesson, and he will probably have nightmares about sapphires," he added with a dark grin.

I nodded, gathering my thoughts back to the matters at hand rather than the Hades business. I needed to save Izzy now that Dracula was no longer an immediate threat. "Do you have any advice on how to deal with the twins? Or which Olympians I might be able to trust?"

He shook his head. "I have done all that I can. It is vitally important that you tell no one of your visit here, or about your new ring. Right now, it is your only bargaining chip. Well, Dracula as well, of course."

"Figured as much. Can you show us the door?" I asked. Then another thought hit me. "Will we meet again?"

He grinned mirthlessly. "Everyone has an appointment with me, Sorin. Some day."

I folded my arms. "You know what I mean."

He nodded without answering my question. "It has been a pleasure to officially meet you. Remember that the world up there is full of cheats and liars. Us being seen together could cause problems. There are, however, some exquisite mushrooms in upstate New York if the situation warrants it. As long as no one else learns where these mushrooms are, of course."

"Of course," I agreed.

Persephone approached, holding out her arms. "If I can't have a Sorin, I'll at least hug one," she said, flicking a playful glare at her husband. I smiled, wrapping her up in a hug. She rested her head on my shoulders and breathed into my ear so softly that I almost missed it. "You really should have taken Aphrodite up on her offer," she whispered, sounding heartbroken.

Then she squeezed me and extricated herself, turning to Nero and Lucian to give them matching hugs. I managed to keep my face composed after her chilling message. How had she learned about me refusing Aphrodite's gift when she hadn't known earlier? And what the hell did she mean?

Hades was studying me thoughtfully. I extended my hand, hoping to distract him by trading grips. "Goodbye, Hades."

Instead of shaking my hand, he snapped his fingers, and we were suddenly back on the ledge in the middle of Nowhere, New York. I blinked, reeling at the abrupt dismissal.

Nero stared at me, then down at his hand. He let out a breath of relief, clenching his bone fist. "Well, that was abrupt," he said, scratching at his head with his bone claw. But he was smiling. "You don't need to feel terrible anymore, Sorin," he said, brandishing the bone claw. "I got an upgrade." I stared at the purple, crystalline joints, still troubled by Persephone's words.

I turned to find Lucian in wolf form again, but now only twice the size of a typical mountain wolf. I bit back my frown so as not to discourage him. "We will figure it out together, brother."

He shook his scruff, meeting my eyes for a long moment. Then he caught the scent of something and slowly turned to look behind us towards the forested slopes of the parent mountain, a gentle, bubbling growl rolling out from his throat as his hackles began to rise.

Whatever it was, he didn't look like he anticipated any immediate danger. He continued staring at the woods, his growl fading.

I turned to find Stevie staring at us. He wore a crooked smile as he stared back at us and then off to the edge of the cliff where he had seen us disappear—only seconds ago, by his estimation.

His smile faltered at Lucian's smaller size and then his growl. "Did it not work?" he asked, looking puzzled. Lucian padded closer, sniffing at the air as if he'd lost whatever scent had caught his attention. Perhaps it had been a bear wandering through the forest?

Nero smiled at Stevie. "It worked. All is good." He glanced at Lucian, licking his lips. "It will take time to fully correct, but he's on the mend."

Stevie smiled in relief. He stroked his beard. "He already feels different from when you left a few seconds ago—which is still hard for me to wrap my head around. How long were you gone?"

I thought about it. "An hour? Maybe more?" Nero gave me a vague shrug.

Stevie shook his head with a grunt. "Well, you only just left, from my perspective." He turned back to Lucian again. "He no longer feels like a wild beast. Whatever you did worked. I have heard stories of men who spent too long in wolf form. It took them years to return to normal."

I sighed impatiently. "We do not have years, but he has already resumed his human form once, so perhaps he will heal quicker."

Stevie grinned excitedly to hear Lucian's progress. "Everyone will be so excited to see him. Lucian..." he whispered reverently, shaking his head. A phone rang and he jumped in alarm, almost dropping the phone in his hand. It was mine. He held it out with an embarrassed chuckle.

I approached, answering it without looking. "Sorin."

"He betrayed us!" Nosh growled, breathing heavily as if running. I heard explosions, screaming, and malevolent laughter in the background. I stiffened with alarm.

"What?" I demanded, all thoughts of Lucian scattering from my mind.

"Benjamin!" Nosh rasped, cursing as an even louder explosion almost blew out the speakers. It was followed by a beastly roar that sounded like Nosh's spirit bear. "Okay," he wheezed. "I'm back. It's fucking chaos over here. The bear should distract them long enough for me to get the hell out."

"How did Benjamin betray us?" I demanded, motioning everyone closer to me by snapping my fingers. How the hell had anything gone wrong? We'd left the city half an hour ago if I was judging time correctly—which was questionable, given all the time changes I'd experienced.

"Benjamin would *never* betray us," Stevie argued adamantly.

"Nosh!" I snapped into the phone impatiently, hoping he could hear me through the chaos on his end. "Where are you? We're on our way back."

Nero nodded grimly, flexing his new skeleton hand. Lucian was scanning the woods warily, keeping an eye out for the nearby predator he had smelled, not seeming interested in our panic.

"I'm here," Nosh grumbled, panting as if running. "Benjamin broke us into groups to search for Izzy. He went with Victoria and Natalie and I went with a few others. But it was a trap."

My blood suddenly ran cold. "What do you mean? The Cauldron knew you were coming?"

"No, Sorin," Nosh snarled. "Benjamin kidnapped Victoria and Natalie. He's gone."

Everything muted and I heard a high-pitched whine in my ears. I blinked, wondering if I'd misheard him. "Kidnapped? That's...not possible. He must be trying to protect them!"

"Listen to me, Sorin!" Nosh shouted at the top of his lungs. "I saw it with my own eyes! He tossed them into the back of a van and took off. The Sisters of Mercy were driving. Then more Sisters attacked us, covering their escape. It was fucking coordinated."

I stared into the middle distance, horrified and unable to make my voice work. Persephone's parting warning taunted me. *You really should have taken Aphrodite up on her offer...*

I wanted to rush back to the Underworld and demand an explanation, even if I had to drown the Queen of the Underworld in the Soul Spring and scream Hades name. But every second counted.

"I'm five minutes away from the museum, but I'm sticking to alleys," Nosh said in a quieter tone, still breathing heavily.

"We'll meet you on the steps. Find out where they're taking Natalie and Victoria!"

"They're going to Trinity Church. It was on the side of the van," Nosh growled, the sounds of fighting fading dramatically. "I think they were upset that you left town rather than meet their High Priestess. Benjamin must have told them, but I can't fathom why. Did you say something to piss him off?"

"No!" I snapped.

"It doesn't make any sense," he muttered, sounding frustrated. "I'll see you at the museum." He hung up without waiting for a response.

Stevie was panting furiously, his eyes distant and wild as he suddenly began to pace. "No. Benjamin would never—"

Lucian cut Stevie off with an abrupt snarl, lunging as if intending to rip his arm off. The tip of a gleaming silver arrow erupted out of Stevie's open mouth, halted by the back of his skull.

If he hadn't moved, the arrow would have hit me directly in the chest.

He blinked once before falling forward at my feet, coming to a final rest on his side. Lucian grunted, shaking his head with a slightly dazed expression and almost losing his balance. Panic briefly rose in my chest, fearing he'd been hit as well. Then he hunkered low, snarling and spitting as he glared at the distant woods in the direction of the unseen archer. It hadn't been a bear he'd sensed out there. It had been this assassin. He had tried to warn us, but we hadn't heeded him.

That arrow had been intended for me.

I called up my cloak of shadow and blood, whipping it out ahead of us just as three more arrows slammed into it with sounds like breaking glass, making me wince. Because the heavy impacts caused me pain despite my shield.

"Silver arrows," Nero growled, holding an orb of smoke in his palm as he peered over the cloak, searching for the threat.

I nodded grimly. "Artemis!" I shouted, my voice echoing through the mountains.

"I missed you, brother!" a distant, merciless voice laughed harshly from the depths of the forest. "I thought it was time we got reacquainted."

"Your sense of humor certainly missed the mark!" I shouted.

## 31

S tevie stared lifelessly at me, the silver tip of the arrow jutting out of his mouth, and blood painting his long beard. Lucian and Nero hunkered low behind my cloak wall, occasionally risking glances out the side or over the top. Which was almost immediately followed by them frantically ducking back down as more silver arrows pelted my cloak. We were pinned down.

And now the alpha werewolf of New York City's Crescent was dead.

How had she found us? Only a few people knew of this mountain. Stevie, Natalie, and—

An icy chill rolled down my spine. Benjamin. He and Natalie were the only other people who knew about this mountain, according to Stevie. Damn it. Was Benjamin working for Artemis? The Sisters? Both? Maybe Artemis was working with the Sisters of Mercy.

"Come out, coward!" I challenged, risking a quick glance to scan the forested face of the mountain. Two more arrows simultaneously slammed into the ground on either side of my cloak, letting us know that even splitting up and running was not an option—and removing all potential doubt that Artemis was the best archer in the world. The best hunter in the world.

"Benjamin was incredibly helpful," she called out, sounding much closer. I peered over my cloak, ready to drop in an instant. No arrows came. "Benjamin was not a fan of being second-in-command. I told him I could make an opening in the werewolf hierarchy for him if he told me where you'd run off to. Nailed it." She had killed Stevie to help Benjamin? I thought she had been aiming for me—she'd implied as much. "He said something about visiting a big wolf, but this canine doesn't look that big to me," she said, exiting the woods without the sound of even a crunching twig, smirking at Lucian as he peered out from the side of my cloak.

She looked exactly the same as the first time I had seen her in Greece so long ago. She had long, golden brown hair, but it was tucked back in a bun so as not to get in the way of her aim. Her features were cold and beautiful, and her eyes were cruel and cunning. She wore jeans and a light jacket and clutched an ornate silver bow at her side with one hand—the same intricate weapon I had once tried to steal. The same bow Hades had so adamantly warned me about.

It was nocked with another gleaming arrow, ready to loose if we made a run for it. She walked sideways, grinning. "You may as well stop hiding. There's no sport in killing men hiding under a blanket," she said, eyeing my cloak. She kept her distance, though.

"What do you want, Artemis?"

"You bleeding out at my feet, whimpering my name, sweet brother," she said in a sickly-sweet tone. She even licked her lips. "And Apollo witnessing it all."

Lucian began slinking away on silent paws as if hoping to outflank her. Three silver arrows suddenly sailed past my face close enough to feel the wind of their passing. They hammered into Stevie's lifeless form—right in his heart—each arrow splitting the haft of the one preceding it. The skin around the arrows blackened and smoldered. "Movement makes me jumpy," Artemis warned. "You don't want me jumpy, brother."

I gritted my teeth, motioning for Nero and Lucian to remain behind the cloak. "If you have everything under control, why convince Benjamin to aid the Sisters of Mercy?"

She lowered her bow, frowning as she cocked her head. "What?"

She looked genuinely puzzled. "He kidnapped some friends of

mine earlier. He's working for the Sisters of Mercy. And you, apparently."

She laughed bitterly. "Well. Little Benjamin has more spunk than I realized." She shrugged dismissively. "No matter. My only concern is your death."

Nero murmured uneasily behind me. I didn't know what he said, but I was pretty sure we were on the same page. "You expect me to believe that's just a coincidence?" I scoffed. "Rather than the much simpler angle—you're working with the Sisters of Mercy as well."

She froze, her good humor shattering in an instant, and punctuated by three silver arrows hammering into the ground directly between my feet. They struck so hard that they sunk into the earth, leaving only the fletching visible.

"Work. With mortals. How *dare* you," she seethed, quivering with outrage at the suggestion. "Only a coward would draw filthy mortals into their godly disputes. Mortals are merely for sport, created for us to play with, torment, and discard."

Nero growled angrily but remained hidden.

I studied her, frowning. I...believed her. No one could fake that level of arrogance. She and her brother had severed the thumbs of Hephaestus without help. I couldn't imagine her accepting the aid of mortals—not even to command them. It would be...degrading to her.

Had Benjamin kidnapped the devils simply to get some leverage against me for Stevie's assassination? I remembered him looking me in the eyes, promising to save Izzy. I realized I was panting, my fury ignited by his straight-faced lie. He'd known he would betray me even then. He'd shaken my *hand*. I bit back most of my anger, directing all that was left at Artemis.

"If you wanted a fight, all you had to do was ask."

She seemed to have overcome her own anger, and a slow smile crept across her cheeks at my words. "Oh, we do not want to fight. We want to *ruin* you, first, my dear Sorin. We want to drag your name through every mud puddle we can find. We want to hurt you down to your bones. We will take Dracula and tear you apart one memory at a time, because you embarrassed us in front of Hera. Now Zeus knows, so we must make an example of you to reclaim our honor. You should have just had the decency to die," she snarled, spitting on the ground. "You are not cut out to stand among true Olympians, no matter your bloodline. Just because a King fucks a donkey, doesn't mean the kingdom can expect a prince—just a braying ass. Hee. Haw." She was smiling now, sensing my almost blinding rage. I was clenching my fists, wanting nothing more than to rip her tongue out as she so crassly referenced my mother. "The actual fight will be your final release from the mountains of pain we wish to gift to you," she said with feverish anticipation, licking her lips again.

I very carefully steadied my nerves. "You should probably know from the outset that it's really not going to work out how you envision. Donkeys don't care about kings. They only know how to work. Rain, sun, or storms. They get the job done either way."

Nero laughed maniacally. "Hee-haw, bitch. Hee-fucking-haw!"

I smiled as her face darkened in fury. "You're about to die. I'll give your regards to Apollo."

I held out my hand for Lucian to remain hidden behind the shield. She had already hinted at wanting a wolf to hunt, so I didn't want to give her any ideas. I was pissing her off plenty, and this was between us. To that effect, I let a long, wickedly barbed blood crystal form in my hand, ready to throw it at Artemis the moment she was distracted.

Nero was ducked down behind my cloak, staring at my dagger. "She's blocking my magic," he whispered softly.

"I am, little magician," Artemis snapped, clearly hearing him.

I focused on her. "This is between us, Artemis. You said it yourself —only cowards use mortals in this game."

She pursed her lips. "Fine. I have no intention of killing the magician and wolf. Yet. Much too easy. I will wait until you are already drowning in depression over the corpses of your women before I heap their bodies onto your guilt."

I stared at her. Hard. "Swear it."

She curtsied theatrically. "As long as they don't attack, I won't kill them," she said, sneering at where Lucian and Nero ducked behind my cloak. "Much like I don't bother crushing the ant that just walked over my boot," she said, pointing at her feet.

I let out a small sigh of relief, masking it from my face. "Why do you want Dracula? The real reason. He's almost as worthless as the mortals."

She smiled delightedly. "I think you know, brother. Oh, and in case it wasn't obvious, you will not give him to these childish witches. Or everyone you have ever loved will die. Horribly. Slowly." Her threats were remarkably repetitive. "I'll see you back in the city." She blew me a kiss and then turned her back on me, making her way back towards the woods. I dropped my cloak and hurled my blood dagger at her spine, immediately shifting into crimson mist since I had seen how fast she could shoot. She couldn't hit me in this form, and I was hoping she would hold to her word not to hurt Lucian and Nero; I was ready to whip my cloak back out in an instant if that wasn't the case.

If I didn't take her down now, I would have to face both her and her brother at the same time.

This was my best shot.

The dagger sailed true, but she instinctively spun out of its path, already unleashing a silver arrow at my mass of mist. And she was grinning, letting me know she had anticipated my attack.

Her arrow slammed into me—an impossible feat since I was mist rather than flesh. I gasped, grunting as I lost control of my mist and collapsed to the grass with an arrow sticking out of my ribs. Nero suddenly lunged forward and snatched another arrow out of thin air, catching it with his bone hand. He glared at her with a snarl and I saw a flicker of surprise cross her face. I somehow managed to fling my cloak up to protect us despite the pain screaming through me. My brothers huddled over me, shaken to see that her arrow had somehow struck me in my mist form. I gasped, struggling to bite down my agony and keep an eye on the Goddess of the Hunt. Artemis lowered her bow, plastering on a forced, triumphant smile to wash away the look of surprise she'd shown upon witnessing Nero's arrow-catching ability.

Nero dropped the arrow he had caught and began checking the one still sticking out of my abdomen with a worried look on his face. Lucian whined anxiously, torn between wanting to help me and destroy her, even though the silver arrows would be fatal to him. No matter how good Lucian was at hunting, Artemis was better. Hands down.

"Nice catch, magician," she said, smiling at Nero. "See you back in the city, brother. Might want to put a bandage on that, although I should warn you that it won't stop the bleeding."

"How?" I rasped, trying to breathe through the pain. Nero leaned down and snapped the tip of the arrow off behind my back. Only then did he extract the haft from my front. The skin was blackened and covered in frost, and I heard a rattling sound in my lungs.

Artemis hung her bow over her shoulder. "I fucking made you. You think I can't take you apart with my eyes closed?" she muttered. "Every gift at your disposal was given by me. I will take great pleasure in slowly ripping them away like the wings of a fly."

I didn't give my newfound knowledge away—that she hadn't actually given me anything. She disappeared in a puff of white vapor, and even that dissipated fast enough that it could have been dismissed as a figment of my imagination.

Nero held his hands over my wound, and I felt the heat from his flesh. He stared down at me after a few moments, looking troubled. "It won't close, Sorin," he whispered. "Not all the way. It's rejecting my magic. Not that I was ever any good at healing," he admitted angrily. "Maybe Izzy could help—" He cut off abruptly, cursing.

Because Izzy had been taken captive by the other fucking witches—the Cauldron.

I glanced down, gritting my teeth at the pain. The wound was smaller, but a hole the width of an arrow shaft still remained, blackened and frosted over. Even as I watched, hot blood dribbled out of it.

Most alarming was the fact that it wasn't necessarily my blood leaking out. I could feel my blood reserves dribbling out just as fast as my actual blood. Artemis hadn't wounded me. She had wounded my source of power—just like she had promised. My reserve tank had a puncture in it, and I could already feel how severe the impact was. Enough to make me wonder if we stood a chance, even against a handful of witches.

Let alone Artemis and her brother, Apollo. I needed help. A lot of it.

Nero helped me to my feet, Lucian pressing against me to support my weight as I wobbled precariously. "Get us out of here, magician," I rasped.

He didn't even react to my quip, his eyes locked onto my wound. He placed a hand on both of us, staring down at Stevie with a sad frown. Lucian bent low, licking Stevie's cheek with a sad whine.

"That bitch needs to die," Nero whispered.

I nodded, unable to peel my eyes away from the dead alpha. My friend. "We will come back for him," I whispered. I discreetly glanced at my soulcatcher ring, wondering why I felt nothing from it if a soul had just been taken away right beside me. My friends hadn't even acknowledged it either.

I frowned. Neither had Artemis. In fact, she'd shown no indication that she knew where we had really been. That we had gone to the Underworld. I let out a weak sigh, wincing as pain ripped through my wound at even that small of a motion. My secret was safe.

A new thought struck me as I stared out at the cliff. "Although, he couldn't have asked for a better final resting place," I said, turning to Lucian.

Lucian met my gaze, his golden eyes blazing with fury. Then he lifted his head and let out a heart-wrenching howl. The sound tore through the mountains, cold and alone.

Nero clenched his jaw and grabbed hold of both of us. The world snapped to black as he took us back to the city.

## 32

The world snapped back into focus, revealing the blood-stained steps of the museum. Several of the stains were still damp, reminding me that it had been less than an hour since we left. Several bonfires blazed in the nearby park. I did my best to ignore the smell, having a good idea what was burning—bodies. A few vampires had been scrubbing down the stone, and they jumped back with alarmed hisses upon seeing us appear out of nowhere.

Lucian hacked, coughing up drool as his stomach adjusted to the abrupt method of travel. I'd been expecting the sensation since I'd done it a few times now. Lucian took notice of the surrounding vampires and let out a polite but warning growl, like a neighborly *Hello. Fuck off.*

Strangely enough, they obeyed him, backing away very slowly.

Nosh jogged our way from the sidewalk leading uptown. I let out a breath of relief to see that he was safe, and then I waved at him to come join us. I gasped, my knees buckling as the act of lifting my arm set my wound on fire. Nero grabbed me with a concerned look on his face, but I managed to bite down the pain and straighten.

About twenty feet away, Nosh slowed upon seeing Nero but no Stevie. Then he noticed Lucian and froze altogether. He stared at the new wolf, cocking his head. There was no mistaking Lucian for Stevie's werewolf form. Also, Lucian was twice the size of any wolf or werewolf anyone had ever seen.

I realized I was fingering my soulcatcher absently, frustrated at what I was supposed to do with it. Hades had been alarmingly obscure, telling me not to talk to anyone about it. Was the Soul Spring already back inside Castle Ambrogio? If so, did that mean Dracula could find it?

Because I still needed to reclaim my soul from it after it had mysteriously disappeared on me. I needed to get inside my castle to find out, but that meant confronting Dracula.

Except my blood reserves were still weeping power down my side, thanks to Artemis' arrow. Even with Dracula weakened as he was, did I still have the strength to stand against him? Were we both weakened to the same extent, or was I weaker after my new wound? I could always rely on the Nephilim vampires to back me up and keep Dracula busy while I got my soul back.

A new thought hit me, and my heart skipped a beat.

With this strange, impossible hole in my side, would my soul just leak out like my blood reserves were doing? I let out an uneasy breath. How the fuck had she hit me in the first place? Her arrows hadn't penetrated my cloak, but they could penetrate my mist? It made no sense.

I realized that everyone was standing eerily still. Even the vampires who had fled were staring at Lucian and Nosh with concerned looks. I turned to see that Lucian was staring at Nosh, his body entirely motionless, his every muscle locked rigid. He hesitantly sniffed at the air in Nosh's direction and then he sneezed violently. He let out a low whine, lowering his head and tucking his tail between his legs.

"Um," Nosh said nervously, eyeing the massive wolf's strange behavior. "Who is that and what is he doing?" he asked, looking as if he was on the verge of making a run for it.

Lucian looked torn between hyper-violence and meek submissiveness, like an abused dog approaching his owner. That's when it hit me, and my heart almost ripped in half.

Lucian...was seeing *Boy* for the first time. The unnamed boy he thought he had failed to save.

My son...lived.

He'd recognized *Boy's* scent, even five-hundred-years later.

And I was watching it slowly destroy him, in the most heart-wrenching, heartwarming manner imaginable. My breath caught and I found that I couldn't speak. I suddenly felt like the world's biggest asshole.

Because I hadn't had time to tell Lucian that *Boy* had survived. That *Boy* was now Nosh.

Nero gripped me by the arm hard enough to make me wince. I turned to him with a panicked look and he shook his head firmly. "Let this play out. Trust me."

"Guys?" Nosh asked, slowly holding up his hands as if to show the wolf that he was unarmed. Because Lucian was now approaching him with hesitant, slinking steps, looking just as scared as Nosh. Or maybe it was shame, not fear. As he drew closer, he began to growl in a faint, continuous tone, warning Nosh not to make any sudden movements.

His tail slowly began to twitch back and forth even though it was still tucked firmly between his legs—a hesitant attempt at wagging his tail. But his head remained low, and he continued growling faintly, keeping his throat protected and approaching Nosh sideways, eyeing him from the corner of his vision. With each step, he seemed to lose a bit of his concern, his tail gradually extending back out behind him and his head rising.

Without warning, he exploded forward in a powerful lunge and tackled Nosh to the ground, whining frantically as he pinned the shaman down.

"Gah! Help!" Nosh bellowed. "He's going to *eat* me!"

We didn't help him.

Instead, Nero and I watched Nosh get slobbered, not slaughtered. Nero wrapped his arm around my shoulders, tugging me close to his side as he grinned at...

The *Boy* and his *dog*.

I smiled, my throat still tight, ignoring the flare of pain in my side from Nero's gesture. Lucian's whine had risen in pitch and was now cracking and rasping as his entire body vibrated and trembled. He frantically licked Nosh from throat to forehead, nuzzling his massive snout into his cheek hard enough to give Nosh whiplash, his whine now practically a screaming wail.

Lucian rolled over onto his back, wiggling back and forth across Nosh's chest with his paws up in the air, knocking the breath out of the baffled, terrified shaman. He yipped and barked playfully, pumping his paws at the air as he stretched the back of his head into Nosh's face, dangerously close to suffocating the poor man.

Then Lucian suddenly leapt to his feet, prancing back a few feet before slamming his front paws down and stretching forward, pointing his rear in the air, His tail was wagging violently enough that I feared it might snap free. He barked loudly enough that I felt it, like drums beating inside my chest.

Nosh cautiously sat up, his face pale and his eyes wide as he stared at the giant wolf play-bowing before him. His hair stuck straight up from great big gobs of wolf drool, and his cheeks glistened with even more of it. "What does he want?" he hissed in an anxious whisper.

We ignored him, grinning at our brother, marveling at what might be the happiest night of his life. The best hunt he'd ever had.

Lucian let out a trio of sharp, loud barks, and then suddenly sprinted away at top speed. Nosh sensed his opportunity and scrambled to get to his feet.

"Wait for it..." Nero murmured.

Lucian skidded to a halt, spun around, and saw his prey attempting to escape. He instantly sprinted towards Nosh at a truly startling speed, his claws somehow gouging the pavement in deep furrows, and barking the whole time. Lucian tackled Nosh, knocking the breath from him in an audible expulsion of air. Lucian rode him to the ground and promptly sat down on top of him, wiggling in a desperate attempt to get his entire body into contact with Nosh all at once.

Nero burst out laughing, and I soon joined in.

My brother had finally found the boy he had once sworn to protect. My son was finally safe.

I watched as unseen muscles in Lucian's body seemed to relax and let go of the burden that had weighed him down for hundreds of years. Abandoning the cause of his madness. Opening his heart back up to the fact that he wasn't a failure. He panted happily, his tail thumping into the pavement with powerful thwacking sounds.

Lucian eventually scooted back to lay beside Nosh, but he rested his chin firmly across the man's chest, pinning him down. His tail suddenly stopped wagging and a menacing, coughing growl bubbled out from his throat, his ears suddenly pinned back and his hackles doubling in size.

I followed his attention to see that he was glaring at Adam and Eve —who had rushed over upon seeing the massive wolf running around and barking like a demented lunatic. The Nephilim vampires stood motionless, staring at Lucian pinning Nosh to the ground, torn between fierce loyalty and confusion. Because Nero was cackling like a madman.

Adam leaned back, scratching at his beard as he reconsidered his threat assessment.

"He's very dangerous," I assured the imposing Nephilim vampire.

Lucian lifted his head, realizing that the Nephilim were not a threat. He yawned wide enough to let out a long whine. Then he began panting, slapping one of his large paws over Nosh to keep him trapped.

"Can someone explain this for me?" Nosh asked tiredly, finally abandoning any attempt at escape. "Am I in danger?"

"Grave danger," I said, shaking my head and smiling at Adam and Eve before they took me seriously. Eve had a hand over her mouth, reminding me of the adoring mannerisms Persephone and Hecate had shown for the Cerberus puppy.

Nero was grinning from ear-to-ear. He folded his arms satisfactorily. "I think we did it, Sorin. We saved him."

I smiled, nodding. "*You* saved him long ago, Nero. In the cave. Without that, none of this would have been possible."

His smile faltered. "You saw that?" he whispered. I nodded. "Oh. Well, what else was I supposed to do. He's my brother," he said, smiling sadly. "I'm sure he would return the favor and chain me up if I ever needed it." He turned to give me a dry look. "Oh. Wait. That was you."

I grinned, nodding. "Yeah."

He chuckled, turning back to Lucian. "Can't rebuild a house without a solid foundation," he agreed. "But you snapped him out of his funk with an ass whooping, and then this," he said, gesturing at Nosh.

"What the *hell* are you two talking about?" Nosh demanded, his voice muffled beneath Lucian's furry bulk.

We ignored him.

## 33

Lucian had needed both of his brothers to save him. And then my son to bring it all together. Lucian's unexpected reaction to Nosh's scent finally gave me solid evidence that Nosh was truly my son. No one could fool Lucian's sense of smell.

"He's still a wolf, though," Nero said in a concerned tone.

I nodded nervously. "Give him time."

He patted me on the shoulder reassuringly. "Well, at least you don't have to hide him. Just have him stand next to Adam and he will look like a normal-sized dog."

I grunted. "If I give Adam a wolf, I have to give Eve a wolf. And that terrifies me."

"I'm getting a *puppy*?" Eve whispered, suddenly quivering with excitement. She smacked Adam in the shoulder with the back of her hand, the sound of marble striking marble coming across like a gunshot. Lucian flinched, tucking his ears low as he glared up at the Nephilim.

"No. No one is getting a puppy," I said loudly, but Adam and Eve were already talking animatedly and debating names.

"What are they doing?" Nero asked, suddenly wary as he spun in a slow circle. I looked up to find werewolves surrounding us. All of them stared at Lucian with awed, somber expressions, and many of them had already fallen to their knees, tears streaming down their cheeks.

Howls erupted throughout the park. The werewolves had come to pay homage to their ancestor. The original king of the werewolves.

Who...was still cuddling with the shaman. Stevie's death suddenly hit me in a new light, and I stiffened. Were the wolves paying homage to their new alpha? Not Benjamin, but Lucian? If so, it verified that they all knew of his death. They all would have felt the pain of it, and now they were witnessing the miracle of Lucian's return.

Lucian slowly lifted his head to silently address the circle of werewolves surrounding us. Every single one of them wilted beneath his gaze, instantly submitting to the alpha of all alphas.

Good god. Hecate and Nero had been right.

If Dracula had managed to gain power over Lucian, he really would have gained control of every werewolf. Even now, I wondered if werewolves from all over the country were suddenly flocking towards New York City.

Maybe even from all over the world.

With the path Hades had set me on, I would need every single one of them.

To tear down Olympus with tooth and claw, christening it with blood.

If I didn't die from my wounds, because I could still feel my power dribbling away.

"Not very monumental," Nero commented, snapping me out of my thoughts. "It's actually kind of embarrassing."

I laughed hesitantly but immediately winced, clutching at my side. Adam and Eve rushed over, looking alarmed. "You're bleeding!"

"I'm fine," I muttered. "It's just a little cut. I'll be fine after I feed," I lied.

Nero pursed his lips, not pointing out my lie to the others. But he did cast me a stern, disapproving glare. I averted my gaze. "We have work to do," I told them. "Come on, Lucian. Let the poor boy up."

Lucian grumbled unhappily as I made my way up the stairs towards the museum. I needed blood if I was going to be of any use.

"Lucian?" Nosh hissed in disbelief, sounding alarmed.

I continued walking up the steps, spotting an envelope attached to the door. My name was written on the front. I frowned, ripping it off and tearing the envelope open.

*Trade Dracula for the girls. Trinity Church. Eight o'clock tonight.*

*Bring no more than three others or the deal is off.*

*—Benjamin*

"Sorin?" Nosh asked from over my shoulder, finally catching up to me. "What is it?"

"A suicide note," I growled, handing it back to him without looking.

Nero read it with him, his lips pursed, and his cheeks darkening. Nosh narrowed his eyes, his hand shaking. "Tonight," he growled, thoughtfully. Sunrise was hours away, so it was technically tomorrow, but I knew what he meant.

"What's the plan?" Nero asked, studying me. His eyes flicked down to my wound in a silent warning—that I wasn't at full capacity.

"We're going to go do what heroes do. We're going to go save the girls. Izzy first. Right the fuck now."

Nosh nodded gratefully, but his gaze shot to my wound. My shirt was liberally caked with blood. I ignored it. He met my eyes with a grim frown. "You can't take on the witches by yourself, Sorin. You're hurt." He leaned closer, speaking in a breathless whisper. "What if more wolves are secretly working for Benjamin?"

I gritted my teeth to hide the increased pain caused by climbing the steps. It felt like someone was tugging at my wound with their bare hands. "I can guarantee that the wolves will be better behaved from now on. Right, Lucian?"

Nosh jumped to find Lucian standing directly beside him, protective of his charge. The wolf met my eyes with a stern glare. I took it as an affirmative.

"When we save Izzy, maybe she can help heal my wound. Maybe she can tell us a way to talk the Sisters down. Let them know why I left town," I lied, remembering Hades' warning about not mentioning any Olympian involvement. "That must be why they kidnapped them."

"That doesn't explain Benjamin's betrayal," Nosh growled.

"If nothing else, she might know how we can break into the Sisters' church. How they set up their defenses. How many witches they really have," I said, thinking out loud, wondering if I was fooling myself. Because I also knew that, without healing myself, I was on borrowed time.

"And the Cauldron?" Nosh asked angrily. "We don't even know where they are, thanks to Benjamin turning coat."

"We will find her, Nosh. Even if we have to burn the city to the ground. The wolves will find her with Lucian's help."

Lucian licked his lips, baring his fangs in the process.

I sensed Nosh's shoulders tightening. "Don't even think about it," I warned him. "Giving yourself up will just get you both killed."

Lucian growled forebodingly.

Nosh scowled in frustration. "We need to accept realities here. I won't hide from the facts. If it comes to that, I will do what needs to be done."

"No," I said firmly. "You will *not*."

Lucian suddenly bumped Nosh warningly, almost knocking him down. I nodded in relief, hiding my hands behind my back. They were shaking. I wasn't sure if it was entirely from anger or a result of blood loss. Nero seemed to notice, judging by the alarmed look on his face. I subtly shook my head at him.

He nodded, glancing down at Lucian with a faint smile. Lucian would keep Nosh safe...even from himself, if necessary.

"Right now, I need blood." I entered the lobby and immediately froze, squinting against the assault of colors stabbing at my eyes. "What the fuck?" I hissed, lifting my arm to shield my vision. Bright, colorful streamers hung everywhere, along with signs and banners and tables laden with decanters and a tower of crystal champagne glasses. Red-eyed vampires were building another tower on a second and third table, and they were smiling, talking to each other in excited tones. They saw me and one of them stiffened, knocking down the tower. The crystal fell and shattered into thousands of pieces.

They shot horrified looks my way, but I waved a hand before they decided to kill themselves for offending me. They set about cleaning up the mess as if the fate of the world depended on it.

Couches and pillows and other furniture had been moved into the lobby, and I saw rows of speakers with bundles of cable stretching away from them. Another pair of vampires was studying a large cube with a curtain for a door. It was open and I saw a bench inside. I frowned.

"Is that a picture booth?" Nero hooted, pointing at the box. "They really are throwing a party," he chuckled. I'd completely forgotten about the social mixer for the vampires. Yet another thing to worry about. I'd hoped to dance with my devils tonight...

I pressed on towards the elevators, dismissing the party decorations.

"I'm going to get something to drink and see what the executive management team is up to," I said. "Other than finding new ways to blind us, that is. Maybe I will find someone to take care of my cut since Nero is utterly incompetent," I said dryly, patting my wound gently. "We can head out in twenty minutes to find Izzy."

Nosh nodded. "I'll go grab my weapons," he said stiffly.

I motioned for Nero to head towards the elevator ahead of me. "Nosh," I said, halting him before he had time to storm away. He met my eyes and they were full of fury and unspent rage. I knew what he was thinking, what was tearing him up inside. And it would continue to do so until someone else said it out loud—a job that fell upon parents and leaders of armies.

In both cases, me.

"You failed three times today," I said in a matter of fact tone. His eyes widened ever so slightly, and his shoulders tensed, surprised that I hadn't attempted to reassure him and justify his failures with a pat on the back. I nodded. "Izzy. Natalie. Victoria." I watched as each name hit him like a punch to the gut. "Right now, you are letting that fact tear you up inside, right?" He nodded stiffly, his cheeks red. "Stop. Or you will add a fourth failure to the list. Focus on the solution rather than the problem. Self-pity will not fix anything. Will not save anyone. It is the gleaming armor of a coward. You are better than that."

He stared at me, looking shaken. "Okay."

"And for the record, I'm confident that I failed more than three times today, so the same advice applies to me."

He gave me a hesitant nod before turning away, striding towards the stairs rather than taking the elevator down with us.

Lucian followed Nosh without even a backwards glance.

No one was getting close to Nosh with Lucian in the way. The king of the werewolves would make good on his promise to keep Nosh safe.

He'd only waited a few hundred years to do so.

"Let's see how good you are at healing," I told Nero, approaching the elevator.

His nod was not even remotely encouraging.

## 34

I had spent a few minutes wandering around the catacombs in search of Renfield, but a fledgling vampire informed me that he had located the Cauldron's hideout after Benjamin's betrayal, and was keeping an eye on the building in an attempt to gauge how many witches were inside and what kind of dangers we faced when we went in to save Izzy. He had about a dozen of the reborn vampires with him, but they were keeping a safe distance so as not to alert our enemies.

Which was an incredible weight off my shoulders. We had a location.

Hugo, Aristos, and Valentine were similarly absent, overseeing the groups of vampires guarding Liberty Island or the sprawling perimeter of Central Park. Which had also been a relief. To see them focused on the dangers, yet still making sure everything was ready for their social mixer tonight.

I would be missing the party, going after my devils instead.

Nero had taken a long look at my wound before testing it again with his magic. The blackened wound was puckered and still coated in ice. "It won't respond to anything."

"Bandage it up as best you can, then. Anything that will help keep the blood inside."

He studied me for a long moment. "You have armies, Sorin. Maybe it's time for you to sit this one out and figure out exactly what that arrow did to you."

I stared at him, my face blank. "I already know what happened and sitting around on my ass won't make me die any slower. Bandage. It. Up."

The curiosity in his eyes was undeniable, but I didn't want to talk about it.

He pulled out a hard candy on a stick, tearing off a plastic wrapper. "It's a lollipop. I give them to anyone bold enough to call me their doctor. Real doctors give them to kids so they aren't as traumatized by the experience," he said with an amused grin, holding it out to me.

I narrowed my eyes at the candy and then snatched it away from him and stuck it in my mouth. I arched an eyebrow. It was surprisingly good.

I bit the candy off and flicked the stick at him, hitting him in the forehead.

He chuckled as he set to work on my wound.

The lollipop helped, actually. It kept me distracted.

I was fairly certain that the only way I could heal my wound was by reclaiming my soul from the Soul Spring like Nero and Lucian had already done. If I was wrong, I didn't have a contingency plan. Hopefully, the Soul Spring was safely tucked away inside my castle but checking on it would require me to confront Dracula, and I wanted to save Izzy, first.

Because Izzy was in danger, and I wanted Nosh to see me back him up after my harsh—but necessary—reprimand a few minutes ago. He needed to see his father step up. As an example, for him to do the same. And...I wanted her opinion on my wound in case I was wrong about my soul helping.

I also wasn't sure if I had the strength to confront Dracula right now. Even though he was weakened after Hades finished with him, I was also weak. Potentially, much weaker. My damned blood reserves were weeping out of my wound at a steady, alarming pace.

My wound looked almost exactly like the silver wounds I'd received from some expanding silver bullets not too long ago. Victoria's potent blood had helped me heal that. Her blood had done much more than heal the wound, in fact—it had temporarily woken up my latent vampire abilities that were *still* dribbling back after my long slumber.

When Nero had been collecting bandages for me, I'd retrieved a bag of Victoria's blood that she had left me in the event of an emergency. It wasn't much, but it was significantly stronger than regular blood. If I was going to encounter the twins tonight—which seemed more than likely—I would need every added power I could muster.

Except Victoria's blood hadn't helped. It had boosted my power, refreshing me greatly, but I was confident that I'd only consumed a third of the small bag's contents—the rest of the precious liquid spilling out of my wound in a jet of blood. Luckily, I'd chosen to drink the blood in the shower, so all the lost blood went down the drain.

Otherwise, Nero might have returned to think I was actively bleeding out.

As Nero set to work bandaging me, I racked my brain for any other solutions I might have overlooked. I ran back through my conversations with every Olympian. Why had Persephone told me I should have taken Aphrodite up on her offer to spend romantic time with Natalie and Victoria? She hadn't known it the first time we spoke—prior to my private talk with Hades. What had changed? Had she known they would be abducted? What else did she know about Victoria and Natalie's current situation?

I took a calming breath before my emotions began to dictate my actions. If I thought too hard about Natalie and Victoria, I would end every heartbeat within a mile of Trinity Church, consequences be damned. Even if it killed my own armies. Even if it doomed the world. If it saved my devils, I would even sacrifice myself.

Exactly what I'd warned Nosh not to do.

I let out a sigh. Going after Izzy first was the smartest move. Get the Cauldron off our backs, once and for all. Hopefully, Izzy would have information that would help me save my devils.

And heal my wound.

Next was Dracula and my soul. Now that I knew my soul wasn't up for grabs—even if I wrapped Dracula up and delivered him to Mount Olympus—I no longer cared about my own personal vengeance.

Dracula was just a bargaining chip. And the Sisters were in the lead when it came to leverage—they had abducted my devils, and I would do anything to get them back.

Which would really piss off the twins.

So, my to-do list was fairly simple.

Save Izzy. Hopefully have her heal my wound. Get my soul back. Trade Dracula for the devils. Deal with a pair of pissed off twins. Not die in the process.

Maybe go to a vampire dance party afterwards.

Easy.

I formed a mental list of Olympians who might be involved in the drama from behind the scenes, but there were simply too many to consider without any proof. Aphrodite had intended to reach out to me with answers, but I hadn't heard from her.

I was thankful that Lucian was keeping an eye on Nosh, but if the shaman was anything like his father, he would be wallowing in guilt no matter what I said to him, and I was very concerned about him giving himself up to save Izzy.

It almost seemed like the witches were all working together rather than as two opposing forces.

I had been roped into a direct fight with the Sisters, and many of them would die as a result. We should have been allies. They were so intent on acquiring Dracula—for whatever reason they truly had—that they were willing to go to war with the man who could have been their staunchest ally.

All because Benjamin had chosen to side with them. How long had he been playing both sides? Had he hoped to become alpha in Stevie's place? Was this really all about power?

I knew the werewolves were no longer a concern now that Lucian had returned, but it was still troubling. I began thinking back on Hecate, wondering who her third gift had been given to. I now knew it wasn't Nosh, but that had been a shot in the dark anyway.

I considered her various gifts, wondering which gift was unaccounted for. She had given her knowledge of magic and necromancy to Nero, and she had given her affinity to dogs to Lucian. Other than that, I was fairly certain that she was known for ghosts and other powers related to the dead—but necromancy was merely a different form of magic.

Although Hecate had let slip a hint about skinwalkers and their cursed blades, she'd bluntly said Nosh wasn't the third recipient. Damned riddles everywhere I turned.

Nero finished winding white tape around my waist to hold the pad of gauze in place. "There you go. It should hold unless you do stupid things, like invading a witch stronghold," he said dryly. "You should get some more blood in you, brother."

I nodded, climbing to my feet. "I already did."

My phone rang from the side table. Nero handed it to me before collecting his supplies and cleaning up his mess from tending to my wound. He began tossing bloody pads into the fire, knowing the value of my blood in the wrong hands.

"Sorin," I said, answering the phone.

"Where are you?" Renfield whispered urgently.

"At the museum. Why?" I asked. Nero paused, glancing back as he read the concern in my voice.

"Nosh just walked into the Cauldron's hideout, appearing out of thin air before we could stop him. A huge fucking wolf arrived a minute later, and he looks like he has already decided who to blame. And he's got enough werewolves with him to succeed," he said with forced calm. "I don't think I can keep them away from the building."

"Don't!" I snapped. "If you attack, the witches will kill Nosh and Izzy!" I hissed. "The big wolf is Lucian." I explained, ignoring his gasp. "Tell him Nosh is dead if they attack. He can understand your words."

"Y-yes, Master Ambrogio," Renfield stammered. I heard him speaking sternly in the background and then he came back on the phone. "Okay. I think that worked. But you should get here as fast as possible. He has a crazy look in his eyes and the other wolves are mirroring him."

"Nosh didn't say anything?" I demanded, climbing to my feet with a hiss.

"No. And we didn't sense him until it was too late, so he must have used magic of some kind. I'm guessing this was not part of your plan?"

he asked, speaking loud enough for those near him to hear his question —and my response.

"Absolutely not," I growled. "He's giving himself up to save Izzy. Damn it! I told him that it won't work. They'll just kill both of them." Nero clenched his fist and an orb of black smoke coalesced around his bone digits. He gave me a firm nod. "Tell Nero where you are, so he can see how fast we can join you." I handed Nero the phone and reached down to toss on a new shirt and jacket I had set out. I tugged them on as Nero spoke to Renfield.

He hung up, shooting me an encouraging look. "I can teleport us there. Well, a block away. We don't want to show up on their front door and set off any alarms they may have set."

I grabbed a fresh bag of blood from the side table and bolted out the door.

"What about your wound?" he demanded, racing after me.

"I'll manage." I muttered, guzzling blood as I moved. I was relieved at the sudden burst of energy, but also greatly alarmed at how rapidly I felt it draining from me. Like I'd only managed to ingest a third of it, at most. Just like I'd felt with Victoria's blood in the shower. I ignored the sudden wet sensation over my wound, hoping Nero didn't notice it. "Much better," I lied, licking my lips.

Nero studied me nervously, wincing at my wound, and I knew he didn't buy my lie.

## 35

We jogged through the dark streets, thankfully close enough to Central Park that no humans resided nearby. They had all left once I brought my castle to the city. I saw Renfield and Lucian peering around the corner of a building at the intersection ahead of us, careful to observe without being seen. We ran past a couple dozen wolves on the sidewalk, all of them hanging a safe distance back from where Renfield and Lucian were scouting the building. Four reborn vampires dipped their heads upon seeing me, clapping fists to hearts. Their faces were barely restrained fury, and I knew that they wanted nothing more than to storm the building. The wolves were even worse, pacing back and forth impatiently.

Lucian and Renfield heard my approach and pulled back from their vantage point to meet me twenty feet away from the intersection so we could talk without being seen by the witches. "They are holed up in an abandoned theater. We have the building surrounded, and no one has spotted any sentries. All the witches are inside, but we're staying back in case anyone is looking out of a window," Renfield reassured me. "It's strange," he said, frowning. "There really aren't very many of them. Not enough to try to pull this off with any hopes of a win."

I frowned, glancing at Nero. He looked just as uneasy. Did that mean we were overlooking something? Were they spread out across different buildings in the city?

"How did Nosh get away from you?" I asked, turning to Lucian.

The wolf lifted his nose to me and sniffed pointedly. Then he shook his head, sneezing. He lifted his nose back in the air, sniffing left and right. Then he continued sniffing, slowly spinning the opposite direction and took a few steps, wagging his tail. He glanced over his shoulder at me, nodding one time.

"He cast his scent in a different direction?" I asked.

Lucian nodded with a frustrated growl.

Renfield eyed Lucian, and I could tell he had at least a dozen questions about how the king of the werewolves was not dead like we had all thought this morning. But he knew that now was not the time. "Some type of shaman magic?" he asked, turning to Nero.

The necromancer considered the question, his eyes growing distant as he stared at the corner of the intersection ahead. He slowly lifted his new skeletal hand, causing Renfield's eyes to bulge in surprise. The purple tendons and joints began to glow faintly, and Nero let out a surprised grunt—as if he hadn't anticipated such a thing. "I'm surprised he didn't set off the dozen wards surrounding the theater. I've never been able to pick up wards from so far away before," he murmured, studying his bone hand with an excited smile. Sensing everyone staring at him, he looked up at us. He shifted his attention back to Renfield and Lucian, lowering his bone hand. "Good thing you didn't try invading or everyone would have died. The wards are nasty."

I punched my fist into my palm. "Can you take them down without alerting anyone?"

Nero stared down at his new bone hand with a dark grin. "You know, I think this is the type of job for a man and his hand. I can probably bang out a pleasant outcome with the right elbow grease, but I'm not sure how quick it will be."

Renfield coughed into his fist, making Nero grin proudly. I rolled my eyes at his crass joke, wondering what else his new hand was capable of doing.

"What are the wards designed to do?" I asked him, knowing we didn't have time to sit around.

"Destroy anything denser than a piece of paper."

"What about my mist?" I asked.

Nero grimaced, not liking my suggestion one bit after how poorly it had worked with Artemis, but I shot him a defiant glare. "That will work," he finally admitted. "But you can't take them all on by yourself," he said carefully, not wanting to point out my injury. I'd already seen Renfield glancing at my side with a suspicious frown, so it wasn't exactly a secret.

I was standing on the street with a gang of monsters who hunted by scent, and blood was one of the most enticing scents available. But I didn't want Nero talking about exactly how serious my wound was. Not minutes before an assault.

"Then you better take down those wards fast. I'll get in there and keep an eye on everything at least. But Nosh is walking out of that building one way or another," I promised in a solemn tone.

Nero motioned for Lucian to lead him towards the intersection so he would have a better view as he began tearing down the wards. Renfield glanced at my side, even though the wound was covered. "It smells serious, Master Ambrogio," he murmured in a very soft tone.

"It is, Renfield. It is." His face paled at my honest answer. I shrugged. "So, I would appreciate you sending in reinforcements as quickly as possible. I might need you to save me, too."

I became mist, wincing at even that slight usage of my power. But I had to save my son, consequences be damned. I shifted past Lucian and Nero, crossing the street to approach the old three-story theater. The doors were boarded up with a foreclosure sign, but doors and walls were no impediment to my mist. Some wards could have prevented me from crossing them—even when in my mist form—but the witches must not have known them.

I chose the high ground in case any of the witches were using their eyes to complement their wards. I might be mist, but it was a crimson shade that would be very noticeable if I appeared within clear view of anyone. I drifted through the lobby and then through a set of double doors leading to the rows of seating with a stage at the far end of the space. Red, tattered curtains hung from the wings, and the wooden stage was warped and uneven. I hung back against the wall, concealing my mist as best as I could.

Nosh was already on the stage, facing a semi-circle of twelve witches. Thankfully, no one was trying to kill anyone. Yet.

The witches all looked to be in their middling years, but with witches, that could mean nothing. Especially dark witches who could steal years of their youth back from helpless humans.

Twelve wasn't an overwhelming number of witches, but it wasn't an underwhelming number of witches either. Plenty enough to be dangerous. But Renfield made a good point. It wasn't enough to risk picking a fight with me. What was I missing?

Izzy was chained and gagged off to the side, held by two additional witches, her face streaked with dried blood from the fight earlier tonight. I recalled how it had only been two hours ago, at most. To me, it felt like it had happened a few days ago, what with my trip to the Underworld. This night had contained some of the longest hours of my life.

They had been long hours for Izzy as well, because I could tell that some of the blood on her face was fresh. They hadn't been kind to their captive. Not overly cruel, but not kind.

Also, everyone had a bleeding nose since light and dark witches had that effect on each other. It was all rather messy.

I saw no way for me to move fast enough to protect both Nosh and Izzy. If I went for either, the other would likely die as a result—and neither would forgive me for making them the lone survivor. And my magic was fading alarmingly fast, even though I was barely doing anything.

The main advantage in my favor was that the witches looked as run-down and ragged as I felt. Many of them were wounded, bandaged, and filthy, wearing tattered coats and rags. But they all wielded long knives or vials of deadly potions in their hands. It didn't matter so much that most of those blades were warped, chipped, and rusted—that just meant they would hurt more than absolutely necessary when piercing flesh. They must have lost more of their number in the fight outside the museum than I'd thought. Why did they want these tomahawks so badly? They were clearly risking everything to get them.

Nosh glared at one witch in particular who was standing in the center of the semi-circle. "I am here, witch. Let her go, and you can have me." He hesitated. "And next time, get your shit together with your ransom notes. You didn't tell me where to find you."

The witches all watched the shaman, glancing furtively about the theater, verifying that he truly was alone and that this wasn't some trick. One of the witches backhanded another witch, chastising her for her note-writing skills. My mist quivered with disappointment at their incompetence.

"I am alone. Sorin has much bigger problems to deal with than cleaning up his shaman's mess," he said tiredly. "In case you have forgotten, your extended family is also in town."

A woman in the center of the gathering of witches stepped forward. She was tall and thin, with inky black hair, looking like more of a scarecrow than a woman. A once pretty scarecrow, to be fair. A plump witch behind her tugged at her sleeve and then whispered something into her ear before stepping back. The tall witch cleared her throat, speaking in an officious tone. "My name is Rowan, leader of the Cauldron. It is fortunate that you...passed our test with the note." The plump witch nodded her approval. "Only a true shaman would have been able to find us."

Nosh stared at Rowan and then at the plump witch who had provided the cover story. "Is that right?" he said, deadpan. "Go, me. I'm a true shaman." He yawned. Loudly.

If mist could laugh, I would have been shaking and crying like a thunderstorm. If I had to pick one Cauldron witch to survive, I would have picked the plump one with the quick—but dull—wit. She looked fun. A real go-getter.

Rowan nodded primly. "We were about to begin torturing this one in case she was the true skinwalker," she said, pointing a bony claw at the ex-communicated Sister of Mercy. "She refuses to hand over her blade." Izzy strained furiously, trying to shout through her gag. One of the witches guarding her cuffed her upside the head hard enough to make her groan and sway.

Nosh kept his face composed—somehow, because I had wanted to give up my secret and rip the guards in half. "I merely let her hold onto it for safekeeping. You saw right through it, Rowan, which is rather impressive. The Sisters of Mercy did not notice it," he said, meeting her eyes. "Only a truly powerful witch could have seen through it," he said tightly, as if struggling to keep a straight face.

Rowan nodded appreciatively, obviously not picking up on his blatant sarcasm. But the plump one had cocked her head thoughtfully, furrowing her brow. I could almost hear her brain squealing with effort to solve the mental puzzle before her. "Show us the other skinwalker blade, shaman," Rowan said.

The witches were nitwits. Nit-witches.

But as much as I wanted to burst out laughing at the lack of criminal geniuses in the room, there was one very important rule that should never be overlooked or dismissed.

Genuine idiots made up for a paucity of intelligence with a plethora of violence.

Nosh held up his hand and his tomahawk of light flared to life, casting the stage in a dim blue glow that made the witches look even more sickly and pale. He lowered it to his side, and the tomahawk lengthened to resemble a long-handled axe—no doubt to subtly prove that it was the real deal and not some other magic axe, in case there were several of those floating around the city.

"How do we retrieve the other?" Rowan demanded, shifting her glare towards Izzy. Because that was how this whole altercation had started—them kidnapping Izzy when they sensed that she had one of the blades. Because I had given it to her.

Which was another reason I couldn't let Nosh handle this on his own, although I hadn't said it out loud to anyone; I knew they would have bent over backwards to reassure me that I was not at fault.

But I was at fault. Heartfelt lies to appease my guilt were as useless as nipples on a sword.

Nosh studied Rowan openly, no longer teasing the nit-witches. "Are you the sacrificial lamb? Do you know what you're really asking for? Not just the benefits, but the price?"

She nodded resolutely, not looking triumphant but resigned instead. What was Nosh talking about? What was the price? And how did this transfer of power even work?

"Before I turn myself in, tell me why this is so important to you," Nosh said curiously. "I often wish I didn't have this curse. Why would you go out of your way to acquire it? I can assure you that it's not a gift."

Rowan curled her lips venomously. "The Sisters of Mercy must fall. They claim they pursue goodness, but their deeds would make even me blush. It's all a façade." I blinked. The Sisters definitely had a dark side, but she almost made them sound...evil.

Had the nit-witch been drinking too much of her own brew?

I hoped reinforcements were coming quickly, because the blood was about to spill.

## 36

N osh looked just as baffled as I felt. "The Sisters of Mercy are evil?" he asked doubtfully. "You don't need to lie to me. I'm obviously not walking away from this—not if one of you truly desires to become a skinwalker. I'm genuinely curious. Speak the truth."

Rowan spat on the ground. "They *lie*. The High Priestess is a poison. She used to be one of us before she switched sides! Who do you think helped us establish the Cauldron in the first place? She established our quest for the pursuit of power so that weak women everywhere could never be defenseless again!" she seethed, spittle flying from her lips. "Then she abandoned us and turned her new, pious, gullible Sisters of Mercy against *us*—her *real* sisters!"

I stared, dumbfounded. Nosh looked just as stunned. Izzy's eyes were practically bulging out of her sockets—not in anger, but as if suddenly concerned for her captors' sanity.

"Which is why we need the skinwalker blades," Rowan snarled. "She will die for her crimes. Die for her backstabbing nature. To hold her accountable for what she has done. To show the world what she truly is. That she led us down our current path and then abandoned us, forming her new coven and turning her old family into the enemy. We were forced to keep studying our dark arts—hiding in caves like rodents—so we could withstand their constant attacks. Especially after she gained the favor of the church! The dark arts were all we had left to protect ourselves! The dark arts she taught us!"

Izzy was shaking her head adamantly, denying the claims with muffled protests.

Nosh cocked his head. "What does your vengeance have to do with the skinwalker blades? Why not just kill her?" he asked, frowning.

Rowan smiled eagerly, happy to oblige his question and vent. "Your skinwalker blades will allow me to slip into her precious coven unseen, appearing before her as Dracula, bound and chained. Hell hath no fury like a woman scorned."

My mist shuddered in alarm. That...could ruin everything. *I* needed to hand over Dracula in order to save Victoria and Natalie. If Rowan succeeded with her insane plan...

Natalie and Victoria were as good as dead.

Nosh grunted. "Are you saying that the High Priestess was once in love with Dracula?"

Rowan nodded. "Yes. But then he shamed her and cast her aside. She's been trying to destroy him ever since."

I stared incredulously. This whole thing...was a lover's spat? It had nothing to do with custody over him, like Hazel had told me. It was straight retribution over an old flame tossing her to the curb.

A woman who couldn't move on was a deadly foe.

Rowan continued. "Dracula is the only target important enough to draw her out—or maybe this new vampire working for Dracula." I gritted my teeth. If I heard one more goddamned person claim I was working for Dracula, I was going to lose it. Not only had he stolen my reputation, but even after I woke from my slumber, people thought I was his new minion.

And they still didn't know my name.

"I hear she hides from everyone, even her own sisters," Rowan continued. "No doubt so that no one's nose begins to bleed in her presence," she snorted. "Appearing as Dracula with the aid of your skinwalker blades, I will finally get close enough to kill her before all of her precious Sisters. I will bathe in her blood, laughing even as her Sisters torture me for my crime. Justice will be served."

"What about the others?" Nosh asked, glancing at the row of witches.

Rowan smiled lovingly at them. "We are the downtrodden—women from different countries, cultures, beliefs, and walks of life. Women who merely wanted to learn and experiment with our powers. But our communities shunned us, so we banded together for protection to prevent them from hunting us down and killing us. And the woman who helped us see that was lying to us the whole time. She must pay. At any cost."

"You were the *good* witches?" Nosh asked, trying very hard not to sound cynical.

Rowan scoffed. "Neutral. Not necessarily good or bad. We just wanted to work without judgment. A fair chance at freedom rather than a life of running from superstitious allegations. The *High Priestess*," she emphasized the title with a sneer, "offered us that. She didn't demand obedience to any set way of life, she simply fed our hunger for knowledge and power so that we could never be dismissed by the world again. We wanted respect, even if we had to claw our way up the mountain to get it."

"You hate men?" Nosh asked, in an overly cautious tone.

Rowan laughed. "We *adore* men. As many as we can get our hands on," she said, eyeing her fellow witches. They were all nodding eagerly, licking their lips. "The women were worse than any of the men. Their jealousy of our powers and the attraction we garnered from the men emboldened their hatred. They united, declaring us demons and worse. You've heard it all before," she gestured dismissively. Nosh nodded knowingly. "Without the women, the men wouldn't have cared one way or another about our private experiments and magics. Back then, men only cared about war, whores, and warhorses. The terms have since changed, but the underlying subjects remain the same. Men are overly emotional creatures, easily swayed by popular sentiment."

I considered Rowan's claims. She wasn't entirely right, but she was pretty damned close. This High Priestess was shaping up to be a real piece of work, and I had already begun to think so before hearing the Cauldron's opinion on the woman. The fact that she never visited with her own coven actually lent credence to the claim that she had started off as a dark witch and hadn't wanted her fellow Sisters to catch on when their noses constantly bled around her.

She had already convinced Benjamin to kidnap Victoria and Natalie—when I had done nothing to directly offend her. Well, nothing unprovoked anyway. They had attacked the museum. We had just defended ourselves. But if she thought I was aiding her old lover...

That would be enough to set her off.

"Enough of this. Hand over the blades or your woman dies. This only ends one way."

Nosh hesitated, holding up his free hand. "Wait! What if I agree to kill her *for* you? This High Priestess has done me no favors, and she has definitely caused problems for more than a few of my friends. Your story rings of truth, despite...popular sentiment," he said with a guilty smile, hoping that a little humility could turn the tide.

Several of the witches chuckled, buying it. But not Rowan.

She sneered at Nosh. "As if we would ever trust a shaman again. No. This is family business. I wouldn't trust you not to betray us at the last moment." She stormed over, snatching a dagger from Izzy's captor and holding it to the ex-Sister's throat.

Nosh held out his hand in a surrendering gesture. "Okay! Take me. Just let her go, first. It's obvious that she is just as much of a victim in this as the Cauldron is. And the Sisters ex-communicated her this morning anyway, once she refused to toe the line and blindly follow the zealous demands of the High Priestess you despise. She's closer to your coven than the Sisters of Mercy. Look at her face. It's obvious that she didn't know about the true history of your order before now, and she was already kicked out of their circle of trust. That has to count for something, right?"

Rowan waited, not replying as she pressed the dagger harder against Izzy's throat.

Nosh crashed down to his knees, holding up both palms. His toma-hawk already rested in one hand, and the second tomahawk suddenly appeared in the other, both blades crackling with a steady blue glow. He held them out to Rowan. "Let her go. Please. Let your choice show her that your claim is true. That you aren't as evil as the High Priestess led the world to believe. And...she doesn't need to see what comes next. Not if you meant any word of your story."

Rowan handed the dagger back to the witch guarding Izzy, and slowly approached Nosh, looking wary of an attack. Nosh remained motionless, staring down at the ground. Rowan carefully accepted the blades, and the crackling blue light winked out. I momentarily panicked, but the row of witches behind her gasped collectively, practically quivering with anticipation. Was the blue power associated only with Nosh? Just like the tomahawk had been red in my control?

*Come on, Nero,* I thought to myself. *Now, while everyone is distracted.*

Rowan shuddered at the power and control of wielding the tomahawks. She slowly inspected them, holding them up to the light. They looked just as they had on the mantle above the fireplace in the Griffins' Penthouse.

She lowered one of the tomahawks to her side but lifted the other to press against Nosh's scalp, right at the hairline. I began to panic, realizing that I was the only one able to put a stop to this—even if I felt sluggish and drained. I hugged the wall, drifting closer to Izzy in hopes that I could kill her captors and at least shove her to safety so that Nosh could reclaim the blades with his magic.

Unless...it was already too late for him to do that. Had he already given them up, or did some ritual need to take place? Like the one Rowan looked ready to start upon his scalp. Nosh had mentioned not wanting Izzy to see what came next, which implied there was a process to passing on the blades. Probably a very bloody process, judging by Rowan's first use of the blade.

I drifted closer, careful not to move fast enough that I drew the attention of the other witches. I was only ten feet from Izzy when Rowan smiled sadly at Nosh.

A lone drop of blood rolled down his forehead, and I abruptly felt a weakened, but white-hot, fire blazing within my heart. My son was bleeding.

"I don't think so, shaman," Rowan said. "We can't afford any witnesses or any mistakes. We're already on the verge of failure. There are barely any of us left. I'm sorry, but I just can't take the chance."

And I actually believed her.

Nosh's eyes widened in fear.

## 37

Out of nowhere, a wolf leapt up onto the opposite side of the stage, barking wildly and drawing everyone's attention. I solidified, ready to destroy the guards in one fell swoop. Instead, I abruptly crashed to my knees as the strain of maintaining my mist form for so long hit me all at once. I felt dizzy and alarmingly weak. My hands shook violently, and I knew I didn't have the strength to do more than wrestle—and even that seemed like a dubious attack plan in my current state. At least the barking wolf had masked the sound of me heroically collapsing onto the stage.

So, I did the unexpected. I dove in front of Izzy, landing on my knees as I reached for the rusted dagger the witch guard had been holding a few inches away from her throat. Luckily, I moved faster than she could react. Unluckily, I grabbed it by the blade. With no other option but to proceed, I wrapped my fingers over the sharp edge so that even if the witch pulled against my puny strength, all she would accomplish would be to press my knuckles into Izzy's throat.

And potentially slice off my fingers, of course.

I stared into Izzy's bewildered eyes as the witch violently tugged against my grip, causing her blade to bite deep into my flesh. I gritted my teeth, focusing on the older wound in my side to ignore the fresh new pains on my fingers. Hot blood dripped over my knuckles, making my grip slippery. I squeezed tighter, panting in both desperation and agony. "Think of the tomahawk in your hand!" I hissed at Izzy, trying to keep both her guard and Rowan in my peripheral vision.

Rowan began sliding the tomahawk across Nosh's scalp, sensing that her time for conversation was at an end. Blood spilled from his hairline, and the air suddenly pulsed with heavy magic, making my teeth rattle.

I saw furry shapes zipping about the edges of the stage, dodging exploding potions, but I ignored them. I wasn't sure which tomahawk Rowan was currently using—Izzy's or Nosh's—but it was all I could think to do without relying on the wolves and Nero. Potions continued exploding in the air and I sensed more vampires and werewolves battling it out, filling the air with the sharp tang of witch's blood and the agonized screams as some of my soldiers burned from a thrown potion.

"Now, Izzy!" I snapped, swallowing the pain from my bleeding fingers.

The tomahawk against Nosh's scalp abruptly winked out of existence and appeared in Izzy's bound hands. Rowan cursed, lifting the other tomahawk to resume her work on Nosh. Izzy spun, swinging the tomahawk at her captor. The witch guard was agile enough to jump back a step—

And right into a pair of werewolves. They tore her in half before she could even scream, striking from two different directions at two different heights to liberally shower Izzy in blood.

I let out a breath of relief, clutching my lacerated fingers to my chest, wondering if I would ever use them again. I definitely couldn't bend them at the moment. I couldn't even feel them. I did my best to position myself between Izzy and any threats, even though I was utterly useless at the moment. I couldn't even call up my cloak, I felt so drained of power. I felt hollow.

"She's safe, Nosh!" I shouted weakly, checking on him amidst the chaos.

Upon hearing my words, Nosh snarled and the tomahawk in Rowan's hand disappeared, making her stumble in alarm as her momentum caused her to slow-punch Nosh in the bloody forehead—which was understandably slick, so she almost fell to the ground.

Nosh exploded up from his kneeling position to grab a fistful of hair on the top of Rowan's head. He sliced his tomahawk across her throat in one swift motion, the blazing blue fire of his skinwalker blade instantly cauterizing the wound as he separated her head from her neck. He held her severed head before him, screaming and chanting at it as his own forehead painted his face in a sheet of blood that looked like war paint. Nosh dove towards us, seeming to hang horizontal in the air as his spirit bear exploded out from beneath the stage, sending shrapnel and planks of wood in every direction.

The bear's arrival knocked down a tight grouping of witches who seemed to be causing the most harm. The bear roared, lunging forward and...

Well, he bit the tits off one witch. That caught me *entirely* off guard. Not more than her, of course. Then it began playing dirty, swiping a massive paw at any witch who tried to run away.

Nosh landed before me with a grunt, ignoring the still-falling pieces of the destroyed stage. He quickly climbed to his feet, panting heavily. His blood-soaked face was nightmarish.

He looked like the shaman of death.

Apparently, he felt he needed to live up to that image. Both tomahawks appeared in his hands, and he began hurling them at any potion flipping through the air. Except they didn't explode upon contact; they simply evaporated, along with his tomahawk. Then the blades were suddenly back in his hands before he threw them at more airborne potions, nullifying the threats.

Vampires and werewolves darted through the battle, and I saw two vampires drinking deeply from the same witch while a werewolf gnawed on her leg.

One witch hurled a potion toward the spirit bear's back.

Lucian appeared through a cloud of smoke about ten feet above the shattered stage, sailing towards the bear. He struck the spirit bear's shoulders with all four paws hard enough to knock him clear of the thrown potion before he rebounded with perfect precision to strike the witch's stomach with his open jaws.

He clamped them shut, crushing the witch's waist in a spray of blood. And then he flung his head back and forth, relishing in the witch's dying screams as I heard her flesh tear and bone snap. Lucian flung the broken witch into the front wall of the stage, knocking one of the tied curtains free so that it swung closed over half of the stage.

The spirit bear appraised the blood-drenched werewolf king, and the two beasts dipped their heads in a silent acknowledgment of respect before resuming their individual battles.

"Come on, Sorin. Let's get away while they're all distracted," Nosh urged, grabbing me from under my armpits and hoisting me to my feet. Then he gently shoved me after Izzy towards the steps that led down to the seating area of the theater. I nodded woozily, trying not to listen to the death screams behind me as I focused on placing one foot in front of the other.

I made the first step without issue, but the second one broke under my weight. I tumbled into Izzy, sending us both crashing down the stairs as I silently cursed the spirit bear for breaking the steps. I cracked my head on something hard on the way, but I wasn't lucky enough to fall unconscious.

"What the hell did he trip over?" Nosh demanded, rolling me onto my side and off Izzy.

"There was nothing to trip over. The stairs aren't damaged. I think he's just exhausted."

One of them helped me to my feet, not listening to my incoherent mumblings about the bear breaking the steps.

I heard Izzy gasp, but I couldn't see her face clearly. "Nosh. He needs help. And who the hell is throwing silver around in here?" she hissed. I felt her shove a fire poker into my wound and I dropped like a dead weight, dragging her down with me.

This time, she fell atop me, straddling my hips and staring into my eyes with a look of panic. Her gag hung around her neck, but her face was still caked with dried blood.

"Hey, you," I murmured, squinting my eyes at the attractive, red-headed blur. "I really should have listened to Aphrodite..." I mumbled.

The room tilted on me and suddenly Nosh was hauling me to my feet again, staring into my eyes. "Where is Nero?" he demanded. "We need to get him back to the museum. Now!"

"What did he mean about Aphrodite?" Izzy asked, sounding flustered. "Did she do this to him?" Then she hissed. "Good god! Look at his fingers! That one is barely even attached! He saved my life!"

"Go!" I heard Renfield shout from somewhere nearby. "I'll wrap up this mess and meet you back at the museum."

"Hey, Sorin. I've got you," Nero said, slipping under my arm to support my weight, and making me feel like we were all wrapped up in one big tangle since I could only make out voices, not faces. Everything was moving so fast that it was just a blur. I felt a large furry presence press up against my thigh, supporting my weight from the other side with a nervous whine. "Hold on, everyone," Nero shouted.

The theater winked out of existence, but the screams of the last surviving member of the Cauldron came along with us, echoing into the void of nothingness like the sweetest lullaby.

## 38

I woke up in my bedchambers, tucked under my silk sheets and feeling vaguely alive. I managed to prop myself up into the next best thing to a seated position, leaning back against my headboard as I groaned at the wave of various pains that rolled throughout my body as my wounds reintroduced me to the land of the living with their sadistic cheers. I waited a moment for them to subside, and then I took a shaky breath. "Who's the lucky guy?" I murmured out loud, realizing that I wasn't wearing a stitch of clothes beneath the sheets.

Someone fell off the couch with a grunt. Izzy popped up a moment later, a blanket wrapped around her shoulders and her hair a damp, tangled mess. "That would be me," she said, blushing. "Everyone else was busy."

I grunted, shifting my weight slightly. "They just didn't want to be embarrassed by my epic manliness—" I yelped in pain as I tried to grip my sheets with my fingers, feeling like I'd just torn half of them off my hand.

"Right," Izzy said, sarcastically. "Epic. Don't use your fingers yet, Mr. Macho."

I nodded, taking a look at my wounded fingers. They were red and swollen, but at least they were attached rather than hanging by strips of flesh. The wound in my side felt better—if I was comparing it to having an exploratory, white-hot, fire poker scraping it clean.

I glanced down to see that my sheets were drenched with blood from where the bandage had soaked through. Izzy was now sitting on the bed beside me, leaning over to frown familiarly at the sodden bandage. "I'll need to replace it. Again. While I work, you can tell me why it's not healing, and why you didn't tell anyone how bad it really was." She leaned back upright and stared at me with an accusatory frown. "And don't give me any bullshit about how it must have happened at the theater. You left an alarmingly thick trail of blood everywhere you went, and the bandage I first replaced had plenty of dried blood. As did your jacket and shirt. And your pantleg. Your shoe was even filled with blood. Nothing that would have happened from five minutes of exertion."

My mouth clicked shut. "Where is Nero? He gives lollipops with his heaping judgments."

Izzy laughed, folding her arms. "Nero is a shit doctor and almost got you killed. Lollipops are bad for your health."

"Preach, sister," Nero said, walking into the room.

Izzy's face clouded over at the word *sister* and I winced.

Nero paused, seeming to realize what he'd done. "Sorry, Izzy. I didn't mean it like that." She nodded stiffly, masking a tear rolling down her cheeks by keeping her back to him. "I brought fresh bandages. And lollipops," he said lamely.

I waved at him over her shoulder. "Thanks, Nero. Could you give us a few minutes?"

"Of course. Lucian won't let anyone else besides Nosh inside the room, but most everyone is sleeping anyway. It's the middle of the afternoon."

I stiffened in panic and Izzy placed a palm on my chest, pinning me down with alarming ease. "Thank you, Nero," she said in a polite tone that was clearly a dismissal.

I heard the door close and Izzy pressed down on my chest harder, using me to assist her to her feet. She made her way over to the supplies Nero had set on the table, and I noticed how stiffly and lethargically she moved. I hadn't considered how tired she must be after being held captive and...whatever that had entailed. It was also a measure of how weak I currently was that she had so easily restrained me.

I licked my lips, realizing that I was ridiculously thirsty. I hadn't even expected to survive, let alone wake up feeling better. Izzy must have taken incredible care of me to bring me back from the brink without risking my bloodlust. When I was as injured as I had obviously been, my appetite could be positively fatal to anyone within a mile of me.

To *everyone* within a mile of me.

"Are you okay?" I asked her. "Nero brought lollipops if you're hurt," I reminded her.

She nodded. "I'm fine. They slapped me around a little, but nothing major. Nosh came just in time. As did you. Your intended martyrdom really cinched the deal." I could tell she was frustrated at me for putting myself in danger, and she wasn't wrong to feel that way, so I didn't try to defend myself. She let out a breath. "That being said, I would be dead right now if not for you. I don't think they would have waited until the ritual was over to kill me. So...thank you, Sorin."

I shrugged. "It's what heroes do," I said with false bravado, smiling to show her that I was mocking myself in an attempt to downplay my actions.

She smiled, carrying Nero's supplies over. She had one of his lollipops in her mouth, but she didn't carry one over for me. I scowled unhappily. She pretended not to notice.

"I had to start turning down blood donors after we hit fifty," she said, shrugging off the blanket from around her shoulders and sitting back down on the bed beside me. "They all wanted to help—every single vampire, every werewolf not on patrol, and even the Nephilim. It would be easier to count how many didn't want to offer you a drink—which was zero."

"I'm the most popular girl at the bar."

She laughed, peeling off the tape over my bandage with extreme caution. I lifted my arms above my head, lacing my fingers—very carefully—behind my neck so as to give her more room to work.

"Is everyone okay? I didn't kill anyone in my bloodlust, did I?"

She shook her head. "I kept you pinned down. You were as weak as a kitten—and just as angry," she murmured despite the lollipop in her mouth, leaning close enough for me to both feel her breath and almost taste the candy as she peeled the stuck bandage away. I didn't even need to look down at it. I could *feel* how bad it looked—even better than if I had physically looked at it.

Rather than getting defensive about her comment, I let out a sigh of relief to hear that no one had died trying to feed me while I had been in such a blood-crazed state. "Just imagine how much better I'd feel with a lollipop," I said wistfully.

She smiled, fixing her attention on my wound even though her face was mere inches away. The fact that I didn't instinctively want to take a drink from her neck spoke volumes about my condition. She really had brought me back from the brink. I hadn't even thought about biting her neck until I'd thought about the fact that I *hadn't* thought about it.

She leaned back and bit the lollipop off, tossing the stick onto the pile of soiled bandages. Then she began dabbing around my wound with a damp cloth. "So. What am I looking at here? Nero grows suspiciously silent whenever I ask, and Lucian pretends to be asleep anytime I look at him. I know it's a silver wound, but none of the typical silver treatment seems to be having an effect. I can't figure out what else it is on top of the poisonous metal. That mystery is preventing me from healing you completely."

I nodded, thinking over Hades' warning about not bringing up the Olympians. "Whatever you've done has helped. I feel much better—"

She turned to lock eyes with me from only inches away. I almost wilted beneath her withering glare. I hadn't ever realized how big and bright her eyes were. Or how scary she could look.

"Oh, no you don't," she said softly, pressing her damp cloth down on the peripheral of my wound with slightly more force. It was enough to make my entire body lock rigid. She released the pressure almost instantly, arching an eyebrow at me in a daring manner, knowing that my anger would only prove her point. Here she was, inches away from a monster who could easily destroy her with a single look, and...

It was *her* look that was terrifying. It was a look of tough love, filled with a concern so deep that she was willing to push me in order to protect me—to heal me. She hadn't broken eye contact or even blinked while causing me pain. "Okay," I rasped. "You made your point."

She sniffed doubtfully. "I fed you three times more blood than you needed once I noticed that two-thirds of what you tried to drink fell right out the hole in your side," she said stiffly. "How do I plug up the hole? Because even now, the blood you did manage to keep down is leaking out rather than fully healing your body."

What Artemis had done wasn't going to be healed by more blood or magic. If she hadn't found a solution yet, my only hope was to reclaim my soul from the Soul Spring in my castle. Which meant confronting Dracula. Other than that, all I could think to do was to go back to the Underworld and beg for help from Hades. I did not want to do that. At all.

Because I wasn't sure what kind of price would be asked. That was a last resort.

Since it was the middle of the day, confronting Dracula wasn't an option. But Izzy had managed to heal my hands, at least. I decided to stay in bed and rest, hoping that Izzy's continued care repaired more of my other wounds while I waited for night to fall. Which meant that I would need a lot of blood to tide me over. Because even without the Soul Spring, Dracula was my next stop—so I could trade him for Natalie and Victoria.

I would need to fuel up.

## 39

"I feel better, Izzy. Really. I doubt there is anything you can do about the hole, but I've got a few ideas. They will just have to wait until tonight." I smiled, hoping to deflect her concern. "Think you can keep me alive that long?"

She stared at me with a doubtful frown. "Let me check your fingers. They were pretty rough. I honestly expected you to lose a few," she said with a serious tone.

I grimaced, holding out my hand and staring at the black stone ring Hades had given me—my soulcatcher. Despite my wounded fingers, Izzy hadn't mentioned anything about it. I frowned thoughtfully. *No one* had commented on it.

"Tell me if it hurts," she said. I watched as she moved from finger to finger, checking each with a gentle squeeze and a mild stretching motion. It was uncomfortable, but not debilitating. She finally moved onto my thumb and I watched as her fingers sunk *through* the soul-catcher—as if it didn't exist.

I gasped in surprise, caught off guard as the ring flared ice cold—letting me know that it definitely existed.

Izzy pulled back with an apologetic frown, letting go of my thumb. "Sorry, did that hurt? I barely even squeezed."

"Just...tender," I lied, licking my lips. What the hell? She hadn't felt it? Not even when it turned cold? Her fingers had gone right through it.

She nodded, looking lost in her own thoughts. Her hand drifted towards her throat as she stared at my fingers—probably recalling how they had prevented the blade from slicing her throat. She licked her lips. "I bullied Nosh into telling me what the Cauldron intended with his tomahawks," she whispered in a haunted tone. "Specifically."

I arched an eyebrow, knowing I wasn't going to like the explanation. I had a pretty good idea based on the witch starting to slice his scalp, but I was confident Nosh would downplay it if I asked for details. He got that from his father. "I don't know much about skinwalkers. I don't know anything, actually. Just what he's told me, which is a whole lot of nothing."

She nodded, her eyes distant. "They were going to skin him alive, Sorin. Right there. That's how you transfer the power. Skin a skinwalker with his blades and then wear his body over yours." She swallowed, looking like she was about to vomit. "Nosh went into that theater all by himself to save me, knowing what it would cost him—that he would be skinned alive. *That's* why he begged for them to let me go, first." She looked up at me, her eyes brimming with tears. "If you hadn't shown up...you saved more than my life, Sorin."

I placed my hand over hers. "But I did show up, Izzy. We all did. Because Nosh is family," I whispered, trying to sound confident and unfazed. Inside, my stomach was roiling so violently that I wanted nothing more than to run to the bathroom and vomit. And not just because of what Nosh had almost gone through.

I was thinking further back. Was...that how Nosh had first become a skinwalker, or had he inherited that ability from my bloodline somehow? Some unintended consequence of mixing the blood of me and Deganawida? Vampire and shaman.

Olympian and shaman.

Hecate and Aphrodite had both commented about skinwalkers as well. Not that it meant anything more to me now than it had when they'd first said it.

"I heard about the devils," Izzy said, snapping me out of my thoughts. "I'm so sorry, Sorin. I've never heard anything like it—the

Sisters do not hold people hostage. I would have left their order a long time ago if they resorted to such things."

I nodded. "We can thank Benjamin for that."

She frowned dangerously, pursing her lips. "Yet another bizarre event. What the hell is going on lately? Why are so many unexplainable things happening?"

I shrugged. "You get used to it." Inside, I was wondering if my actions were somehow to blame. That my existence was somehow to blame. That the natural order of the world sensed the bigger problems brewing behind the scenes.

Much like how wildlife would suddenly scatter when they sensed a major storm coming, even though no one else knew about it.

That the fabric of existence sensed the man who was coming to tear it up.

That I was considering destroying the Olympians.

Perhaps the supernatural wildlife was beginning to scatter. The question was, did I care?

Hecate had said that exact thing when I pressed her on harming my friends with her gifts.

*Do I care?*

I decided to change the subject. "What do you think about Rowan's claims that the High Priestess is one of Dracula's old lovers and that she used to run the Cauldron?"

"Her story cast enough doubts to make it sound true," she admitted, scrunching up her nose thoughtfully, "but I don't see how it can be possible. The High Priestess is devoted to capturing Dracula, but I've never heard anything to corroborate a tragic love story." She shrugged. "It sounds like a conspiracy theory to say she is a dark witch. Enough snippets to make it sound believable, but there is no damning proof."

"There is the nosebleed thing, and how no one is allowed to see her," I suggested.

She shrugged. "That's like saying yesterday's sunrise caused a wreck on the highway today. Both events happened, but that doesn't establish any real relationship. Just two unrelated facts."

I nodded. "We will learn the truth tonight when we bring her Dracula."

She glanced over at me. "Is that what you've decided?" she asked softly. "To forgo your own vengeance?"

I nodded easily but chose my words carefully. "It's not even a question. If it saves Natalie and Victoria, they can have him."

Izzy nodded grimly. "Then we will soon know for certain. And we will deal with the facts at that point," she said in a low growl. "Definitively." She assessed me critically. "You should get some rest. We can't do anything until after sunset."

I nodded, sliding down into my sheets. "Okay." I didn't intend to sleep, but I did want to clear my head now that there was no immediate danger. To choose how I wanted to proceed tonight.

Izzy left, closing the door softly behind her. I let out a breath, staring up at the ceiling and listening to the crackling fireplace for a few minutes to make sure no one else was coming.

Then I slowly sat up, staring down at my soulcatcher. I took it off to make sure it was in fact real, even though I could sense the vast powers swirling within. Although I knew it was powerful, I still wasn't entirely sure how to use it. I had a few ideas, but Hades hadn't given me any explanations or directions.

I frowned down at it, wondering again why Izzy hadn't noticed it, even when she had touched it. I dropped it on the table, and it splashed like smoke, but then it instantly reformed into the ring. It even made a *clinking* sound on impact. I shuddered, putting the ring back on.

Why couldn't anyone else see it? Or feel it? Illusions could be invisible, but contact often broke the allure, making it visible to the naked eye. Except...my ring hadn't done that.

I abandoned thoughts of the soulcatcher, thinking about my brief, unpleasant altercation with Artemis, and the lovely parting gift she'd given me. At some point, the Olympians were going to get involved. Artemis and Apollo wanted me dead, and they still thought they could use Dracula to do it. Boy, were they going to be upset once I handed Dracula over to the Sisters of Mercy.

That's when the real fight would start. After I got my devils back.

The bed was cold on either side of me, a silent, screaming accusation of my failure to protect Natalie and Victoria. Persephone's strange parting comment came back to me—that I should have taken Aphrodite up on her offer.

I sighed. "No shit," I muttered, closing my eyes for just a moment. Maybe I would take a quick nap. Just a short one.

Despite my confidence, I began to fall asleep, feeling weak and afraid. I had almost died today. I needed Natalie and Victoria's blood if I wanted to stand a chance against either Apollo or Artemis, let alone both. I needed something powerful if I was going to save everyone.

The soulcatcher was cold around my thumb...

But it wasn't empty...

## 40

I stood on a beach of black sand so fine and dry that it felt more like powder between my toes. I stared out at an endless array of twinkling, amethyst lights bobbing up and down in a sea of rich black velvet. The sky was a blanket of thick white clouds, but a bright, luminous moon shone down upon the black sea, creating shifting slivers of white on the surface of the water.

Steady waves crashed into the shore before me in a soothing, hypnotic, rolling tempo, lulling me into a calm sense of peace and tranquility. The power behind those tides was unassuming and overwhelming, backed by the quiet, unstoppable force of the infinite ocean beyond.

*Crash—CRASH! Crash—CRASH! Crash—CRASH!*

The steady double beat reminded me of something, but I couldn't quite place it.

I was the master of this strange, unexplored realm. The very air was thick in a pregnant pause, holding its breath in hopeful anticipation. Distant lightning illuminated the skies miles away, too far to even hear the thunder. But I could feel the growing power of that storm. I knew it was a warning.

I didn't see a single person on the beach, but I felt like I stood in a crowd. I didn't see any buildings in the distance either. Just me, the sea, and those purple lights floating in the water beyond the waves. I was certain that it was not a real place, at least not as it was now. This land was virginal.

I started walking down the beach, sweeping my attention over the pulsing amethyst lights floating in the water. I had never visited this area of New York City.

Maybe it was Brooklyn? I'd heard all sorts of wild stories about Brooklyn.

What was I doing here? I'd been thinking about my soulcatcher when I'd fallen asleep.

I paused, spinning in a slow circle. I was asleep. This was a dream.

I felt my soulcatcher grow chilly and I glanced down. I gasped to find that it was glowing with a dull golden light. As I stared, it began to grow brighter, pulsing in tune to the beating waves.

And the amethyst lights in the water suddenly seemed to all focus on me, almost like walking through a crowd of strangers when everyone suddenly stops and stares directly at you. None of those lights moved, but they were suddenly all watching me.

I let out an uneasy breath, wondering what the hell kind of dream this was. I'd been thinking about the door in the Underworld. At what I had accidentally taken from the other side. Accidental might be the wrong word. I had intended to do...something, but that realm of fire and ice had been a raging storm of anguish and emotion.

I hadn't actually seen anything, and I hadn't spoken with anyone.

But I hadn't been alone. The realm had been teeming with life. It had almost been a living being in its own right, and it had given me something—somehow reading the desires in my mind without bothering to ask me, first.

And although my thoughts had been vague and barely half-formed —definitely not committed to any specific course of action—the wild entity beyond those doors had made the decision for me, filling my ring with two spirits who hadn't walked the world in...

A very, very long time.

Without words, it was hard to be certain.

But I was pretty sure I had two Titans living within my soulcatcher.

And those unnamed Titans wanted new hosts—not to possess their bodies and minds, but to aid and empower them.

Wind picked up, and I stifled a gasp to see two large orbs of blue and red light bobbing towards me, hovering over the sea—which had grown wilder at some point. The waves were now limned with white, frothing water and I could taste the salty spray in the air as the distant storm loomed alarmingly closer.

The blue and red orbs drifted nearer, unaffected by the screaming wind and frothing water, finally coming to a halt before me. My soul-catcher blazed with golden light.

I stared at the two orbs, wondering why they felt familiar. They were each blue, but crimson striations like infinite lightning crackled across their surface, making them look like the two colors were attempting to mix but could not.

"Master Ambrogio?" two familiar voices asked, emanating from the orbs.

I gasped, my eyes shooting wide. "Adam and Eve?" I whispered incredulously, staring at the two orbs. My two Nephilim vampires. "Why do you look like this?"

"Yes, Master Ambrogio," Adam said. "It is us."

"You are seeing our souls, Master Ambrogio," Eve said. "I did not know you could communicate with us in this way."

"I'm asleep," I said numbly. Their spirits?

They seemed to be focused intently upon my soulcatcher, although they had no eyes for me to assume any such thing.

"Why do you trap two of our brothers?" Eve asked, sounding on the verge of tears.

My soulcatcher suddenly crackled with desire, feeling like nothing more than a dog tugging at a leash upon seeing a familiar dog in the kennel.

I slowly lifted my arm, showing them my ring. "Brothers?" I asked softly. "I think they are Titans, not Nephilim."

They were silent. The storm continued to rage.

"The Titans are our brothers," Adam said. "Or maybe cousins is more accurate. It is why we despise the Olympians so much. They betrayed us."

I stared at the two of them. The Titans were...Nephilim? That was almost as fucked up as...

Every other romantic relationship in the Greek pantheon. With all their incestual relationships, the family tree was a ball of knotted string if one attempted to draw it out. Was it really impossible to think that the Titans were related to the Nephilim?

Nephilim were the children of Angels. Unless...Angels were just another term for Titans.

If I took theology and religion out of the discussion, I was looking at two ridiculously powerful beings with similar power sets—Angels and Titans.

Was it truly possible?

I licked my lips, remembering my conversation with Hades. The storm was almost directly upon us, now, whipping my hair wildly. Adam and Eve remained still, unaffected by the wild forces. Just like they'd been unaffected by the effects of me turning them into vampires. They were resolute and steadfast, able to handle most anything thrown at them.

"The Titans are looking for hosts," I said carefully.

Adam and Eve's orbs suddenly began to bob up and down in an excited manner. "Oh, this is much better than a puppy," Eve whispered anxiously.

"I would consider it an honor to look after them for you, Master Ambrogio. They are wounded but strong. They need to recover. We can nurture them. Bring them back."

My soulcatcher was crackling with golden light, my arm vibrating.

Whatever this was about, I could sense that this moment was tied directly to the storm above. I couldn't tell how, but the next few moments were critical. Would my decision cause the storm to crash down upon us or dissipate to nothing.

I knew I could always send the Titan souls back with my Soul Spring if I changed my mind. And I felt absolutely no malevolence from the Titan souls. I felt only a desire to help. And the glee of encountering their long-lost brother and sister, Adam and Eve.

"Are you certain you can control them?"

Adam grunted. "They are the same as us. You already have two Titans in your employ, Master Ambrogio."

"What's two more?" Eve said eagerly. "We can manage them."

So, I held out the soulcatcher and touched Eve—I wasn't sure how I knew which one was her, but I was confident that I was correct. Golden light ripped out of my ring, numbing my arm. Eve's orb blazed like a golden sun, basking me in light. She gasped and cried and laughed.

I did the same to Adam. He groaned with pleasure as more golden light screamed out of my ring, crackling across the surface of his crimson and blue orb, making him swell with power.

The storm above roared down upon us and instantly struck an invisible dome of power over Adam and Eve. The skies and clouds evaporated, and I saw a distant red glow on the horizon.

Sunrise was coming to this dark world. I smiled at my Nephilim.

"Do not utter a word of this to anyone."

"Yes, Master Ambrogio," they said in unison. "We live to serve."

And then I told them my plan for tonight.

## 41

I stared at the fire, trying to ignore the pain in my side and the already spreading wet sensation in the new bandages Izzy had just replaced. At least my fingers were back to normal, no longer swollen and tender. I felt almost back to my usual self, but I knew that would rapidly change once I began moving and using my powers.

I had woken up from my bizarre dream with the Nephilim to find Nosh, Nero, Izzy, and Lucian waiting for me, sprawled out on the couches around the fire. Izzy had immediately forced me to consume thirty bags of blood; the entire museum had donated while I slept, amassing a large store of blood to help heal me. Izzy had then changed my bandages again, checking me over to make sure that I was as ready as possible for tonight's events.

As she had worked, I had gone back over my dream. As concerning as the situation seemed, I felt only a calm sense of peace over my decision. That I had done a good thing.

The right thing.

And I could not tell anyone about it. I needed this secret up my sleeve in order to stand a chance against Artemis and Apollo later tonight. I would need Adam and Eve's newly increased strength.

Because Titans were the only beings strong enough to help me take on Mount Olympus.

Hades had known it. He was banking everything on it.

Nero sat in the chair across from me, staring into the fireplace, lost in his own thoughts. He absently flexed his skeletal fingers, marveling at the new hand. Lucian was lightly dozing before the fireplace at our feet, but his ears twitched at every little sound, letting me know he was ready for violence at a moment's notice. Nosh and Izzy were cuddled up together on the couch, smiling contentedly. I couldn't blame them. They had survived near death in the early hours of this very morning.

I leaned forward, watching Izzy and Nosh as I subtly slid the soul-catcher from my thumb, pretending to dry wash my hands in an idle, distracted manner. Neither of them looked over.

I dropped the ring on table, the soulcatcher making a dull clinking sound. They didn't seem to notice the sound, and they definitely didn't notice the strange visual effect of the shadows rolling outward from it and then sucking back inward to reform the ring. Lucian and Nero remained oblivious as well.

"What are you doing?" Nosh asked, frowning at my hands absently.

I held the ring in my palm in full view, but he didn't seem to notice it. "Fidgeting. It's not polite to point out nervous tics," I said sternly.

He shrugged, turning back to the fire. I put the ring back on with a thoughtful frown. Nero was shaking his head absently, muttering under his breath.

"Do your fingers hurt again?" Izzy asked.

I shook my head. "They are fine. Just restless with all this...resting."

Nosh indicated Lucian, pointing his chin at the massive wolf. "I'm glad you finally believe I'm your son," he said, smiling. I could tell that it wasn't a bitter comment. He meant it. "What's a son have to do to earn his father's attention?" he added, chuckling. "Befriend his dog."

I glanced down at Lucian with a fond smile, nodding. "It's reassuring to see him recognize your scent. So many people have lied over the years that I can't trust my heart. The skinwalker aspect really threw a wrench into the truth," I added.

Nosh nodded, still looking at Lucian. "Do you think he'll return to normal anytime soon?"

I nodded. "Pretty sure he's just milking it so he can take naps while we do all the hard work."

Nero chuckled, nodding his agreement. "Lucian always was a lazy bastard."

Lucian chuffed and lifted his head, glaring at Nero and me with those chilling golden eyes. Izzy grinned brightly.

"I think it's incredibly sweet that he made such a strong oath. And I'm all for an extra set of eyes to keep watch on Nosh. He makes terrible decisions when left unattended." I winced. Unattended, like him being raised without parents? That hurt, even though she hadn't meant any such thing.

Nosh frowned, pinching her side playfully. She giggled, nuzzling her cheek against his.

Lucian lowered his head back to the floor with a tired groan.

"You know," I said, turning to Nosh, "I was an orphan, too. Lived on the streets for most of my childhood."

He stared down at Lucian with a distant smile. "I lived in the woods, and for much longer than my childhood. Solitude was preferable."

"Is Nosh even your real name?" I asked, genuinely curious.

He shrugged. "I've had many throughout my life." I nodded, waiting. "Nosh means *father*. It's what I was always looking for. It was the first name I thought of when filling out the orphanage paperwork for my adoption to the Griffins."

I let out a pained sigh, shifting my weight to lessen the pain in my side. "I wish it could have been different, Nosh. We missed a lot that we can never replace."

He nodded his agreement, but then shrugged. "We are together now. That is better than what we had before. And it is almost time for Dracula to die." He glanced over at me and then the wound in my side. "Are you going to be okay?"

I waved off his concern. Nero shifted in his seat but didn't look over, pretending he was just getting more comfortable. He was very concerned about my wound.

I was, too.

"Why did you tear those pages out of Deganawida's journal?" I asked, thinking back on his time spent with his shaman grandfather. Nero glanced up sharply, curious to hear the answer.

"He was researching stories about a creature in the woods killing vampires. And bad humans," he added with a shrug. "He came closer to learning the truth than I ever knew. I didn't want anyone finding out about our blood relationship that way. I wanted to tell you myself."

I nodded, having expected as much. "If you knew all along who I was, why didn't you say anything earlier?"

He averted his eyes, staring down at Lucian. "I wanted to see what kind of man you really were. Just because we were related didn't mean I wanted a relationship. Especially if you were like Dracula. There were no real stories to go on other than the ones I learned from Deganawida —and I couldn't ask too many questions of him without making him suspicious. I figured I would get to know you myself. As a man."

Nero eyed Nosh. "You're one brave son of a bitch, Nosh. Mind telling us how you came to the brilliant conclusion that it would be wise to confront the Cauldron all by yourself?"

He sighed, kicking his boots up onto the table. "Because Sorin was right. I failed Natalie and Victoria. I failed with Izzy. I didn't see Benjamin's true colors until it was too late."

I winced, feeling like shit. He'd needed to hear the admonition in order to rise above it. Not to go sacrifice himself. I wisely kept silent, sensing that I had done quite enough already.

Nero grunted. "No one saw that coming."

Nosh shrugged. "But it wasn't up to anyone else at that moment. It was up to me. I'd already hurt enough people with my mistake. I wasn't going to add to the toll. Sorin was wounded and needed his strength to save Natalie and Victoria." He slowly looked up. "And...even though it's obvious that you all had full faith in my abilities," he said dryly, "I had a plan. I might have even been able to pull it off by calling the toma-hawks to me at the right moment. Maybe. You guys might have shown up to find Rowan wrapped up in a silk bow," he said, flicking his gaze at me in a meaningful way when no one else was looking.

I frowned. Silk bow...

I managed to keep my face composed when it hit me. Aphrodite's ribbons. How she'd gotten him to say *bonds* and trapped Nosh. He still had them. If he could have found a way to get Rowan to say the word, he very well might have pulled it off all by himself. There had to be more to it than someone saying the word, otherwise the ribbons would have been flying all over the place with this crowd and their constant abductions.

I cast him an approving, but subtle, nod. "Well, don't do anything that stupid ever again," I said pompously.

He grunted and Izzy smirked, staring into the fire. I could tell that she didn't like the topic of Nosh's heroic act, even though it was a testament to how deeply he cared for her. Everyone liked to hear that their partner would walk through hell to save them.

Until they lived up to their words.

"For the record," Izzy said, "if you had told me that I could actually use the tomahawk, I might have just saved myself. You heroic idiots."

The three of us males turned to look at each other, frowning as if she had said the sun was black. She rolled her eyes.

"I'm sorry about Stevie," Nosh said, changing the topic as he studied Lucian at his feet. "The wolves silently mourn him, but it's overshadowed by Benjamin's betrayal and now Lucian's return. Very mixed feelings as a result."

I nodded, glancing down at Lucian. I sensed an opportunity—a chance that I didn't want to take, but that I needed to know for certain. Hecate had flatly stated that the third recipient of her gifts was not Nosh. But...her skinwalker compliments were really bothering me. "I can't be certain," I said as if thinking out loud, "but Stevie's fall might be tied to Benjamin's betrayal."

Nosh frowned. "How so?"

"The only other people to know about that mountain were Natalie and Benjamin. And suddenly Benjamin betrays us." I watched his reaction very carefully—as did Nero. If Nosh really was the third person to go to that mountain to make a deal with Hecate, he wouldn't be able to tell us. But I was hoping his body language would give something away.

Nosh frowned down at Lucian. "That's where you found him?" he asked. I nodded. "I thought you were trying to get your soul back, not find Lucian." He looked very confused.

Izzy's eyebrows almost climbed off her forehead upon mention of me getting my soul back. She slowly turned to glare at me—and then my wound.

I pretended not to notice. "That's taken care of. I'll tell you about it later."

Nosh studied me with a suspicious frown. "Right..." He took a calming breath, placing a palm on Izzy's thigh to calm her obvious annoyance regarding the soul topic. "So, you found Lucian on this magic mountain when you were looking for an entrance to the Underworld." I groaned at Izzy and her practically twitching glare. "Is that why only the top three werewolves knew about the spot? Because of Lucian?"

Nero cleared his throat. "I knew about the mountain as well, but not about Lucian."

Nosh cocked his head, looking even more puzzled. "Why would you know about it?"

Nero studied him, flexing his claws. "Necromancy stuff. And they have good hiking trails there."

"You hike?"

"Nope. But they have good mushrooms there, too."

Izzy was practically quivering with anger and unasked questions, but she also looked suddenly uneasy at the strange new tension in the conversation brought on by Nero's clipped, cryptic answers. Nosh finally began to pick up on it as well. "Mushrooms," he repeated. "Are we talking about recreational mushrooms?" he asked.

Nero grunted. "You could say that."

Try as I might, I sensed nothing but confusion on Nosh's face. I knew he was a good liar when necessary, but he sounded genuine.

I cleared my throat. "Stop being creepy, Nero."

He chuckled good naturedly. "Just feeling out the crowd's take on hallucinogenic mushrooms. I only tried them twice," he told Nosh. "And they gave me a hell of a trip. I wouldn't advise it."

Nosh pursed his lips. "No thanks. I don't even like real vision quests, let alone hallucinogenic ones," he said, crossing his ankles. "Thanks for the warning, though."

He glanced over at me from the corner of his eye, and I could sense the unasked question. He knew we weren't just talking about mushrooms or hiking trails. But it was also apparent that he assumed it had something to do with Lucian. The coincidence of Nero knowing a good mushroom spot and it being the same mountain coveted by the werewolves was an impossibility.

"Well, it's sundown," he finally said. "I'm going to go get ready. We have a long night ahead of us." He rose to his feet. Izzy joined him.

I nodded. "I'll be right out."

The two of them made their way to the door, but Nosh paused at the threshold. "For the record, mushrooms usually grow in valleys, not on mountains. Whatever that was about, you should find a better story to go with it. A good cover needs enough truths to lend credibility."

Then he left.

Nero grunted. "Clever little shit."

I grunted, smiling proudly. "What do you think? Is he lucky number three?" I asked, referring to the third recipient of Hecate's gift of choice.

Nero thought about it for a few moments and then sighed. "I would say no, but he just proved how good of a liar he is."

"Yeah. That's my take as well," I admitted. "he has a point, though. It is time to end this."

"You sure about your plan? The parts you haven't blatantly lied to me about, anyway. And the parts you outright refuse to tell me," he added with a humorless smirk.

"To save Natalie and Victoria," I whispered, thinking about how Nosh had been willing to sacrifice himself to save Izzy, "I would give up my revenge." With no hope of Izzy healing me, my next best bet was to go to my castle and hope that the Soul Spring was there. And I wasn't even sure if that would be enough—what if my soul also leaked back out of me from Artemis' wound? If the well wasn't there...I might just have to go back to the Underworld; that was my last option. Whatever Artemis' arrow was capable of, only Hades seemed to know.

Thankfully, Artemis hadn't realized I had gone to the Underworld. When she saw me handing over Dracula to the Sisters, she would be livid. Because she still thought he held value.

Dracula didn't know it yet, but he was no longer valuable to anyone but the High Priestess for a very brutal lesson in scorning past lovers. That was good enough for me.

I needed to keep Olympian involvement a secret for a little while longer, per Hades' warning. After tonight, I would make my own decisions on the matter. Hell, after giving the Nephilim Titan souls, maybe I'd already started making my own decisions. Hades had never specifically stated that he knew what my plan was.

"All that matters, is that Dracula dies. I don't care who swings the blade."

"In a way, you are still tricking someone into swinging the blade for you, so it's still on your terms," Nero said supportively.

"Second-hand vengeance. I'll take it. Let's get to work."

## 42

I approached the fog surrounding Castle Ambrogio. Lucian and Nero walked a dozen feet back, sensing that I wasn't in a talkative mood. I frowned to see Nosh walking towards me from the wall of fog. Behind him, right at the edge of the fog, Adam and Eve seemed to be arguing quietly but animatedly. I instantly tensed, fearing revealed secrets that would put him in danger.

Whoever learned about me giving them Titan souls would become a target of every Olympian. And my wound was evidence that one of them was an excellent archer.

I held up a hand, signaling Nero and Lucian. "Give me just a minute to figure out what the hell he's up to. Damned kids and their curiosity," I muttered.

"Ooooo, somebody's in trouuuubble," Nero chuckled.

I approached Nosh alone, scowling. "What did you do? Why are they arguing?"

He scowled back, looking a lot angrier than when I had seen him in my rooms only minutes ago. "I asked them to at least let me hit Dracula after you brought him out," he admitted, kicking an errant pebble into the nearby playground. It struck the metal slide with a loud clang and Lucian spun, glaring at it. "Before you give him up for good," Nosh finished. He was breathing heavily, and power was radiating from him, letting me know he was on the verge of losing his cool.

"You need to calm down, Nosh. This is about more than our vengeance. This is about saving Natalie and Victoria. There is no room for emotion in this. I can't afford to indulge even my own emotions. And trust me," I snarled, "it's taking a toll on me as well. But adding another failure to my list won't help," I said meaningfully.

Nosh's cheeks flushed red and he huffed remorsefully, kicking at a stick on the ground this time. "I put them in a tough spot. I'm sorry," he said, lowering his eyes. "This whole thing just pisses me off. Handing him over to the Sisters after everything they've done—rewarding them for turning Benjamin. You and I should be the ones to kill Dracula."

I shrugged, studying him thoughtfully. Was he really ready for tonight or was he going to be a liability? "What if they held Izzy captive right now?" I asked softly.

He froze, slowly looking up at me with a strangled look on his face. After a few moments, he gave me a stiff nod. "I know, you're right," he finally sighed. "I'm going to go take a walk."

I nodded, stepping to the side. He stood there for a second, not moving, looking as if he had more to say. I waited. Finally, he walked past me. "I'm sorry, father," he said, sounding much more sincere this time.

I shot a look at Nero, shaking my head so he didn't try to antagonize or tease Nosh. Then I motioned them to follow me as I turned and walked the rest of the way over to the Nephilim. They grew silent at my approach, studiously staring at the ground, looking guilty as all hell. I rolled my eyes. "Did you tell him about the beach?" I asked cautiously.

They flinched, immediately shaking their heads. "Of course not, Master Ambrogio."

I let out a breath of relief, recognizing the situation for what it was. Nosh had asked them to do something that might go against my wishes. To punch Dracula in the face. "Do as Nosh asked you," I told them, deciding that it couldn't hurt and that it might be good for morale.

They stared back at me, stiffening in surprise that I knew of their plight.

I shrugged. "What's one more secret among friends? I'll act

surprised."

They nodded uncertainly. Nero stepped up beside me, scrunching his nose up at the wall of fog. "I'm going to need a piggyback ride," he said. "From the pretty one," he smiled at Eve.

"It would be my pleasure," Adam said, grabbing him by the waist and propping him up on his shoulder, ignoring Nero's angry squawk.

"What's up with the gray crystals? Is that like Nephilim back hair?" Nero complained, frowning at the occasional gray tendrils shifting back and forth across Adam and Eve's bodies. I'd noticed them as well, but I hadn't had time to ask about them. I was betting they were a result of the secret souls I had given them. "Are our Nephilim not bathing? Growing lichen?"

Adam and Eve remained stoically silent.

I shrugged. "When Dracula was trying to break out and sacrificed all of his vampires in the attempt, it weakened the Nephilim a little bit."

"Not enough to break us," Eve growled, clenching her fist.

Adam nodded. "I feel excellent now. Better than ever."

Nero frowned, glancing out at the white and black castle in the distance. "I still can't believe he took such a stupid gamble. His whole army?" He shook his head. "Idiot."

I nodded. "There are a few vampires left. For the next few minutes, anyway." Nero frowned curiously. "His brides," I elaborated. "But poor Dracula is about to become a widower. As long as you guys don't mind getting your hands dirty."

Lucian wagged his tail happily and everyone else smiled, nodding along.

Eve clapped her hands and then held them out towards Lucian with an eager grin on her cheeks. Lucian happily bounded up into her arms. She straightened, holding him in the crook of her elbow, making him look like one of those canine-rodent hybrids that humans liked to carry around in purses. I walked into the fog towards the gate, smiling as the fog recoiled away from me, forming a clear path. It did the same for Adam and Eve as they flanked me.

I hadn't dared bring anyone else to the castle. I couldn't risk anyone hearing Dracula mention any Olympian interference—what he had attempted with Hades.

The fog billowed around us, keeping everyone else far back. There were about two hundred werewolves and vampires gathered on the streets surrounding the park, all watching the momentous event of me entering my castle for the first time in hundreds of years.

I placed my palm on the gate and it instantly vibrated warmly, opening on silent hinges. The castle no longer felt strained and weak. Instead, it felt hyper-aware of the unfolding events. I strode a few paces inside, motioning for the Nephilim to follow me. Once clear of the gate, I closed it and motioned for them to put Nero and Lucian down. Because the fog remained just outside the gate, unable to enter the castle grounds.

Lucian and Nero took deep, satisfied breaths and nodded at me. I didn't speak as I began to walk down the long, bridge of land connecting the gates to the castle itself. I didn't look down at the yawning chasm to either side of me. But I did smile.

I was coming home.

The very air seemed to quiver and hum with anticipation, waiting for me with bated breath.

"This...is a very long fucking driveway," Nero complained, kicking a rock over the edge and down into the endless darkness. The rock let out a muted wail as it fell, and I glanced back to see Nero's face paling.

"It wasn't a rock," I said. "You just kicked some poor bastard's skull into infinite darkness."

Nero winced guiltily. "Sorry, pal!" he called out, cupping his hands around his mouth to apologize to the skull. It continued wailing, still falling.

A few minutes later we reached the massive wooden front door. It was tall enough for even the Nephilim to walk through without concern. I marveled at the ivory and ebony columns rising all around me. I'd been so used to the black stone that it almost felt like a new castle rather than my old one.

In a way, it *was* a new castle. One touched by the Nephilim. Now, it was also touched by Titans. Then again, if the Nephilim were also Titans, nothing had changed. I pounded my fist on the door. It sounded like a hammer striking an anvil, echoing throughout Central Park.

"Did you get my cards, old friend?" I called out.

Rather than hearing Dracula answer, the door opened to reveal three ancient, almost desiccated women in once elaborate velvet dresses. Their skin was as fine and dry as aged parchment. Nero hissed, lifting his claw. His bone hand flared with purple light and their rheumy eyes began to glow the same color.

Although, they hadn't been doing anything threatening. They had just been standing there.

I held out my hand to Nero. "Who are you?" I asked, even though I was fairly certain that I already knew. I'd seen them in my vision of the castle, helping Dracula kill off all his vampires for his ritual. Except they had been a lot more...youthful then. Had Hades done this to them, or was Dracula now so deprived of blood that he had been forced to drain his own trinity to survive?

Could this happen to Natalie and Victoria if I drank too much of their blood?

One of them shifted her attention to me, her skin cracking and letting out faint puffs of dust. Lucian sneezed loudly, pawing at his nose as he inhaled some of the particles.

"You killed our Mina," she said in a dry rasp. There was pain in her voice, but no anger.

"One of my fondest evenings since returning," I admitted with absolutely no shame. "She deserved much worse. You must be the Brides I've heard so much about. Dracula's trinity. Sorry that I missed the weddings."

The three nodded in unison. "Yes. We are all that remains to him, now," they said in unison. "Please, show him mercy, Master Ambrogio."

I stared at them without reacting. "Where is he?"

"He is...indisposed."

"Grab them."

Nero grinned wickedly. "Nah. They look like they're resisting." The women shook their heads frantically, holding up their palms in innocent gestures.

Nero clenched his fist and all three women went flying into a massive pillar inside the castle. They shrieked as bones broke upon impact. They squirmed weakly, pinned down by a purple force emanating from Nero's claw.

Lucian trotted up to them, wagging his tail. One of the brides lifted a hand, begging for mercy from the happy wolf. He clamped down on her offered hand, sinking his fangs deep into her flesh, still wagging his tail. Then he began trotting over to me, dragging her along behind him.

Eve bent down and tentatively poked one of the brides with a finger. The vampire winced in terror and Eve spun back towards Adam, hooting triumphantly. "You owe me a five-minute massage!"

I stared at her, baffled.

Adam snorted, turning to look at me. "I could have sworn the vampires would blow up the moment we touched them," he told me, shrugging. "But a five-minute massage is an easy price to pay," he murmured, licking his lips.

I stared at the two of them. "You're just now telling me this?" I demanded, wondering why I hadn't considered the risk earlier.

His smile faltered. "I wanted it to be a surprise."

Eve nodded. "You mentioned making Dracula a widower, so we didn't think you'd care."

Nero began to laugh. Hard.

The Brides were openly whimpering and begging now that Eve had mentioned making Dracula a widower. I remembered the Nephilim telling me that, in the past, vampires attempting to drink from them would be destroyed, but Eve poking them brought up an interesting topic. How much had the Nephilim changed? They had changed the castle, but had the castle also changed *them*?

If we survived all of this, I would have to find out.

Eve bent down over the vampire she had just poked and gripped a fistful of her hair. She tugged it sharply enough that it tore some from the scalp, forcing the gasping bride to follow or lose what little hair she had left. Adam grabbed the last vampire by her leg, bringing up the rear as I made my way to the throne room. I reached the familiar wooden door, glaring at the absence of my crest. Dracula must have torn it down.

I glanced back at Eve with a mild frown. "I do not see an attendant. Nor do I see a door knocker to announce my presence." I frowned up at the door. "And this is not my original door."

Eve nodded obediently, striding up to the door with her vampire.

"What is your name?" she demanded, baring her teeth at the dazed vampire bride.

"Akeldama," she wheezed.

Nero whistled. "Hell of a name."

She nodded with mild pride. "It means field of blood."

Nero grunted. "Of course."

Eve nodded. "Announce our imminent arrival, blood-field whore."

Nero hooted. Akeldama stiffened instinctively but was wise enough not to show offense. Instead, she nodded eagerly. "O-okay. What are your n-names?" she stammered.

Eve sighed. "Pitiful creature. I said *imminent* arrival." Akeldama had time to widen her eyes before Eve palmed her face and slammed the back of her head into the wooden door once. "Knock," she said, ignoring Akeldama's muffled cries and the strange squishing sound from her skull. She repeated the gesture with a squishier thud, lessening the muffled whimpers. "Knock." Then she put her back into it for a third and final motion. "KNOCK!" The force of her strike shattered the wood and ripped the door from the hinges, sending it skittering into the throne room.

Akeldama's head also exploded like a burst melon, splattering me with pale, almost pink blood and gore. Eve bent down to wipe the gore off her hand on one of the surviving vampire's dresses. The pair of terrified brides shied away in sobbing horror at her proximity. Eve straightened back up, unsheathing her scythe. She frowned at the open doorway. "There. Whore-knocker." She beamed at her joke.

"We will find your original door," Adam said absently, studying the new opening through the dust and falling debris.

"So hot," Nero commented, appraising Eve. The surviving vampires whimpered and sobbed, too weak to fight back against their abductors. Eve smirked at the necromancer, curtsying.

Adam drew one of his blood scythes and used it to swipe away excess wood and debris from the frame. Then he held out a hand and bowed formally, motioning me to enter first.

I strolled inside.

## 43

They followed me into the vast but spartan throne room. A bright green glow in the far corner of the room behind the throne drew my attention, but I pretended not to notice it. Inwardly, I let out a breath of relief.

The Soul Spring. Even though it was no longer purple. What did that mean?

But my attention riveted onto the sad shell of a man facing us with his head hanging down to his chest. He was kneeling at the base of the steps leading up to the raised dais that held my ornate, inky black throne of polished marble.

Hellish wings fanned out to either side of the back, and the lush red velvet looked just as soft and pristine as the day I'd first acquired it. I sighed longingly.

Lucian jerked his head violently, tearing off the vampire bride's arm. Her instant wail of anguish snapped me out of my reverie. Dracula gasped as if impaled, his shoulders shaking as the amputated vampire screamed, clutching at her wound with her free hand. Her screams echoed off the marble walls like a cat's hiss and nails on a chalkboard.

Lucian gobbled down the arm without fanfare, and then licked his lips a few times. Then he began barking excitedly, circling the wounded man kneeling before my throne.

Dracula finally managed to lift his head, and I kept my face blank as I stared into the pale, misty eyes of the usurper.

His cheeks were hollow and gaunt, much like I had looked upon waking after my centuries-long slumber. His breathing was a steady wheeze and rattle, like dead leaves rustling through a forgotten graveyard. I thought about a pile of sapphires and a riverbank to bolster my resolve and smother the desperate desire to kill him myself. Right here. Right now.

I came to a halt five paces away from him, staring at him with a cold smile.

"Welcome to New York City, old friend."

"If you could call the return of an ingrown cock hair an old friend, anyway," Nero muttered, stepping up beside me. Lucian stepped up to my other side, his head hanging low and his golden eyes blazing. He licked his lips—slowly and loudly, not even blinking.

"P-please," Dracula wheezed, extending a hand towards his two remaining vampire brides. "They are all I have left." He fell into a wet coughing fit.

"Adam? Eve?" I asked, not breaking eye contact with Dracula.

The vampire brides began screaming louder as Adam and Eve stepped up to my other side, each holding one of the brides by the neck. "Master Ambrogio," they said subserviently.

"What are their names?" I asked Dracula.

"Polona and Thana," he croaked. "They have nothing to do with our feud."

I stared at him. "Feud," I repeated flatly.

Dracula nodded, clapping his hands together in a begging gesture. "They are all that kept me chained to my human side. They are gentle women, and they have great magic. They can help you. They know how to make magical artifacts like bracelets," he said, noticing the nullification chains hanging from Nero's belt—the ones he had brought to restrain Dracula for when we took him to the Sisters of Mercy.

A voice suddenly rang through the halls, but no one else seemed to hear it.

*Vile, merciless, and cruel, but spineless in the face of real threats. Polona experimented on pregnant mothers, initiating the turning at the last possible moments in the hopes of producing a vampire child for her husband. Thana worked on babies, trying to turn them at the moment of birth. They worked tirelessly in their efforts to help Dracula's conceive a child and threw the discarded bodies into the depthless moat leading to the castle. Thousands of innocent women and children...*

Castle Ambrogio was speaking to me. Judging by Dracula's intent focus on Polona and Thana, he hadn't heard the castle's commentary either.

I slowly glanced over at Adam and Eve. They were trembling furiously, and I knew that they had heard the castle's warning. I used our connection with the castle to give them a command.

They clenched their jaws and I turned back to Dracula in time to observe his face. I might not be able to get my ultimate revenge, but I could do much worse. In a way, this was better. I could assassinate his heart long before the Sisters ever got their hands on him.

"Dracula says you can make powerful bracelets. Is this true?" I asked the brides.

They began speaking so quickly that their words were just a waterfall of consonants and vowels.

"Now," I said, cutting them off.

Eve hoisted Polana up into the air by the base of her throat, holding her face inches away from her own nose. "Mothers," Eve accused, her fiery crimson eyes blazing. I sensed golden lightning now in those depths, but I kept the observation to myself. Then Eve used her other hand to grip Polana under the chin. There was a moment of stasis, and then she ripped Polana's head off in such a way that her spine remained attached, ripping out of her body cavity like a straw lifted from a drink.

She discarded the body, hurling it at Dracula's feet. She inspected her work, studying Polana's head and the dripping, gory spine dangling from her neck.

Dracula let out an agonized sob, his shoulders slumping as tears poured down his weathered, bloodless cheeks.

Thana screamed, panting wildly as Adam repeated the process, lifting her up to his face. "Babies. Fucking *babies!*" he roared, the force of his voice blowing Thana's hair back from her face. She continued screaming, begging and pleading in terror. Adam ripped her head off the same way Eve had done, also managing to keep Thana's spine intact. He also tossed the body before Dracula, nodding satisfactorily as the man cried out in physical pain.

"Don't let him die, Nero. It's not his time yet. The night is young."

Nero nodded. "He will live, but that greatly wounded him. I think he was relying on them to survive. That's why they looked so drained."

Adam and Eve were swinging the spines in the air playfully as Lucian leapt up, barking and trying to catch the tail ends.

Nero was staring at the Nephilim with a frown. "You two on steroids or something? I thought you were weak and hungry."

Eve glanced over at him. "We are always hungry, but after Sorin put a stop to Dracula's nonsense ritual, we felt much better." Adam grinned mischievously, nodding.

I very carefully kept my face blank. The Titan souls were working wonders.

Nero shifted his attention to study the spines with great interest rather than amusement or disgust. "I think I can use them," he said, glancing down at his glowing bone hand. The spines began to glow with a matching purple light.

I studied the necromancer and his new hand. "How so?"

"To make personalized nullification cuffs," he said, licking his lips. "And I think they will work better than these," he said, patting the cuffs on his hip. "Because these are already bound to Dracula." He approached Adam and Eve, holding out his hand. Adam held out his prize to the necromancer with an interested smile. Nero studied it clinically. "I don't need the head."

"Trophy," Adam said, plucking the skull free with almost no effort. Nero took the spine and his bone hand began to glow brighter. He held the two ends together and I watched as purple fire crackled to life, fusing the vertebrae together so that he held a loop rather than a long string of bone. He twisted the two ends so that it formed an infinity symbol.

He carefully set it down on the ground, crouching before it. His forehead glistened with sweat, and his bone hand began to glow a deeper shade of purple. I watched as strange, ancient runes flared to life over each vertebra. Finally, he let out a tired breath, brushing his hair back with his good hand. "The other one. Quickly!" he snapped without looking away from his work.

Eve tugged off the head with a sickening pop and handed him the spine. The moment Nero touched it with his bone hand, more of the runes flared to life, again racing down each vertebra like a lit fuse of violet flame. He was panting as he looped one end of the spine over the center intersection of the infinity loop.

There was a deep thump to the air and Dracula gasped, trembling as he stared at Nero's work in horror. The spine came to life, winding around that intersection of the other spine so that it resembled a leash attached to the twin loops. Then Nero sat back, his shoulders shaking.

Eve pulled him to his feet, staring into his eyes nervously. "Are you okay, warlock?"

Nero grinned weakly. "Magician, toots. I'm a fucking magician."

She smiled at their private joke—how she had called him a magician when we had first raised the castle. She shoved him towards Dracula, laughing. "Let's see how they work, magician."

Everyone watched as Nero scooped up the macabre spine cuffs. Dracula climbed to his feet, not even remotely resistant. He held out his hands and Nero slipped the loops over them. Then he stepped back, tugging on the leash portion. The loops tightened over Dracula's wrists, the jagged points of the vertebrae jabbing into his skin. Dracula's eyes widened in pain and he bit his lip. The entire setup glowed with dull, purple light. Then it slowly dimmed to nothing.

The castle walls suddenly seemed to relax and settle. As if they had been holding their breath. Dracula was no longer her problem. Master Sorin Ambrogio was officially back.

I smiled, nodding to myself.

Nero nodded smugly, staring into Dracula's eyes. "Karma is a bitch, Dracula. The leash-holder becomes the leashed." He leaned close, affectionately petting Dracula's matted hair. "What's your safe word?" he whispered.

Dracula stared at him, shaken to his core. "Hubris," he rasped. Purple arcs of electricity abruptly ripped out of the spine manacles, scorching his flesh from head to toe and he screamed wildly. They winked out after only a moment, but Dracula's echoing cries continued on for a few more seconds. His flesh was charred and steaming where the electricity had burned him. He whimpered, trying to catch his breath.

Nero grinned maliciously. "I forgot. Safe words won't work until the next software update." He tugged at the spine with a frown. "Well, spine-ware update, I guess."

Dracula shuddered, lowering his eyes. "I'm sorry, Nero. I was only doing as commanded—"

"Strip," Nero commanded.

Without hesitation, Dracula began tearing off his clothes. But...his face looked confused and startled. As if...he was obeying against his will. His eyes had turned a solid purple, just like...

How Dracula had once used Nero's collar to control him against his will. Nero's eyes had turned red when Dracula used the collar that way, but since Nero's necromancy power was purple, Dracula's eyes had turned purple.

I shook my head, marveling at his creation. "That's incredible, Nero," I breathed in a sincere compliment. "How did you learn that?"

Nero glanced over at me as Dracula continued shredding his clothes off, tearing the fabric rather than unbuttoning anything. "It just came to me," Nero admitted. "I studied the collar a lot over the past few days, trying to make a duplicate, but I hadn't been successful. Until now." He stared down at his bone claw with a wondrous smile. "It's as if everything I studied suddenly clicked into place. Kind of like when you go to sleep with an impossible problem on your mind and then suddenly wake up with the solution."

I considered that in silence, wondering what Hecate had truly given him. I frowned, assessing Dracula. He had known when Nero would return from the Underworld so that he could instantly collar him. "I heard you met a friend of mine recently," I said to Dracula.

He shuddered at the memory, nodding weakly. "Yes. He drained me of all the blood I had spilled." He looked troubled, likely wondering why his ritual had not worked. "If not for my brides, I would already be dead."

"I see he made his delivery," I said, jerking my chin towards the Soul Spring.

Dracula tensed, whimpering as if expecting an attack. Realizing that he wasn't in danger of immediate harm, he glanced over his shoulder, and then back to me with a nervous twitch. "What?" he asked, obviously not seeing the Soul Spring.

## 44

I studied Dracula. He couldn't see it? I glanced at Nero and Lucian, who were also frowning in the direction of the Soul Spring, but it was apparent that they couldn't see it either. They knew Hades intended to deliver it, though, so they both shot me considering looks, understanding the situation. Adam and Eve, on the other hand, were staring directly at the Soul Spring, sniffing the air and licking their lips hungrily. "Clever bastard," I said, smiling. Hades had only made it visible to those who could use it. I turned to Nero. "Keep an eye on him. I need to talk to the Nephilim in private."

Nero nodded in understanding, shooting another brief glance in the direction of the invisible-to-him Soul Spring. "Need me to interrogate him?" Nero asked me, jerking his chin at Dracula. "For you."

Dracula whimpered again. I stared down at him, disappointed to find him such a pathetic disgrace. What the hell had Hades done to him? He'd never been remarkably brave, but he hadn't been such a sniveling waste of life either.

I shook my head. "I wouldn't trust a word from his mouth. Even though he seems broken, he lied about Polana and Thana."

Nero nodded grimly. "Maybe my new hand can help teach him some honesty."

"Start with how he found you after you learned necromancy. He said he'd been following commands." I stared at Dracula, who was wilting dejectedly. "Take the answer with a grain of salt. Now is his last chance to be helpful. I imagine the last few hours of his existence will be truly wonderful to witness. Those are the only sounds I care to hear from this...creature. We'll leave in just a minute, so be ready."

"Where are you taking me?" Dracula whispered numbly.

"Snitches get handed to witches," Nero muttered. "You really shouldn't have tried to summon Hades to sell out Sorin."

Dracula shuddered, but didn't offer a response. Nero set to work, growling at Dracula in low tones—under the close, watching glare of Lucian—as I walked over to the Soul Spring, motioning for Adam and Eve to follow me. My fingers were tingling at the prospect of getting my soul back. I glanced back to find that I had left an alarming trail of blood in my wake. I saw Dracula licking his lips as he stared at it, but his fear of Nero—and his spine leash—kept him in line.

"You understand your earlier instructions, right?" I whispered meaningfully.

They nodded uncertainly. "Kind of," Adam said in a low whisper.

I nodded. "And you feel healthy? No ill effects from...your reunion?"

Eve smiled. "Quite the opposite, Master Ambrogio. They are sleeping peacefully—for the first time in many, many years—but their power is ours to use at will."

Adam nodded. "It is...humbling. I thought we were the same, but they are much stronger."

I nodded uneasily. "They were the worst of the worst—according to the Olympians. Which really means that they were the strongest and most feared." I pondered that for a moment. "Do you know which Titans they are?"

Eve shook her head, sharing a glance with Adam. He shrugged. "Mine just sleeps."

I let out a breath. At least it wasn't bad news. In my dream, the storm had evaporated upon giving the Titans over to Adam and Eve, so I took that as a favorable sign.

"Okay. Be vigilant." They nodded.

We drew close to the Soul Spring, and I managed to get my first clear look at it. It was decorated much like vases from Ancient Greece, but one thing on the front drew my attention like a moth to a flame. *Ambrogio* was written on the front, but the first and last letters were the Alpha and the Omega symbols.

*The beginning* and *the end*. I frowned uneasily. Had those been on the Soul Spring in the Underworld? Surely Nero would have noticed and told me about it later. I maintained my composure and held out my hand. "This is a Soul Spring, courtesy of Hades."

Their faces stiffened to anger. In our shared dream, I'd told them everything about my meeting with Hades. I'd come entirely clean with them, trusting their unwavering loyalty. But no one else knew about that, so we were forced to maintain appearances. They did well.

I held up a hand, forestalling their fake anger. "I know how you feel about the Olympians, but I expect you to keep that to yourselves for the moment. Hades is on our side, and his gift already saved Lucian and Nero."

They nodded stubbornly.

I gestured at the Soul Spring. "It's tied directly to the Underworld so that you can always have nourishment without having to kill anyone."

They studied it curiously, genuine smiles breaking out on their faces. Even though they had the Titan souls inside them, I knew they were still very hungry. Starved, even. The Titan souls had given them power but had done nothing for their hunger.

"Watch closely so I can show you how it works." I picked up the golden chalice sitting atop the fountain and scooped up some of the green liquid, my fingers trembling. My soul was within. I was about to be reunited. After so long.

I took a drink of the thick, almost chewy soul juice.

I dropped the chalice as power tore through me, making me clench my fists tight enough for my knuckles to crack. The power was wild, furious, and violent—a beast willing to do anything to escape this new mortal cage. Letting me know that it definitely wasn't my soul.

And then the foreign soul drained straight out of my wound, zipping back into the Soul Spring, taking the momentary power along with it. I bent over, slapping my hands onto my knees, panting wildly. That...wasn't *anything* like Nero and Lucian had experienced. The fountain had given me the wrong soul! Where the hell was mine if not inside the fountain?

And what the fuck had Artemis done to me? I managed to mask my concern as I shot an amused look at Adam and Eve. They were staring at me intensely.

"I don't see how you two can stomach the stuff, but to each their own," I said with a hollow grin. "I don't consume souls, so it doesn't work for me. Why don't you try?"

They nodded warily, and Adam scooped up the chalice, bumping Eve back as if to protect her. She rolled her eyes. "Hurry up, you big lump. I'm starving," she complained, patting her taut stomach with a hungry gleam to her eyes.

Adam nodded, scooping up a drink and pouring it down his throat. The vapor dribbled down his chin and his eyes flared green for a moment. The crimson crystals abruptly crackled to life over his body, doubling and expanding with renewed vigor. I saw a few new green tendrils shifting over his shoulder, looking like an infant compared to the mass of red.

Huh. Red, gray, and now green. How many colors could they acquire? They were starting to look like rainbows. Adam let out a loud belch, licking his lips. "Maybe the Olympians are not so bad," he said carefully. "Hades knows how to make a good apology, at least." His eyes still glowed with crimson fire rather than the brief green I'd seen after he consumed his cup.

Eve snatched the chalice from his hand and followed suit. She gasped, her body going through similar reactions with the thin tendrils of green crystals and the momentary green glow to her eyes. She blinked, her legs shaking as she turned to stare at me, her eyes red again. "Wow," she breathed. "I feel like it's my first meal in weeks. This is so much better than what we get from killing someone. And without the after-guilt."

I grimaced, wondering what kind of souls they had just consumed. "Like fat-free chocolate," I said, recalling Aristos' love of the sweet— and for the same reason. They grinned, nodding.

Lucian trotted over to us, sniffing at the air curiously. Then he sat down and stared at me, obviously hinting that he was bored and wanted to go kill something. I sighed, casting one last look at the Soul Spring. I momentarily considered visiting the Underworld to see if Hades could help with my wound.

Then I turned away, masking my lightheadedness, and motioned for Adam and Eve to follow me. "Let's go. It's time for Dracula to meet his adoring fans." I would at least get him out of the castle before I decided what to do next. It was almost time to meet the Sisters, so traveling upstate might be cutting it close. What if Artemis was waiting for me there?

Or Apollo?

Lucian watched me approach, his tail tucked between his legs. He probably sensed the lack of my soul, but I didn't want them worrying about that.

Nero glanced up, smiling at me hopefully. "Did it work?"

I plastered on a smile. "I feel like a new man."

He eyed my wound dubiously. Then he glanced back at the unseen Soul Spring, squinting his eyes. "Why can't we see it? Is it because we got our souls back?"

"Maybe."

He turned to me with a frown. "If you just got your soul back, why can you still see it?"

I shrugged uneasily, hoping my Nephilim didn't ruin it. "Because this is my castle."

He nodded after a few moments. "That makes sense." He clapped his hands together, scooping up the spine leash and tugging Dracula forward to get him moving. "I'm so excited. More excited than my first farmgirl in my first barn. I think even my magic has an erection right now," he said, openly readjusting his pants as he grinned at Dracula.

I rolled my eyes.

"You ready to meet up with your old girlfriend, Drac?" Nero teased. "Because she's dying to see you. You're going on a date, loverboy!"

Dracula slowly turned to look at him with a puzzled frown. "What?"

Nero smiled. "The High Priestess of the Sisters of Mercy. Or maybe you knew her from her wilder, more rebellious stage with the Cauldron witches. You look like you enjoy naughty girls."

Dracula stared at him as if he'd spoken a foreign language. It was the first sign of a backbone I'd seen from him. It wasn't anger, but it was something. "We are all dead."

Then he stared ahead blankly, resigned to his fate. He truly was a broken man. I scratched at my chin, his words and demeanor sending a slight chill down my neck.

Nero glanced at me. "You were right. He's a closed book. I got nothing from him."

I wondered again about what had caused his change of attitude from the man I had once known. Was it a result of Hades' torment? Maybe we'd hit him with one too many sapphires.

Was this foreshadowing of what I could expect if Natalie and Victoria came to harm? I licked my lips nervously, more afraid than I had been a moment ago.

We walked out of my castle, leading the naked Dracula towards Central Park. I could already hear the roar of the crowd from the distant streets, despite how far away they were.

## 45

I stood outside the gates to Castle Ambrogio, staring at the wall of impenetrable defensive fog protecting my home. Crowds of my monsters huddled on the far side. The rest of my party remained within the castle grounds, waiting.

I held out my hand, drawing on the power of the castle. *Form a clear path.*

The fog rolled back, forming parallel, twenty-foot-tall walls on either side of the wide path leading towards the street. Nosh and Izzy waited near the playground on the other end, staring at us in disbelief. I motioned for my party to join me. "Close the gates," I said.

Lucian loped beside me, and Nero followed us, leading the bound, naked Dracula through the new path. He walked obediently, his head down, not even acknowledging the sounds of the crowd, the fog, his nudity, or anything else. Not in shame, but in acceptance.

I shook my head. And the world had thought this man was the world's first vampire.

It was laughable.

I realized that everyone further back—hundreds of vampires and werewolves—had jogged over to Izzy and Nosh, all of them screaming like they were an invading army. Dracula didn't even flinch at that. He was entirely numb to everything.

I turned back to Adam and Eve. "Keep an eye out for any Olympians and guard the gates." I warned them. "Remember the plan. If you see anything, find a discreet way to let me know."

"Yes, Master Ambrogio," they said, clapping fists to their hearts. But Adam wore an uneasy frown. Eve elbowed him with a stern glare. "Man up, Adam. This is what is best for Master Ambrogio. He already told us to let it happen," she hissed in a low tone. And I suddenly remembered giving them permission to let Nosh punch Dracula.

A promise was a promise. Even if it felt excessively cruel, given his current state. But Nosh deserved to get his own taste of vengeance against the man who had destroyed his family.

Adam nodded hurriedly. "Of course."

Nero was still holding Dracula's leash, and he cast me a nervous look as Nosh walked up to Dracula. I waved off the necromancer's concern, watching my son. The crowd hushed, all leaning forward to watch.

"Do you know who I am?" the shaman snarled.

Dracula gave a faint nod, not meeting Nosh's eyes. "Yes."

Nosh reared back and kicked him straight in the nuts. Dracula dropped to the ground, gasping for breath. I winced, shifting from foot-to-foot. I'd been expecting a punch to the face. Not this.

"Damn! I think I felt that through the spine," Nero said, jangling the leash.

Nosh glared down at the groaning vampire. "You are getting better than you deserve for the crimes you've inflicted upon my family. Upon this world. I wanted to make sure you had a proper send off. Before your romantic date."

Nosh spit on him and then stepped to the side. Izzy motioned me to join her, waving a satchel of blood bags she was carrying. I glanced down at my side, wincing at the blood soaking my shirt and pants. I muttered a curse as I made my way over to her.

"You need to drink as much as possible, Sorin," she said, shoving a blood bag into my hands. I tore it open and began to drink, turning back to the crowd and Dracula's current predicament. They had formed an angry tunnel of monsters, forcing him to walk between them.

Dracula climbed to his feet—hurried along by Nero's tugging of the leash. The necromancer pointed ahead, silently commanding Dracula to lead the way between the walls of vampires and werewolves. Dracula began to walk, his shoulders wilting under the glares from hundreds of monsters.

Then they began pelting him with trash, vegetables, paint, and other bundles of filth. Sticks, rocks, anything they could get their hands on. I sucked down the blood faster, approving of his walk of shame.

Izzy cleared her throat, speaking softly. "Nosh was very upset about how easily he's getting off," she said, staring at Dracula.

I nodded. "I can see that. He set all this up?"

Izzy nodded, and I saw that her eyes were red-rimmed. "He was... uniquely motivated." She saw that I was finished with my bag and handed me another one—already opened. I took it, studying her. "What's wrong, Izzy?"

She hung her head. "I'm just so pissed off right now. The Sisters threw me to the curb for absolutely no reason, the Cauldron says the High Priestess might be corrupt, and who ends up winning the grand prize at the end of the day? For doing absolutely nothing!" she hissed, clenching her teeth. "And Dracula's getting off easy! Nosh isn't even talking to me. He puts on a brave face whenever you are around, but he turns dark the moment you look away," she whispered, sounding frightened. "I've never seen him like this. He's a wreck."

"Like what?" I asked, lowering my drink. Nosh had seemed angry, but not in any alarming way. I turned to see that Nosh was now walking beside Nero, a safe distance behind Dracula, who was walking with his head down and eyes closed, flinching at every impact. His naked body was covered in splashes of paint, filth, and even glitter. He looked absolutely ridiculous. Nosh walked in quiet fury, glaring daggers at Dracula's back.

Staring with pure murder.

"He was *crying*, Sorin," Izzy whispered. "Angry, violent sobbing. I... think he's going to do something reckless at the church. If the Sisters don't handle Dracula in a way that Nosh approves of..." she trailed off meaningfully and let out a sob of her own.

I grimaced, suddenly frustrated. Nosh would ruin the exchange. That was what she was saying. I couldn't have that. It would put Natalie and Victoria in danger. If he didn't have his head right, I couldn't risk bringing him. "This is the best way out of our problem. Do you have any idea how badly I want to torture that man? I want to rip his finger-nails off one-by-one, let them grow back, and then do it again. Over *years*, Izzy. But this is the only way to get the devils back safely."

She shrugged. "I know, Sorin, and I accept it. I tried telling Nosh that. He's like a brick wall."

The crowds were inching dangerously close to Dracula, and alarm bells started ringing in my mind. Was Nosh trying to do something right *now*? A happy accident?

I spotted Renfield frowning warily at the crowd, and that's when I saw the dagger in Nosh's hand. He lunged for Dracula's unprotected back, and werewolves suddenly began to howl as all hell broke loose, everyone diving towards Dracula—my only bargaining chip.

Izzy gasped in alarm. In seconds, there was a pile of bodies swamping the pair. Two thoughtful werewolves dumped their cans of paint on top of the pile in hopes it would break up the chaos. "Disperse, you idiots!" they shouted, casting panicked looks my way. "Dracula is not yours to kill!"

No one listened.

Izzy shouted, flinging her hands into the air. A brilliant white light flared to life, brighter than the sun, followed by a thunderous crack. It worked significantly better than the two cans of paint. Werewolves and vampires fled in every direction, hissing and whining as they scattered away from the concussive blast and flash of light. I saw Renfield standing over the pile, throwing people off to get to Nosh and Dracula.

"Renfield! Get Nosh out of here! Put him in the museum prison. Now!" I hissed, hoping no one else overheard me. Then I raised my voice loud enough that it echoed throughout the park. "If I see one vampire within one hundred feet of Dracula in the next five seconds, I'm ending them myself!"

The rest of the vampires scattered. Lucian howled one time and the werewolves loped away as if his fangs were nipping at their heels.

Nero climbed to his feet, covered in paint. His skeletal claw glowed with infernal light and his glare was furious enough to murder upon contact. Renfield shrugged out of his long coat and grabbed Nosh by the arm, yanking him up to his feet. He was covered in paint and jerking, his attention seemingly everywhere at once. Renfield threw his coat around Nosh's shoulders to keep the chill from the wet paint off him. Also, to hide the fact that he was abducting my son. Because if anyone saw Nosh in chains, they might react first and think later—especially after Benjamin had recently betrayed us.

They might think Renfield was *another* traitor.

Renfield glanced around warily and then discreetly slapped a pair of nullification cuffs over Nosh's wrists. He also swatted the dagger out of his hand before Nosh got any bright ideas. Then he was shoving him away, back towards the museum.

Nero waited until Nosh was safely out of reach before tugging Dracula to his feet by the spine leash. I let out a sigh of relief to only see a long gash down his shoulder from Nosh's blade. He looked terrified, his eyes darting back and forth as if expecting another assault.

Izzy was openly crying, staring at Nosh being marched away. "I told you," she whispered.

I took several deep breaths, trying to mask my rage. He'd almost gotten my devils killed. "He will be fine, Izzy. He just needs to cool his head and see reason. He'll be better when we get back. When he sees Natalie and Victoria safe and sound."

She nodded shakily. "I'm sorry, Sorin. All this just brought too much back to the surface." I nodded, placing a hand on her shoulder. She clutched her hand atop mine, looking mildly embarrassed but appreciative for my physical touch. "Thank you for your concern, but I'll be fine," she reassured me, squeezing my hand.

"No. I was going to ask if you have any more blood bags." I said.

She choked out a laugh and nodded. She reached into her satchel to hand me another bag. I tore off the top and guzzled it, accepting another—the last one in her satchel—before I turned back to Nero. He had the spine leash draped over his neck and was fitting the nullification cuffs he had brought into the castle over Dracula's wrists.

I frowned. "Thank you, Izzy. I think we're going to leave before anything else happens."

She nodded. "Another bizarre event," she murmured, thinking out loud. I grimaced, recalling her earlier comment about the same thing. The storm of oddities crackling throughout my forces. As if someone was orchestrating it.

I glanced back at the Nephilim to find them clutching both of their scythes, casting hooded glares over the insanity, but proving their cool headedness by continuing to guard the gates. They noticed my attention and dipped their chins at me. I waved my hand and the fog crashed back together, closing the tunnel of clear space as I approached Nero and Lucian—who were both guarding Dracula with murderous dedication.

"What is this?" I asked, frowning at the nullification cuffs and then the spine bracelet hanging over Nero's shoulders. "Why switch out the spines?"

Nero shook the cuffs firmly, making Dracula wince as they bit into his flesh. "I didn't want to have to explain the spines to the Sisters and risk harming their delicate sensibilities," he muttered. I shot him a frown. "I also don't want them knowing just how capable I am—you have a lot of undead friends, and I would hate for the Sisters to learn how they are made." I winced at the thought of that. "These will work fine. Tried and true. I could use a fishing line on the poor bastard right now."

Dracula's filthy face was filled with terror as he glanced back and forth, still expecting another mob attack. I grunted, feeling absolutely no empathy, but a whole lot of frustration.

"What the fuck was all that about, Sorin?" Nero demanded. "Nosh is a pretty mellow guy. He could have ruined everything."

I gritted my teeth, finishing off my bloodbag and ignoring the instant gush of blood down my side. It almost felt pointless. "Which is why we are leaving. Now."

"Come on, Lucian. We're going to church."

The werewolf growled warningly at Dracula. Nero waved him off.

"What about the spines?" I asked, since Nero still had them draped over his shoulders.

Nero grunted. "Right," he muttered, sounding embarrassed. "Um..."

I turned to the Nephilim and let out a sharp whistle. Eve came running over, looking as if she expected an attack. Dracula immediately crumpled to the ground and curled into the fetal position.

Nero chuckled.

"Can you take the spine leash for me and keep it safe?" I asked Eve. "We don't want anyone knowing about them." She nodded, plucking the spines off Nero's shoulder. She studied me for a few seconds as if waiting for another command. "That will be all. Thank you, Eve."

She nodded slowly. "Yes, Master Ambrogio."

Then she turned, jogging through the mist towards Adam. Nero pulled Dracula back to his feet and sighed longingly at Eve's rear through the eddying fog.

"The worst thing about death, Drac, is that you'll never again get to see something so beautiful as a bare Nephilim ass frolicking through the fogs of hell."

Dracula slowly turned to look at him with a strange look on his face.

Nero shrugged. "Sucks to be you, eh?"

"Let's go," I muttered, rolling my eyes.

Izzy ran up to us, panting. "I want to go with you. I'll take Nosh's place."

I frowned at her, considering. It would be helpful to have a witch on our side, and Nosh definitely wasn't welcome.

"I want to see the High Priestess who exiled me," she said firmly. "And you could use another fighter," she said, lifting back her coat to reveal her two pistols.

I glanced at Lucian and then Nero. "You two do not have guns, so she's coming."

Nero smiled. "We are going to church, and I've always loved nuns."

I nodded at her. "Don't pick a fight. I want an easy exchange, and then Nero is getting us the hell out of there. I have somewhere to go immediately after this," I said, feeling the blood spilling from my side. I currently felt full of power, but my blood reserves were steadily leaking out. I needed to visit Hades and find the solution to my wound. Before Artemis killed me by bleeding me to death.

The vampire mixer would have to wait.

"Bring it in," Nero said, motioning for us to all touch each other.

## 46

Nero teleported us to a dark alley a few blocks away from Trinity Church. The Financial District was far from Central Park, near the southern tip of the island, so for the first time in a week, human witnesses became a concern. And by concern, I meant a huge fucking problem, because Dracula was naked and filthy.

Lucian was sniffing the ground, walking back and forth across the alley as his first real taste of city life filled his nostrils. I smiled absently at him. I remembered how new it had all been to me after I woke up from my long slumber. It had been overwhelming. Lucian's tail was wagging, so he seemed to be handling it better than I had. He lifted his head to stare deeper into the alley, his ears pricking up as he cocked his head. He sniffed curiously and then went back to sweeping the ground, walking back and forth with endless curiosity.

I glanced deeper into the alley just to make sure he wasn't dismissing a very real threat. I saw only a sleeping homeless man covered in a makeshift blanket of filthy newspapers. Definitely not a threat, so I dismissed him as well.

I glanced the other direction. The streets beyond the alley were packed with lines of honking cars, hundreds of shouting drivers and pedestrians, strings of discordant music from every genre, whiffs of exotic food from both restaurants and street vendors, and the putrid stink of excess waste, courtesy of civilization.

But beneath it all, blood. Every flavor imaginable from the melting pot of humanity that was Manhattan: spicy, sweet, tangy, mild, thick, thin, peppery, smoky, and everything between. It made me both violently hungry and nauseatingly ill.

I shot Nero a concerned look, pointing my finger beyond the alley at the bustling city life, and he nodded his agreement. "Probably why the Sisters of Mercy chose the spot."

Despite the difficulties this added to my plan, there was a potential benefit. It meant the Sisters did not want a full-blown battle or else they would have chosen an isolated location. They wanted an uneventful trade. This observation did little to appease my frustration, though. Thanks to Nosh's inability to control his temper outside my castle, I had been pushed into immediately handling the situation with Dracula rather than heading to the Underworld and seeking out a potential remedy for my wound.

I let out a frustrated breath, silently admitting that I was just making excuses, heaping additional blame on Nosh's shoulders out of anger over his decision. Disappointment, really. Because even if he hadn't attacked Dracula, I doubted I would have entertained the idea of leaving Nero and Lucian on the mountain where Artemis had shot me —even with the knowledge that time would be frozen and they should be relatively safe.

Now that I had Dracula in my hands and out in the open, I was uncharacteristically paranoid that something terrible was about to happen. The prize I had sought for so long was finally in my grasp, and I was about to give him away. If anything—anything—ruined my handoff with the Sisters of Mercy, Natalie and Victoria would die.

Period.

I was barely able to keep Dracula out of my peripheral vision without my pulse ratcheting up. I'd spoken with Izzy for about a minute—outside my own castle with no enemies in sight—and Dracula had almost died. I had almost lost my chance to save Natalie and Victoria.

I realized that I was—again—checking to make sure that Dracula was still safe in our custody, and I let out a frustrated sigh. "Why the fuck did you have him strip?" I demanded, rounding on Nero.

He winced guiltily. "It seemed like a good idea at the time," he replied very carefully, sensing how lame his excuse sounded when said out loud. "I wanted to demoralize him."

I sighed, waving a hand dismissively. "I'm just tense, is all. I'm so focused on saving Natalie and Victoria, that my emotions are getting the best of me," I admitted. "I feel like we're going to lose him before we have a chance to use him."

I remembered how Nero had possessed him with his spine leash, making Dracula's eyes turn purple, and I shuddered. Was that a gift Nero had over any vampire or had it been a facet of the leash? Could he, for example, do that to me right now?

I decided to ease up on Nero until I found out.

Nero was studying Dracula uneasily, licking his lips.

Izzy cleared her throat meekly, squeezing my shoulder fondly. "Let's all take a deep breath and focus on what really matters. Trading this worthless sack of shit for your devils. Then we leave with them in hand and go to the vampire dance." She smiled reassuringly, swiping her palms together in a familiar gesture. "Easy, peasy."

Nero nodded, still looking uneasy. Maybe my paranoia really was rubbing off on him. I decided some levity was in order. I cast Izzy a disapproving smile. "Nuns shouldn't swear."

She smiled, batting her eyelashes. "You're right. How about this? His mother should have swallowed."

My face purpled and Nero let out a choking, high-pitched laugh, sputtering incredulously.

Dracula looked up, snapping out of his depression to cast the ex-Sister a deeply hurt look.

Izzy's smile faltered and her cheeks flushed. "I'm sorry. Perhaps that was too much—"

I burst out laughing, shaking my head. "No. I just...didn't know you had it in you."

Her shoulders relaxed in relief. "Nosh is a bad influence on me, I guess."

A sound from deeper in the alley drew my attention, and I turned to see the homeless man staring at us with a nervous frown. "Remind me to talk to him about his foul mouth," I murmured to Izzy, eyeing the homeless man as he climbed to his feet and began gathering up his papers.

I turned to look at the naked Dracula, sizing him up and down. He was currently huddled in on himself to avoid the faint chill to the air. The wound on his back was filthy. Long term, I didn't care about his well-being, but I wanted to make sure he didn't die before I got a chance to trade him for my devils. He was already severely weakened after Hades had drained him of blood and we had killed his brides. Now he was wounded, wet, naked, and afraid.

"This is going to be an issue," I said, indicating his lack of clothes.

Nero scratched at his stubble, eyeing Izzy's long trench coat side-long. "We could cross-dress him," he said, smirking. "Count Drag-ula."

Dracula blanched, but kept his face aimed at the ground, knowing better than to argue.

"Not with my coat, you won't," Izzy argued.

I didn't understand the terms Nero had used, but I assumed they meant putting Dracula in female clothes. Since a coat was hardly a female garment, I ignored the pair.

"Do either of you have any money? Because that man's coat could resolve our problem."

Lucian was panting at the homeless man, wagging his tail in a friendly manner as Nero and Izzy looked over at him. He flinched at the sudden attention, looking ready to make a run for it, but Nero was already waving a sheaf of cash at him in one hand. "Hello, friend. Two-hundred-dollars for your coat?"

The man hesitated at the large amount of money. He licked his lips suspiciously, glancing left and right as if fearing some trickery. "Is that monster of a dog friendly?" he asked in a rough voice, eyeing Lucian. "I used to have a wolf-mix," he added sadly. "Miss the mangy bastard."

Lucian hunkered down to the ground, thumping his tail into the filthy pavement. It helped make him look somewhat less threatening, but he was still impossibly large.

I nodded. "Best wolf-mix I've ever seen," I reassured him, realizing that it was the truth. Werewolves were technically wolf-mixes.

Izzy snatched the cash from Nero's hand and snapped her fingers at her side. Lucian leapt to his feet, following her as she approached the homeless man with a dazzling smile. "You can pet him if you want," she said in that tone that all women use to dismantle a man's wits.

His face crumpled into a joyous smile at her suggestion and he swiped back his hair in a hurried gesture to make himself more presentable to the bombshell deviant. He instantly began shrugging off his coat. "It's nothing fancy," he said, looking embarrassed, "but it's kept me warm on some of the longest, coldest nights. And your friend doesn't look picky," he added, glancing at Dracula's filthy body.

"It's perfect," she said. She gripped his arm, establishing human contact to make him feel like the luckiest man in the world, and made the exchange with her undivided attention. It was magical to watch—a man given the proper attention from a beautiful woman was like watching a flower unfolding. She let him pet Lucian a few times, and Lucian had the courtesy not to sneeze at the man's stench. Then she was walking back to us, draping the coat over her forearm.

The homeless man whistled as he collected his things and departed deeper into the alley, his back straight and his shoulders squared, looking a foot taller than he had minutes ago.

I smiled, recalling how I had done much the same with the home-less people in the underground tunnels, earning their trust by treating them like humans rather than nuisances. Of course, I hadn't looked as good doing it. But I knew for certain that there was an entrance to the underground nearby. In fact, it was in the basement of an adjacent building to Trinity Church, as fate would have it.

The Nephilim knew all the routes of the underground; it had been their home long before anyone else. Even now, Adam and Eve should be making their way here, with none the wiser. There was no longer any reason to guard my empty castle—no one could penetrate the fog, and there were no more prisoner vampires inside. I had given Adam and Eve specific instructions not to interfere unless I used our unique bond to summon them, or if they sensed reinforcements coming to trap us from outside the church.

But that was my own little secret contingency plan in the event that the exchange with the Sisters didn't go as planned. After Benjamin's betrayal and Nosh's little stunt, I wasn't feeling particularly trusting. The formal plan was to get the devils and have Nero immediately teleport us out. He had seemed nervous about the idea, knowing well that plans never went off without a hitch, and that getting us all together in a huddle would be its own complication.

Especially if the Sisters felt buyer's remorse and decided that they wanted two vampires for two devils, adding me to the negotiation. There was nothing for it, though. Worst case, Nero could take the devils first and leave the rest of us behind with the Nephilim to cover our escape.

Izzy wrapped the long, filthy, threadbare coat around Dracula's shoulders, and then stepped back with an approving nod. "Good enough."

Dracula wrinkled his nose, gagging reflexively at the stench, but that was the extent of his complaint. He was walking to the figurative gallows and seemed eager to get it over with already. If I had trusted him to tell me the truth, I would have peppered him with questions, but I couldn't afford the added time or the distraction of sifting through ultimately worthless information. The only comment he'd made that had given me a chill was when he had learned we were handing him over to the High Priestess. That we were all going to die.

Foreboding, but I didn't trust him to elaborate. And I had as much backup as I dared without breaking the rules of the exchange. He hadn't reacted at all to the rumor about him once being romantically involved with the High Priestess either. Perhaps he no longer cared one way or another. Either way, it wouldn't change my plan in the slightest. Hades had already made it abundantly clear how worthless Dracula was in the larger scheme of things.

I winced at the amount of blood already pooling beneath my boot. "We need to move. Each passing moment diminishes the amount of help I'll be able to provide." Nero nodded, tugging Dracula's chain and muttering at Lucian to look friendlier. "And don't forget to paw at the floor if you smell anything off," he reminded Lucian. "Other than this godforsaken coat, of course. Phaw! It's so unbelievably *foul*! Like the pungent lust of the most ambitious girl at the second-cheapest brothel in a busy port town."

Izzy chuckled with a grimace, keeping her distance. "Why not the cheapest brothel in town?"

He glanced at her somberly. "*No one* goes to the cheapest brothel in town. Better to die a virgin during the plague than go *there*." He shuddered and made the sign of the cross.

Dracula glanced up at him with a disgusted look. "What is *wrong* with you?"

"If you can wear it, I shall bear it," he intoned. Then he shoved him forward. "From way the fuck back here," he clarified, letting the leash grow taut.

I motioned them to lead the way since I wasn't familiar with this part of town. Izzy apparently was, so she confidently led us out of the alley and turned us onto the bustling sidewalk. If I was willing to use my dwindling blood reserves, I could have made it so that crowds subconsciously gave us a wide berth, avoiding us altogether. But I was conserving every drop of blood I could.

The plan was to make the exchange, put a stop to their threats of war, and leave.

My blood reserves should not come into play unless things went terribly wrong.

Even knowing that we would likely see Benjamin here, I had told everyone to let him be—unless Lucian was able to use his undeniable alpha status to instantly subjugate him and silently force him to follow us back home. Maybe even turn him and use him as a meat shield if we needed to beat a hasty retreat with the devils.

Otherwise, we would leave him for a later date. He wasn't worth the trouble.

Izzy's bright red hair and bubbly smile drew a lot of attention from young men in suits and expensive shoes, but the giant wolf at her side sent them swiftly changing course. Or the stench of Dracula's coat. Or the pissed-off warlock. Or the even angrier, wounded vampire leaving a trail of blood in his wake. Izzy rested her hand on Lucian's neck, making it look like she was holding a collar. She glanced at me from over her shoulder. "I feel like I'm walking down the street with a cocked and loaded shotgun. I've never frightened so many people before."

"You get used to it, and it gets old fast," I told her in a low tone.

Dracula nodded absently but maintained his silence.

Even in our alley, the nearby skyscrapers towered over us, impossibly tall. I found myself staring at the hundreds of windows within direct eyesight. It was hard not to feel like every single one of those was a threat—like standing beneath arrow slits in castle walls.

Death watched over us as we made our way to the church.

## 47

I stared up at Trinity Church, marveling at the exquisite detail cast in stone. It looked like a castle and was larger than I had thought. All around it, modern skyscrapers, and video screens glowed, seeming as if they were trying to beat down the quiet old pile of bricks.

The children beating down the parents, shouting loudly that their time had come and gone.

I grunted.

The foot-traffic had died down considerably, as if everyone was subconsciously avoiding the area surrounding the church. Eyeless Sister Hazel, the Speaker to the High Priestess, stood on the steps of the church, glaring at us. Two unfamiliar Sisters in dark, hooded cloaks flanked her, attempting to match her pose and her generally unpleasant demeanor.

Until they saw Dracula cuffed and leashed. The subordinate Sisters suddenly looked anxious and excited, even though they tried to hide such an obvious reaction. Dracula was finally within their grasp—after however long they had been hunting him for their High Priestess.

It was obvious that they were terrified of messing up the victory for their boss.

Sister Hazel did not even remotely smile; her empty eye sockets seemed to narrow infinitesimally, seeing the man as another dog that needed to be put down. I could not tell if that attitude included me, but I was fairly certain I knew the answer already.

Their reactions told me much. They were just as desperate as me for this exchange to go off without any hiccups. Or Nero was right and they were excited to see both of their prizes walking towards their doors. That wasn't going to happen.

I was confident that the Sisters had picked the location for the very reason that my army of vampires would be prohibited from providing me backup; many could not set foot within a church. On that note, I turned to Dracula, frowning. "Can you even enter a church?"

Nero answered for me. "The nullification cuffs will keep him from sizzling. Unfortunately. It's another reason I switched them out," he said guiltily. "I had no idea how the spines might interact on Holy Ground since I made them from his brides."

Dracula let out a short breath of relief to hear that he wasn't walking into a veritable oven. I was mildly surprised he hadn't thought of it on his own and asked me about it. I would have said he simply hadn't cared, but...he had let out that nervous sigh. I studied him suspiciously until he began to fidget.

"I was more concerned about the other forms of imminent death I was facing," he mumbled.

I watched him for a few more seconds and then I turned away. "Let's go."

I strode briskly across the crosswalk and stepped onto the property. I watched Dracula, relieved to see that he didn't spontaneously combust. The whole religion topic was now a basket of worms in my mind. If Nephilim were really Titans, why was any vampire impacted by Christian artifacts? Was it just Faith in general that harmed us? Why? None bothered me, and I had started the vampire bloodline. Shouldn't they all be immune?

I set the question on a mental shelf, out of reach.

Speaker Hazel studied me from head-to-toe, looking as if she had succeeded in confirming how much blood I had consumed in the last hour. I could tell she still hated me for embarrassing her outside my museum. She shifted her scrupulous gaze to Lucian with noticeable concern, and then the rest of my party, blanching at Dracula's current state. His hair was stiff with paint in places, and the smell was strong enough that I could almost see tendrils of vaporous rot rising from his coat. It was truly eye-watering, and that was with the gentle breeze of city air diluting it.

"He resisted arrest," Nero explained, tugging the chains and making Dracula stumble. "I highly recommend exorcising the coat. Then Baptizing it in Holy Water for twelve Gentile cycles because there is no *way* that thing is kosher."

The two attendants burped out unexpected laughs before wilting under Sister Hazel's withering glare. Even Dracula let out a reflexive chuckle, but it cut off abruptly.

Hazel turned her nose up at Nero—and likely the coat. She studied Izzy longer than the rest of us, and she didn't even bother hiding her blatant disdain for the ex-communicated witch.

"I missed you, Hazel," I said, feeling protective of Izzy in Nosh's absence. "Must be the twinkles in your eye sockets." Izzy beamed, absently petting Lucian's neck.

Hazel turned to me with an unreadable expression. "You came," she finally said, by way of introduction, sounding almost disappointed. Maybe she had been dreaming about warring against me instead of having a peaceful meet. Her eyeless gaze somehow took stock of the wound in my side and the obvious trail of blood behind me. "That looks serious. Want me to have one of the Sisters look at it?" she asked, shooting a thoughtful glance at Izzy, likely wondering why she hadn't already healed me.

"Thank you, but no. It's just blood. I wasn't about to miss a second meeting over it."

She studied me thoughtfully. Finally, she turned to Dracula and advanced a step, reaching out for the leash Nero held. "I will take the prisoner."

Nero tugged it—and Dracula—away from her. "Not until we have the devils," he warned, showing her his teeth. "Like we agreed."

She regarded him in brittle silence. Then she sniffed, motioning for us to follow her into the church. "So be it. Let's get this over with." She turned her back on us and entered the church. Her attendant Sisters did the same, but backwards, so they could keep an eye on us.

Izzy held the door and they openly sneered at their ex-Sister. Izzy paid them no mind, motioning for us to follow, as she scanned the streets reflexively. We entered the church. Sister Hazel walked down the center aisle a safe distance before us, and her attendant Sisters continued their backwards shuffle. I ignored them, reminding myself not to pick a fight.

Upon the altar ahead, the rest of the Sisters of Mercy awaited our arrival. They let out small murmurs of muted excitement to see Dracula walking towards them in his filthy, tattered coat. They probably smelled him before they saw him. I gestured for Nero to get rid of the cursed coat; I was having a difficult time focusing through the smell in the relatively confined space. He tugged it off and threw it into the pews. Dracula shuddered in relief.

The Sisters all wore dark, hooded cloaks, matching the first two we had seen with Hazel. On that note, Hazel's bodyguards joined the ranks of their Sisters, slipping into the long double line of shrouded faces.

None of them were holding weapons, at least; they each had their hands clasped before them.

I clenched my fists to see Benjamin standing guard over Natalie and Victoria, a safe distance apart from the Sisters. He stood closest to Natalie, holding a pistol to her head in such a way that if he squeezed the trigger, the bullet would kill both of them. He knew how fast I was.

Izzy shot the devils a panicked, anxious look.

I steadied my breathing. They were seated in wooden chairs, but they were slumped over, blinking with dazed, groggy expressions on their faces. They wore nullification cuffs, much like Dracula, but they weren't necessary. They couldn't even sit up straight. They had been beaten, although nothing that appeared alarming. But they were alive.

I shifted my glare to Hazel, ignoring Benjamin entirely, knowing it would rankle him. "What have you done to them?" I seethed, careful to keep my anger in check.

"They have been sedated. Nothing more. In the event that you demanded we take the cuffs off, we didn't want to hand you two capable fighters. We want this over swifter than even you. And you have a penchant for overwhelming bloodshed, according to our associate," she said, jerking her chin towards Benjamin.

This time, I did force myself to meet his eyes. To let him see the promise of his future doom. The usually comical werewolf showed no humor, but he did portray an almost grandiose aura. The self-declared, heir-apparent alpha of the Crescent.

Lucian's golden eyes glowed as he stared down the unrepentant werewolf, and a bubbling, hacking snarl like a hand saw against knotted driftwood rumbled out from his barrel chest. Benjamin sneered at him, which surprised the living hell out of me.

*No one* could out-alpha Lucian. Literally.

Benjamin slowly drew another pistol and aimed it at Lucian, thumbing back the hammer. "Silver bullets. The Sisters gave me a necklace to shrug off dominant wolves in the likely event that you brought my old boss, Stevie." He flashed a chilling smile. "Told them he probably wouldn't make it." Lucian coughed, his growl livid as he bared his teeth at the incriminating comment. Benjamin laughed. "So. Sit. Or bang-bang." I waved a hand at Lucian and he backed down. "*Good boy,*" Benjamin cooed, laughing raucously.

I had never heard of such a necklace, but the proof was right in front of me.

"Benjamin is merely here for security purposes," Hazel said primly. "You can address your personal grievances with him at a later time. For now, pay him no mind. We surely don't," she murmured dryly, not even bothering to look at him. Benjamin stiffened at the slight. "Now, hand Dracula over," she continued. Her voice practically oozed zealous fervor.

Lucian was no longer paying Benjamin any mind, but he was sniffing at the air curiously. I shot him a questioning look and he sneezed. He didn't paw at the floor, so he wasn't sensing any immediate danger.

I stared at my devils and then Dracula, considering all the angles. "We came under your terms, traveling halfway across the city to face overwhelming numbers," I said with polite authority, indicating the row of witches. "Give me the devils and you can have your prize," I said, pointing at Dracula. "Given our lack of numbers, I will not hand him over first."

Hazel studied me thoughtfully before finally nodding. She turned to Benjamin. "Walk them over, Benjamin. If you *dare* jeopardize this, you will pay *dearly*," she warned. I noticed that her fingers were actually shaking. I didn't care why. This was almost over. I could play nice.

I turned to my party. "Same rules. Don't even look at him wrong," I snarled.

Benjamin snorted, holstering his pistols.

"Uncuff them. They are already sedated—you said so yourself."

Benjamin glanced at Hazel, who nodded anxiously, gesturing for him to comply.

Benjamin drew a key from his pocket and uncuffed them. He tossed the manacles to the side and then crouched down between them. He draped one of each of their arms over his shoulders—a devil on either shoulder—and they groaned sleepily as he rose to his feet, lifting them with him. They moaned at the disturbance, but they did maintain their footing. Then they began to shuffle towards us at a glacial pace.

## 48

I held my breath, hoping that I didn't look manic as I watched Natalie and Victoria, both drooling slightly, as their shoes scuffed across the wooden floor, bringing them to safety one quarter or half-step at a time. Their eyes locked onto me and they both whimpered, seeming to regain some measure of coherence. Their backs slowly straightened, making it easier for Benjamin. Their eyes were severely dilated, and their pulses were slow, but nothing suspiciously so. Lucian watched their feet, not trusting himself to meet Benjamin's eyes.

Nero held Dracula's leash, shifting from foot-to-foot with a frantic look on his face.

Izzy stepped ahead of me, knowing that as badly as I wanted to take them, I couldn't safely support them with my wound. Also, I couldn't afford to be burdened. It wasn't over yet.

Izzy dry-washed her hands impatiently, looking like she wanted to close the last few feet herself, rather than wait for Benjamin to reach her. Surprisingly, Benjamin angled his approach so that he came to a final stop beside a pew. He used his hip to wedge Natalie—his old friend, and fellow second-in-command—against it so that he could safely hand over Victoria to Izzy.

He still gripped one of his pistols close enough to kill any one of us
—leverage.

Izzy gasped in relief as she ducked under Victoria's arm, taking her
weight and murmuring soothing words to the vampire hunter.
Benjamin swiftly extricated himself and straightened with Natalie,
drawing her away from the pew. I let out a soft breath, my fingers
tingling—from blood loss or anticipation, I didn't know.

His finger rested on the trigger and Lucian watched him closely
enough to count every hair on his eyebrows. He did not blink. He did
not even seem to breathe as he stared at the werewolf.

Benjamin angled himself enough to help Natalie without putting
his back to us, and Izzy ducked under her arm. More soothing words.
Victoria and Natalie's legs shook ever so slightly as Benjamin swiftly
backpedaled, holding his pistol down but ready to raise and fire in half-
a-heartbeat if we advanced. Lucian licked his lips and then let out a
sharp whine of frustration.

Benjamin smirked faintly. "Nice and easy," he murmured, slowly
backing away.

Izzy began to guide the devils past me at the same, impossibly slow
pace. I licked my lips, turning to Nero. He was our way home. "Advance
ten steps and drop the leash."

Sister Hazel slowly began to approach, nodding her agreement.
"Agreed. Once he is in my hands, you are free to teleport them away."

Nero nodded stiffly, but he shot me a desperate look, double-
checking that I was sure.

I nodded. "Go. This is almost finished," I reassured him.

He nudged the naked prisoner forward, murmuring wordlessly
under his breath as if saying a prayer. Dracula walked forward with his
head held low, resigned to his fate.

I eyed Izzy and my devils, marking their sluggish progress. Nero
would need to hurry back so we could get the hell out of here.

Right before Nero reached Hazel, he let out a forced laugh. "This is
it, Dracula. Any last words before we leave you here with the witches?
Maybe a *fuck you*, or a damn these nullification bonds?" he asked
tensely.

Hazel slipped close as quickly as a striking snake and snatched the leash from Nero by the middle of the chain. She stared at him for the space of a second before she flicked her other palm up into the air just below Dracula's face. I saw a tiny puff of powder and I instantly tensed. Dracula coughed and sneezed in surprise, and then immediately became silent, his mouth opening wordlessly.

Nero had leapt back, dropping the chain reflexively. He side-stepped so as to be certain not to come near the faint cloud. Everyone shared anxious looks back and forth, but Hazel held up her hands to show they were otherwise empty. "Just a silencing potion. You had your chance to talk with him, and the necromancer was acting suspicious."

She risked a glance at me, and I nodded my agreement before shooting Nero a dark scowl. "That is fine. We are finished here. Agreed?"

She nodded stiffly, backing away with the silently shouting Dracula.

Nero slowly turned to stare at me, licking his lips in a stunned expression, his entire body rigid. "Can I at least get my cuffs back? I only have one pair."

"No," Hazel said, drawing Dracula further from the skittish necromancer.

I frowned. "Nero. It's *fine*. Let's go," I said, through gritted teeth, pointing at Izzy meaningfully. He dry-washed his skeletal hand against his real one and stiffly made his way back, angling for me.

Lucian suddenly began to whine, but he did not paw at the ground. Was he concerned for Nero? Upset at the situation in general—giving away his favorite bone? What the hell was going on with these two?

"Easy, Lucian," I said, maddeningly patient. "Calm down. Let's leave."

He did the opposite of calming down. His whine grew *more* persistent and longer. I frowned, scanning the witches suspiciously, wary of an attack—even though he still wasn't pawing the damned floor. The witches were stirring anxiously, and I saw a woman in a rich silk dress with a black, gauze veil covering her entire head, approaching the altar from the wings of the church with a shuffling handmaiden at her side. She paused, seeming to stare at Hazel and her prize, Dracula, although it was impossible to tell through her veil.

I froze. The High Priestess. It was *definitely* time for us to leave. We had what we came for.

Hazel pursed her lips, looking angry as her grip tightened on the leash. Benjamin had a dark grimace on his face as well. I frowned suspiciously. If this was some sort of power play between the High Priestess and Hazel, we should have left an hour ago.

Hazel—almost begrudgingly—curtsied, clearing her throat. "The High Priestess and her handmaiden," she said officiously, her voice echoing throughout the church. "Do not fret, Sisters, at your bloodied noses. The High Priestess' handmaiden is a Cauldron witch—a sign of our superiority over our cruel, dark sisters."

My eyes darted to the handmaiden, and I winced to see that she was attached to a dainty chain held by the High Priestess. She was also missing her eyes, and her lips had been sewn shut. I glanced at the altar to see that every Sister now sported a bloody nose, and none of them dared look in the direction of the High Priestess.

"Kneel and avert your eyes or suffer the wrath of the High Priestess!" Hazel warned.

All the Sisters obeyed without question or hesitation.

It was...*exactly* like the Cauldron witch, Rowan, had said. The High Priestess kept a dark witch as an attendant. Was that truly to hide her own dark magic? With a dark witch always in her presence, no one would ever know. No one but the blind attendant with the sewn-up mouth, of course—a woman who could not see or talk. The situation guaranteed a bloody nose from her audience either way.

Nero was grimacing, shuffling closer to me as discreetly as possible even though his face was pale. He'd finally realized the danger of hanging around.

Thankfully, the High Priestess approached Dracula, not even glancing in our direction. She had discarded her handmaiden's chain without a backwards glance. The dark witch knelt submissively, not daring to move. The High Priestess snatched Dracula's leash from Hazel.

I discreetly gestured Nero to hurry up and I began backing away, closer to Izzy—who was still supporting Natalie and Victoria. Nero's panicked expression turned to outright frustration as I increased the distance between us—as if he had intended to get me out of here at all costs. But I wasn't leaving without my devils. The aisle was already slick with my blood, so I had to be careful not to slip and fall. My toes were tingling now, as well. I was losing entirely too much blood to spend even one more second here.

Lucian yipped loudly, threatening to make my heart burst from my chest. He was standing between us and the witches as the first line of defense. Except...he didn't look very defensive.

The High Priestess looked up sharply at the sound, hesitating warily as if anticipating an attack from the massive wolf. She shifted her attention to the shuffling Nero like a hawk spotting a fleeing rabbit. She stared from him to Lucian, the rest of her body locked rigid.

"Come on!" I growled at Lucian, my shoulders suddenly tense as all hell.

The High Priestess gasped as she stared at me. She lifted a shaking hand to her veil, tearing it off and flinging it to the side as she took a step forward. My heart froze, and the two of us stood entirely motion-less—thirty feet away and five-hundred-years apart from each other.

"Sorin," she breathed, dropping Dracula's leash. Her voice hit me like an arrow to the chest. She...hadn't aged a day. Nero spun to look back at her, letting out a laugh of relief for some reason. Lucian whined, his tail wagging furiously.

"Bubbling Brook," I whispered, staring at my wife. The mother of my child. Deganawida's daughter lived! My knees trembled violently, both from blood loss and raw, unbidden pain.

## 49

**B**ubble stared at me, and I couldn't help but marvel at her thick, inky black hair, remembering how she would dry it on the rocks after we went swimming in the river. I remembered our heated arguments. I remembered the infuriating debates we had—most often inflamed by a lack of a shared language, leading us both to anger.

I remembered my last sight of her...

Holding Nosh's hand, teaching him how to walk. The night of Dracula's attack.

"You're alive?" she whispered in perfect English, not even a modicum of an accent after centuries of use. "*You* are the vampire behind all of this madness?"

I momentarily narrowed my eyes as it dawned on me. My goddamned name was too difficult for anyone to remember, and it could have prevented all this insanity? It was enough to make a man lose it. A man needed a name, or the world spiraled into chaos.

I stared at her, nodding. "How is this possible?" I asked, struggling to remain standing as I felt my blood pooling beneath my boot. Since Benjamin and Hazel were the only ones looking—or standing, for that matter—they stared at the unfolding situations with puzzled frowns.

I ignored them. Nothing else mattered but this.

Tears fell from her eyes and she was unable to speak. "Our son..." she rasped, trembling. "I never found him. I never named him," she whispered.

"He lives," I whispered back, nodding urgently to calm her. "His name is Nosh. I will take you to him." Then I laughed, pointing at Izzy. "Sister Isabella is—"

I abruptly cut off, realizing that I had inadvertently wandered off the safe trail of social norms and into the unforgiving wilderness of speaking about someone else's relationship—to that person's own mother. I might as well have draped Izzy with a dress made of raw meat and tossed her to the wolves. I cleared my throat, smiling at the thought in spite of my mistake. That I suddenly had the ability to *make* such a mistake—our family was reunited!

"Sister Isabella is good friends with Nosh. A member of your own coven!" I added, laughing at the ridiculousness of it all.

Dracula shifted uneasily, realizing how much worse his situation had suddenly become. He was now dealing with two vengeful parents. Bubble's sad smile evaporated and she backhanded Dracula across the jaw. She gripped him by the chin before he could even recoil, panting lividly. "You. Took. Everything. From. Me."

"From *us*," I growled, realizing that I now had the chance to participate in his destruction. Bubble nodded with a bemused smile, staring into Dracula's terrified face.

She snapped her fingers and he abruptly went as stiff as a board, unable to even move his head in addition to being mute. I felt terrible about it. Truly.

I took a step forward and slipped in my own blood as a wave of dizziness struck me. I caught myself, letting out a sharp breath. Nero had spun at the sound and Lucian growled nervously.

I waved off their concern. "I slipped. It's fine," I murmured, annoyed. Nero was shaking his head ever so slightly, his eyes darting about wildly. Izzy cleared her throat gently and I glanced back. She had an anxious look on her face as she continued to support Natalie and Victoria.

I was suddenly torn—not wanting to abandon Bubble, and not daring to abandon my devils until I knew they were healthy.

I was in a room full of witches, damn it, and we were no longer enemies. One of them had to know healing. I spun back to Bubble, opening my mouth. The words died on my tongue as I saw her staring at Victoria and Natalie suspiciously. That's when I understood how far off the path I'd wandered.

I'd donned my own cloak of steaks and thrown a rock at the Queen wolf.

Now I knew why Nero had looked so nervous. *Old meets new, and everyone lived happily ever after*, was not how that particular story ended.

"Who are those women to you?" Bubble asked, her voice slicing like a razor.

*Those women*, was not a great start to this conversation. "Good friends," I said. "And they are hurt. Your Sisters gave them—"

"Good friends," Bubble interrupted, her words falling like shattered glass. "Like my son's *good friend*."

I tried to think of some way to say it without hurting her. I wasn't embarrassed of our budding relationship in the slightest, but I had briefly entertained a more productive reunion. I glanced back at Natalie and Victoria. Izzy had managed to prop them up in one of the pews rather than continue holding them upright. They were frowning, but definitely still dazed and confused. Izzy wore an unhelpful blank mask, leaving me to my own devices after almost accidentally sacrificing her to Nosh's mother. I turned back to Bubble. "Yes. They are very good friends," I said gently but confidently. *Not one, but two*, I thought to myself. That certainly wasn't going to make this any easier.

"You. Love. *Them*." Her voice fell like an executioner's axe.

"They are hurt, Bubble," I said, hoping to shift the topic. "Your Sisters drugged them—"

Lightning abruptly struck the church, blasting a hole through the ceiling and making everyone jump in alarm. I almost lost my footing as debris crashed all around me, destroying the pews. I was thankful that the blast hadn't brought the whole building down upon us or harmed any of my friends. Everyone was shaken but unharmed. I instantly assumed my father had come to either save me or team up with Bubble to teach his son a lesson on how to respect a woman.

But Bubble had not flinched, and I knew beyond a shadow of a doubt that it had been her. Her face was frozen in a rictus of inner pain. I focused on her whispered words, thankful for my enhanced senses. "Why do you punish me so?" she whispered amidst the sound of crashing timbers and shingles as the gaping hole cast the aisle in pale moonlight between me and my devils. "I have served you well, Hecate," Bubble continued. "Why offer me a dream only to turn it into a nightmare?" she whispered in a flat, hopeless tone.

I stared at her, unable to move. Hecate?

Bubble had been the third person to acquire Hecate's powers? Not Nosh. Not Deganawida. I had even entertained the idea that Dracula was the third recipient. I had never, in my wildest dreams, considered Bubble.

Bubble. The woman I thought dead. My wife. The mother of my son.

Like Lucian and Nero, she must have found herself on that mountain, desperate and alone. And Hecate had taken pity on her, offering her a blessing and a curse. Making her immortal. That was how she still lived and didn't look a day older than that fateful night I last saw her.

Apparently, witchcraft was a much different magic than necromancy—the gift Hecate had given Nero. I'd considered the two in the same category, so I hadn't anticipated a witch to be the third recipient of Hecate's blessing.

I suddenly realized the truth to Rowan's story about the nefarious High Priestess. It wasn't as a scorned lover of Dracula. It was worse. The fury of a surviving mother hunting down the man who had destroyed her family. It was not a romance like Rowan had claimed, but it was an obsession resulting from a tragic love story.

Our love story.

That Dracula had destroyed our family. Bubble had devoted her entire existence to hunting him down—and destroying every vampire she could get her hands on along the way. She had formed both the

Cauldron and Sisters of Mercy, doing the good work of Hecate with her new gift—witchcraft, Hecate's core power.

Bubble had spent her life acquiring power to ultimately defeat Dracula.

Nosh had chased rumors and legends, hunting down answers in hopes of finding the truth—learning who his parents had been and could he bring them back?

I'd been running around the last month doing everything in my power to bring down Dracula.

Vengeance and pain had consumed each member of our family, and none of us had ever needed avenging because we had each *survived*, unbeknownst to the others.

Bubble seemed to snap out of her daze, and the first thing she saw was Dracula.

I took a hesitant step closer, nodding. "Do it, Bubble. Avenge our family," I whispered.

Nero spun to me, shaking his head. "No!" he shouted. "That's not—"

Bubble flung a hand at him without looking, and a glass band suddenly slapped over his mouth, silencing him. "You always did talk too much, Nero," she said fondly but firmly, not looking at him. "Even when I did not speak the language well, I knew this. Our family has waited five hundred years for this moment. I will not let you ruin it."

Then she turned to Dracula, and I licked my lips in anticipation. Bubble hadn't been wrong. Nero often went off on tangents.

The necromancer screamed through his gag, shaking his head at me, his eyes bulging. He began clawing at his cheeks, gouging his flesh in his desperation to remove the gag. I frowned uneasily, reconsidering Bubble's decision as I saw blood spilling from his self-inflicted cuts. What had he been about to say? He flicked his eyes towards Dracula and shook his head adamantly.

I slowly turned to Dracula and frowned. What was he trying to tell me?

Bubble gripped Dracula by the hair and yanked his head back. "You destroyed everything I loved. Everything. I never knew my own son because of you. I have waited five hundred years for this single moment."

Dracula stared back at her, his face pale. He could not speak or move, but...

He was sobbing.

"Tears?" she laughed. "I know tears, vampire."

I frowned, approaching Nero before he managed to hurt himself. Killing Dracula's brides had been the last straw for the man, breaking his morale entirely—taking away the last things he cared about. He had been resigned to his fate. Why the sudden remorse?

I reached Nero and flinched as he stabbed a bone finger down onto the floor near my foot. He sketched a hasty symbol into the wood, using his own blood. Green magic incinerated the gag in a puff of vapor and he retched loudly. I managed to crouch down, almost toppling onto him in the process as the room tilted wildly.

Nero gripped me frantically, his bone claw digging deep into my arm. "You do know that's not Dracula, right?" he whisper-shouted at me, flicking his eyes at Dracula.

## 50

I stared at my friend with a baffled look, wondering if he'd hit his head. "Nosh said you knew, and then Eve confirmed it, saying it would be *your little secret*." He glanced over at Bubble, who was walking in a slow, wide circle around the motionless vampire, tapping her lips with a dark grin as if debating how she wanted to punish him first. "Nosh staged the fight outside the castle to make the switch. He's a *skinwalker!*" My lips tingled as what felt like a bucket of frigid water rolled down my scalp. Nero was staring at me, jostling me. "I thought you knew until I saw how anxious you were to leave him here!" he hissed. "Then Bubble showed up and I thought it might have been your plan all along! But then you told your *wife* to kill your own fucking *son!*"

"Oh my god," I whispered. I hadn't approved of *this*, I had approved of Nosh *punching* Dracula. Not becoming his double!

I spun to find Bubble spinning a wicked dagger in one palm. But she was frowning at Dracula's—no, *Nosh's*—nullification cuffs.

"Stop!" I shouted at Bubble, fighting against a sudden wave of dizziness. "That's not—"

"What is beneath these cuffs?" Bubble demanded in a shout, interrupting me as she rounded on Hazel. The Speaker stared at her with a blank look. "What trickery is this?" She touched a pink ribbon poking out from beneath Nosh's right shackle, and she instantly recoiled, her face darkening with fury as she lifted her dagger in alarm. "They reek of magic. These are magical bonds—

The ribbons that Aphrodite had given Nosh whipped to life at the command word, *bonds*, immediately slithering over Bubble's body and arms, trapping her in place with her hands overhead. I let out a breath of relief. Bubble hissed like a caged cat. The ribbons began to choke her in an attempt to knock her out, because Nosh could not physically escape and was doing everything in his power to keep his deadly mother at bay.

"It's Nosh!" I shouted weakly, my blood loss making the entire room seem to wobble and tilt.

Nero was shouting right along with me, and I heard Izzy racing towards us, abandoning the devils in order to help save the man she loved. Except Bubble was lost in her own rage and could not hear us over her own choking shrieks.

Lucian began barking furiously, but I couldn't look away from Bubble.

I saw her use the dagger to slice into the meat of her other palm before the ribbons could stop her. She choked out a harsh word, and her fingers suddenly flared with dark flames. I tried to stand but I couldn't make my legs work properly. Hazel gasped in alarm, her gaze swiveling towards the witches at the altar. One-by-one, all down the double line, the kneeling Sisters gurgled and clutched at their throats. I stared as rich, crimson blood gushed from their wounds, briefly fanning across their necks before they slumped over with dull thuds like dominoes.

Dark magic. Bubble had just slaughtered her own coven, using their stolen powers to try and break free of her bonds. The fire over her hands grew wilder and louder, and Aphrodite's ribbons began to smolder and burn.

Oh my god.

Her own people. She'd sacrificed them as her first option! Much like the *real* Dracula had done with his vampires. Bubble was no longer the same woman I had once loved. And...if she had been willing to do that to her own Sisters, what was she capable of doing to the man she *thought* was Dracula? The man who was actually her own son.

Rather than dying along with the other Sisters, Hazel stood unharmed, her face as pale as a ghost. It was proof that Bubble cared for—or was practical enough to leave—at least one survivor and ally. Hazel, although eyeless, was staring at her High Priestess and then Dracula with a shocked expression. For the first time, I realized that her nose wasn't bleeding.

I watched as her features slowly darkened to a quiet, depthless rage. Was she upset that her superior had just killed all of their Sisters, or because her leader was in pain?

Nero was still shouting that it was Nosh, not Dracula, in the nullification cuffs.

Bubble couldn't hear. But Hazel seemed to hear him just fine.

A long, elegant silver bow shimmered into existence in her hand and my heart threatened to implode within my chest.

Not Hazel...

Artemis.

How many fucking disguises were there in the church? First, Nosh, and now Artemis?

In crystal clear terms, I comprehended her sudden rage. Dracula... was not Dracula.

The prize she coveted—the prey she hunted in order to destroy me —was an imposter.

The eyeless Hazel slowly turned to stare directly at me, leading with her bow, and her body shimmered to reveal Artemis in all her glory. She reached over her shoulder and slowly grabbed a brilliant silver arrow, nocked it to the string, and then drew down.

On me.

Lucian was barking and snarling in the distance, but I had eyes for only the arrow pointed at my heart. I kicked my feet, slipping in my own blood as the edges of my vision throbbed with darkness.

Izzy suddenly leapt between us with a shout and I saw golden liquid erupt from her arm as Artemis' arrow ripped through her flesh, glancing off bone with a solid *crack*.

And then the arrow slammed into my shoulder with the force of a hammer striking an anvil, sending me sliding back into a pew. Izzy lay on the ground between us, clutching at the golden liquid oozing from her wound. I could hardly breathe through the pain of a second silver arrow wound, let alone thank Izzy for trying to save my life.

Or yell at her for trying to save my life.

My blood reserves began to leak even faster—so fast that it slipped from my grasp even as I pathetically tried to harness it, like I was using a sieve. I had already been too weak to do anything with it, but now I couldn't even *hold* it.

How had Lucian not picked up on Hazel really being Artemis? He'd sensed Bubble without issue. I hissed in agony as I struggled to scoot away, trying to use my pain to get a second wind. My thoughts were groggy, but the answer to my question came to mind almost immediately. Artemis was the Goddess of the Hunt. She knew a thing or two about scents. She must have masked hers, knowing Lucian's abilities after seeing him on the mountain—how he had been the first to notice her.

And then she had muted all sounds from Nosh—another hunting trick—preventing him from speaking. Artemis stepped into view, sneering down at Izzy. Even looking at her true form now, I couldn't sense that she was an Olympian.

She drew a second arrow and aimed it at my head. Izzy grabbed her ankle with her good hand and yanked hard, sending Artemis crashing to the ground—and her arrow slamming into the pew an inch away from my ear rather than the center of my forehead. My eyes widened and I managed to lean away with a groan. Nero was suddenly looming over me, yanking the arrow from my shoulder with a blinding flash of pain. The next thing I knew, he was dragging me down the aisle by my ankles, racing for Natalie and Victoria and away from Artemis.

"Izzy," I whispered pathetically, feeling slightly punch-drunk. "Nosh!"

Nero tripped over some debris and struck the ground with a loud expulsion of air and a *thunk* as something of his struck an object that was harder than his something. He dropped my ankles in the process.

I heard him groan, but I was more interested and concerned with Benjamin squaring off with Lucian almost directly in front of me.

Lucian lunged and missed, giving me a clear view of Benjamin's face as he spun my way. Benjamin wore an expectant grin as he noticed me with a look of surprise.

"Fuck it," he said, baring his teeth at my helplessness. His eyes began to glow, and the room suddenly grew warmer. I watched in horror as his features shifted to reveal an entirely different man—a face I knew very well.

Apollo, God of the Sun.

I was saved from trying to process that revelation as the front door of the church suddenly exploded inwards off the hinges and slammed into Apollo, sending him flying. I let out a shuddering breath as I glanced over at the open doorway, blinking away my slowly shrinking tunnel vision to see...

A *second* Izzy surveying the carnage and gripping a blazing tomahawk in her fist. "WHERE IS NOSH?" she roared. With that tomahawk in her hand, it was irrefutable proof that she was the genuine Izzy. And she apparently knew about Nosh's ruse to double as Dracula.

Naturally, I turned to assess the first Izzy who had tried but failed to save me from Artemis' arrow. She was currently fighting Artemis one-handed alarmingly close to Nosh and Bubble, hurling blasts of pink magic at the Goddess of the Hunt while deftly dodging return fire. Even though her arm was broken and leaking golden liquid, she looked to be holding her own. Artemis flicked her attention towards the door, and she instantly stilled to see the second Izzy with the blazing tomahawk.

Artemis' eyes widened and she drew another arrow, glancing from one Izzy to the other with a befuddled expression. Whoever the fraudulent Izzy-of-the-golden-blood was, she'd at least tried to save my life, so I liked her a lot. And her blood was shiny, which was also nice.

Nero swore. "I'm so confused that I feel like I understand it all," he grumbled woozily.

"Apollo got hit by a door," I mumbled absently.

"That's funny," he slurred.

I nodded weakly as I turned back to the real Izzy at the entrance to the church.

Her eyes locked onto the only target that mattered to her—the High Priestess. Bubble loomed over Nosh—who still looked like Dracula, for some reason—with her flaming hands. The ribbons smoldered, almost entirely burned away, now.

"NO!" The real Izzy screamed, bolting into the room and hurdling debris as she closed the distance to the apparent threat to Nosh, not realizing that the threat was really his own mother.

I watched, feeling my vision dwindle as I used every scrap of energy to simply remain conscious.

The fake Izzy—not wanting to be out-Izzied, I guess—screamed. "You will pay for what you did to my Hephaestus, you vile, virgin!" she shrieked at Artemis. And between one moment and the next, she shimmered, revealing her true form—Aphrodite, and she was wearing... battle lingerie. I barely had time to appreciate it before she flung a blast of pink magic at the utterly confused Artemis.

The Goddess of the hunt leapt clear of the pink magical attack with a startled curse—both at the obvious danger and the shock of seeing the Goddess of Love trying to murder her with hate. With Artemis out of the way, Aphrodite's blast was lined up to perfectly strike Bubble.

Izzy reared back and hurled her tomahawk with both hands in an overhead throwing motion.

Bubble finally burned through the last of her ribbon restraints and immediately flung up a visible dome of power around her entire body to block both attacks.

Her shield blocked the flare of pink magic with a concussive, sparkling *thump* that sent both Artemis and Aphrodite cartwheeling across the room and into the wall of the church.

But that tomahawk tore through the shield and struck Bubble in the chest, knocking her down to her back with a huff of air.

I stared at Bubble as she fell to her knees, my heart torn in two. "No!" I whispered weakly, my vision throbbing smaller and smaller.

Then everything flickered strangely and winked out.

## 51

I woke with a panicked gasp as something grabbed me, but I was too weak and delirious to jerk free. Instead, I stared down to find a hand dripping with golden blood gripping my ankle. Aphrodite was lying on her stomach, lifting her head to stare up at me, her beautiful face contorted in pain and firm resolve. Her lip sported a fresh cut, oozing with golden blood.

"I tried, brother," she whispered. "I really wanted to make you happy," she said sadly.

I stared at her, horrified, unable to do more than weakly prop myself up on my elbows so that I wasn't lying prostrate. Even that threatened to do me in, making my vision flicker with sparkling lights. I felt hollow. So hungry that I wasn't even hungry. So weak that I only managed to twitch my thumb as I stared at her with wide eyes.

Rather than wait for my response, Aphrodite grunted as she propped herself up to a seated position with only one arm. Her other hung limp at her side. She winced, panting breathlessly, and closed her eyes as she sat facing me. She had lost her battle lingerie while I'd been unconscious. Her naked torso was spattered with golden blood, as if she'd been splattered by paint. Two silver points poked through the flesh below her collar bones, like strange body piercings.

Except they oozed golden blood in matching, steady drips that splashed down her chest.

She opened her eyes and smiled weakly. "A big sister can get you the rest of the way, at least." Then she grunted, using her good arm to swivel her body so that her lower back pressed up against the flats of my boots. I managed to sit up, confused by both her words and her actions. She took a deep breath, strained with her good arm, and methodically slid me backwards down the aisle, shoving me like a cart with her back. I winced as I got a close-up view of two silver arrows jutting from her shoulder blades, like wings with the silver fletching on the ends. Golden blood oozed from the wounds. Now I knew what the silver points on her chest had been.

*Heave. Slide.*

Aphrodite's shoulders bunched with each motion, causing her muscles to flex, the arrow shafts to wobble, and more blood to spill from her wounds, painting a horrifyingly beautiful tapestry on her sinfully-smooth back.

*Heave. Slide.*

"I love a happily ever after, don't you, Aphrodite?" Artemis said with mock sweetness from somewhere in front of us. My big sister ignored the taunt, keeping herself firmly between me and my enemies.

*Heave. Slide.*

Apollo rose into view over Aphrodite's taut shoulders. "Oh, there you are, baby brother," he said to me, grinning darkly. "We thought you were still asleep."

*Heave. Slide.*

Aphrodite ignored them, continuing to slide me back, even with the use of only one arm.

*Heave—*

A silver arrow ripped through my big sister's arm, and ricocheted past my ear, knocking out her only support and halting our movement. "Stop dragging this out, whore," Artemis snarled.

Aphrodite shuddered, biting back a sob as she lost the use of her other arm. Then I felt her lower body shift, and we were moving again. Slower, and my big sister's back twitched and spasmed in pain from the effort. The arrow shafts in her back wobbled and shook more violently.

*Heave. Slide.*

"Stop," I whispered, tears brimming in my eyes and my lower lip trembling as I watched my big sister being torn apart, arrow by arrow. "Please, stop, Aphrodite. You have done enough."

Aphrodite took a deep, shaking breath. "I. Have. Not."

*Heave. Slide. Shudder.*

"Oh, for crying out loud," Artemis snapped, looming into view again. She grabbed Aphrodite by the hair and flung her to the side.

I began to panic, seeing Aphrodite struggling to her feet from a pile of debris.

Apollo drew a large, reddish-brown bow and shot Aphrodite in the thigh, dropping her with a cry. "Stay down, and I'll stop."

This time, my heroic big sister did not get back up, and a lone tear spilled down my cheek.

Using her steadfast resolve as inspiration, I managed to prop myself up all the way, focusing on one arm at a time. I did my best to ignore my pain, just like my big sister had done.

For whatever reason, she'd given her all to slide me backwards down the aisle.

I shied away from Artemis and Apollo standing a few paces away from me. They watched me with feral, merciless grins.

I bunched up my knees and planted my boots on the ground. Then I strained, seeing stars burst across my vision as I panted and pushed.

*Heave. Slide—*

My back bumped up against something soft and I flinched in surprise. I was limned in moonlight.

"You will never have your trinity," Apollo snapped, scowling down at me. "The Olympians shall never fall."

I blinked at him, discreetly reaching back with one hand to feel warm flesh. Natalie and Victoria. Why had Aphrodite wanted me here? They seemed to be unconscious, and I saw fresh blood on their faces in my quick glance. Had she been trying to get me to drink their blood?

"Let us end this," Artemis muttered. "There is no sport in such pathetic prey. I don't even know why we were ever so concerned about this one."

Apollo nodded. "He dies last. Let us at least get some enjoyment for our efforts. He's already crying over Aphrodite. Let him cry some more over the dead bodies of his women."

"Then we can deal with the other rodents," Artemis agreed, her eyes narrowing as they locked onto Victoria. "She abused my gift. Did you know her bloodline was designed to destroy *you* above all others?" she asked, meeting my eyes with a bored smile. I was too tired to do more than twitch in surprise. "Yet you turned her against me. You die last, baby brother. But you won't have a long wait," she said, eyeing my wound.

And she was right. She didn't even have to bother shooting me. I was spent.

They both drew arrows and took aim at the unconscious Devils over my shoulders.

With an instinctive gasp, I scraped the dregs of my blood reservoir, and gathered enough power to call up my cloak of shadow and blood, but it was wispy and threadbare. My vision exploded with painful light at the pathetic attempt, right as Apollo and Artemis released.

The arrows hit my cloak and spun me to the side. I crashed down beside my devils, propped up against a pile of debris at a slant, my vision dwindling as my pulse dropped to almost nothing.

I stared at Natalie and Victoria from inches away, spotting the still quivering arrows sticking out of their hearts like staked flags—*Apollo and Artemis were here*. I blinked, struggling to lift my hands towards them. I felt our bond sever, snapping back into me like two blows to the chest, making me grunt. That sensation, more than the arrows, told me the truth.

A screaming wail heralded a trio of malevolent green spirits, chasing Apollo and Artemis away with frustrated hisses. I saw Nero race by with his bone claw out, seeming to be directing the spirits. As the gods retreated, I saw arrows whipping through the spirits, causing no harm.

My vision faded to a tighter circle as I shifted my gaze back to Natalie and Victoria's motionless forms. I saw no pulse in their throats. I finally managed to set my hands on their chests as Izzy skidded up beside me. She slapped her fingers over their throats. "Their hearts have stopped!" she wailed, on the verge of tears. Then she gasped. "You're almost dead!"

I drew absolutely everything I had left, silently begging to use the last beats of my own heart if necessary...to make lightning. And it worked.

Lightning crackled from my numb fingertips and latched onto them. Their bodies rocked and arched wildly. "Oh my *god!*" Izzy shouted, cringing from the sudden blast of power.

But the look on Izzy's face as she touched their throats with her fingers told me the truth. It hadn't worked. The lightning winked out of me.

I closed my eyes, still touching Natalie and Victoria. We would all die together, it seemed.

I died. I didn't fall asleep. I could feel the difference.

## 52

I opened my eyes to find everything slightly...green. Hades, the God of the Underworld, loomed over me with a triumphant grin, laughing excitedly. "I knew it!"

I stared at him, confused as all hell. "Then I really am dead."

"Not for long!" he crowed, rearing back with his fist.

"Wait. What—" He punched me in the forehead, his ring burning like fire as it struck my skin and knocked me down through the center of the planet. Yet I clearly saw everything zipping past me, and none of it could be described as cavernous.

I flew.

About one thousand miles in the span of a few seconds. Through trees, walls, boulders, buildings, cars, and even people, judging by the shouts and sounds whipping past my ears too fast for me to individually process.

And it didn't hurt at all. In fact, it felt like...I was getting *bigger*.

Something abruptly snatched me out of the air, hoisting me up by the neck. I stared into the fiery crimson eyes of a large, somewhat homely, perfectly smooth face. I hung limply, unable to move my arms or legs. Despite him holding me by the throat, I didn't feel any pain or discomfort at being choked. It took me a moment to recognize him.

"Adam!" I snapped incredulously, wondering what the hell was going on, and why it was all so...green.

Adam gasped, dropping me to the ground. "It's him! He's not dead!" he hissed. I landed with a wet splat, forming a small puddle at his feet.

Someone else grabbed me off the ground, holding me upside down by my ankles as they hoisted me high in the air. I stared at a pale expanse of gloriously gigantic breasts made of polished marble. "Higher, Eve," I said, unable to make myself move since I had no actual body.

She did, gripping me by the waist. In a truly sickening sensation, I felt my lower body fold in half over her fist, collapsing in on itself to kick myself in the back of the head.

But it didn't hurt, at least.

Like...I was a wet towel. "What the fuck is going on?" I snapped.

Eve stared, stunned. "Master Sorin? We just felt you die!"

Adam growled. "No. We felt him die for a second, and then I felt him back at the castle gates."

I was beginning to panic as they debated semantics. "What the fuck is going on?" I repeated in a frantic shriek.

"It's his *soul*!" she gasped, shifting me back and forth like she was inspecting a bundle of silk.

I began to panic even more at her words. Hades had just punched me in the head with...his soulcatcher. Had he been holding onto it this whole time? I decided that it did not matter at the moment. "Gah! Don't hold me like that! I've been looking for this thing everywhere! Put me back!"

She glanced over at Adam with a puzzled frown.

"Maybe we could charge him up enough to at least stand on his own? Give him some spirit bones, or something?" he asked.

Eve turned back to me, pursing her lips. "I want a puppy."

I stared back at her, wondering if she was joking. She continued to stare at me, and I began wondering if there was only a limited window that my soul could withstand the real world without a body. "Fine! Just give me some damned spirit bones!"

"This is all very strange," Adam said uncertainly.

Realizing that I was in no position to threaten them since I was technically dead, I hung limply, doing my best to hang appreciatively. "You are exceptional guardians, and I need your help before anyone else dies in there."

He thought about it, poking me with a finger. "Can I have a puppy, too?"

"Fine! Just give me some spirit bones so I can walk back to my body! I was well on my way before you snatched me out of the air."

"I didn't realize it was you," he argued defensively. "I wasn't about to let a soul just slip past me. You told me to guard the church!"

"So how did Izzy sneak in?" I argued.

Eve pursed her lips. "She said she was here to save Nosh."

I winced, not actually sure if she had succeeded or not. "Okay. Give me bones. I have to get back and see what's happened."

The two of them touched me, and their eyes suddenly blazed with burnished gold. I felt myself solidify, bone-by-bone, in a sickening, jerking series of movements. It didn't hurt at all, but it made me want to empty my stomach. I think. Adam and Eve's eyes slowly dimmed, and they studied me nervously, eyeing me up and down. Triumphant grins slowly stretched across their cheeks. "I told you letting us watch the Titans would be helpful!" Adam hissed, setting me down on my feet with exquisite care.

I took a few hesitant steps, shivering at the prickling sensations across my...soul. I could feel my physical body inside the church, beckoning me. Now that I had bones—of a sort—I was able to withstand the almost magnetic pull. But it gnawed at me like the fiercest, hollow hunger.

"Puppies!" Eve cried out, slapping palms with Adam.

He turned to look at the open doorway, his humor fading rapidly. "Do you want us to come inside and break things?" he asked, his eyes crackling with golden light again. "I've got a puppy, now. I'm feeling uniquely parental."

Eve nodded, slowly drawing one of her crystal scythes. "*No one harms Lady Applesauce.*"

I stared at her. "Who is Lady Applesauce?"

"My puppy. Of course." Then she took a step towards the open doorway, her face set in a stern grimace.

I flung my hands up, motioning for them to stop. "Neither of you have puppies yet! And I do not want you to enter the church. I don't want the Olympians seeing you. I don't want them knowing about the Titan souls inside you!" They relaxed slightly. Eve sheathed her scythe with a disappointed grumble.

"Now I have to come up with a new name," Adam complained, under his breath, but loud enough for all of us to hear.

I closed my eyes, wanting to scream.

"I'm going to send everyone out. Do either of you have healing powers?" I asked eagerly. "From your new souls?"

They shook their heads sadly. "No."

I sighed regretfully. "Just keep them safe, then. And don't hurt Aphrodite. She's a friendly," I said, hoping she was still alive after her numerous arrow wounds.

Their faces hardened and they looked suddenly violent. I winced, having almost forgotten their hatred of Olympians—likely made worse, now that they were harboring Titans.

"Aphrodite might even have some games she can teach you," I added. "*Private* games."

Adam blushed, shuffling from foot-to-foot. "Oh? I like games..." he said shyly.

Eve licked her lips. "I can stay my execution if she can help us with our...romantic executions," she said, grinning suggestively as she eyed Adam up and down.

He smirked, boyishly.

"Great. Fantastic. Keep everyone safe. I'll see you back home later," I said, eager to get back to my friends inside the church. I was hoping that since I had just encountered Hades, time was not a concern. Adam had hinted that only seconds had passed, but he wasn't the best judge of time.

Only one way to find out. I strode through the open doorway of Trinity Church.

Even with so many dead, my work was not finished. I could feel it in...

My soul.

## 53

I entered the church with a new perspective on life, much as leaders of such noble religious institutions might theoretically hope for from a first-time visitor. However, my perspective was not a quest for meaning or purpose. I was not noble. I was not humble.

And I was not even remotely repentant or apologetic.

Rather than entering on my knees, I was here to bring Artemis and Apollo to theirs.

Even though I was currently a wandering soul, when I saw that everything and everyone was frozen in a dim green glow, I let out a sharp breath of relief. My newly acquired spirit bones, if that was what they truly were, permitted me to feel much like I was back in my own body.

Except I wasn't. I could feel my physical body pulling at me, begging to be reunited with my restless soul. I resisted the sensation, feeling...restless.

Like a captured light-painting, no time seemed to have passed since I died.

Victoria and Natalie lay where I had last seen them, arrows jutting out of their chests. Izzy's illuminated hands hovered over my wounds, and her red-rimmed eyes were locked onto my lifeless face. She was weeping and angrily screaming at me as she worked to save me.

The four of us were bathed in pale moonlight from the gaping hole in the roof of the church.

I smiled vaguely at a sudden thought. Trinity Church. Of course it was. I hadn't even considered that. But...this was where our trinity had died.

Most surprisingly, I suddenly noticed another person in the church who was unaffected by the stoppage of time, although I didn't understand how or why she was here.

Selene stood over the three of us, crying softly. She seemed to sense my presence at the same time I sensed hers, and she slowly looked up. Her breath caught, and her eyes widened. Her lower lip began to tremble, and her shoulders shook. "Ambrogio," she whispered, her voice cracking with relief.

"Selene," I said, unable to make myself move as I tried wrapping my head around her presence. Rather than the violent version of Selene who I had last encountered in my bedchambers with Natalie and Victoria, the woman before me now was gentle and compassionate, her eyes windows to a depthless well of sympathy and patience.

She was a vibrant, seemingly young woman with long, silvery white hair. She wore a white silk toga that was clasped with a crescent moon brooch over her left shoulder. It draped down her chest at the diagonal to leave her other shoulder bare. She wore a loose belt of interconnected silver hoops that seemed to portray the phases of the moon. As above, so below—the bottom half of her shimmering white garment seemed to hitch up over her left hip before cutting down at the same angle, revealing almost her entire thigh, but ending just above her opposite knee.

Metallic lace sandals trailed up and around her calves, ending just below the knee.

Her skin was pale and almost seemed to emit a faint sheen when caught out of the corners of the eye. I was unable to avert my gaze in order to verify that, but I remembered it well from the past. This was the Selene I had first fallen in love with. The priestess who had been used as a tool by her own god, Apollo, to systematically and emotionally dismantle me from the foundation up.

After a few endless seconds, I felt a tear spill down my cheek, startling me. My soul...was crying. Seeing my tear, Selene let out a heartbroken sob. She immediately extended her hand towards me, her wrist shaking.

I let out a shaky sigh and joined her to stand over Natalie and Victoria. I enveloped her small hand in mine, sucking in a breath at the warm sensation of flesh on flesh, even though I was currently a soul without a body. She reacted the same way.

But neither of us let go. We squeezed tighter.

We cried silently—internally. Together.

"How are you here, and how can we touch if I'm a spirit?" I whispered.

"Lord Hades helped you more than you know," she whispered, eyeing the soulcatcher around my thumb. It throbbed with faint, green light. "And moonbeams are my domain. They are like bridges to me," she said, lifting her palm to indicate the moonlight shining down on us.

I nodded silently, not wanting to look a gift horse in the mouth.

I stared down at my broken body. As I stared down at the arrows sticking up from Natalie and Victoria's chests. "I tried," I finally whispered. Aphrodite, my protective big sister, had said that to me as well. Before she had shoved me down the aisle towards...moonlight.

Selene let out a whimper. "I know, Sorin. You always do."

Persephone's words drifted into my mind like whips to my back. *You really should have taken Aphrodite up on her gift...*

Not just Aphrodite...It had been Selene's gift, too.

And here she was, standing over my devils. Paying her last respects.

"You knew," I whispered, the severity of the situation dawning on me. "You all knew they would die tonight."

Selene shook, gripping my hand tight enough to hurt. "We feared," she finally whispered. "We broke rules to try to change the course of events. But the twins broke rules, too," she admitted.

I glanced back at Aphrodite, recalling how she'd doubled as Izzy, adamant about wanting to accompany me to the church. "That's why

she joined me tonight? To try and kill the twins before they could do...
this. It's why she gave Nosh the ribbons."

Selene nodded. "Yes."

"So, she knew Dracula was really Nosh?" I whispered.

Selene shook her head firmly. "No, but she wanted to give your son
—her nephew—a gift of protection. She did not know he would need it
so soon," she said sadly.

"Why are you here?" I asked gently.

She sighed. "Lord Hades said that he could save your soul but not
your heart. That only I could save you from letting rage consume you.
That justice was different from vengeance." She paused. "I'm not
certain that I was the best person for the job. Rage
sounds...appropriate."

I turned away, gritting my teeth. I swept my gaze throughout the
church, noticing the others paused in the middle of their fight. Artemis
and Apollo stood on the altar, each with drawn arrows. I glared at
them, the green glow to the room momentarily replaced with red
before snapping back. "I...am going to *hurt* them," I stammered,
shaking.

Selene nodded. "If you don't, I will. They have taken everything
from us."

My attention drifted to Bubble's dead body. "I cannot fail again," I
rasped. I had lost four women to the twins. And now, I was standing by
the first. The woman who truly owned my heart. The woman who
always would. The woman I could never touch. Until now.

"Do not focus on the failure, Ambrogio," she whispered. "Do not
cry. Get *mad*," she hissed with a quiet, gentle, bottomless
malevolence.

Her words were a balm to my wounded heart. Like a wife putting on
her husband's armor before a battle. "I can do that," I breathed, taking
one halting step towards the twins.

Then another.

I sucked in a breath to see Aphrodite in the process of rising from
her stomach. Her taut stomach and legs looked rooted to the ground,
but her previously useless arms were planted before her and locked
rigid, supporting her bare upper body so that she looked like she was

pressing herself up from the ledge of a river bank, emerging from the water after bathing.

Her gaze smoldered with determination as she gritted her teeth against her obvious pain. She was staring at my body further down the aisle. With the silver arrow fletching looming over her back, her pose reminded me of phoenix rising.

She must have heard Izzy's shout as I died and forced herself back upright. Damn. She didn't know the meaning of the word *quit*. And she had suffered all that pain simply to get my body closer to the moonlight.

Lightning abruptly crackled over my clenched fists. I looked around the room at the dozen arrows currently in flight—all aimed at Lucian and Nero, who were doing their best to advance without getting killed. My lightning lashed out and incinerated the airborne arrows to faint puffs of floating ash.

The three green spirits sprinting forward from Nero's hands slowly swiveled their heads to watch me as I passed. I'd seen them right before I had died, chasing Artemis and Apollo away from me. They nodded appreciatively but didn't speak or approach. Not knowing what else to do, and appreciating them trying to save me, I nodded back.

I reached my son—who was still trapped in the guise of Dracula. The nullification cuffs Nero had put on his wrists must have trapped his powers—all of them. He'd been relying on Aphrodite's ribbons to get him out. That was why Nero had been so adamant about asking if he had any last words before we abandoned *Dracula* to his fate.

Except Artemis had silenced him with her hunting powder, preventing him from goading his abductors into saying the activation word, *bonds*.

I calmly reached out and snapped the nullification cuffs. They exploded into pieces and then immediately froze in midair a fraction of a second later—little clouds of chaos kissed by order.

His Dracula guise didn't disappear, but that was because no time passed here.

The spirit tomahawk Izzy had thrown was buried in Bubble's chest, and there was no question that she was dead. I knelt down and brushed her hair from her face. My tears splashed onto her cheeks. We had only just been reunited. Her vengeance had consumed her long ago, making her a darker person, but I could have helped her with that. Like I had with Lucian. And Nero. And Nosh. I gently closed her eyes. "They will pay, Bubbling Brook. They. Will. All. Pay."

Then I closed my eyes as I pulled the spirit tomahawk out of her chest with a sickening sound.

I let out a breath, feeling the power of the spirit tomahawk vibrating against my palm, marrying the wild, erratic crackles of lightning dancing over my knuckles. I stood.

I approached Artemis and studied her from inches away. I could kill her. Right now.

But a swift, unseen death was too sweet and gentle of an eternal embrace for my dear sister. I stared at her silver bow and considered slicing the string. But weapons were not dangerous in and of themselves. The danger came from the person wielding the weapon. I stared down at the fingers holding the string. They were attached to her hand.

I calmly stepped back and swung the tomahawk down. It severed her wrist instantly, cauterizing the wound, and ruining her ability to use her bow. I stared at her, frowning. Then a dark smile split my cheeks. "Do you think I have time for one last drink?" I called out, glancing back at Selene.

I was surprised to find her standing directly behind me with a supportive smile. Her eyes glittered. "You have time for two."

I grinned back at her.

I turned and brushed an errant strand of Artemis' hair out of my way. Then I sunk my teeth into the soft flesh of her neck. I didn't know how it was possible to do such a thing as a spirit, but I was hoping it hurt her more than when bitten in real life. Molten blood struck my tongue and I gasped in surprise. I hadn't even been sure it would work, but I definitely hadn't anticipated such raw power! The lightning around my fists stabbed down at the ground with sharp cracking sounds like snapping bones.

I released myself, not wanting to kill her. Yet.

The puncture wounds on her neck oozed golden blood—just like I had seen from Aphrodite. I licked my lips. They were tingling and hot, and my mouth was salivating at the heady taste of a god's undiluted blood—significantly stronger than the blood she had once gifted to Victoria's father to turn their bloodline into assassins aimed at me.

I approached Apollo and stared at him for five long seconds, recalling every feature on his face from the first time I had met him so long ago—when he had cursed me so that sunlight scorched my flesh. I remembered how he had been the last one to shoot my big sister, Aphrodite, in the thigh, ultimately ceasing her interference.

I wondered where the real Benjamin had gone. The real Hazel.

As I pondered this riddle, I calmly sliced off both of his hands with the spirit tomahawk. Then I sunk my fangs into his neck and took a deep pull of Olympian blood. The hairs on my arms stood straight on end, and I saw tiny arcs of electricity dancing around them.

My eyes momentarily rolled back into my skull, and I had to force myself to stop feeding.

I stepped back, breathing heavily. Then I appraised my work, glancing from Artemis and Apollo. The tomahawk hissed in my fist, hungry for more action. I frowned after a few moments. "I feel like I'm forgetting something."

Selene stepped up beside me and rested her cheek against my shoulder with a contented, nostalgic sigh. She studied them in silence, and I wouldn't have minded her taking as much time as she needed. She pointed at Artemis. "They are twins." She released me and stepped back.

I followed her finger to see that Artemis still had one of her hands.

I nodded. "That's it." I walked up to Artemis and severed her other hand.

Finished with my work, I glanced back at Selene with a dark smile. She was holding her hand out imploringly, her cheeks damp and her eyes regretful. "It is time for us to part...Sorin," she said, as if tasting the name on her tongue. She had always called me Ambrogio. She was smiling wistfully.

I nodded woodenly and accepted her hand. The lightning enveloping my hand danced over hers, making her smile. "That tickles," she murmured.

We walked back towards my body and I paused beside Nosh to put the tomahawk into his hand. I closed his knuckles over it and sighed.

Izzy had just killed his mother to save him. That...was not going to be easy for him to accept. But I would help him.

I walked back with Selene, savoring these precious few moments. I had so much I wanted to say to her. Hades had been right. Her presence had helped focus me. My heart was full to bursting at the simple act of holding hands with my first love—an act that had been denied us in life. No matter how many things I wanted to say to her, simply touching her flesh with mine said more than any words could have. She squeezed my hand tightly, seeming to read my mind.

We paused over my body, both of us staring down at it. It was beaten, bloody, and broken—both inside and out.

But it was all I had. For better or worse.

"I love you, Selene," I whispered. "Always have, and I always will."

She stiffened, squeezing my hand hard enough to hurt. She lifted my hand to her mouth and kissed it, letting out an emotional sound. "I love you, too, Sorin," she whispered as another tear fell down her cheek. I smiled at her using the newer name.

Then she released me and took a step back. I knelt down and touched the wound in my side. The lightning slipped into the puckered hole and sucked me down with it before I had time to shout out in alarm.

## 54

I slipped back into my body with the stealthy nature of a young man sneaking into his lover's bedroom while her parents were asleep in the next room.

Then I tripped over the figurative empty chamber pot, sending it clanging across the floor.

The Olympian blood I had just consumed crackled out of me all at once in a concussive blast of internal lightning. Those wild bolts tore through my body, sewing up the hole in my blood reserves with threads of golden light, and then filling it up to overflowing with the godly ichor.

Next, it shredded my physical wounds, scraping off the black ice to clean the inflamed flesh. Finally, it pulled the edges closed with more golden threads, leaving both wounds glowing and pleasantly warm.

I opened my eyes and gasped to find myself back in the church. Back in the land of the living, since I saw no haunting green glow to the air.

Power raged through me, bringing back the full extent of my latent abilities for the first time since waking up from Deganawida's slumber. I wasn't just back to life; I was back with every vampiric power I had ever wielded. Stronger now than I had ever been, because my blood reservoir was pregnant with Olympian blood. The golden ichor was much thicker than any blood I had ever tasted—heavier, denser, and exceptionally more powerful.

Izzy squawked in shock. "SORIN!" she shrieked in relief, shaking me to verify that I was real. "You were just d-dead!" she stammered. "And why are your wounds *glowing?!*"

I leapt to my feet without any effort whatsoever, clenching my fists at my side.

I didn't look down at Izzy.

I didn't look at my wound.

I said four words.

"I found my soul."

My eyes locked onto Apollo and Artemis in time to see them suddenly bellow in pain and shock as their bows clattered to the ground. The airborne arrows I had destroyed simultaneously popped, emitting faint puffs of dust into the air. Lucian and Nero flinched in surprise, and then turned to gawk at me. I dipped my chin and lifted a finger to my mouth, requesting their silence. They nodded uncertainly.

I glanced to my left as Aphrodite climbed to her feet on unsteady legs. Her maddeningly beautiful nudity was marred with ghastly wounds and copious splashes of golden blood, but as she saw me appraising her, she squared her shoulders and lifted her chin high. Her eyes were wild with dark promises and whispered secrets of unbound pleasures.

But it was not directed at me. It was a result of her wounds—her innate powers were raw and close to the surface in order to embolden her and keep her alive. She stared at me with relief and unquenchable love. I dipped my chin and gave her a proud smile. She had saved my heart and soul. Her cheeks warmed as she flashed me a dazzling smile that made Nero begin a murmured rant about injustice and a general lack of appreciation from the opposite side of the room. Aphrodite shot him a smoky wink and his tirade cut off with an abrupt squeak. Then she slowly, painfully, made her way toward Izzy.

I turned back to Artemis and Apollo and smiled to find them both staring down at their missing hands. Then their stumps flew to their necks, sensing my bite.

I began to laugh. Loudly.

They jerked their attention up and stumbled back a step to see me alive and well. I watched their eyes closely, so I saw the *exact* moment they mentally chose to retreat—no doubt intending to use the vaporish puff that I'd seen Artemis utilize at Lucian's mountain.

I had been ready for it, and I instantly lashed out with fingers of lightning, gripping onto their ankles like shackles. Then I expanded it to surround them in a cage of electricity, preventing them from using magic or any other power. I wasn't sure how I did such a thing, but the stunned looks on their faces told me that it worked as intended.

I realized I clutched a bundle of glass daggers in one fist—identical to Zeus' lightning bolts. The twins blanched in horror, recognizing the glass daggers and what they signified—that I was no longer their mortal toy but a capable Olympian in my own right. Or the scariest demigod they had ever met, depending on who my mother truly was. The arcing tendrils of electricity crackling down my knuckles and forearms was icing on the cake. They couldn't flee and they couldn't move; their feet were rooted to the floor. And that also terrified them.

"Leave us," I said to my gathered friends. "Aphrodite will help you. She's already saved my life twice tonight," I said, shooting her an adoring smile. She'd helped me learn strength, dedication, and commitment—all forms of love, now that I thought about it. "She is my big sister, and she is my hero," I said firmly. Aphrodite sucked in her bottom lip and she nodded fervently. As she turned to the bodies of Natalie and Victoria, I saw a heartbroken frown drift across her momentary joy, smothering it. I turned to Lucian and Nero. "I will clean up here."

They nodded obediently, eyeing the electricity swarming over me. They'd seen it once before on the mountain, but not to this extent.

I turned away to find that Nosh no longer looked like Dracula, having shifted back to his true form while I had addressed everyone else. He was naked and kneeling over Bubbling Brook with a blank look on his face, although his cheeks were damp with tears. His tomahawk crackled in one fist, the blade resting against the wooden floor in a slowly expanding, charred ring. His wrists were bleeding from the shattered nullification cuffs, but it didn't look concerning.

Nosh slowly lifted his head to stare at Izzy across the room. My heart melted at the warring emotions in his eyes. He'd finally found his mother, only to have his girlfriend kill her. Rationally, I believed that it had been the singular moment that saved us. She had been so enraged, that she would have killed Nosh, thinking him Dracula. Then she would have begun killing everyone else in sight, flinging around the powers of Hecate and possibly tipping the scales towards Apollo and Artemis before they ended up killing her.

Then again, who knew how it would have played out? Maybe Hades had.

Either way, I knew that it would be some time before Nosh came to any such conclusion.

Nosh watched Izzy for a long moment before turning back to his mother. His hand trembled as he pinched her hair between his fingers. "Mother..." he rasped. "I tried to find you."

I grimaced at his pain. I turned back to my friends. "*We* will clean up here," I amended. "Go. Adam and Eve are waiting outside if you need their help carrying...Natalie and Victoria," I said, biting back the sudden swell of emotion—that I was sending them away rather than carrying them myself. "There is an entrance to the underground next door." Nero frowned at my mention of the Nephilim outside, but the rest took it in stride. I smiled at Aphrodite. "I promised Eve that you would teach them the ropes on their newfound...hobbies. I told her it was your specialty."

Her face split into an excited grin and she nodded. Then she scooped up Victoria in her arms, obviously refusing to let the Nephilim carry the both of them. This was a job for the big sister. Everyone shuffled out of the church where Nero would teleport them to safety, half of them supporting the others. I approached Nosh, ignoring the restrained Artemis and Apollo.

"Izzy didn't know," I said after a few moments of silence. "She was trying to save you."

He nodded numbly. "I...know."

"Why did you pretend to be Dracula?" I asked gently, kneeling down beside him.

"I got the idea from the Cauldron. Their grand plan," he laughed bitterly.

I grimaced. "It wasn't necessary. You could have just left it all alone."

His shoulders stiffened. "No. I could not. *You* deserved to kill Dracula. No one else. Not the Sisters, and certainly not the Olympians," he growled, glaring at Artemis and Apollo. "His death was *yours*. And... you risked your life to save Izzy from the Cauldron. I wanted to do the same for you, father." He was trembling as his eyes settled back on Bubbling Brook. "I had no idea that my own mother was leading the Sisters of Mercy. She...was beautiful," he croaked.

I hung my head tiredly. "I know, son. She *was*," I said, emphasizing the past tense. "But she let vengeance consume her. She let it *change* her. She formed the Cauldron and then the Sisters of Mercy—all to get a chance at killing Dracula," I whispered, recalling my conversation with Selene with a sad smile. "Don't let the fires of vengeance change you into something worse than the target of your hatred. Vengeance must be cold and rational—it must become *justice*."

Selene really had saved my heart tonight, just like Hades had intended. Because despite the emotions warring inside of me, I felt calm and detached about what would come next. They had earned their punishment, just like Hades had told me in the Underworld. I merely intended to give them a glimpse of their forthcoming eternal torture ahead of schedule.

I was sure Hades would not mind, the sick bastard.

Nosh nodded affirmatively. Then he slowly stood, and we walked down the aisle in tense silence. Nosh stared down the twins, suddenly twirling both tomahawks in his hands. Their edges were already blackened with crusted, Olympian blood.

His face was utterly blank, and his pulse was lower than I'd ever felt— which was saying something for him. "Justice. Okay." An ephemeral headdress shimmered into existence over his head, making him look twice as tall. Huge, glowing feathers fanned his face and trailed down past his tailbone. A matching, vapory set of buckskin pants covered his lower body, and his chest was suddenly glowing with war paint of the same magical hue.

I arched an eyebrow and then turned to gauge Artemis and Apollo's reactions. I was pleased to see the fear of the unknown in their eyes. Olympians weren't familiar with Nosh's flavor of badass. Neither was I, really.

I was eager to change that inadequacy. Maybe by watching and learning now.

A spirit bear suddenly rose up behind Nosh.

Apollo and Artemis looked equally alarmed to suddenly remember that they had no hands to fight off the bear. Incapability was its own fear, I'd found. Knowing that even if unrestrained, they couldn't do so much as claw their enemies with their fingernails was a poison that seeped down into their souls, murdering all semblance of courage and dignity. You couldn't even die fighting.

"You will never be an Olympian, boy," Apollo growled defiantly.

"I agree. I will end the Olympians," I said in a cold, flat tone, realizing that I meant it.

They scoffed incredulously.

"It is better than cowardly hiding behind mortals," I said, flashing Artemis a mocking smile.

She bared her teeth at me and then shot an accusing glare at Apollo. "I told you it was foolish to debase ourselves by associating with mortals."

"I'll make it a fair fight," I said, removing the electric cages, "but I'm not letting you run away. This ends here." With a thought, I made it so that the electric manacles on their ankles no longer impeded their ability to move within the church, but they could not escape the building.

Apollo did not waste time with words or threats. He flung his stumps at me and hurled the full might of the sun at me. Artemis bolted towards us, looking ready to bludgeon me to death with her stumpy arms. But she was fast and clever, so that could still be deadly.

I spread my arms wide and my cloak of shadow and blood flared out behind me, protecting Nosh from the scorching, unbearable heat of the sun. Church pews incinerated in puffs of embers and ash, and sections of the wooden floor simply ceased to exist in its wake.

That sunlight hit me, brushing my cheeks like a lover's kiss, and I let out a deep belly laugh. The sun...no longer harmed me.

That once-cursed light hit my cloak and rebounded, sending Artemis and Apollo both crashing back into the altar with a shout. I glanced over my shoulder to find Nosh huddled low in anticipation of the heat.

Everything behind my cloak was entirely unscathed. Nosh looked up at me, realizing this fact. Then he frowned. "I was just tying my spirit shoe. Are you ready to fight yet?"

I chuckled and turned back to our foes. Artemis was flat on her ass, clutching her side, but Apollo stood upright, eerily stiff and motionless. They both stared at us in stunned disbelief. The altar smoldered around them.

I frowned in disappointment as Nosh straightened beside me. I released my cloak and frowned at him. "I think the fight is already over," I said, pointing.

Nosh was quiet for a few moments and then he sighed. "That actually works for me," he said letting out an exhausted sigh.

I arched an eyebrow at him. He'd hardly done anything tonight. Unless maintaining his skinwalker guise was taxing.

"There's a dance back at the museum," he said very slowly, "and there is a girl I'm thinking about asking. If we hurry."

My heart skipped a beat and I smiled in relief. Izzy. He had forgiven Izzy—or at least he wanted to do so.

I wrapped my arm around his shoulders and jostled him lovingly. "Then let's get this over with. To be honest, after five hundred years, I think this fight is over as well. They don't even deserve the time and effort of a slow death. An unremarkable execution is more fitting. To let the other Olympians know that they are nothing special, and that they will be dealt with like pests."

Justice, not vengeance.

My heart, although broken, was full. The cracks from Natalie and Victoria's deaths were being held together by silver threads, rather than the golden threads that had healed my wounds from Artemis' arrows.

Threads of moonlight, thanks to Aphrodite bringing me to Selene.

Thanks to Hades for bringing Selene to me.

## 55

I walked up to the Olympians. They stared at me, seeming unable to move. Or unwilling. Artemis had a massive hole in her side from the ricocheted sunlight, and Apollo had—

"Holy shit!" Nosh cursed, pointing at Apollo. "Wasn't there a crucifix attached to that pedestal?" he hissed, pointing at the marble block Apollo was straddling. The Olympian's face was red with both pain and embarrassment.

I nodded slowly, crouching down to assess the somewhat melted pole rising up from the pedestal. Golden blood was trickling down its length where it suspiciously disappeared near Apollo's ass. I blinked.

Then I straightened with a grimace. "I'm pretty sure the crucifix is still there. We just can't see it, because it's...well, *in* there," I said meaningfully, gesturing at Apollo.

"Holy shit," Nosh repeated. Then he laughed. "Literally, as a matter of fact."

I nodded. "Now we know what took the fight out of him," I said, shrugging.

"Yeah," Nosh chuckled. "He's too full of the Holy Spirit to fight. Puts a whole new take on turning the other cheek."

Apollo gritted his teeth furiously, doing his best not to move an inch in any direction, but especially not up or down. His firmly planted feet were the only thing saving him from further torture, but his legs were shaking and trembling as blood oozed down the pedestal.

"Your trinity is dead. You are finished."

"A fact you should probably not bring up right now, given the circumstances," Nosh suggested dryly.

Apollo moved only his eyes. "Hera will destroy you," he rasped.

"I'm not hiding, so where is she?" I asked, snickering.

He pursed his lips. "You have no idea what you've done. All of Olympus will unite against you for this."

I nodded. "That will make things easier. I'd hate to have to hunt them all down."

Nosh nodded at my logistical assessment. "That is both taunting and factual."

"I could turn you," I told them, turning from one face to the other. "I've already bitten you once. Drink my blood and I can protect you from Hera. You could have a new chance, no longer forced to be her pawns. I turned the Nephilim," I said with a shrug. "You could help me rebuild."

"And we could help get that crucifix out of your ass. Not hands-on help," he clarified with a grimace, "but we could cut the base off the pedestal and let you figure out the rest."

A flicker of hope danced in Apollo's eyes.

"We could work together to make Olympus what it always should have been." I met his eyes, smiling gently. "Did you know Sorin means sun?" I asked, hoping to persuade him.

He gave a stiff nod. "Yes." Then he spasmed at a fresh pain. "What do we need to do?"

"Tell me where the real Hazel and Benjamin are."

He nodded. "The San Remo," he said, rattling off the address, suddenly extremely helpful now that he had a chance to escape his torture. "The northern corner penthouse on the top floor."

Nosh grunted. "You put them in one of the most expensive penthouses overlooking Central Park?" he blurted, baffled.

Artemis cleared her throat. She was holding a large portion of her stomach in place, looking like nothing more than a field-dressed animal, which was oddly poetic. "It is our penthouse. We moved into it when the humans fled the area after you brought your castle to the park," she spoke softly. Obviously in great pain. "It let us keep a close eye on you, and we needed Hazel and Benjamin close so we could ask them questions to better our disguises."

"A true son-of-a-bitch lived there," Apollo grunted. "Prick named Shayne—with a *y*—the pretentious asshole."

I cocked my head. "It's not like he picked his own name. Who cares about the spelling?"

Apollo grimaced. "He offended me."

"This I have to hear," Nosh murmured. "Have you even met this man?"

"No. Or he would be dead," Apollo said.

Artemis hissed in pain as she tried to shift her weight. Some of her organs slipped out and her face paled.

Nosh blanched. "Good lord. That is disgusting. Stop moving it!" he snapped.

She nodded weakly. "Shayne has a statue of my brother in the penthouse, and it is...defaced."

Apollo licked his lips urgently. "I don't want to talk about it. I agree to your terms," he snapped, sounding desperate.

I turned to Artemis, arching an eyebrow.

"I never wanted to work for her in the first place," she whispered, barely able to even breathe. "I agree."

I nodded, studying their faces as I considered the potential. Turning them, I could make them obedient whether they wanted to be or not. I could use them—their contacts, their powers, their knowledge. I could get answers.

And...I would be just like the other Olympians.

A slow, devilish grin split across my cheeks. "They thought I was serious, Nosh," I said softly. Because I had *never* intended to follow through. I'd entertained the benefits, but more as an idle curiosity than anything else.

I burst out laughing at the shame on their faces. That I'd gotten them to openly admit how easily they would turn coat. I'd just destroyed their honor on top of everything else.

"How?" Apollo whispered.

I knew what he truly meant. "I got my soul back," I said. "Even if you had won tonight, Dracula wouldn't have been able to help you. My soul was safely tucked away, and none of you knew it."

He blinked rapidly. "Hades," he breathed. "He's behind all of this?" he asked, his eyes darting behind me towards the church.

I shook my head. "No," I lied. "He just helped me even the odds. Told me to do as I pleased, but that you two pieces of trash were tarnishing the family name."

I turned to Artemis, recalling something all of a sudden. "You told me that you wanted me bleeding out at your feet, whimpering your name. And that you wanted Apollo to witness it all."

She grimaced at my sudden smile.

"I think that's a marvelous idea." I calmly knelt down before her. Then I drew a claw down my finger and let my blood drip onto her toes. "Artemis!" I whimpered in mock terror. "Artemis, no! Artemis, please!"

I glanced back at Nosh to gauge his review of my performance. He had stepped up beside Apollo, draping an arm over the god's shoulders. The added weight forcing Apollo down onto his implement of impalement had to be pure murder. Then Nosh patted him on the back forcefully, smiling at his fellow audience member's gasp. "Who knew he could act?" Nosh asked. Then he patted Apollo on the shoulders one last time, stepped away, and spun back to the God of the Sun.

His tomahawk severed Apollo's head from his shoulders so fast that the head fell forwards, bumping into Artemis' feet. She screamed. Apollo's body slowly slid down the pole as his legs finally gave out. I turned away, not wanting to see what would eventually rise out of Apollo's gaping neck. It definitely wouldn't be a sunrise.

More like a *son* rise. I hadn't noticed if a depiction of Jesus Christ had been on the crucifix.

I let Artemis' scream continue for a few moments. Nosh finally bent down to scoop up Apollo's head and shoved it into her arms. "Cut it out, would you? He gave you what you asked for, you ungrateful hag. You've done far worse to countless others, and all of them better than your brother. And that is before we begin to recount the atrocities you've directly and indirectly inflicted upon my own family."

She held her brother's head, unable to drop it for fear of the imagined consequence of dishonoring her brother, but also not wanting to
hold such a macabre trophy.

Rather than drawing it out, I met Nosh's eyes. He gave me a resolute
nod. I turned back to the Goddess of the Hunt. Justice, not vengeance; I
would not mention my devils or Selene. I'd already paid them for that
by slicing off each of their hands—one for Natalie and one for Victoria.

"This is for Stevie."

And I decapitated her, swinging my claws through her throat with a
growl. The church fell peacefully silent as the two heads rolled, finally
coming to a stop at my feet, their cheeks pressed together. I let out a
sigh of relief. It...was done.

Everyone who had cursed me had paid for their efforts. Well, Hades
had been protecting me.

But I had granted the twins the justice they deserved—Hades'
method of justice.

I scooped up both heads and met Nosh's eyes. "Let's go—Gah!"

My soulcatcher suddenly hummed against my thumb, instinctively
making me clutch the heads to my chest. I stared down at my hand in
alarm, only for the ring to suddenly calm.

Nosh was frowning at me. "Are you okay, father?" he asked
nervously.

I nodded stiffly. "Felt like one of them moved," I said quickly. "Startled me."

Nosh nodded slowly. "Okay."

"That was a mercy killing. Trust me. I've fantasized about much
worse."

"I know. They deserved it." He glanced back at his waiting spirit
bear. "Guess I didn't need him after all. Thought that was going to be a
lot more difficult," he said, waving a hand. The bear evaporated into
fog, looking crestfallen.

"They are just gods, Nosh. Nothing to get worked up about." I
glanced at the destroyed church and sighed. With the fight over, I realized I had nothing to do. Natalie and Victoria were dead. No great
victory waited for me, and I suddenly felt rudderless at my bitter win.
"We have a long walk ahead of us."

Nosh nodded wearily. Then he paused, glancing down at the ground. Two ornate bows rested there. The deadly silver bow Hades had warned me about, and Apollo's thicker, sturdier bow. Nosh glanced up at me with a smile. "Mementos."

I nodded, and he bent to scoop them up.

"How did Izzy get here?" he asked, slipping the weapons over his shoulder.

I slowly turned to look at him, frowning. "I don't know. She drove, probably."

Nosh grinned. "She has a hide-a-key!" He was already urging me towards the door. "And Nero took them back the fast way."

I let out a breath of relief. "Let's go check. We can send someone up to Shayne's penthouse to collect Hazel and Benjamin."

"Don't you want to at least see the statue?" Nosh asked, smirking. "You *know* you do..."

I smiled, hefting Apollo's head. "I think we've done enough defacing of Apollo, if beheading counts." Nosh grinned, shrugging. "Now that the penthouse is vacant, maybe you and Izzy should check it out."

That drew him up short.

But he was smiling.

# 56

We had made it back to the museum fairly quickly after successfully finding Izzy's spare key.

I'd tucked the spare heads under my arms as we slipped into the back entrance of the museum so as not to crash the social mixer or be swamped with hundreds of questions. We made it down to the catacombs without encountering anyone, eager to find our party from the church, rather than attending the party raging above.

I had promised Nosh that I would send someone out to Trinity Church to collect the bodies we had left behind. Especially Bubbling Brook's body. I wasn't sure how no humans had noticed us destroying the place, but I was betting it was related to the odd repelling spell I'd initially felt outside the church that had seemed to keep bystanders back. I didn't know how long that spell would last, so I wanted to get someone back there before anyone else found the murder scene.

Stevie had contacts to help with body removals and crime scene clean up, but Stevie had died. I was hoping that Benjamin could step up to help me. To help his new boss, Lucian.

We came to a stop outside my bedchambers to find Nero waiting for us. He opened his mouth, and then he noticed the severed heads under my arms for the first time. "Oh. That's...pleasant," he said.

"Can you put them on a shelf for me?" I asked, shoving them into his arms before he could say otherwise.

He watched me with a sad expression on his face, knowing the pain I was in. "Of course."

"Where are they?" I asked softly.

He hung his head. "I will—"

"I will take my brother," Aphrodite said, stepping up from behind me.

Nero nodded in understanding. "The real Dracula is nice and comfy in the prison, so you can interrogate him at your leisure."

I nodded absently. "Some other time." I turned to Aphrodite, waiting. She held out her hand and I took it, realizing that she was still bloody from battle, but that she wore one of my robes. She'd gotten the arrows taken out of her back, at least. She held a mug of some spicy tea in her other hand, and it seemed to be healing her. She noticed my attention and smiled. "Ambrosia."

I grunted. Ambrosia was the nectar of the gods, and my namesake. "It healed you," I said, taking her hand in mine, needing to feel hot flesh against mine, rather than the cold flesh of Apollo and Artemis' heads.

"Yes. My *Ambrogio* is healing me," she said with a gentle smile.

I returned the look with a smile of my own. She had said Ambrogio, not Ambrosia, indicating that I was healing her, not the drink.

"Let's go grab a drink and compare notes," Nosh told the necromancer, hefting the newly acquired bows over his shoulder. "You're never going to believe what happened to Apollo, and we have a statue we need to steal for Șorin..." I smiled absently at the idea of them stealing the defaced statue of Apollo as they walked out of earshot.

Aphrodite watched them leave, eyeing the bows with a proud smile. "Much better in your hands, brother. Although you don't need two."

I nodded. "Want one?"

"No," she said, smiling. "But thank you. Perhaps you will find someone worthy of it, some day," she said thoughtfully.

We turned and made our way towards the storage rooms, of which there were hundreds. We walked in silence, both saddened and relieved. We had survived, but others had not.

"You've changed things," she said softly. "I don't see you like I saw you yesterday. I've never looked at a handsome man the same way I look at you. It is strange."

I arched an eyebrow. "It is strange to see a man and not desire to have sex with him?" I asked.

She nodded seriously. "For me, yes." She smiled. "But it is oddly fulfilling in a different way," she admitted. She glanced down, indicating our joined hands. "This feels nice."

I studied our hands for longer than I needed to, trying to formulate a serious answer. She was trying to have a meaningful conversation about something she didn't fully understand. Mocking her would be cruel.

"Family," I said, thinking out loud. "Trust." I met her eyes. "Love."

She nodded thoughtfully. "I like them. Very much. They offer different, lasting pleasures."

I absently stroked the soulcatcher around my thumb. I was almost entirely certain that it had consumed Apollo and Artemis' souls, but I didn't want to claim so until I spoke to Hades again. I had questions for him. Like, where the hell had my soul been the whole time, and how had I gotten it back? Adam had claimed sensing me at the gates to Castle Ambrogio right before he'd snatched my soul out of the air. But I'd briefly seen Hades and he'd punched me with his soulcatcher. So, had my soul been inside the Soul Spring at Castle Ambrogio or inside Hades' soulcatcher? Or somewhere else.

I sighed and soon found myself catching her up on Artemis and Apollo's final moments.

Aphrodite spewed her Ambrosia all over my face upon hearing about the crucifix impalement. She was also laughing too hard immediately after to apologize for it. I found my scowl fading and I began to laugh along with her. Before long, the two of us were coming up with inappropriate slogans and phrases to memorialize the occasion with a t-shirt or new coffee mugs.

When we'd exhausted our creative juices, I let out a sigh, realizing that we were now far removed from public halls where another vampire might have interrupted us.

"There will be repercussions for their deaths, but we will handle it together," she said.

I nodded. "Thank you for coming to the church tonight."

She smiled, squeezing my hand. "Of course."

"You inspired me. Shoving me across the floor like that, even when the twins were taking shots at you."

She smiled faintly, looking surprisingly shy. "Someone needed to do it."

"Do what, exactly?" I asked, wondering if I would hear a solid answer.

She considered her response. "Hades told me that moonlight was your salvation."

I watched my big sister. Her eyes were tight with pain, and glossy with tears. I could tell she was hurting inside, knowing my next words. The self-blame was obvious. "I know it wasn't your fault, sister. Natalie and Victoria. But I want to know how you knew they would die. You knew back when we first met. Selene told me."

A tear fell down her cheeks. "Selene can be blind as a bat at times," she said with a cracked sob, her shoulders slumping. "I wanted so badly to save them for you, but I failed. We all failed. I thought I could at least get you to taste happiness once before they died," she sobbed, crying messily. Then she abruptly hurled her empty mug against the wall, shattering it. "All I wanted was your happiness!"

I drew her to a halt and wrapped my arms around her, hugging her tight. She sobbed into my neck, her entire body shaking. "You did make me happy, Aphrodite. I was able to talk with Selene. I even held her hand," I whispered.

She cried harder.

And...I let her.

One day, I might need her to do the same for me. To stand there like a boulder in a raging river and keep me grounded.

She would probably do so naked and beautiful, which was a sight better than my current filthy state. She finally pulled back, wiping at her eyes. "I'm sorry."

I gave her a warm smile, waving off her concern. I glanced around us as she composed herself. "Are they close?" I asked.

She nodded, pointing at a nearby door. "It is a refrigerated room the museum once used for certain specimens, apparently. Hugo showed it to me."

I stared at the door, gathering my courage. "Okay. I might need your help," I admitted, recalling how I had been there for her moment of grief a few seconds ago.

She nodded determinedly, gripping my hand again. We approached the door, and she opened it for me, ushering me inside what seemed part surgical room and part library. Natalie and Victoria lay on a long, wide table in the center of the room. Candles were burning, filling the room with the familiar scent of fennel and anise.

I glanced over at Aphrodite curiously, indicating the candles.

She smiled. "They were burning in the bathroom when I first met you. They lit them, expecting a happier turning of events. You went in there the last time you touched them, so I thought it would be... comforting," she admitted sadly.

My throat tightened at her kindness.

I slowly approached the table, staring down at Natalie and her short, blonde hair. Her eyes were closed, and her face looked peaceful. I imagined her inappropriate jokes and crude humor, the fiery passion she kept stoked like a blacksmith's forge.

I turned to Victoria, the would-be assassin who Artemis had aimed at me centuries before. I remembered meeting her at the auction and laughing.

Both faces brought a smile to my own, remembering the good times we had shared. The things we had learned together. We had only known each other a month, but it had felt like much longer. I'd kissed them once or twice, but nothing more. Only once or twice...

Why not three times?

I slowly bent down and lightly kissed their foreheads. There. My knees buckled and Aphrodite caught me, holding me upright.

I had missed out on the finer things we could have shared. I'd finally had a chance to explore love, and I'd squandered it *myself* this time.

I wasn't sure how long we stood there, but I remembered that Aphrodite never broke physical contact with me. Not once.

Even when I cried and fell asleep with my head in her lap to her murmured words as she lovingly stroked my hair with her fingers.

"I will never leave you, my Ambrosia. Your sister will help you find happiness, brother. Happiness or blood..."

## 57

**M**any days passed in a numb, uneventful haze. I went through the motions of being the most powerful vampire in the world, not finding anything particularly pleasant about it.

It wasn't even necessarily the loss of Natalie and Victoria, although that had hit me hard. We had known each other such a short time, but it felt like so much longer. It hadn't even been a week since we had decided to become romantic. It wasn't even Bubbling Brook's death that shook me. Three women who had dared to get close to me, and all had suffered for it. Their funerals had taken place on the lawns of Castle Ambrogio, so that they were always close to home.

It was more that I couldn't find anything to truly care about. No matter how hard I tried, love always escaped me. Usually violently and with deep pain.

I hadn't met with Dracula, leaving him to ripen in the museum's prison instead.

Izzy and Nosh were looking into acquiring puppies for Adam and Eve, which was made difficult since the Nephilim could not go inspect the offerings themselves. The act of puppy hunting had served to bring her closer to Nosh, the two of them working together on the task. Their laughter and warm embraces soon filled the halls of the museum. When they weren't enjoying their new penthouse, anyway.

The vampire mixer had gone off to great success, and I soon saw reborn vampires socializing with the present-day vampires, forming friendships and bonds together.

I kept to myself.

Lucian had left the wolves to Benjamin after he'd been recovered from the penthouse with Sister Hazel. Dr. Stein had taken a liking to the eyeless monster almost immediately, and we had hardly seen the pair since.

Lucian preferred to work with Benjamin rather than hundreds of werewolves. He also hadn't regained his human form, so he wasn't much help in talking to the pack. Well, he growled at them often. He had spent centuries away from others, and had grown grouchy in his old age.

I empathized with him. In fact, Lucian and Nero hardly ever left my side. Aphrodite was practically my servant, bending over backwards to do anything I asked quicker than I could ask it. The four of us played a lot of board games to pass our time—well, Lucian watched or dozed while we played—as we waited for Olympus to respond to the murder of Apollo and Artemis.

They did not respond.

So, we played more games. A hellish number of games. And we waited. And I grew darker.

I sat before the fire in my outer rooms, absently sipping a Bloodee as I watched the dancing tendrils latch onto a fresh log. It reminded me of the lightning over my knuckles. I hadn't experimented with it. I also hadn't experimented with my reclaimed vampire powers.

A sudden crash in the hall outside drew my attention. "Sorin!" Nero shouted, sounding panicked. He and Lucian had only just left the room five minutes earlier. "Hurry!"

I set my mug down and bolted for the door. I flung it open and raced out into the halls—

And I was suddenly outside. I flexed my claws, snarling as I whipped my head left and right. No one attacked, and I was all alone.

And I stood atop Lucian's mountain.

I narrowed my eyes suspiciously, turning back around. A rectangular hole in the air showed me Nero and Lucian on the other side, back in the museum. Lucian was panting, wagging his tail, and Nero was grinning like a maniac. I took a step towards him, snarling. "What is—"

"See ya, brother!" he hooted, and he snapped the fingers of his skeleton hand. The door back promptly winked out, leaving me miles from civilization in upstate New York. I didn't have a car, and I didn't even know which direction to walk to get back to the city.

I gritted my teeth in frustration. Was this some kind of prank? A joke to lift my spirits?

"Oh, I'll lift his spirit alright," I promised, growling under my breath. "I'll lift it right out of his body." My eyes flicked to the soul-catcher on my thumb and I shuddered, realizing that it was something I could accomplish with little effort. I closed my eyes and took a deep breath of the clean mountain air.

I turned back to the cliff, staring up at the night sky. The moon hung high overhead, looking impossibly large.

"Sorin?" a new voice shouted, sounding startled.

I turned to see a woman in a white toga standing at the edge of the cliff. The moonlight shone down on a familiar woman, making my breath catch as it seemed to enrich her natural beauty. My anger flickered away and died, and my heart skipped a few dozen beats.

"Selene. What are *you* doing here?" I asked, jogging towards her.

She waited for me to approach, and I slowed to see that she was scowling into the middle distance. She punched a fist into her palm and began to pace. "That sleazy, good for nothing—"

I instinctively smiled at her angry shuffling, having seen it a time or two when we had been together, long ago. "What is it?" I asked, trying to hide my amusement.

She rounded on me. "I was having tea with the girls—"

"Because it's Friday," I said without meaning to, nodding.

She stopped in her tracks to stare at me with a wary look. "How did you know *that*?" I sensed an undertone of surprised appreciation—that I'd somehow known a private aspect of her life.

"One of them mentioned it in passing." I smiled wider at her sudden discomfort. At the way the moonlight cast her blushing cheeks in a soft, purplish glow.

She studied me in silence, looking curious and suspicious. "If it was said in passing," she said, walking closer, "how did you remember it so quickly?"

I lowered my eyes, trying not to become distracted by old emotions. "It stuck, for some reason," I said softly.

"Did someone trick you into coming here, Sorin?" she asked.

I glanced up sharply. "Yes. Did the same thing happen to you—"

I froze as the pieces clicked together.

Selene gave me a slow, dramatic nod. But a warm smile was stretching across her cheeks. "I think your dear, foolish sister is up to her old tricks," she said almost nervously, clasping her hands and staring down at the ground.

I nodded uncomfortably, not entirely sure what to say. Aphrodite had tricked her into coming here at the exact same time Nero had tricked me into coming here, forcing us to meet.

Together. In private.

"Maybe we could talk?" I suggested, feeling just as uncomfortable as Selene looked.

Selene let out a faint laugh, pointing at the cliff. There, near the edge, was a table with two chairs, a bottle of wine, and two chalices. A large fur blanket rested in the grass beside it, piled with pillows, blankets, and a platter of food. On the table was an electronic timer, counting down from eight hours. Propped up against one of the boulders were the bows I had taken from Artemis and Apollo.

And I suddenly remembered how Aphrodite had vowed to find me happiness or blood. Since no Olympians had attacked, she'd chosen to hunt down a little happiness for me. I stared at the silver bow pensively.

She had also mentioned that I might find someone worthy of taking one off of my hands.

Someday.

It looked like Aphrodite thought that *someday* was *tonight*. At least for the next eight hours anyway.

"They are not subtle," I said, biting back a smile. "Do you still remember how to shoot?" I asked, unable to look directly at her.

"Yes. I quite enjoy it, actually," she said with a shy smile, not looking at the bows.

I nodded, rooted to the ground. "That is good." I continued staring at her, feeling something for the first time in days. My heart felt like a muscle being stretched—hesitantly—after a long run. A familiar, soothing balm being rubbed into old, tired muscles.

She stared back, her smile widening at my obvious trepidation.

"I brought Artemis and Apollo to justice," I blurted.

She dipped her chin. "I know. I am no longer banished."

My breath caught. "Banished?"

"I was not permitted to show my face anywhere on Earth without their permission," she said very slowly. "Tea with Hecate, Persephone, and Aphrodite has been my only escape, and even that was a significant risk. We often went to the Underworld so as not to draw their ire."

I flinched as if struck. Her visit to me with Hephaestus' chains brought on a whole new meaning—the danger she had risked to deliver a message to me.

"Was," I said, my hands shaking. "You said *was*."

She nodded very slowly, licking her lips. "Yes. I am banished no longer."

I stared at her, my heart beating wildly. An impossible hope screamed through me, followed with just as much apprehension. "We can talk. Two Olympians. Have tea." My eyes shot to the bows. "Shoot arrows."

She smiled shyly. "Yes."

"I feel very nervous right now," I admitted, realizing that I was sweating profusely.

She bit back a laugh. "I am also nervous. Perhaps we could sit down?" she suggested.

I nodded jerkily, uprooting my feet from the ground so that I could stomp closer.

We sat down on the fur blanket and stared out at the moonlit valley. Neither of us moved.

We did not look at each other. We did not touch. We just sat beside each other, much like we had done when we had been married so long ago.

But the tension...

Was unbearable. Not in a physical manner, but in a thick cloud of unspoken conversation. All the things we didn't say, were too nervous to say.

"Do you think Hades knew?" I asked softly.

She didn't look over, but we could clearly see each other in our peripheral vision. "Hades always knows more than he lets on." She let out a flustered breath. "Before all of this began, Hades told me something in passing, and I'm only beginning to think it might have meant more."

I turned to her with a frown. "Oh?"

She met my eyes and I almost gasped, forced to avert my eyes. She was so close...

"He said it in such a way that it felt like part of the conversation, or maybe a frustrated curse. After the church, I wonder if it might have been something more," she whispered uneasily.

My heart beat wildly in my chest. "What did he say?"

"Olympus will fall when the sun kisses the moon." She was silent for a time. At the word *kiss*, I flinched, because I had been staring at her lips with entirely too much interest.

Selene grinned briefly. "This is serious, Sorin. Focus."

I nodded. "What do you think it means, Selene?"

She shook her head, a strand of hair falling across her collarbone. "I do not know. But I think we need to find out so that we can use it as a weapon. To strike them first."

I nodded, smiling at the sudden fire in her voice. "I agree."

"Hades is obsessed with constellations because he is stuck in the Underworld. But all I can think of is an eclipse," she murmured, speaking so softly that I almost couldn't hear it. I was too busy staring at her lips again to be of any help, but I knew little about constellations anyway.

I thought about Apollo, and how I had turned his own sunlight against him.

I thought about Artemis, and how silver no longer harmed me.

The two of us stared out at the valley, smiling at the moonlight painting the forest in a pale, silvery glow. It would be just as breathtaking with the sunrise. I froze at the thought.

I turned to Selene. "Do you know how to get back, or are you stuck here, too?"

She smiled brightly, making her eyes sparkle. "I am stuck here, but I do not mind. Why? Is my company not enough?" she asked, glancing over at me.

I shook my head adamantly. "I've never seen a sunrise with you," I whispered, pointing out at the valley. "Would you like to change that?" I asked.

Her breath caught and her eyes glistened. She clutched my hand tightly. "I would love to see a sunrise with you, Sorin."

I squeezed her hand, not daring to do more.

"We're going to need more arrows if you're going to break in your new silver bow tonight," I murmured.

She smiled. "It is mine now?" she asked, smiling excitedly.

I nodded. She shifted closer, leaning her head against my shoulder. I had to force myself to continue breathing. "Thank you," she whispered.

*It always has been yours, Selene.*

And I wasn't thinking of the bow. I was thinking of second chances. Of focusing on the things that really mattered. I wasn't ready for new love. I was still hurt and wounded.

But...old love?

Maybe...someday.

For now, I would enjoy a sunrise and a full heart.

Sharing a first with...my first.

**The Devil of New York City returns in 2020**

*Turn the page to read a sample from Shayne's other worldwide bestselling novels in* **The TempleVerse**—*The Nate Temple Series.*
*He worked really hard on them. Some are marginally decent—easily a solid 4 out of 10.*

# TRY: OBSIDIAN SON (NATE TEMPLE #1)

There was no room for emotion in a hate crime. I had to be cold. Heartless. This was just another victim. Nothing more. No face, no name.

Frosted blades of grass crunched under my feet, sounding to my ears alone like the symbolic glass that one would shatter under a napkin at a Jewish wedding. The noise would have threatened to give away my stealthy advance as I stalked through the moonlit field, but I was no novice and had planned accordingly. Being a wizard, I was able to muffle all sensory evidence with a fine cloud of magic—no sounds, and no smells. Nifty. But if I made the spell much stronger, the anomaly would be too obvious to my prey.

I knew the consequences for my dark deed tonight. If caught, jail time or possibly even a gruesome, painful death. But if I succeeded, the look of fear and surprise in my victim's eyes before his world collapsed around him, was well worth the risk. I simply couldn't help myself; I had to take him down.

I knew the cops had been keeping tabs on my car, but I was confident that they hadn't followed me. I hadn't seen a tail on my way here, but seeing as how they frowned on this kind of thing I had taken a circuitous route just in case. I was safe. I hoped.

Then my phone chirped at me as I received a text.

I practically jumped out of my skin, hissing instinctively. "Motherf—" I cut off abruptly, remembering the whole stealth aspect of my mission. I was off to a stellar start. I had forgotten to silence the damned phone. *Stupid, stupid, stupid!*

My heart threatened to explode inside my chest with such thunderous violence that I briefly envisioned a mystifying Rorschach blood-blot that would have made coroners and psychologists drool.

My body remained tense as I swept my gaze over the field, sure that I had been made. My breathing finally began to slow, my pulse returning to normal, as I noticed no changes in my surroundings. Hopefully, my magic had silenced the sound and my resulting outburst. I glanced down at the phone to scan the text and then typed back a quick and angry response before I switched the cursed phone to vibrate.

Now, where were we...

I continued on, the lining of my coat constricting my breathing. Or maybe it was because I was leaning forward in anticipation. *Breathe,* I chided myself. *He doesn't know you're here.* All this risk for a book. It had better be worth it.

I'm taller than most, and not abnormally handsome, but I knew how to play the genetic cards I had been dealt. I had shaggy, dirty blonde hair, and my frame was thick with well-earned muscle, yet still lean. I had once been told that my eyes were like twin emeralds pitted against the golden-brown tufts of my hair—a face like a jewelry box. Of course, that was two bottles of wine into a date, so I could have been a little foggy on her quote. Still, I liked to imagine that was how everyone saw me.

But tonight, all that was masked by magic.

I grinned broadly as the outline of the hairy hulk finally came into view. He was blessedly alone—no nearby sentries to give me away. That was always a risk when performing this ancient rite-of-passage. I tried to keep the grin on my face from dissolving into a maniacal cackle.

My skin danced with energy, both natural and unnatural, as I manipulated the threads of magic floating all around me. My victim stood just ahead, oblivious of the world of hurt that I was about to unleash. Even with his millennia of experience, he didn't stand a chance. I had done this so many times that the routine of it was my only enemy. I lost count of how many times I had been told not to do it again; those who knew declared it *cruel, evil, and sadistic.* But what fun wasn't? Regardless, that wasn't enough to stop me from doing it again. And again. Call it an addiction if you will, but it was too much of a rush to ignore.

The pungent smell of manure filled the air, latching onto my nostril hairs. I took another step, trying to calm my racing pulse. A glint of gold reflected in the silver moonlight, but the victim remained motionless, hopefully unaware or all was lost. I wouldn't make it out alive if he knew I was here. Timing was everything.

I carefully took the last two steps, a lifetime between each, watching the legendary monster's ears, anxious and terrified that I would catch even so much as a twitch in my direction. Seeing nothing, a fierce grin split my unshaven cheeks. My spell had worked! I raised my palms an inch away from their target, firmly planted my feet, and squared my shoulders. I took one silent, calming breath, and then heaved forward with every ounce of physical strength I could muster. As well as a teensy-weensy boost of magic. Enough to goose him good.

"*MOOO!!!*" The sound tore through the cool October night like an unstoppable freight train. *Thud-splat!* The beast collapsed sideways into the frosty grass; straight into a steaming patty of cow shit, cow dung, or, if you really want to church it up, a Meadow Muffin. But to me, shit is, and always will be, shit.

Cow tipping. It doesn't get any better than that in Missouri.

Especially when you're tipping the *Minotaur*. Capital M.

Razor-blade hooves tore at the frozen earth as the beast struggled to stand, grunts of rage vibrating the air. I raised my arms triumphantly. "Boo-yah! Temple 1, Minotaur 0!" I crowed. Then I very bravely prepared to protect myself. Some people just couldn't take a joke. *Cruel, evil,* and *sadistic* cow tipping may be, but by hell, it was a *rush*. The legendary beast turned his gaze on me after gaining his feet, eyes ablaze as he unfolded to his full height on two tree-trunk-thick legs, hooves magically transforming into heavily-booted feet. The thick, gold ring dangling from his snotty snout quivered as the Minotaur panted, and his dense, corded muscle contracted over his human-like chest. As I stared up into those brown eyes, I actually felt sorry...for, well, myself.

"I have killed greater men than you for less offense," he growled.

I swear to God his voice sounded like an angry James Earl Jones. Like Mufasa talking to Scar.

"You have shit on your shoulder, Asterion." I ignited a roiling ball of fire in my palm in order to see his eyes more clearly. By no means was it a defensive gesture on my part. It was just dark. But under the weight of his glare, even I couldn't buy my reassuring lie. I hoped using a form of his ancient name would give me brownie points. Or maybe just not-worthy-of-killing points.

The beast grunted, eyes tightening, and I sensed the barest hesitation. "Nate Temple...your name would look splendid on my already long list of slain idiots." Asterion took a threatening step forward, and I thrust out my palm in warning, my roiling flame blue now.

"You lost fair and square, Asterion. Yield or perish." The beast's shoulders sagged slightly. Then he finally nodded to himself in resignation, appraising me with the scrutiny of a worthy adversary. "Your time comes, Temple, but I will grant you this. You've got a pair of stones on you to rival Hercules."

I pointedly risked a glance down towards the myth's own crown jewels. "Well, I sure won't need a wheelbarrow any time soon, but I'm sure I'll manage."

The Minotaur blinked once, and then bellowed out a deep, contagious, snorting laughter. Realizing I wasn't about to become a murder statistic, I couldn't help but join in. It felt good. It had been a while since I had allowed myself to experience genuine laughter.

In the harsh moonlight, his bulk was even more intimidating as he towered head and shoulders above me. This was the beast that had fed upon human sacrifices for countless years while imprisoned in Daedalus' Labyrinth in Greece. And all of that protein had not gone to waste, forming a heavily woven musculature over the beast's body that made even Mr. Olympia look puny.

From the neck up he was entirely bull, but the rest of his body more resembled a thickly-furred man. But, as shown moments ago, he could adapt his form to his environment, never appearing fully human, but able to make his entire form appear as a bull when necessary. For instance, how he had looked just before I tipped him. Maybe he had been scouting the field for heifers before I had so efficiently killed the mood.

His bull face was also covered in thick, coarse hair—even sporting a long, wavy beard of sorts, and his eyes were the deepest brown I had ever seen. Cow shit brown. His snout jutted out, emphasizing the gold ring dangling from his glistening nostrils, catching a glint in the luminous glow of the moon. The metal was at least an inch thick, and etched with runes of a language long forgotten. Thick, aged ivory horns sprouted from each temple, long enough to skewer a wizard with little effort. He was nude except for a beaded necklace and a pair of worn leather boots that were big enough to stomp a size twenty-five imprint in my face if he felt so inclined.

I hoped our blossoming friendship wouldn't end that way. I really did.

**_Get your copy of OBSIDIAN SON online today!_**

# MAKE A DIFFERENCE

Reviews are the most powerful tools in my arsenal when it comes to getting attention for my books. Much as I'd like to, I don't have the financial muscle of a New York publisher.

But I do have something much more powerful and effective than that, and it's something that those publishers would kill to get their hands on.

**A committed and loyal bunch of readers.**

Honest reviews of my books help bring them to the attention of other readers.

If you've enjoyed this book, I would be very grateful if you could spend just five minutes leaving a review (it can be as short as you like) on my book's Amazon page.

Thank you very much in advance.

# ACKNOWLEDGMENTS

I couldn't do this without my readers—those wayward souls who crave adventure, encouragement, tears, laughter, danger, and confidence. You are all enablers to my madness.

And I love you for it. I'll keep wording, you keep reading. I'll do my goodest.

Also, take a gander at that kick ass cover! I know a wizard, obviously. Check her out here:

*Cover Design By Jennifer Munswami - J.M Rising Horse Creations*

# ABOUT SHAYNE SILVERS

Shayne is a man of mystery and power, whose power is exceeded only by his mystery...

He currently writes the Amazon Bestselling **Nate Temple** Series, which features a foul-mouthed wizard from St. Louis. He rides a blood-thirsty unicorn, drinks with Achilles, and is pals with the Four Horsemen.

He also writes the Amazon Bestselling **Feathers and Fire** Series—a second series in the TempleVerse. The story follows a rookie spell-slinger named Callie Penrose who works for the Vatican in Kansas City. Her problem? Hell seems to know more about her past than she does.

He coauthors **The Phantom Queen Diaries**—a third series set in The TempleVerse—with Cameron O'Connell. The story follows Quinn MacKenna, a mouthy black magic arms dealer in Boston. All she wants? A round-trip ticket to the Fae realm...and maybe a drink on the house.

Shayne holds two high-ranking black belts, and can be found writing in a coffee shop, cackling madly into his computer screen while pounding shots of espresso. He's hard at work on the newest books in the TempleVerse—You can find updates on new releases or chronological reading order on the next page, his website, or any of his social media accounts. <u>Follow him online for all sorts of groovy goodies, giveaways, and new release updates:</u>

*Get Down with Shayne Online*
www.shaynesilvers.com
info@shaynesilvers.com

# BOOKS BY SHAYNE SILVERS

*CHRONOLOGY: All stories in the TempleVerse are shown in chronological order on the following page*

## *SHADE OF DEVIL SERIES*

*(Not part of the TempleVerse)*

DEVIL'S DREAM

DEVIL'S CRY

DEVIL'S BLOOD

## NATE TEMPLE SERIES

*(Main series in the TempleVerse)*

FAIRY TALE - FREE prequel novella #0 for my subscribers

OBSIDIAN SON

BLOOD DEBTS

GRIMM

SILVER TONGUE

BEAST MASTER

BEERLYMPIAN (Novella #5.5 in the 'LAST CALL' anthology)

TINY GODS

DADDY DUTY (Novella #6.5)

WILD SIDE

WAR HAMMER

NINE SOULS

HORSEMAN

LEGEND

KNIGHTMARE

ASCENSION

## *FEATHERS AND FIRE SERIES*

*(Also set in the TempleVerse)*

UNCHAINED

RAGE

WHISPERS

ANGEL'S ROAR

MOTHERLUCKER (Novella #4.5 in the 'LAST CALL' anthology)

SINNER

BLACK SHEEP

GODLESS

## *PHANTOM QUEEN DIARIES*

*(Also set in the TempleVerse)*

COLLINS (Prequel novella #0 in the 'LAST CALL' anthology)

WHISKEY GINGER

COSMOPOLITAN

OLD FASHIONED

MOTHERLUCKER (Novella #3.5 in the 'LAST CALL' anthology)

DARK AND STORMY

MOSCOW MULE

WITCHES BREW

SALTY DOG

SEA BREEZE

HURRICANE

## CHRONOLOGICAL ORDER: TEMPLE VERSE

FAIRY TALE (TEMPLE PREQUEL)

OBSIDIAN SON (TEMPLE 1)

BLOOD DEBTS (TEMPLE 2)

GRIMM (TEMPLE 3)

SILVER TONGUE (TEMPLE 4)

BEAST MASTER (TEMPLE 5)

BEERLYMPIAN (TEMPLE 5.5)

TINY GODS (TEMPLE 6)

DADDY DUTY (TEMPLE NOVELLA 6.5)

UNCHAINED (FEATHERS... 1)

RAGE (FEATHERS... 2)

WILD SIDE (TEMPLE 7)

WAR HAMMER (TEMPLE 8)

WHISPERS (FEATHERS... 3)

COLLINS (PHANTOM 0)

WHISKEY GINGER (PHANTOM... 1)

NINE SOULS (TEMPLE 9)

COSMOPOLITAN (PHANTOM... 2)

ANGEL'S ROAR (FEATHERS... 4)

MOTHERLUCKER (FEATHERS 4.5, PHANTOM 3.5)

OLD FASHIONED (PHANTOM...3)

HORSEMAN (TEMPLE 10)

DARK AND STORMY (PHANTOM... 4)

MOSCOW MULE (PHANTOM...5)

SINNER (FEATHERS...5)

WITCHES BREW (PHANTOM...6)

LEGEND (TEMPLE...11)

SALTY DOG (PHANTOM...7)

BLACK SHEEP (FEATHERS...6)

GODLESS (FEATHERS...7)

KNIGHTMARE (TEMPLE 12)

ASCENSION (TEMPLE 13)

SEA BREEZE (PHANTOM...8)

HURRICANE (PHANTOM...9)

Made in the USA
Coppell, TX
24 October 2020